FEAR ON THE FENS

A gripping crime thriller with a huge twist

JOY ELLIS

Detective Nikki Galena Book 13

Joffe Books, London
www.joffebooks.com

First published in Great Britain in 2021

ISBN: 978-1-78931-976-7

CHAPTER ONE

It had been unusually quiet in Greenborough CID. Arrest rates were up, and crime rates were down. Even so, DI Nikki Galena noticed that with every passing week, her friend and superintendent, Cameron Walker, seemed to develop more worry lines and he'd lost his ready smile.

Today, as she and DS Joseph Easter sat in his office waiting for orders, the lines were more apparent than usual. 'Okay, Cam, as it's just us, your door is closed and as far as I know, your office isn't bugged, what's eating you?'

'Straight to the point, as ever!' said Joseph, rolling his eyes.

Cam gave him a weak smile. 'Well, she's never been one to mince her words.'

'Then an answer would put us all out of our misery, wouldn't it?' Nikki looked at him hopefully. She liked Cam. He had been a good friend over the years and was now a good boss, and he was clearly troubled.

Cam sat back and gave a long sigh. 'Just the usual, really. Sometimes all the red tape gets to me. I miss the days of being active and actually *doing* something, rather than organising and delegating. But,' he threw his hands in the air, 'that's my job now. I suppose someone has to do it, so it might as well be me.'

1

'Point taken and we do commiserate.' Nikki stared harder at him. 'But what's the real reason for the long face?'

'Okay, Galena, you win.' He leaned forward, elbows on his desk. 'We've inherited a bit of a tricky problem and it might need kid gloves.'

'That lets me out,' muttered Nikki.

'Sorry, but you might have to hone a new skill and develop diplomacy for this one.' Cam pulled a face, clearly not expecting too much by the way of success in that quarter. 'Do either of you recall the name Hopwood-Byrd?'

Nikki and Joseph both nodded, although Nikki was struggling to recall the context.

'British scientist, said to have worked with the CIA on some secret project,' said Joseph.

'Ah, and got himself killed, right?' Nikki suddenly recalled the headlines from the time. 'Yes, he got topped in a psychiatric hospital.'

Cam nodded. 'Julian Hopwood-Byrd was seconded to the CIA in the early 1990s to work on a classified project. When he returned home to London, it became instantly apparent that he was not the man he was when he left England.' Cam's expression darkened. 'Colleagues and friends expressed fears for his sanity, but evidently not enough was done, because in 1998, he murdered a man who worked for him. Following an assessment, he was taken, under section, to a psychiatric unit. After being convicted of murder, he was moved to a larger permanent secure facility in Surrey, where, as Nikki said, he was murdered by another patient.'

'He had no connection with this neck of the woods though, did he?' asked Joseph.

'No,' said Cam. 'He lived in Highgate village in London, a nice old house in a quiet, leafy road.'

'So, interesting as this is, what has it got to do with us, Cam?' asked Nikki, with a hint of apprehension.

'Quite a lot.' He took a fat folder from his desk and pushed it towards them. 'Bit of light reading for you — although maybe not so light. It gave me a mammoth headache,

I can tell you!' He let out a long sigh. 'Not long ago, the CIA uploaded millions of declassified documents to its site. Some of them reveal the kind of thing that Julian Hopwood-Byrd was involved in. If I tell you that millions of dollars were spent on this programme, and that it ran from the mid-seventies and went under at least six different code names, it will give you an inkling of the scale of it. The scariest thing I noticed was that the participant consent form for this project read, "Potential for injury during some training cannot be conclusively ruled out." As it was not an actual physical military exercise, that bothered me. Anyway, I'll leave that for you to digest and tell you about our involvement.'

He handed Nikki a memo with some contact details written on it. 'This morning you two are going to visit this gentleman — Harry Byrd. He's Julian's son and he's staying at Corley Grange Hotel on Saltfleet Road. He's expecting you at ten thirty. He's an interesting man, and what he has to tell you could be a massive issue for us.'

Nikki still didn't understand why they were required to read a dauntingly thick file on some defunct CIA project, but she decided to sort that out after they'd spoken to Harry Byrd. 'Any clues, Cam, or do we walk in blind?'

'Julian had two sons, Harry and Lucas. Lucas was a troubled child. He ran away from home at the age of thirteen. Harry hadn't seen or heard from his brother in twenty years, but now he thinks he's back, on our turf, and he has a propensity for killing.'

Joseph puffed out his cheeks and exhaled loudly. 'Great. Just what we need.'

'Isn't it?' Nikki breathed. 'I was rather liking not having a killer stalking the streets of Greenborough for once.' She groaned. 'Proves you should never get complacent.'

'Indeed,' said Cam grimly. 'I haven't met Harry Byrd myself, just spoken to him on the phone. I'm certain this isn't some sort of hoax, and naturally I've checked that he is who he says he is. He's worried, Nikki, very worried. I'd like you to report to me the moment you've spoken to him, okay?'

Nikki nodded and glanced at Joseph.

'Here we go again!' Joseph gave her an encouraging smile. 'Back on the roller coaster.'

That smile lifted her spirits. She couldn't deny the tiny flutter of excitement. After all, that's what they were there for — the roller coaster.

She gathered up the file. 'Right. Corley Grange, here we come.'

* * *

Shelley House Arboretum was a little gem of a place. Maybe "arboretum" was a little ostentatious, but it was a beautiful, wooded oasis in the flatlands of the Fens. It had been the passion of a wealthy landowner back in the late 1800s, who had visited various grand parks and determined that his own estate would provide a similar setting for native and imported trees and shrubs. It had been a labour of love, often beset with problems, mainly deriving from the unrelenting and often brutal winds that hurtled across the fields from the east. But he persevered and, thanks to careful planting, the selection of varieties that had a chance of surviving, as well as the placing of windbreaks and protected areas, he succeeded in producing a relatively small but beautiful park, with a collection of magnificent specimens.

Sean Cotton had never worked anywhere else. He had arrived as a skinny teenager looking for a way to earn a bit of cash so he could take his girl out, and he had never left. Sean was now edging towards thirty-five, still skinny, but strong as an ox. He had weathered, tanned skin and strong, calloused hands that could wield an axe as well as they could handle a tiny sapling — without breaking a single delicate bud. His girl was now his wife of some fourteen years, and he lived with her in a tied cottage in the grounds of Shelley House. Sean was the head gardener and a recognised and respected arboriculturist. He'd turned up, all those years ago, believing, like most lads, that trees were there to be climbed and not much else. Having been put to work he found, to his surprise, that he'd fallen in love with them. The Morton family, who owned Shelley House, saw it in him. As Joel, their long-serving gardener, was approaching retirement age, they invested a considerable amount of money in Sean's horticultural education. Luckily, Joel had taken to the boy from the word go, and as a parting gesture to the Mortons, he bequeathed everything he knew to his eager young apprentice.

This morning, Sean was heading out to one of his favourite areas of the garden, a spot that he called Sean's Pinetum, a section dedicated entirely to conifers. This summer they were opening the gardens to the public, and he was both happy and worried in equal measure. It was something of an achievement, and he would be pleased to welcome truly interested people — people come to see and enjoy the results of years of hard work — but he dreaded the prospect of having to host bored kids with penknives in their pockets, vandals or litter louts.

As he walked, the sun streamed through a latticework of leaves, and Sean smiled to himself. His lot really was a happy one. All in all, they had had very little trouble here over the years. Once, some idiot joyriders in a stolen 4x4 had rammed the front gates, crashing through and then spinning off the drive and gouging up the lawn before being brought to a halt against the trunk of an ancient horse chestnut tree. Sean recalled tending its wounds like a mother bathing a child's grazed knee, gently cutting away the damaged bark, talking to it as he worked. Sometimes the human race was beyond contempt, and he felt a sneaking pleasure that the tree stood firm, while the vehicle was a write-off.

The only other trouble had occurred last week. His face lost its smile. A group of young people had climbed the estate wall and made their way to a small, sheltered glade. From the number of cans of lager and stray items of clothing that he found the next day, the idea had clearly been to get rat-arsed and shag each other silly in the moonlight. Worse, some halfwit had decided that the night was chillier on his naked arse than he liked and had lit a fire.

At the back of the glade was an arched arbour with bench seats, where you could sit and look out into the clearing and enjoy the peace. It wasn't the best spot to pick for a bonfire. Sean supposed that half a gallon of Triple X might have impaired their thinking somewhat. The result, on tinder-dry grass after a baking hot day, was a conflagration that probably warmed a lot more than the halfwit's arse.

It was just lucky that Sean was a light sleeper and that the local fire station was in the next village, only a couple of miles down the road.

The damage could have been much worse, but even so, it pained Sean and his three helpers to see the destroyed arbour and the blackened and burnt vegetation surrounding it. The only serious casualty was a beautiful golden-foliaged robinia — a false acacia tree. Sadly, they had had to take it down.

It had taken the four of them two days to clean up, prune the damaged plants and make the site presentable again. Arthur Morton had ordered another arbour, and hopefully it would be delivered in time for the public opening.

He walked along the wide pathway towards the Pinetum, then paused at a narrower leafy lane that led to the clearing. Something had caught his attention.

He sniffed. A kind of cooking, barbecue smell. At nine in the morning? Out here?

Sean veered off the path and headed for the clearing. It wouldn't hurt to just check the area and make sure all was ready for the new arbour.

Just before he reached the clearing, he stopped and stared. What was one of their large metal wheelbarrows doing there? He could have sworn everything had been cleared away days ago. They mainly used powered barrows these days — they made carrying the heavier loads a piece of cake and, with the distances they walked on the estate, they were invaluable. But this was one of their old traditional wheelbarrows. He squinted in the early sunlight. Was that smoke? Something was being burned in it!

Angry and puzzled, Sean marched up to it, then stopped short. He gave a choked cry of horror.

Hanging over the side of the barrow was a hand. At the base — the handle end — were two blackened sports shoes.

With his hand clasped over his mouth, Sean turned and ran until he was back on the main path. There, he pulled out his phone and with a shaking hand, dialled 999.

* * *

Corley Grange Hotel had a relaxed, old-fashioned air to it. Nikki could almost see croquet being played on the lawns, and bright young things sipping cocktails and listening to the latest tunes on a gramophone.

Harry Byrd met them in reception and suggested that they sit outside on the veranda since, at present, it was devoid of guests.

He was a rather ordinary-looking man of perhaps thirty-five years. He had light-brown wavy hair and greenish-brown eyes and was dressed in casual slacks, a pale check short-sleeved shirt and a light cotton sweater draped across his shoulders.

'I took the liberty of ordering a pot of coffee, hope that's okay?' he said, smiling at them.

Before Nikki could answer, her phone rang. She apologised and checked the display. It was DC Cat Cullen. Cat knew where she was and wouldn't have rung unless it was important, so Nikki apologised again and said she needed to take it. She would join them in a minute or two.

'Boss? Sorry to interrupt, but we've got a murder.'

Why did she instantly connect it to the unremarkable young man who had just offered her coffee? She had no idea, but the thought stayed with her. 'Okay, what do we know so far?'

'Ben and I have attended, boss. We have one male, burnt beyond recognition, on the private estate of Arthur

Morton. It's called Shelley House Arboretum, not far from where you are now.'

Nikki nodded, frowning. She knew it. She knew Arthur Morton too. He was a staunch supporter of the local police and a good friend of the commissioner, and she made Cat aware of it. Cat was a great detective but did have a habit of telling it like it was. 'We'll do what we have to here, then come over. Will you be okay until then?'

'All in hand, boss. Forensics are held up but should be here within the next thirty minutes. We've cordoned the site off, and uniform are with us, so we're all cool.'

'Unlike your victim,' muttered Nikki. 'Sure it's not some freak accident? Remember the drunk that burned to death after dossing down in a skip for the night? He lit a cigarette after drinking too much cider and hadn't realised the skip he'd chosen was full of something flammable, poor guy.'

'It's murder, no question.'

Nikki didn't press the point. 'Okay, we'll see you as soon as.'

She hurried outside to where a waiter was placing three individual cafetières on the table. Well, that would make a change from the station vending machine. She had a personal coffee machine in her office, but it needed replacing and was often out of action.

They introduced themselves, then, coffee poured, Nikki asked Harry Byrd to explain his strange statement to Superintendent Walker.

'We know a little about your father's history,' she said, 'but only what the media tells us.'

'Well, DI Galena, there is a whole lot more to my father than most people imagine.' He stirred his coffee. 'But my immediate worry is my brother, Lucas.'

'Okay, from the top,' said Nikki, helping herself to a shortbread biscuit.

He nodded. 'I'll try and keep it succinct, given the complexities. Firstly, I have to say that what you believe or do not believe about my father and what he did in the States is irrelevant. The only thing that matters is that my little brother had absolute faith in our father. Father was God to Lucas and when he died, Lucas, who'd been psychologically troubled all his life, was devastated. Six months after Dad's murder, he ran away, and I've never seen him since.' He looked at them apologetically. 'Filling you in on all the background will take time, but it *is* relevant. If it would help, I'll come to the station and give a full statement.'

'That would be brilliant,' said Joseph. 'As soon as you are able would be good.'

'I'll come later this afternoon. I have some commitments immediately after this, but I thought you should know the basics as soon as possible.' He took a breath. 'Lucas has a strangely childlike view of the world, Officers, and he also lacks the ability to reason why some things have to be a certain way. He cannot comprehend grey areas, or personal points of view or opinions. Lucas sees everything in black and white, and only his perception is the correct one as far as he's concerned. Frankly, I cannot see that having changed as he's grown up.' He sipped his coffee, then quietly said, 'I suspect he was instrumental in my father's killing of our gardener.'

Nikki let out a low whistle. 'Why do you think that, Harry?'

'Dad was not the same after his work abroad finished. There was something terribly wrong with his mental health. I'll explain what I believe when I come to the station. Suffice it to say that I think his rage, which culminated in his killing Bruce, our gardener, was ignited by Lucas telling a lie about Bruce.'

'Something pretty serious, I assume?' asked Joseph.

'Lucas told Father that Bruce had abused him.' Harry stared down at the table. 'I would swear that wasn't true. Bruce was a gentle man, kind, and he'd been a good friend to both of us boys. I didn't believe him then and I still don't.'

Harry almost gritted his teeth, as if he hated saying this, but knew it had to be said.

'You believe that Lucas told him that dreadful lie knowing what might happen?' asked Nikki.

'I believe he deliberately did it, knowing what *would* happen,' Harry replied flatly. 'I saw his face when he heard what Dad had done. He was triumphant. He would have punched the air if others hadn't been there.' He looked Nikki directly in the eyes. 'I swear he orchestrated Bruce's death only because he was too small and too young to carry it out himself.'

'What on earth do you think Bruce did to cause Lucas to want him dead?' Joseph sounded shocked.

'It could have been something very simple, Detective Sergeant. I told you he had a childlike attitude, but it was more than that. He believed in magical things, especially in the natural world. He saw faeries and pixies and magical beings everywhere he went. He believed in woodland spirits and water sprites. Bruce could have accidentally trodden on a cowslip, or pulled up some bluebell bulbs, and if they were special to his faery kingdom, Lucas would have hated him for it. Simple as that.'

'Did he receive any help for all these delusions, Harry? Or were you the only one who knew about his fantasy world?' asked Nikki.

Harry shook his head sadly. 'Father made sure he saw plenty of doctors, but Lucas always managed to charm them with his little-boy routine. He was basically assumed to have some learning difficulties and a trait that might evolve into fantasy prone personality disorder, but they always followed this up with, "he'll probably grow out of it."'

'And now you believe he's back and in this area? Why?' Nikki was impatient to cut to the chase and get over to the Arboretum.

'I still live in Highgate, DI Galena, in the family home. My mother is still alive and loves the old place, even though some of our memories are less than happy. Anyway, I got a letter from him, completely out of the blue. It was a terrible shock — I had come to believe he was dead.' He reached into his trouser pocket and withdrew an envelope, which he placed on the table. 'It came a fortnight ago. After almost two decades.'

'May I?' asked Nikki, indicating the letter.

'Go ahead. Although it won't mean much to you.'

She slipped some gloves from her pocket and pulled them on. 'Just in case,' she murmured. 'Don't want to add mine to whoever else's prints are on it.'

She slipped a single sheet of paper from the envelope and read:

I'm going to find the Elf King and slay him.
Join my quest, my dearest brother.
I'll see you in Shrimptown.

She stared at the paper, utterly perplexed. 'And that's all? Where's Shrimptown?'

'We had a special game. I used it to calm him if he got upset over something. I found a big wall map of the British Isles and cut out the shapes of all the counties in plain paper, and stuck them on to the map. We then renamed them and transformed the towns and cities into Lucas's own kingdom. Lincolnshire was Reedmire and its main town, Greenborough, was Shrimptown, on the River Staghorn. That's how I knew he was here.'

'Dare I ask who the Elf King is?' asked Joseph tentatively.

'According to Lucas, he had many faces. He was a trickster, a malevolent spirit who could take on different shapes at will.' He looked from Joseph to her. 'I'm afraid it's anyone who has disturbed Lucas's fragile little world, anyone who has transgressed against it and committed a cardinal sin.'

'Like treading on a cowslip,' said Joseph softly.

Nikki groaned. 'I hate to be so blunt, Harry, but bottom line, you're telling us we are going to be looking for a nutter, and any one of the thousands of inhabitants of the Fens could be his victim, yes?'

Harry looked pained but nodded miserably. 'A little harsh, DI Galena, but yes, that's about the long and the short of it.'

CHAPTER TWO

'Very nice indeed! How come I didn't know about this exquisite property before?' Professor Rory Wilkinson gazed about him at the house and gardens of the Arboretum and sighed with pleasure. 'It's a dream!'

'I first came here a long time ago,' said Nikki, who had arrived at exactly the same time as the Home Office pathologist and was now walking with him down a long tree-lined avenue towards the crime scene. 'The owner, Arthur Morton, had a garden party here in aid of a police charity. I brought Hannah and she loved it. She could have only been about six or seven, and there were stalls and lots of kiddies' games. I remember she won a furry dog, a poodle-like thing and hell, she adored it! Called it Fluffy.'

'Original!' commented Rory, with a smile. 'I would have expected something more along the lines of Sebastian, or Bartholomew.'

Nikki laughed. 'She may well have done that when she reached her "deeply misunderstood by the whole world" phase, but at six, what you saw was what you got.' She swallowed. Thinking of her darling Hannah was still painful, even after so many years had passed, but at least she could now talk about her without dissolving into tears. She vaguely wondered what had happened to Fluffy.

'I would love to live somewhere like this,' said Rory, tactfully changing the subject. 'Imagine waking each day to such a vista, it's positively orgasmic!' He took on a stern expression. 'I hope the owners appreciate it.'

'Oh, they do, believe me!' Nikki said. 'They're deeply committed to keeping its heritage going. Arthur was telling me how long it's taken some of these trees to get to maturity. He said that with proper care, some can live for many hundreds of years.'

'And yet someone chose this idyll to commit murder in.'

Nikki was immediately beset by thoughts of a deranged young man and his faery kingdom. Wasn't this the perfect place for a man with a penchant for woodland spirits to undertake his murderous acts?

Joseph had gone ahead and was now beckoning to her. He was talking to a tall man who managed to look deathly pale despite a weathered, tanned face.

'This is Sean Cotton, DI Galena,' said Joseph. 'He's the head gardener here and it was him found the body.'

He hadn't had to tell her. The man's expression said it all.

'We've met before, Mr Cotton. Last year, when Mr Morton was discussing plans to open the gardens to the public and wanted some advice on public safety. You kindly walked me around the lake and the wildlife ponds.'

Sean Cotton gave her a weak smile. 'Of course, I remember. Much more pleasant circumstances than today, that's for sure. Still, I suppose you get used to terrible sights like this in your job.'

'Not exactly,' said Nikki sombrely. 'Actually, never — you just learn how to deal with it.'

'All tips gratefully received,' said Sean ruefully. 'I'm used to, er, "gentler" problems in my line of work. This has shaken me to the core.'

Nikki noticed the apprehensive glance Joseph gave him and knew what he was thinking. Some people coped with horrific sights, others didn't. Joseph was concerned about Sean Cotton.

'My sergeant here will have a chat with you in a moment, Sean, and maybe suggest someone you could talk to about this.' She smiled reassuringly. 'It's shock, and it's perfectly natural. Joseph here can point you in the right direction, so you handle it in the healthiest way possible.' She lowered her voice. 'He knows what he's talking about, Sean. From experience.'

For the first time, Sean Cotton seemed to relax a little. 'Sorry. I'm behaving like a total wuss. Look at me — five foot eleven and shaking like a jelly. My wife would be ashamed of me.'

'I'm sure that's not the case at all,' said Joseph, giving him an encouraging smile. 'Now, are you up to telling us something about what happened this morning? No details of what you found, just a timeline of events is fine for now.'

Sean took a deep breath. He described his morning routine and told them what had happened in that same clearing the week before. He returned to that morning and the odd smell that he'd thought was cooking. There, he stopped.

Nikki steered him back to more mundane events. 'You say you'd cleared the site, but someone had left an old wheelbarrow there. Was there anything odd or significant about its position?'

Sean frowned. 'No, it was just slightly to one side of where the arbour had been.' He paused. 'Although, when I think about it, if this had happened before last week's conflagration, it couldn't have been placed where it was.'

'How so?' asked Nikki.

'Because that was where the robinia tree stood, the one I said we had to fell and dig out the root. The barrow was placed squarely on the recently dug and re-turfed patch.'

Nikki threw a swift glance to Joseph. Harry Byrd needed to tell them a whole lot more about his little brother. If treading on cowslips was a serious crime, what would be the penalty for burning a tree?

'Forgive my ignorance, Sean, but was it a special kind of tree?'

Sean looked more himself now he was back on the subject he loved. 'Well, robinias are all very beautiful. They're not rare, like some of the older specimens here, but this one, *robinia pseudoacacia "Frisia"*, was a tree with lovely golden leaves that pass through citrus yellow to chartreuse green before turning to buttery gold.' He sighed. 'It literally hurts to see something so beautiful mindlessly vandalised and have to be destroyed.'

Nikki considered his words. If a simple plantsman could feel like that, imagine how a zealot felt. She rubbed at her forehead. This was going to be a tricky one to explain without looking like a total prat — 'And your motive for murder?' 'He hurt my tree, M'Lord.'

From the moment Cat rang her, she had been certain that Harry Byrd's prophecy was coming true. Now her fears were being confirmed. 'Sean, I'm going to leave you with Joseph for a few moments. I need to talk to the pathologist. If you'd be so kind as to give him details of everyone who helped to clear up the glade after those idiots lit the fire, as well as anyone else who has regular access to these gardens, it'd be a great help.'

She turned to go, then stopped. 'Did you ever hear anything back about the kids that lit that fire?'

'No, they weren't caught, DI Galena, and I guess it wasn't considered important enough to take any further. Mr Morton was more concerned that we just try to repair what damage we could, ready for the public opening.'

She thanked him and went across to the blue-and-white police tape that cordoned off the barrow with its grisly contents.

Nikki pulled on a protective suit. She limited herself to one look at the deceased and returned to where Rory was discussing camera angles with Ella Jarvis, his crime-scene photographer.

'Ah, Nikki. I see my grilled bacon breakfast was a poor choice,' said Rory, pulling a face. 'A crispy critter is never my favourite way to start a day.'

'Me neither. So, what's your first impression?'

Rory pushed his glasses further up on to the bridge of his nose. 'Mmm, well, actually I can tell you quite a lot, even before we extricate him from that barrow. We have a young Caucasian male, probably in his late teens. It would appear from the large depressed fracture at the back of his skull that he was dead, or at least mortally wounded, prior to his woodland cremation. I can't yet say whether he was killed here or brought here to dispose of — some tracks from the barrow might help there, although the ground is probably too dry. But not to worry, dear heart, in the fullness of time, I will reveal all.' He gave her a cherubic smile, then pulled up his mask. 'Sweet Ella and I have to go and do our duty, gruesome as it might be. As soon as I know more, I'll ring.'

Nikki thanked him. She saw Cat approaching, along with her partner DC Ben Radley. 'Anything to report?'

'We've been down to the house, boss, but they were unaware of anything happening until the head gardener raised the alarm. The owner of this here posh drum is dead upset about it. He's a really nice bloke — for a toff.'

Nikki grinned. 'Praise indeed, coming from Cat Cullen.'

'Well, he's not up his own arse like some we've dealt with. He's offered to open up his kitchen so everyone working here can get a drink. I mean, that's proper breeding, isn't it?'

'And he's given us a list of all his staff,' added Ben. 'We wondered if there was a connection between anyone working here and the dead guy.'

'Excellent, well done,' said Nikki. 'Now, as uniform have the scene contained and the SOCOs are in full swing, I think we can all head back to base. I've got some interesting info for you that might well have a bearing on this case, and you both need bringing up to speed.'

'Mr Morton said he'd like a word, if you have a minute. He sounded like he knew you?' Cat looked at her enquiringly.

'He seemed dead chuffed when we told him who our guvnor was.'

'We have met before and yes, you're right, he is a nice man. Now you two get away. Joseph and I will tie up here and follow you back.'

Arthur Morton welcomed them at the house, shaking Joseph's hand warmly. Then he turned to Nikki. 'I'm so sorry we have to meet again in such horrible circumstances. Terrible thing to happen, just terrible. This is such a peaceful place. It always has been. It's always managed to avoid the usual shady goings-on and dark deeds that went on in other old houses. Murder and Shelley House just don't go together.'

'It does have a lovely atmosphere, sir,' said Joseph, 'and the Arboretum is spectacular. My daughter would love it here. She studied ecology and works for the Woodland Trust. She'd do a dance of sheer joy if she saw some of these trees.'

'Then she's welcome to come, any time she likes.' Arthur Morton handed Joseph a card from a small carved box on the hall table. 'Tell her to ring and let us know she's coming, and Sean can show her some of the finer specimens and give her a potted history of most of them. We'd love to see her.'

Joseph took the card and nodded. 'That's very kind of you, sir. Her name is Tamsin Farrow and I'm certain she'll be ringing you.'

Arthur Morton turned to Nikki. 'I know you're very busy, DI Galena, but I just wanted to assure you that if there's anything we can do to help, please, just ask. My family and I are all here at present, so do make use of us. My two daughters have volunteered for twenty-four-hour kitchen duty, so your officers will have drinks available round the clock. And there's a toilet in the stable block that they can use. We feel awful that such a dreadful thing has happened in our grounds, and we want to do all we can to help.'

'I wish everyone was as accommodating as you, sir,' said Nikki with feeling. 'And we do appreciate it. We'll try not to cause too much disruption. Sadly, a crime scene requires a lot of manpower. It's unavoidable.'

'Do what you have to, no problem. We can renovate later. That's the wonderful thing about nature, it will regenerate — unlike human beings.'

As they drove back to the station, Joseph commented that for someone to offer so much assistance at a moment's notice was quite something. 'Men like Arthur Morton are a very rare breed. He's very compassionate, isn't he, and they are clearly a very close family.'

'That's part of it, Joseph. He's always been a pretty fair sort of guy, but he wasn't always as altruistic as he is now. He lost his eldest son in a car crash. An off-duty police officer saw it happen and desperately tried to help. When he realised the lad was dying, he crawled into the wrecked vehicle and stayed with him so that he wouldn't be alone. Arthur was so moved by the man's courage and compassion that his whole outlook on life changed completely.'

'I see. So that's why he supports our charities so much. Even so, he's really going the extra mile. It means a good deal to the troops on the ground. I liked him a lot.'

Nikki did too, possibly even more because, like him, she had lost a precious child. 'I'm going to ask Cam to move heaven and earth to keep the details of this murder out of the media for as long as he can. It's got nothing to do with Arthur wanting to open the gardens to the public this year, it's more about invasion of privacy and wanting to try to preserve the integrity of the Arboretum.'

'You felt it too,' said Joseph, as he carefully negotiated a sharp bend in the road. 'Even though the place was filling up with police and forensics' vehicles, you could still feel its quietude.'

They drove on, Nikki contemplating the effect one man's actions can have on an entire community.

Joseph interrupted these, for her, rather philosophical thoughts. 'If it's okay with you, I'd like to get a peek at that folder on Julian Hopwood-Byrd before his son Harry arrives to give his statement.'

'Absolutely,' she agreed, dragging herself back to the here and now. 'And I suggest that you and I be the ones to take it. As I'm fairly certain little brother is responsible for the "wheelbarrow pyre," I suspect it will be a long session.'

'I was hoping you'd say that.' Joseph glanced across at her. 'I've got a good idea what our mad scientist and his CIA friends were involved in. Ever heard of Stargate?'

'*Stargate SG-1*? That military, space-travel TV programme?'

'No, the real thing,' Joseph said quietly. 'Stargate. Code name for a clandestine US programme that ran for, I don't know, maybe over two decades.'

'Not my forte, as you well know, Joseph.' She gave him a patient smile. 'But you clearly do know about it and you're itching to educate me.'

'I'm not sure I want to try. It's sure to make you throw up your hands and start shrieking, "Don't want to know! What drivel!" and the rest.'

'Joseph Easter! I do not shriek, I'll have you know.'

He chuckled. 'You will when I tell you that Project Stargate was set up in direct response to secret intelligence that the Russians were having some seriously interesting results in training their operatives to spy using psychic abilities.'

'Oh, what utter tosh!' exclaimed Nikki. 'Total cobblers!'

'See? You're shrieking. But before you have a small meltdown, consider this: all through the seventies, eighties and nineties the CIA and the Department of Defence spent twenty million dollars on it. Twenty million! That's a lot of money now, and was a hell of a lot back then. So, quite a lot of people in high places felt it was worth investigating, didn't they?'

Nikki snorted, then thought about it. 'And you believe Julian H.-B. was in on it?'

'It fits Cam's description perfectly. I'd certainly take a punt that I'm right.'

'Well, we'll know for sure when we read that dossier and get to talk to Harry Byrd, won't we?'

'And I for one can't wait.' Joseph turned into the police-station car park, flashed his warrant card at the barrier and watched the gate open. 'Just . . . keep an open mind, if you can?'

'Naturally, Joseph dear! You know me and how eager I am to embrace bloody stupid crank ideas about flaky hocus-pocus.'

Joseph closed the car door and locked it. 'Mmm. Thought so.'

CHAPTER THREE

With twenty minutes to go before Harry Byrd's appointment time, Joseph closed the dossier and exhaled loudly. 'Bloody hell! It'll take a month to scratch the surface of all that.'

'But you were right, Joseph, he *was* involved in Stargate. Although how anyone with a brain cell could take such a lunatic programme seriously is beyond me.' Nikki shook her head.

'Still, it has to be admitted that they had some pretty remarkable intelligence-gathering successes.' Joseph stretched. 'I'm not saying I even vaguely understand a quarter of it all, or believe half of it, but one special project intelligence officer was awarded a Legion of Merit for providing info on 150 targets that were inaccessible using conventional sources. Like it or not, Nikki, some people do have abilities that the rest of us don't. The world might be full of charlatans, tricksters, magicians and hoaxers but, just occasionally, you come across a man or woman whose circuitry is wired up differently.'

Nikki still looked unconvinced. Joseph, who was far more open to such things than she was, said, 'I'm going to ask a favour — well, more like make a suggestion.'

'As long as I don't have to start believing this bunkum, ask away,' she said, crossing her arms.

'Can we bring Spooky in on this? I'm betting she knows as much about this stuff as you do *Butterworths Police Law*.'

'Probably a very good idea, so long as you two heretics don't go all woo-woo and start ganging up on me, okay?'

Spooky, real name Sarah Dukes, was their prize IT consultant. A civilian, her company was stationed at Greenborough Police Station and worked pretty well solely for the Fenland Constabulary. Spooky was a good friend of Nikki's. They had started police training together, until Spooky realised that her talents lay in technology rather than on the mean streets of Greenborough. Besides being respected for her expertise in automation, she also had a reputation for being a UFO enthusiast and was very knowledgeable about astronomy. Joseph was certain that she would have more than a smattering of knowledge about the Stargate Project.

'Go see if she's free, Joseph. At least it'll convince Harry Byrd that we are taking him seriously if we have a couple of like-minded souls sitting in on the statement, other than one crusty old diehard cynic.'

Trying not to smile at the description she had given herself, Joseph hurried to the IT department.

As expected, Spooky had almost fallen over herself to get downstairs to the interview room.

Harry sat opposite them, looking relaxed and rather out of place in the austere box of a room, which was usually home to less salubrious characters than the smartly dressed Harry Byrd.

Having got all the introductions and formalities out of the way, they listened to a potted history of the Hopwood-Byrd family and its two sons.

'From an early age, we were aware that Father was eccentric, but as children we accepted that was just the way he was. He was just Dad — weird and very wonderful to us. Especially to Lucas. He idolised him.' Harry's expression softened at the memory. 'No matter how different to other boys' fathers he was, he was a great dad to us, and we both loved him dearly.'

'Weird and wonderful? But he was a scientist,' said Nikki. 'Surely, by definition they are very practical — a bit like us, really, in that they deal in proven facts and figures.'

'That's actually technically incorrect, because science never proves anything. That's not the way it works. It accumulates empirical evidence for or against various hypotheses.' Harry smiled. 'That was drummed into me from a very early age. My father was meticulous, with a mind like a calculator, but was intensely curious about parapsychology. He quickly moved from quantum biology — his initial field of study — to psi phenomena. This happened before we were born. I was told when I grew up that after he published findings of his controlled experiments, he was contacted by two men from Stanford University in the States. They asked him to join a CIA project that had been set up to close a gap between the US and Russia, who were purported to be using psychic spies.'

'Remote viewing,' murmured Spooky.

'Exactly.' Harry nodded, appearing relieved that someone here knew what he was talking about. 'My father entered the programme as one of some forty men and women with extraordinary abilities. They were used for intelligence collection, espionage, finding missing aircraft, hostages and terrorists. Bit like a cheap radar, really.' His face darkened. 'But some of them paid a heavy price, and my father paid the ultimate one.'

'Forgive me, Harry,' said Nikki. 'My colleagues here seem to understand what you're saying, but I haven't a clue what remote viewing means.'

Harry smiled patiently. 'It's a case of "seeing" things, using your mind to travel. For example, one of the early exercises they were given was to describe what they "saw" at a particular location. They had to draw an image of it. Sometimes they were given clay to mould an impression of what they were seeing. One of my father's first representations of his target was remarkably accurate. He was given co-ordinates, travelled there in his mind and drew a circular device with metal handles in the shape of a hoop at intervals around it. When he was shown an aerial view of the location, it turned out to be a children's playground, and the exact coordinate was a roundabout with metal handles in that same shape for the children to hold on to.'

'And this was for real?' Nikki sounded incredulous.

'Oh yes. They had their successes, DI Galena, and a whole lot of failures too. My brother and I were born in the US after Dad had been moved to a facility in Reston, Virginia. It was pretty, with parks and lakes and lovely trails to walk and play in. We were happy there, but young as we were, we knew our dad was changing. We never knew exactly what he went through with the experiments, he never spoke about them, although I know his curiosity would have made him volunteer for anything. Then, in 1995, just before the project folded, he had a breakdown. We came back to England and Dad got worse.' He shrugged. 'That, as far as his history goes, is that. And as I said before, what you believe about him or his abilities is irrelevant. It's how it affected Lucas that is the real issue.'

'You told us before that Lucas was a troubled child, prone to fantasy,' said Joseph. 'Is it possible that it was caused by your father's, er, unusual talents?'

'Not as such. It was more that a part of him simply never grew up, Detective Sergeant. He retained his childish belief in his magical elvish kingdom, with its creatures that lived in the plants, flowers, trees and rocks. But on other levels he functioned very well. He did fine at school, was never actually challenged academically, but he couldn't integrate with the other kids. It was like they were from different planets.'

'So, did he become insular?' asked Joseph. 'If he had no friends, no contemporaries to interact with, he must have struggled.'

Harry gave a bitter laugh. 'Not exactly. I mentioned that he saw everything in black and white, so, because his contemporaries were not on the same wavelength as him, they weren't worth considering. I think he quite pitied some of them, but he certainly didn't need them. He had his own world, and as long as none of the other kids threatened it in any way, he was fine.'

'And if they did threaten it?' asked Nikki, alert.

'He could become aggressive. He was excluded from one school for attacking another child.'

'A child who threatened his little world?'

'Yes, DI Galena. He saw the child stamping on an ant colony. According to Lucas, ants were soldiers in the service of the Faery Queen. He knocked the boy to the ground and stamped on him.'

'An eye for an eye,' said Joseph, throwing Nikki a worried glance. 'Was the boy badly hurt?'

'Nothing lasting, bruises and scrapes mainly, but that was only because some other kids dragged Lucas off. If they hadn't, I'm not sure how far he would have gone.' He straightened up. 'What you should know, Officers, is that despite what I've told you, I still love my brother. I want him caught for his own safety, as much as to stop innocent people dying. He's not a child anymore. He's a grown man, but he doesn't see things as you and I see them. I'm fully convinced he has developed full-blown fantasy prone personality disorder. You have to find him and stop him before someone gets killed.'

Joseph glanced across to Nikki. She nodded.

'We believe that might have already happened, Harry.' Joseph saw Nikki watching Harry Byrd carefully to see what his response would be.

For a while he said nothing, apparently stunned, and then he slowly shook his head. 'A murder? Can you tell me why you think it is connected to my brother?'

'The woodland location, for a start,' said Nikki. 'And there are clear indications that there is an element of, how shall I put it, retribution?' She stared at him. 'If I take you into our confidence, can I rely on your silence until a formal statement is issued? I'd like you to give us your honest opinion as to whether the perpetrator of this crime could be Lucas.'

Gravely, Harry Byrd nodded. 'Yes, you can, DI Galena. I'll be honest with you. I really do need to know.'

Nikki gave him a brief account of what they knew and what they believed had been the motive for the killing. When she'd finished, he inhaled, his breath catching. 'I consider it very possible that this is my brother's doing. Can you tell me what kind of tree was damaged in the original fire?'

Nikki looked through her notebook and found the name. 'A robinia, with a whole lot of Latin after it. The head gardener said it was also called a false acacia, if that means anything.'

Harry nodded. 'I recognise the name. Lucas had favourite trees. Each had its own deva, or nature spirit, that performed a specific function in helping the Earth maintain its balance. I can imagine that if someone thoughtlessly damaged one of those, it could push him over the edge. And if the transgressor's body was burned, as the tree was, then I'd say you need look no further than my brother.'

It was as they had thought.

Joseph looked at Nikki. 'I think we should get ourselves back to the Arboretum and round up the staff who were working with Sean Cotton to clear the damage, don't you? It seems most likely that Lucas actually worked at Shelley House. He saw what happened and took his revenge.'

'Joseph, will you gather up some uniforms and do that immediately? And ring me with an answer. There are a few more things I want to talk to Harry about.'

He stood up. 'Of course. I'll see you again soon, Harry, and we do appreciate what you're doing. It can't be easy for you.'

Harry gave him a tired smile. 'Oh, you have no idea, Sergeant. It's tearing me apart.'

* * *

Nikki and Spooky got Harry a cup of tea, and she continued asking him about his brother. She needed to get the fullest picture possible of this strange man and his fantasies.

'Would you be prepared to talk to our psychologist about your brother's condition?' she asked. Laura Archer was going to be her first port of call as soon as she was out of this interview room.

'Yes, yes, of course, although I'm not sure what I can tell her. It's a rather poorly named disorder and beyond my understanding, I'm afraid.'

'Our psychologist will understand, believe me. If you can just describe what you know of Lucas and his private world.' She leaned forward. 'I hate to ask this, Harry, but do think this is the first time your brother might have killed someone?'

'I have no way of knowing, DI Galena. Don't forget, he was just a boy when he disappeared. He's been out of my life for so long now I cannot imagine where he's been, or what he's been doing in all these years.' He looked thoroughly miserable. 'I wish I knew, really I do. But for some reason — maybe wishful thinking or a "brother" thing — I don't believe he has ever killed before.'

'Harry, do you have a photograph of Lucas? I know it will be an old one, from when he was a lad, but if it's clear enough, Sarah here can use age progression software and produce a likely image from it.'

'I certainly can,' said Spooky.

'I'm afraid I'm going to disappoint you there,' said Harry. 'There are no photos of our family.'

Nikki frowned. 'What? None at all? No school pictures? No holiday snaps?'

'My father refused to have any of us photographed.' He gave an exasperated shrug, 'As I said, he was an eccentric. He was adamant: no photographs, ever.' He reached into his jacket pocket. 'Only once did I ever disobey him.' He handed her a picture across the table.

Nikki stared at it.

'One night, back in Reston, not long before we were due to leave the States, there was a storm. Lightning struck a beautiful blue pine tree and tore it almost in half. The following day it was taken down and sawn up. Just a stump remained and, although they tried to get it out and practically reduced what was left to matchwood, it refused to budge. Lucas was inconsolable. I woke up early that morning to find his bed empty. I found him curled up, like you see him in the picture, in a foetal position, in the stump of the tree, surrounded by the tattered remains of its branches. The image was so striking that I ran back indoors to get the secret disposable camera that Dad didn't know I had and took a photograph. To my knowledge, it's the only picture ever taken of Lucas.'

Nikki stared at the image and shivered. She handed it to Spooky and noted the look on her face. That devastated child, asleep in the arms of the ruined tree. 'Can I take a copy of this, Harry?'

He nodded. 'But I'd like it back. It's precious.'

'I'll do it now if you like,' offered Spooky, 'then you can have it straight back.'

'Go,' said Nikki. 'And send a copy of it to Joseph.'

Alone with Harry, she looked hard at him. 'What puzzles me, Harry, is how any boy of thirteen can disappear without trace. His family never hear of him again, but he turns up years later as an apparently fit, employable adult. He would have to have had a good deal of strength to kill. If it transpires that he worked at the Arboretum, he must have had certain skills and maybe even qualifications, so where has he been?'

Harry seemed to shrink into himself. 'Since the moment that letter arrived, that question has been burning itself into my brain. But I have no answer. There has been no sign, no sighting, not even a single hint, in all the time that he's been gone. Just once, when I was walking my dog on Hampstead Heath on a frosty winter's morning, I had the strangest feeling that he was there, watching me.' He gave a little apologetic laugh. 'Ridiculous, I know. But I felt as if I could reach out and, suddenly, he'd be there beside me. I could feel the closeness of our boyhood days back in Virginia. There was a woodland trail where we used to play hide-and-seek, and just like in that game, Lucas was there but I couldn't see him.' He shook his head. 'It's never happened again.'

'The day, or night, that he left — can you describe it?' Nikki asked.

'There's nothing to describe. I went into his room at around eight o'clock in the morning, on my way down to breakfast. His bed hadn't been slept in. Lucas had gone. That was it.'

'Was it suspected that he'd been abducted?'

'No. My mother and I knew that was not the case. He had been almost unreachable for days, completely withdrawn into himself. When we checked, his most precious things were gone and a few of his clothes. Enough to fill a holdall and a rucksack — they were missing too.'

'You reported this?' Nikki queried.

'Not immediately. My mother refused. She was convinced he was trying to come to terms with his grief. He needed a little time alone and would be back. She was adamant, and I never went against her wishes. Don't forget, she was mourning too. I couldn't bear to hurt her further.' He looked down. 'We just knew, Inspector. Neither we nor the police would find Lucas if he didn't want to be found.'

'But he had a plan, didn't he?' insisted Nikki, hoping she wasn't pushing too hard. 'He took certain objects and clothes, so it's likely he knew where he was going.' She narrowed her eyes. 'You said "precious things." What were they exactly?'

He frowned in concentration. 'His notebook, first and foremost. It was his record, in words and illustrations, of his magical kingdom. A couple of books, a compass, a small box of things that were special to him — pebbles, crystals, an unusual pine cone, some dried seed heads, shells, stuff like that. Oh, and we discovered that Father's watch and a pendulum made of amethyst on a silver chain were also missing. That's all I can remember.'

Oh, that boy had a plan, thought Nikki. He knew exactly where he was going. This was no moment of terrible mental anguish that sent him dashing off into the night with no direction or thought for the future. Lucas Hopwood-Byrd was in complete control when he left the family home.

Spooky returned and handed Harry back his photograph. 'Would it be in order to ask Mr Byrd a couple of questions, DI Galena?'

Nikki nodded. Byrd was only helping them, he wasn't under caution, but she valued Spooky's intelligence and knew her query wouldn't be flippant. Spooky's mind certainly ran on a different track to hers, but maybe for that reason, her thoughts would be relevant and possibly valuable.

'Did your father encourage Lucas and his fantasies? Did he consider his belief in a kind of spirit kingdom here on Earth as being not childish and silly, but maybe special? As in a gift?'

Harry finished his tea. 'Let's say he never ridiculed him. He listened with apparent great interest and looking back, I suppose, yes, he did seem to endorse a lot of Lucas's stories, even encourage him. He gave him books to read and sometimes printed off articles and images from the internet for him on such things as earth energies, mythical stories and folklore. I'm sure he believed Lucas had something special.'

'Without wishing to hurt, sir,' said Spooky tentatively, 'would you say that Lucas was your father's favourite?'

'Without a doubt. Lucas was different and therefore special, like him. I was Mother's boy, totally grounded. She and I tried to keep everyone's feet on the ground, not that we succeeded. There was no animosity between any of us. We knew we weren't your typical average family, so we clung together. There was a lot of love.' He looked sad. 'That's why it hurt us so much when my father became mentally unstable.'

'Those experiments had a reputation for damaging minds, sir.' Spooky looked angry. 'Some sensitives were pushed too far, and none of the declassified documents include a record of the "unfortunate incidents" that occurred along the way.'

'You've studied remote viewing?' asked Harry with interest.

'In depth,' replied Spooky. 'When I was younger, I took a great deal of interest in some of the more unusual practices initiated in Russia and then developed further by the Americans to stop the USSR getting ahead of them in the espionage race.'

'And that led you to Stargate?'

'It wasn't originally known by that name, but yes.' She smiled. 'And even after it was debunked, it still goes on, you know. Different name, different locations, though officially it doesn't exist.'

'I can believe that. My father told me his work was far too important not to continue. I simply don't want to know any more. It killed my father after provoking him into taking what I believe to be an innocent life. Nothing is worth that kind of sacrifice.'

Spooky sat back, nodding in agreement.

Nikki's phone rang, breaking the silence. 'Joseph? I'll take this outside, signal's crap in this room.' She excused herself and hurried down to the reception foyer. 'Go ahead. I've got you now.'

'He did work here, Nikki, for a whole year. He used the name Luke Elmore and Sean said he was the most dedicated woodsman he's ever met. But he's done a runner.'

'I bloody knew it! We missed a trick there, Joseph. Damn it!'

'Yes, but we now have a clear description of him, and can place him here on the night of the killing. We don't have the man himself yet, but it's a massive step forward. It appears he left a message at the house some time before the body was found, saying he had some urgent family business to attend to, and would they apologise to Sean for him and say he'd be back as soon as possible. Before we even knew there'd been a killing, the bird had already flown, Nikki. When uniform called at his stable lodgings, all his things were gone. I'm gathering all the info I can on him, okay?'

'I'm nearly through here, I'll be with you within half an hour.' She hung up, swearing. She shouldn't have left it to others to find out who worked on that estate. She should have stayed there until everyone had been accounted for, by her. It wasn't that she didn't trust the others, she just felt that she'd let herself down by not personally checking all the staff before she left.

When she returned, Harry and Spooky were talking about something called Area 51, of which she was dimly aware. They both smiled conspiratorially and shut up when they saw her, so she decided it was something for later. She filled in a few more blanks with Harry and, deciding not to tell him yet that his brother probably worked at Shelley House, she thanked him and showed him out.

'I have to get over to Shelley House, Spooky. Can I get you to ask Zena, my office manager, to run off a whole load of copies of that picture?'

'No problem, Nik, but sadly I won't be able to do anything with it. Those old disposable cameras went out with the ark. The picture quality is rubbish and, as the child is asleep and lying on his side, facial ageing software would be useless.'

'It's not important now,' said Nikki. 'We have a whole bunch of witnesses who've been working with him for a year. I'm guessing the next step will be a facial composite.'

'Brilliant. My upgraded EvoFIT system will cope with that, no hassle. Just get me a couple of his mates with good powers of description and you'll have your ID picture.'

'Great. I'll get you your witnesses and leave that with you, Spooks.' She turned to go, then stopped. 'What's Area 51?'

Spooky grinned at her. 'A US Air Force top-secret military base in the Nevada desert. It's a development and test site for military stealth aircraft and for covertly studying Soviet MiGs, purported to be used to study and store alien UFOs.'

'I should have known!' Nikki groaned, threw up her hands and hurried off down the corridor. Behind her, she distinctly heard someone giggle.

CHAPTER FOUR

Joseph found Sean Cotton alone in a sunlit clearing in a small plantation that seemed to be composed entirely of conifers.

'These are my favourites,' he said to Joseph. 'I love everything about them — their constancy, always draped in wonderful forest greens, their shapes, their formation, the fruit they bear in the form of such a variety of wonderful cones and even their amazing smell. To me, a damp pine forest is the best scent in the world.'

Joseph stared around. 'It's not until you see a collection like this that you realise how many different conifers there are.'

'We have a lovely selection — pines, cedars, spruces, firs, cypresses, junipers, yews. And some real treasures too.'

Joseph pointed to a magnificent bluish green tree. 'What is that one? It's incredible.'

'An Atlas cedar, a real beauty. There are only three true cedars: Atlas, cedar of Lebanon and deodar. You can tell them apart because of the way they grow. Atlas tips are pointing up, so A for ascending; Lebanon are flat, so L for level; and deodar tips point downwards, D for descending. Simple.'

'I learn something every day,' said Joseph with a smile. 'But I'm sorry to say I need to talk to you about the man you knew as Luke Elmore.'

Sean's smile vanished. 'You are sure this isn't some awful mistake, Sergeant? Luke is a gentle soul, passionate about nature, and trees in particular. I've truly never met another man with such . . . such empathy with the natural world. I'm passionate about it myself, but mine is born from a more practical interest in cultivation, nurturing of plants and trees so as to produce the best. Luke cared for them in a different way. I'd say his love for nature was more spiritual, possibly even mystical.'

Any doubts Joseph might have had vanished. He knew immediately that Luke was their man.

'I liked him a lot, Sergeant,' Sean said. 'And work! My God. We gave him single-room accommodation in the old stable block, which meant he lived on-site, but whatever time I started, he was already out there, and when I finished for the day, Luke was still finding some "vital" job he had to finish. He never stopped and, to my knowledge, only left here once a week to shop.'

'Can you take me to see his room? I know uniform have checked it, but I'd like to see it for myself, before the SOCOs get here.' Joseph knew that Nikki would want to see it too, but by the time they'd walked back, she should have arrived.

As they left the clearing, Joseph asked Sean to describe Luke's reaction when he saw the damage the youths had done.

Sean looked at the ground, his face crumpled into furrows. 'I was there first, and Luke arrived shortly afterwards. I felt incredibly angry myself, but Luke's expression was almost unfathomable. Now I think about it, he looked like he was in physical pain, if that makes any sense.'

Joseph nodded. 'Actually, it does.'

'Then rage. He was incandescent! I mean, we were all furious, and the language was graphic to say the least, but Luke was boiling. But I'll tell you one thing, Sergeant — I'd forgotten about it until now. When we took the chainsaw to the tree and cut up the trunk, Luke was crying. He swore he got sawdust in his eyes after he took his visor off, but when that tree was finally reduced to logs and branches, Luke was shedding tears.'

'If I told you that Luke saw spirits and faeries in nature, would that surprise you?' Joseph glanced at the stoop-shouldered man.

Sean pulled a face. 'That's a new one on me. I know I mentioned mystical, but I meant the sort of spiritual, "Gaia" kind of feeling that this place gives off — you know, a life force, peace, Mother Earth and all that, but faeries? No. I draw the line at faeries, Sergeant!'

'Most do,' said Joseph dryly. 'Certainly policemen. But you see, Luke has a personality disorder, in which the sufferer believes fantasies. He sees a magical kingdom populated by beings inaccessible to mere mortals like us.'

'Bloody hell! I would laugh, but it's a long way from being funny.' Sean looked up as if suddenly remembering something. 'You might do well to have a word with my missus, Sergeant. She spent quite a bit of time with Luke. She's a yoga teacher, which is where I get my understanding of the spiritual side of nature. He might have opened up to her more than to us lads.'

'Thanks. We'll do that after we've seen his lodgings.'

Ahead of them, Joseph saw Nikki drawing on to the parking area at the side of the house. They hurried over to talk to her.

Luke's room had police tape across the door and a young, uniformed copper that Joseph didn't recognise stood to one side, barring entry.

New he might be, but he recognised the senior investigating officer and immediately offered her a protective suit.

She held up her hand. 'No, it's all right, we'll look from here. It's hardly an extensive des res kind of apartment, is it? We'll leave it for forensics.'

And indeed the whole of the big square room, once a stable, was visible from the doorway. There was a single bed with a wardrobe and a chest of drawers at one end. The central area had a sofa, a coffee table and a bookshelf, and at the far end was a tiny kitchen area with a sink, fridge and a small countertop microwave and oven.

'There's a tiny shower cubicle, basin and toilet next door,' said Sean. 'Mr Morton was going to add a connecting door but Luke said he didn't mind going outside to do his ablutions. The weather never worried him, and it is along a covered way, so he wasn't particularly inconvenienced.'

The place was clean and tidy, with no sign of ever having been lived in. 'Everything of his has gone?' asked Nikki.

'Every scrap. He didn't have much, and he was meticulously tidy.'

'I smell bleach,' said Nikki gravely, sniffing the air. 'I suggest it's not just a good tenant leaving the place tidy for the next person, but more a careful goodbye to fingerprints and DNA.'

Joseph agreed. 'I don't think the SOCOs will be picking up much from this place. Still, we have a description, and uniform are already tracking his car.'

'He could have gone a lot of miles since he rang the house,' said Nikki morosely. 'Or he could be just around the corner, holed up somewhere and waiting for the furore to die down.' She turned to Sean. 'Can you give us a really good description of him?'

He looked a bit uncomfortable. 'Well, to be honest, I, er, don't really notice things about others.' He brightened. 'But my missus Karen will. She's really into people, their faces as well as their characters. She's at home today. Why not have a word with her?'

'Sean told me his wife used to talk to Luke quite a lot,' added Joseph.

'Then let's not waste time staring at a recently sanitised ex-stable and go see her.' Nikki was already turning away from the room.

'Did he have any Wi-Fi access here?' Joseph asked Sean.

'Yes, he could pick it up from the house, although the signal is iffy out here. He used a laptop, and he had a mobile phone.'

'Do you have his number?' Joseph asked.

'Sorry, no. Never needed it. As I said, he was always here. Mr Morton will have it, though, from when he first took him on.'

Joseph made a mental note to ask him as soon as they'd spoken to Mrs Cotton.

'Maybe I should tell you that Karen doesn't know you suspect Luke of killing that boy,' said Sean. 'She knows about the death, obviously, and that Luke has disappeared, but I've not told her any more than that. Mind you, she's a canny lass, she'll probably have put two and two together by now.'

On their arrival at the cottage, Karen Cotton invited them in and offered drinks. While she prepared their coffee, Joseph looked around him at what was every inch an authentic country kitchen, leading into a beamed sitting room with an open fireplace and mullioned windows. Karen seemed rather out of place in a setting traditionally inhabited by a plump, rosy-cheeked countrywoman in a flowered apron. She was tall and slim, with very long, straight auburn hair tied back in a ponytail. Her hazel eyes seemed to change colour from green to gold. She was a very beautiful woman. Joseph recalled Sean — who was thirty-five — saying that they were the same age. Karen looked to be in her twenties.

Sean took them into the sitting room and, after Karen handed round the mugs, told her what had apparently happened.

'We need a clear description of him, Karen,' said Nikki. 'As well as a little bit of your time. We'd like you to work with our IT department to produce a composite likeness of Luke.'

'Of course I'd be happy to help, but I have to say, I'm really shocked that Luke could even consider killing anything. He has such respect for nature. It just doesn't seem possible.' She bit her bottom lip. 'Although maybe not.'

Joseph asked her what she meant.

'I suppose if you are utterly passionate about something and someone destroys it, it will affect you far more than someone who doesn't have the same depth of feeling. And Luke was passionate all right.' Karen sat in an oversized armchair with her legs tucked underneath her. 'We talked quite a lot actually. I think he could open up to me and, while he respected Sean and the other men, he knew he was different to them.'

Sean looked surprised. 'I didn't realise that. He always seemed very much one of the lads, even if he was more dedicated to his work here than the others were. I put that down to the fact that he had no family or wife or partner to go home to, so his work was all he had.'

'I taught him to meditate,' said Karen. 'He asked me if I would. He knew I taught yoga and rather hoped that I could help him relax.'

'He was stressed?' asked Nikki.

'Not exactly stressed, more hyperactive actually,' said Karen. 'He said that the energy from the Arboretum sometimes overpowered him.'

Joseph saw Nikki's look of impatience. She really didn't do esoteric. She was certainly much more comfortable with facts and hard evidence than with earth energies and tree sprites.

'Was he able to master meditation?' Joseph asked quickly, before Nikki could say anything. 'Not everyone can quieten their mind sufficiently.'

Karen looked at him with interest. 'You meditate, Sergeant, don't you?'

He nodded. 'It can help a lot in this job.' He wasn't going to tell her about his travels abroad and how he had immersed himself in a dozen different techniques that might heal his war-damaged spirit, and how nowadays he rarely practised the relaxation exercises that had helped him so much. He wanted to talk about Lucas Hopwood-Byrd. 'And Luke?'

'He was a very apt pupil, actually. He took to it remarkably easily.'

'Did he talk to you about what he saw in his meditations, or keep it to himself?' Joseph asked.

'Oh, he talked a lot. Especially initially. It was like a kind of awakening, and he was keen to share everything he felt and saw.' Karen looked pensive. 'Although it usually ran along the same lines and always against the backdrop of a forest or woodland and the creatures that lived there.'

Nikki's face was getting darker. 'Not bloody faeries?'

'Oh yes,' Karen said.

Joseph looked at her. She had spoken in such a matter-of-fact manner. 'He talked about faeries?'

'How come you never mentioned this to me?' interjected her husband, with a rather hurt air.

She laughed fondly. 'He would never have forgiven me! He was really happy working with you, my darling, but I'm not sure that chatting about his magical kingdom would have done his street cred with the lads too much good.' Karen smiled rather sadly. 'I liked him and I'm so sad this has happened. He had a childlike quality that was very endearing. I don't think I'll ever be able to equate that with a killer.'

'Tell me how he got you to believe in his utter sincerity when he talked of such things,' Joseph said.

Karen picked up her mug of tea and sat nursing it. 'He said that ever since his childhood he had always sensed spirits in natural environments, especially woods, forests and rivers or the sea. The way he put it was very down to earth, as if he were talking more about life and energy than mystical beings. It was almost religious.'

'He suffers from something called fantasy prone personality disorder. He is disturbed, Karen, mentally ill, not just exceptionally spiritual or other-worldly,' Nikki said.

'And dangerous,' added Karen, rather sadly. 'Or so it would appear.'

'Did he tell you anything about his home life, his family, or his past?' Nikki asked.

'Nothing, DI Galena. It was as if, like Rip Van Winkle, he had awoken from a long sleep.' She looked at Nikki. 'Although he did say something strange one day, about *having* to come to "Shrimptown," as he put it. He said he had no choice, because this was where he needed to be.' She gave a little shake of her head. 'It was gobbledegook to me. I had no idea what he meant by Shrimptown, or about his having to come. And before you ask, he never explained and never spoke of it again.'

'He and his brother used to make up names for English counties and towns. They called Greenborough "Shrimptown,"' Joseph explained.

'Oh, right. He never mentioned a brother.'

'Sounds like he never mentioned much at all,' Nikki growled. 'I'm assuming someone took up references, Sean? I mean, surely Mr Morton wouldn't just take someone on for their childlike love of trees, would he?'

'He came from working on a woodland project as a volunteer, I know that much, and Mr Morton would most certainly have made enquiries about him,' said Sean. 'Mind you, his knowledge of the different tree species and their origins alone would have been enough to convince me.' He frowned. 'And up until this terrible incident, he was a real asset to the Arboretum. He'll be sorely missed. Finding some-one with his knowledge and commitment will be damned nigh impossible.'

Joseph could almost read Nikki's mind. She was won-dering how on earth these apparently sensible people could speak so glowingly about a deranged psychopath capable of clubbing a man almost to death then setting fire to him. Maybe it was time to go. 'We are really grateful for your offer of help with assembling an identikit picture, Karen. Would you be able to come back to the station with us now? We'll have you brought home immediately afterwards.'

Karen Cotton glanced at her husband. 'It's fine by me, if Sean doesn't mind. I've not prepared dinner yet.'

'You go, honey. There's always fish and chips, so don't you worry about that. Luke has to be found and you can help there.'

Joseph and Nikki stood up and thanked Karen for the tea. While she went to get a jacket and her keys, Joseph turned to Sean. 'I don't have to remind you, but if you think of anything at all that could help us to track him, please ring me. You have my card.'

Sean nodded. 'I'll talk to the other two lads as well. You never know, he might have said something to one of them. After all, they worked together for twelve months.'

As they drove away from Shelley House, Nikki asked Karen how she liked living there. Karen said it was the best home she could ever imagine.

'We both came from the Carborough Estate, you know. When my Sean became full-time deputy head gardener at the Arboretum, Arthur Morton offered him the cottage and we knew our lives would turn around. I can't imagine anywhere on earth where we'd be happier.'

Joseph would never have put either of them down as Carborough kids, especially the beautiful Karen. She looked as though she came from money and had a serene and well-balanced air to her, which was certainly not synonymous with Greenborough's infamous Carborough Estate.

In any case, that comment served to lift Karen up in Nikki's estimation. Anyone who could survive the Carborough and continue to function was okay in Nikki's book.

'It's not a big country estate, like some in the Fens,' continued Karen. 'It's a family home, but it has this glorious garden that was born in another era and, thank God, they value it. Ours is the only tied cottage. It was built decades back specifically for the Arboretum's head gardener. That living accommodation at the stable was cobbled together when one of the girls' ponies got sick and Arthur Morton finished up spending night after night in a sleeping bag on the stable floor. That's the kind of family they are, DI Galena. They let Luke have it because he had nowhere else at the time, and he was really grateful for it.'

'I know it sounds a daft question,' said Joseph, 'but you told us about him feeling the energies and the spiritual side of nature — when he talked to you about actually seeing faeries and woodland sprites, what form did they take?'

'Well, for a start, not the fluffy little gossamer-winged things you see in children's books. Some he described were rather frightening, more what I'd call goblins, or elves, or possibly trolls. Others did sound beautiful, but not in a Cicely Mary Barker Flower Fairy kind of way, more like an elvish spirit that resembled its host tree or the location it presided over. To be honest, Sergeant, I listened but didn't always take too much notice of some of his descriptions. He believed in them, I knew that, but I also knew they weren't real. It was like listening to a child talking about his imaginary friends.'

'And he never mentioned his family?' said Nikki.

'Never, and I did ask him once. He said, "all dead." No more than that, just, all dead.'

Joseph wondered why Lucas would deny the father he adored. Why deny the family that had been so close? Why deny a brother who had loved him enough to devise a whole new kingdom for his troubled little brother? It didn't make sense to him. It struck him that there were going to be an awful lot more things that defied common sense in this case before it was over.

* * *

'I hate to say this, Cam, but I'm going to struggle with this case.' Nikki looked her old friend and superintendent in the eye. 'CIA psychic spies and bloody faeries! It's like *The X-Files* meets Tinker Bell around here. Whatever happened to good old bumping someone off to get their money? Or going after the wife's lover with a meat cleaver? I mean to say, faeries? Well, honestly!'

Cam fought back a laugh, then gave up. 'Oh dear, oh dear! How about you try to look at him as a psychotic, a very dangerous young man, and try to leave aside the fact that he sees things you don't. And as for the father, well, he was recruited by the CIA for his extraordinary talents, then he burned out. Keep it simple. Don't try to analyse what their damaged minds were thinking.'

'I just like straightforward, Cam. Not all this hocus-pocus. It does my head in.' Nikki rubbed hard at her eyes. 'Joseph seems to sail through all this weird stuff because he understands it. I spend half the day trying to fathom out what people are getting at.'

Cam was still smiling. 'You'll catch this guy quicker than anyone and you know it. You're just annoyed because you don't do spooky stuff. You're out of your comfort zone with anything metaphysical. Just keep in mind that Lucas Byrd, or whatever he calls himself, is capable of doing very nasty things to people. He has to be stopped. He's a loose cannon, a deadly one. Forget the faery crap and look at him for what he is, an unstable killer.'

Nikki exhaled. 'Well, that's told me.' She smiled apologetically. 'But you're right, Cam, of course. I just get so frustrated by flimflam.'

'And don't we know it! Now, what have you got for me?'

'Well, I'm just about to call a team meeting, so how about I do that, then come back and update you at end of play? It's been hinted that Cat and Ben are on their way back to base after chasing up the victim's ID.'

'Okay, sounds good to me. Now, before you go, do you recall a detective called DC Aiden Gardner?'

Nikki nodded. 'Yes, I worked with him a while back. Nice bloke. Didn't he get injured in a drugs raid a couple of years ago?'

'That's the one. He was badly injured in that incident — he was rammed by a getaway car, and it was touch-and-go for a while. Now, although he hoped to be fit to return to duty, it seems that's not going to happen. He's accepted a post as a civilian intelligence officer in Durham. The post won't become available for another three weeks, so I'm going to suggest that as you've lost Dave, Aiden lends you a hand with this case before he gets shipped out. Are you okay with that?'

'Absolutely, Cam. I liked him and, frankly, the quicker we get this sewn up the happier I'll feel, so sure, the more the merrier.'

'Great. In which case, he'll be with you tomorrow. Oh, and Nikki? Anytime you want to sound off about any aspects of this case, the door is always open.'

'Good. It might just save me from taking a swing at the next person who mentions clairvoyant secret agents or their fairy godmothers.'

On her way back to the CID room, Nikki saw Cat and Ben running up the stairs. 'Any luck?' she called out.

'Yeah, we've IDed him, boss,' said Cat. 'Well, as best we can. The parents have confirmed certain items of clothing and jewellery that weren't too badly damaged, but the prof decided that the lad was too seriously burned for them to view the remains. We've arranged a DNA check for proof of identity.'

They went through to the main room where the whole team was assembled. 'Gather round. Let's have a campfire and pool what we have,' Nikki told them. She walked up to the whiteboard. Cam had given her good advice. She'd reduce all they had to the nitty-gritty and stick fast to the facts. With fresh determination, she picked up a marker pen.

In the centre of the upper part of the board was the picture of the child curled up in the stump of his precious tree. It seemed appropriate. Lucas's deep and obsessive love for a tree had caused him to murder a young man — if the evidence was to be believed. She wrote his name by the photograph and tapped it. 'Lucas Hopwood-Byrd. Age thirty-three. Suffers from a personality disorder. He is our prime suspect for the murder of . . .' She looked across to Cat and Ben.

'Stuart Baker, boss, nineteen years old. Lived with his parents in Hartley Close, Greenborough. We found his name thanks to a mobile phone that uniform spotted just outside the clearing. It appears it fell from his pocket as he was being transported to the site of the dead tree.'

'Do we know if he was with the group that scaled the wall into the Arboretum the week before?' asked Nikki.

'Yes, boss.' Ben looked at his pocketbook. 'The parents gave us the name of his closest friend, who admitted they were there. He told us it was Stuart who started the fire.'

'Okay, then we need to ascertain how Lucas found him, and how he went about luring him to a place where he could kill him.' She frowned. 'Do we know where that was yet?'

'So far there's nothing back from forensics regarding that,' answered Joseph.

'Right. Now, at present, we have Karen Cotton, wife of Sean Cotton, head gardener at Shelley House, working with Spooky on a composite facial image. She's very observant, so we are hoping for something pretty true to life. She has also furnished us with an insight into his thought processes, which could be extremely useful. He used her as an outlet for some of his secret feelings, almost like a therapist, so she could be vital to this investigation.'

As she spoke, she wrote the different names on the board along with their various links to the suspect. She started to relax as she wrote. Seen like this, it was beginning to look like any normal investigation.

'So, we need to find Lucas, known at Shelley House as Luke Elmore. The family there are helping us one hundred per cent, which is a godsend. Cat, when you are clear, get back over there and collect all the details that Morton has on file about Lucas.'

Cat nodded. 'Yes, boss. No problem.'

'Joseph and I will stick with Harry Byrd, Lucas's brother. He's our link to the rather bizarre history of their family. Lucas sent him a letter, saying he would meet him in Shrimptown, which is Lucas's name for Greenborough. Hence, we have to keep a close eye on Harry, especially if his little brother contacts him again. Ben? I'd like you to do some digging as to how on earth a thirteen-year-old teenager who, by the way, looked less than that, could pack a rucksack and leave home, and not be heard of for the next twenty years. It beggars belief really, but it happened. You'll need to liaise with Joseph and myself and also with the brother. The whole disappearance thing wasn't helped by the mother, who didn't report it immediately. According to the brother, they were a tight-knit family and when the father was murdered, you would have expected them to become even more reliant on each other. So why walk away?'

She stared at what they had gathered so far. It was coming on. 'At least we don't need to try to analyse why Lucas killed his victim in the manner that he did. He was paying Stuart Baker back for damaging a tree. Not logical or sane, but that's it, folks, that's who we are dealing with. A man who avenges on behalf of nature and the imaginary magical creatures who he believes inhabit trees and plants and water.' She narrowed her eyes. 'Cam said he's a loose cannon, a deranged one. That's exactly what he is, so don't get too tied up with the flaky, other-worldly stuff. We have no idea in whose direction he'll look next, or for what oddball crime they have "committed." The brother Harry said it could be something as simple as treading on a cowslip plant, so be warned. And watch your step.'

'Couldn't he have left the county?' asked Ben.

'We'd know about it if he'd tried. Look, Harry Byrd believes he has an agenda in Shrimptown — Greenborough, that is. He wants to kill someone, a person he refers to as the "Elf King," whatever that means, so no, Ben, he'll be back, I'm sure of it. *If* he went anywhere in the first place. This is a big rural county, easy to hide in.' She looked at the perplexed faces staring at her and sympathised with them. 'Oh, and this is something separate. We have Aiden Gardner joining us tomorrow for three weeks. I think some of you know him already. He was a very good detective and he's heading upcountry to work with the police in County Durham in a civilian role, but we've got him for a short while. If he's amenable, I'm going to suggest that he does some research into fantasy prone personality disorder and anything else pertaining to the mental disturbances in the Hopwood-Byrd family, including that of the father. I've asked you all to disregard the creepy, weird side of this and concentrate on the facts, but we can't ignore what drives our killer. That would be foolish. If Aiden's agreeable, he'll be our go-to man for all things off the wall.'

'Good idea, boss,' said Joseph. 'You're right. The more we understand his twisted thinking the better.'

'Any questions? Anyone got anything else to add?' she asked. Hearing no replies, she said, 'Okay, it's getting towards the end of the shift, but if you wouldn't mind that quick trip to Shelley House, Cat, to pick up the info on Luke Elmore from Arthur Morton? Then we'll call it a day. We'll pitch in tomorrow and work like Trojans to find this killer before some unsuspecting soul takes their late summer pruning one step too far for our avenging plant-protector.'

CHAPTER FIVE

Standing at the mortuary table, Rory looked at the charred remains of Stuart Baker and sighed loudly. 'It's at times like this that I truly wish I'd become a florist instead of a pathologist.'

His two technicians, Spike and "Cardiff" Erin Rees stifled their giggles. They'd heard this numerous times before, but it always made them laugh.

'Don't mock, cherubs. I'll have you know that my David declared my flower arranging good enough for the Chelsea Flower Show. What I can do with three strelitzias and a couple of palm leaves would amaze you.' He sniffed and tossed his head back disdainfully. 'I'm such a loss to the floristry world!'

'Well,' said Spike with a theatrically straight face, 'imagine *our* loss, Professor, if you'd taken that flowery path strewn with rose petals.'

Erin spluttered out a laugh and made a hurried excuse to leave the room.

'Nicely put, dear Spike, and so true. Which brings me back to the job in hand. It's looking more and more as if our young friend here didn't die from being coshed on the back of the head. It's a sad fact that, judging by the damaged and burnt state of his throat and his upper respiratory system, he was probably still alive when our killer set fire to him. Dead men don't inhale smoke and fumes and burning material.'

Spike nodded. 'The pathological evidence leaves no doubt about it, Prof. Poor sod.'

'Indeed, although he would certainly have died anyway, from the blow to his skull. From the kind of injury he sustained, I'd say the killer felled him with the flat of a spade, wouldn't you?'

Again, Spike nodded. 'The stellate fracture certainly indicates that, and considerable force was used to cause the skull to fracture along the lines of stress. He's no wimp, this killer, is he?'

'He meant business, that's for sure. When we remove the brain, I'm pretty sure we'll find serious damage on the opposite side of the brain to the injury site, where the brain bounced against the cranium with the force of the blow.'

'A contrecoup injury, like you see in car crashes? Where the head stops with the impact, but the brain continues to move.' Spike continued to stare at the body. 'Yes, I can see that's probably going to be the case.'

'Right, so go and find your giggling schoolgirl of a Welsh technician, tell her that her untimely exit has cost her the price of three coffees and then, before we all go home and leave this rather gruesome day behind, we'll get to work on the hapless soul that was young Stuart Baker.'

* * *

It was a beautiful end to the day. The wood glowed in the last rays of the sun and the shadows deepened and lengthened. He lay on the ground, on a bed of bracken and spongy, lime-green moss. The smell from the soil was intoxicating. He didn't want this moment to end. There were small sounds around him — the cracking of a dry twig, the rustle of disturbed leaves, scurryings and hurryings — but they did not disturb his peace. Nothing here would hurt him. They knew who he was and accepted him. They welcomed him. He felt something lightly touch his hand, but he didn't move. They were curious, they always were. But if he opened his eyes, they would run from him, and he liked their company. The older spirits allowed themselves to be seen, just for a fleeting moment before disappearing, and he knew he was blessed to have these rare sights. They were hidden from most humans. He had seen the tall, slender, lithe form with the flowing golden hair — the essence of the robinia tree — many times and was astounded by her elegant beauty. He had seen her, twisted, burned and writhing in agony, when they had finally taken the tree from the soil that had nurtured it. He had wept for her and silently promised revenge, and she had smiled at him, finally closing her eyes and finding peace. He had always known he was important to them, but this confirmed his position as the only earthly warrior. He alone was willing and able to restore the balance.

After a while, he sat up and opened his eyes. All around him, the wood was still, with just a gentle evening breeze stirring the leaves, branches and fronds of bracken. It was time to go back to his new abode. He smiled. He liked it a lot. It was much more suited to him than the stable, although even that had been perfectly acceptable. He liked to hear the soft snorting or whinnying of the Mortons' last two ponies. They were gentle creatures, and he would often go and lie in their stalls when the weather was rough and they were disturbed. He knew his presence and quiet voice calmed them. All in all, his stay there had been a good one. He appreciated the Morton family and liked them a lot. They loved the Arboretum and they cared for it. That made them good souls in his eyes, and he would miss them.

He stretched and, smiling, melted into the heart of the wood.

* * *

By ten o'clock that evening, Nikki and Joseph had finally eaten after working late. Now they were standing together

50

looking down the lane towards the river, the marsh and Knot Cottage.

'I'm wondering,' said Joseph, looking at the familiar little cottage, with its single chimney, outlined against a darkening sky, 'if the time has come to let it go.' Joseph lived with Nikki in Cloud Cottage Farm, but still retained Knot Cottage, more as a cover than anything. He never stayed there now, just called in to keep it clean and tidy. 'That would bring problems of its own, though, wouldn't it?'

Nikki didn't answer for a while, then, very sadly, she said, 'I wish things were different.'

So did he! He sighed. 'But they aren't, are they? And the repercussions, should we decide to take things in a different direction, could be, well . . .' The fact was, they simply didn't know.

They didn't even really need to discuss it any more. They had been over and over it. The fact was that unless they were prepared to jeopardise the team and stop working together, their relationship had to stay undercover. 'We *are* together, Nikki. That's what counts. Let's allow fate to take its course. If Cam ever leaves or gets promoted, then we really will have to reconsider our options. A new superintendent would definitely take a different view. Meanwhile, let's enjoy the best of both worlds, shall we?'

She nodded. 'You're right, of course you are, but just sometimes . . .'

'I suggest a small nightcap, then we turn in,' said Joseph. 'We have a killer to catch and an early start tomorrow.'

They went back inside.

'Why Shrimptown?' Nikki asked, as Joseph was locking up. She sounded rather as if she were talking to herself.

'Do you mean why call it that?' he asked.

'No, I mean, why here? What's so special about this place?'

'It's the home of the Elf King, I guess, and our man is out to slay him. Where else would he go?' Joseph shrugged, then frowned. 'Although Harry said the Elf King was many people, anyone who really upset Lucas, in fact, so that wouldn't fit, would it? He could be anywhere.'

'It's odd, isn't it? We aren't exactly the most picturesque county, are we? It's not full of interesting attractions, quaint picture-postcard villages, cities and towns full of culture, the arts or top-notch restaurants. In fact, Joseph, unless you like flat farmland, lots of water, thick mist and copious quantities of mud, we don't have a lot going for us, do we? So why come here?'

Joseph handed Nikki her brandy. 'Another thing we don't have much of, and which our tree-loving killer would have found a necessity, are dense woodlands and forests. I'm beginning to see what you mean.'

'We need to know where that man has been for the last two decades. The mere fact that he survived at the age of thirteen screams out that he went directly to someone, some adult who was either helping him or, well, holding him in some way.' Nikki sipped her drink. 'Someone could have offered to help him, then kept him prisoner. We know he was vulnerable mentally, so it's a possibility. Who knows?'

'It's fortunate that we have an extra pair of hands for a few weeks, isn't it? I get the feeling that Aiden's part in this inquiry is going to be pretty time-consuming and maybe very important.' They wandered into the lounge, where Joseph sank into an armchair. 'To be honest, it's something I'd have liked to take on myself, but I know we're needed at the sharp end.'

'Don't worry, Joseph, if I hadn't been given Aiden on loan, the research would have been all yours. You're quite welcome to anything weird and creepy, thank you.' She eyed him over the rim of her glass. 'I bet you've been checking out faery stuff in your lunch break. You have, haven't you?'

He raised his eyes to the ceiling. 'Might have.'

'I knew it! Anything a bit fey . . . You really are a very different animal to most detectives, aren't you?' She took another sip of her drink and smiled at him. 'Not that I'd have it any other way. So, what have you found out?'

'I rather wondered about his obsession with nature spirits and whether he possibly believed in an actual faery kingdom. People do, you know. They think you can access it through doors, or portals. Glastonbury Tor is the most famous, but they can be found anywhere, if you know where to look.'

'If I said "hogwash," you wouldn't be surprised, would you?' Nikki chuckled.

'Not in the slightest,' Joseph said. 'I'd expect it and, believe me, even I'm not going to be traipsing around the Arboretum hunting for magic portals in a toadstool patch. We just need to try and get a handle on how our killer's mind works, that's all. I've sourced a few informative sites that might give Aiden a kickstart on his mystic journey.' He laughed. 'I wonder if he's open-minded, or more like you in his outlook?'

'A nice combination of the two would be good, but we'll see tomorrow.' She yawned and held up her half-empty glass. 'I'm going to take this up with me, Joseph. I'm out on my feet.'

He nodded. 'Good idea. Let's go. We could be looking at some very late nights if we don't catch this psycho fast.'

As he followed her up the stairs, he was haunted by the feeling that today's horrible death was not going to be the last one to take place in a beautiful garden.

* * *

Ritchie fell into bed, totally exhausted and aching all over. He hoped Sandy wasn't going to be wanting him to perform tonight. Hell, he was usually ready for anything in that department, but please God, not now.

Though he was physically knackered, his mind was racing, and he was filled with excitement. He was on the last leg now. Soon his Sandy would have the one thing she'd always wanted — a swimming pool.

As he lay in the darkness, still hoping his wife would stay asleep, he thought back to all the guys, seven years ago, who had laughed at him when he said he was going to marry the gorgeous Sandra Hislop. They'd said she'd never even look at him. Well, he'd proved them wrong. And he proved them wrong again when they said she'd leave him within the year. And best of all, he'd proved them wrong when they said he was a loser and he'd never hold a job long enough to provide for the extravagant Sandy Hislop. Well, he'd worked his fucking socks off for the girl, which hadn't gone unnoticed by her protective and adoring father. Daddy Hislop, coming from humble origins himself, recognised a grafter when he saw one and had given him a bloody good job in the family business. Now they had their own home. Only one thing remained before his Sandy became the happiest woman in the world — a swimming pool.

Luckily, Daddy Hislop was in the construction business and had sourced a reliable company to do the professional work and installation. Then the adoring father, who could refuse his only daughter nothing, had seen how Ritchie was doing all the overtime he could to pay for it, and had chipped in with the cost. The one proviso was that Ritchie cleared the proposed site in preparation for the work to begin. Result! He was good at that kind of thing. He'd borrowed a mini digger from a mate of his who worked part-time at some private park close by, hired a large skip and, in the space of three days, had done wonders.

Ritchie sighed. One more day and he would be ready to call in the serious excavation machinery. All that was left was to clear a shrubby kind of flowerbed and bring down an umbrella-like tree in the centre of the overgrown shrubs. Then he would be finished. *Job done, over to you, pool guys, and get your fingers out. My Sandy's bought six new swimming costumes already!*

As sleep seemed a long time coming, he worked out the best way to get rid of the tree. It wasn't too big, in fact it was more what you'd call a specimen tree, maybe only fifteen feet high, but covered in broad, pale, yellowy-green leaves. Luckily, he had a shredder, or it would have taken him forever to get rid of all the leafy branches. It was a shame, really, to have to fell the thing, but it was situated bang in the middle of where they were putting a log cabin to house the pumps and a steam room. Oh well, it was only a tree. To make Sandy happy, he would fell a forest! And with that thought, Ritchie Naylor fell into a deep, exhausted sleep.

CHAPTER SIX

Nikki had met Aiden Gardner many times in the past and had even worked with him when she first became a detective sergeant. He had always been a bit of a joker, a real glass-half-full kind of man but with a keen eye for spotting trouble. She wondered how losing his career as a serving police officer would have affected his outlook on life.

There was a knock on her door and she steeled herself. It wasn't easy, deciding what to say to him. Nikki decided forthright was best. Just be herself and see just how much of the old Aiden was left.

She shouldn't have worried. He walked in wearing a big smile and held out his hand. 'Good to see you again, Nikki. You always said you'd have your own office one day. Bit smaller than the one you described, but hey!' If possible, the smile broadened. 'I'd better get used to calling you ma'am, hadn't I? Instead of some of the other more interesting names we used to use.'

She grasped his hand and returned the grin. She was surprised to see how well he looked, and how much fitter than when they last met. He was broader-shouldered and seemed, well, so much stronger. 'Blimey, Aiden, have you been working out? You look great!'

His eyes lit up. 'Comes from marrying my physio. You're looking at a happily married man now.' He gave a little bow.

Nikki laughed. 'Aiden Gardner, married. Well, that's a day I never thought would dawn.'

'Never say no good can come out of bad — I met the girl of my dreams in hospital, and now I have free physio treatment day or night. How good is that!'

Aiden was not exactly handsome, but he was attractive in a funny kind of way. It was his ready smile that made him instantly likeable. He had short, dark hair and close-set, dark-brown eyes in rather irregular features, and Nikki noticed a lot of lines that hadn't been there before. No matter how much he joked, she was sure he'd been to hell and back in the last few years.

'So, guvnor, what little treat have you got lined up for me in my temporary post here in Greenborough?'

Nikki raised an eyebrow. 'Nothing you could have expected, that's for sure.' She stood up and went to the door. 'I'm just getting my sergeant to join us. He understands more about this rather odd investigation than I ever will.'

'Intriguing. I'm all ears.'

She introduced Joseph. The two men shook hands and sat down opposite her.

It didn't take long to give Aiden a brief outline of the case. Then she asked him if he'd take on the task of researching the Hopwood-Byrd family, father and son, especially Lucas's quirky belief system, to give them a better understanding of what made the killer behave as he had. She tried to avoid the word "faery" as much as possible, but because they seemed to be what drove Lucas to murder, it inevitably came up.

For a while Aiden said nothing, then he flashed her a grin. 'Well, assuming this isn't a wind-up, bring it on. Oddly, about three years before my accident, I had a case that involved witchcraft. Believe me, the research on that was bloody scary but fascinating too, I have to say, especially when you try to understand how intelligent and apparently normal people can get involved in that sort of mind-bending stuff. Yeah, I'll be happy to take it on.'

She threw Joseph a relieved smile. 'Well, I'm going to let Oberon here tell you all he knows so far about his faery kingdom, while I get on with some proper police work, like chasing up forensics. I know our Rory was snowed under yesterday, but he promised to do the Baker boy's post-mortem last night. We're quite sure it will hold no surprises, but seeing how our killer works, in black and white, gives us something concrete.' She smiled at them both. 'Nice to have you with us, Aiden. Hope we can keep you amused until you have to head up country. Now fly away and do some research, my little goblins.'

As they left, she heard Aidan mutter in a stage whisper, 'Shows how much *she* knows! Everyone knows goblins can't fly.'

* * *

Joseph led Aiden out into the CID room and introduced him to the team. 'I'm thinking that as you're going to be doing mainly research, you might like my office. It might be little bigger than a shower cubicle, but at least you can close the door on this troop of chattering monkeys and concentrate. I'll take a workstation out here for a while.'

'No need, really,' said Aiden. 'I appreciate the offer, Sarge, but I'll be quite happy out here. I rather like the busy atmosphere. It makes me feel like I'm part of something again.'

His slightly wistful tone wasn't lost on Joseph. This man appeared to be the life and soul of the party, but he had a suspicion that it was a different story inside his head. Joseph had been badly injured himself in the past but was lucky enough to regain his fitness and return to duty. Even that time of waiting, wondering and recuperating had been difficult. What Aiden Gardner had been though must have been a nightmare. He had always had a reputation as an action-man detective as well as a thinker. Now he wasn't even a proper copper and that must be tough.

'Okay, but if you change your mind, just say.' Joseph looked towards an empty workstation, but before he handed it over, glanced at Cat Cullen. Up until now, they had left their retired colleague Dave Harris's desk free, but the time for sentiment was over. Cat nodded. 'All yours, Aiden. Happy researching! Give me five to grab some info and I'll show you what we have so far.'

Aiden sat down — a little stiffly, Joseph noticed — and took some pens and other personal things from a small attaché case.

'Might as well make it home, as I'm here for a few weeks. The pot plant and the framed photos will be here tomorrow.'

Joseph smiled. The funny man facade had slipped back into place. 'Don't forget the stress-busting Newton's cradle.'

'Is it that bad here?' Aiden asked with mock horror.

'Mate,' chipped in Cat, 'there are times when you need more than a bloody Newton's cradle, you need a therapist!'

'Speak of the devil, or should I say angels?' Joseph smiled as he saw the CID-room door open, and Doctor Laura Archer walk in.

Laura was the force's psychologist and partner of DI Jackman of Saltern-le-Fen CID. She was a slim, tall, very beautiful woman with blonde hair and eyes of a startling blue. It was generally agreed that she and Jackman made a very striking couple indeed.

'DI Galena asked me to call in,' she said. 'I hear you've landed up in Fairyland.' The blue eyes sparkled with amusement. 'Sounds a little different to the usual drug-induced psychotic episodes I'm used to dealing with.'

'Hi, Laura.' Joseph turned to Aiden. 'Have you two met?'

'Oh yes,' said Aiden emphatically. 'Frequently, over the last year, and especially after my injury. How are you, Doc?'

They chatted for a few moments before Laura headed off towards Nikki's office.

Joseph sorted out the information he had so far and, as he glanced over it, he thought again what a strange case this was. The human mind was capable of some very strange quirks. The oddest thoughts, should they take a darker path, could lead to madness and sometimes death. Young Baker hadn't deserved that terrible end. When he considered the antics of some teenagers, getting rat-arsed and lighting a fire in an inappropriate place was not grounds for murder.

'I see Nikki's door is shut, Sarge.' Spooky had appeared beside him. 'I've got you the e-fit pictures that we've produced courtesy of your head gardener's wife, Karen.' She grinned at him. 'Wish all witnesses could be like her. What an eye for detail!'

She handed him a batch of images. Joseph almost gasped. 'My goodness! He's very like his brother Harry, only more weathered and obviously a bit younger. These are very good, Spooks. Better than I've ever seen. They could be photographs.'

'I told you the new software was impressive, didn't I?' said Spooky proudly.

'Thank you for these. I'll give them to the boss as soon as she's free. Have you got time to say hello to our new temporary member of the team? He's working on the backgrounds of Lucas and his father, and I told him you should be his first port of call for all things Stargate and the remote viewing programme.'

She nodded. 'Sure, happy to help.'

He gathered up his files and they went over to Dave's old desk.

'This is our resident go-to woman for everything to do with IT, plus anything weird and wonderful,' he said to Aiden. 'Meet Spooky.'

Aiden looked up from the copious notes he was making and stood up, hand outstretched. 'Good to meet you. I was just trying to gen up on Stargate so I don't look a total plank. I knew absolutely nothing about it. Forgive me for saying, but it all looks a bit off the wall to me.'

Spooky laughed. 'To be honest I'd have thought twice about spending millions on something so, well, unorthodox. But then, if you take a look through the lists of declassified programmes, some of them will frighten the pants off you. Excuse the vulgarity, but they range from the truly frightening Project MK-Ultra, which was an illegal human research project investigating mind control, using hypnosis and drugs like LSD to "program" the brains of potential assassins, to the absolutely barking mad training of domestic cats to spy on Soviets in the Kremlin.'

'You're kidding me. Cats?' Aiden was open-mouthed.

'Yup. Look it up if you're bored sometime. Project Acoustic Kitty. I kid you not.'

Joseph shook his head in amazement. 'Well, after that, Stargate will now seem a little less bizarre after all.' He looked at Aiden. 'I'll leave you with Spooks for a while and we'll talk over this lot later.' He pointed to the folder of notes. 'And this is an e-fit of our killer.' He placed one of Spooky's reconstructed images on Aiden's desk. 'I'll put one on the whiteboard, and then see if the boss is free yet.'

He left them talking animatedly and tacked an image on the board, next to that of the sleeping child in the arms of a dead tree. Then he headed towards Nikki's office.

* * *

Ritchie Naylor was sweating buckets. It was half ten in the morning and he'd already cleared away most of the shrubs and bushes from the pool-shed site. The shredder was a real boon, eating up the branches and spewing out fine wood-chips. Another half an hour and he could tackle the tree. He wiped his forehead with the back of his glove and strolled back to the house for a cold drink.

He sat for a moment on the patio lounger, a bottle of Coke in his hand, and looked across the landscaped garden. Not long after they took possession, he'd brought his mum and dad to see it and his mum had cried. His dad just shook his head in disbelief. Ritchie knew that Dad was dead proud of him and what he'd achieved. He too had been a doubter, never thought his son would come to anything much. Well, he'd shown him. He'd shown them all.

Sandy was out with some of her friends this morning, shopping again. Then another lunch at that new snobby bistro restaurant in Greenborough High Street. He smiled. Well, he shouldn't complain. Sure, liked her treats and the company of her friends, but she was a good wife to him too. If she could just master cooking, she'd be perfect.

He stood up and stretched. Better get on. Rain was forecast for later, although it didn't look like it right now.

He pitched back into the shrubbery and took down the last of the shrubs with his big, strong loppers, which sliced easily through the stems and branches. Then he fed them into the shredder. He emptied the collection box into the skip and raked over the exposed ground to collect up the loose twigs. The ground was dry, and the roots came up pretty easily. He barrowed them down to the skip and lobbed them in. In no time at all, the area was clear.

Putting his tools together by the shredder, ready to cut up the felled tree branches into sections for shredding, he returned to the site of the new pump-house shed with his chainsaw.

Right. Now for the tree.

* * *

Nikki looked up as Joseph knocked and entered her office.

Laura smiled at him and then turned back to Nikki. 'So, you've no problem with me bringing my old mentor, Sam Page, in on this?'

Nikki shook her head. 'None whatsoever. Joseph and I would welcome every possible bit of help with this killer. We're certain that he won't stop with one isolated murder.'

'I agree,' said Laura. 'There is usually one incident, or a trigger, that moves the fantasist to that next dangerous step, making his fantasies reality. Then there's no telling what may happen.' Her expression was sombre. 'It's a complex condition but even so, this man is very unusual. You can probably guess what a lot of fantasists dwell on, can't you?'

'I can imagine,' said Joseph. 'And it has very little to do with tree spirits.'

'Exactly. I've had to deal with several cases of people who have alleged sexual assault. False allegations of that nature are becoming rather too common these days. And I've dealt with erotomaniacs too, who stalk people, convinced that their victim is in love with them. They can be very dangerous indeed if thwarted.' She looked a little perturbed. 'Whereas I've dealt with several varied cases, from men who claimed to be doctors to military fantasists, one of the most common types being those who do their best to convince people that they are SAS officers or claim to be hero veteran soldiers or mercenaries. But I've never dealt with a man like your Mr Hopwood-Byrd.'

'Nor have we, believe me,' said Nikki vehemently. 'And I'm getting very twitchy indeed about what he might have in mind.'

'I'll give Sam a ring as soon as I've finished here and get his take on Mr H.-B. and I'll let you know what he says.' Laura stood up. 'I'll have a quick word with your new arrival on my way out.' She stopped for a moment in the doorway. 'When you catch him, ring me immediately. I need to see this man.'

Joseph closed the door. '*When* we catch him? There's been no sign of him anywhere. He's disappeared.'

'Yeah, just like magic,' grunted Nikki and waved an imaginary wand.

He laid the images that Spooky had produced on her desk. 'At least we know what he looks like. I wondered if Harry Byrd might like to see these. They are very like him. I know he hasn't seen his brother for years, but at least he'd be able to say if he thought we were on the right track.'

'You're right,' Nikki said. 'I'd like another word with him too. I know he insisted that it didn't matter what we thought about his father and his beliefs, but I think it does. It seems to me that if young Lucas was "strange" as a child, it probably did him no good at all having an eccentric father. We really need to understand more about that father/son relationship.'

'Why not take Aiden with you?' suggested Joseph. 'He's really keen to get to grips with this background research. I'll hold the fort here in case anything interesting comes in.'

'Good idea. I'll ring Harry now. See if he's free.' She dialled the mobile number he'd given her. 'Midday, at the hotel.'

'Okay, I'll go and warn Aiden to be ready in half an hour.'

'Joseph?' She stared at him. 'Ring me if anything else happens? I mean like immediately.'

He gave a low chuckle. 'Of course I will. You think I want to deal with the woodsman on my own?'

'That's actually a rather suitable nickname,' she said with a frown.

'It's what uniform are calling him,' he said.

'I think I'll stick with his proper name, if it's all the same. It makes him real. Not a fantasy character.'

After all, Lucas Hopwood-Byrd was all too real.

* * *

Ritchie gave the pull cord on the chainsaw a powerful yank. There was a cough and a second of whirring, then a splutter and it stopped. It was a bit temperamental, so he tried again. And again.

'Come on, come on! Not now, you sod! It's just the tree and I'm done here, so come on!' Ritchie cursed and tugged on the cord, to no avail. With a final obscenity he dumped the saw on the ground and stomped off in the direction of the garage. A few minutes later he returned, carrying a bow saw and an axe.

The lower, leafy branches he clipped off with the loppers, using the bow saw on the thicker ones. One or two he severed, close to the trunk, with the axe. It was hot work, but he was getting there. He fed the small stuff through the shredder, then returned to the tree itself.

It wasn't a thick trunk. Damn the chainsaw. The axe would do just as well. He swung the blade against the tree and felt it bite through the bark and into the tree. He pulled it out and swung again, another deep cut making a wedge of fresh wood fly out. Again he swung, and this time he heard a creaking sound.

This would be a piece of cake. He flexed his muscles and prepared to swing the axe again.

The pain that erupted through his whole body was little short of cataclysmic and centred in the small of his back. He didn't even remember falling, but was now lying on the recently raked ground, totally unable to move.

Maybe he blacked out. He didn't know. The next thing he knew was that a man was standing next to him, leaning casually on a long-handled sledgehammer. He tried to beg him for help, but something had happened to his windpipe and no words came out, just a ragged gasp. He tried to focus. He knew this man from somewhere, but where? And why was he here now? Tears welled up in his eyes. That first excruciating pain had dulled down, but he still couldn't move a single limb. Ritchie was frightened. More, he was terrified.

The man let the hammer fall to the ground and hunkered down on his haunches just inches from Ritchie. He gave the saddest of sighs. 'Oh, Ritchie, Ritchie. What were you thinking? How could you?' He looked across to the lone tree and shook his head. 'I should have got here earlier. But now you've inflicted such terrible wounds, ones that I cannot heal, not with all the love in the world.'

What shit was this? Ritchie wanted to scream at him to get an ambulance. He was the one with the terrible injury, for fuck's sake.

'You really don't get it, do you?' He tutted. 'I'd better explain. You see, you've committed a crime, Ritchie, so it stands to reason you have to pay. That's the way it is, simple.'

He stood up and looked forlornly at the damaged tree. 'Now, it's my belief that the punishment should fit the crime.'

Ritchie watched the man, whom he suddenly recognised as one of the men who worked with his mate at that private park, move across to the chainsaw and pick it up. 'You didn't use this, did you? Had a bother starting it? I thought I heard you trying as I ran through the woods at the back of your garden.' He looked at him tolerantly. 'You have to be patient with these things, Ritchie. Treat them sweetly. Look, I'll show you.'

Ritchie didn't think he could feel any more scared than he was already, but those calm words and the man's horrific unspoken intention had notched that fear up a hundredfold.

'You turn it on, Ritchie, then you open the choke. Then you get a nice rich mix of fuel to your engine as you start her, see? Oh good, this one has a primer, so you press it a few times until you see the fuel flow into the bulb. So easy, Ritchie, like tickling a nipple. And then . . .' He pulled the cord, and almost immediately, the saw roared into life. 'See? More haste, less speed, my friend.'

Ritchie stared up at him in horror. He mustered a croak, a cry, a plea for help.

The man turned off the chainsaw.

This might have indicated that the man had relented, but Ritchie had seen his face. His panic mounted. He knew now, without a shadow of a doubt, that he was about to die, right here where, in a month or two's time, his darling Sandy should have been swimming.

'I know all about chainsaws, and the rest of these tools, but the difference between us is that I use them to care for trees — to maintain, protect, conserve them and ensure their beauty survives. It's called husbandry. I don't torture or murder the trees under my protection. And so . . . You probably already realise that your back is broken, like the trunk of this exquisite — but because of you, mutilated and *dying* — Indian bean tree.'

He looked down on Ritchie, his eyes cold as ice. If Ritchie's paralysed body had allowed him to do so, he would have shivered.

'So, in the spirit of "do as you would be done by," we shall replicate your actions. Now, let's see . . . You took heavy pruners and cut back the smaller growth, and then you shredded it.'

He moved to where Ritchie had left the tools.

The stricken Ritchie saw the man walk towards him, his tread deliberate, holding the pruners. In the background, Ritchie heard the shredder's powerful motor growl.

* * *

Just as he turned off the shredder, he heard the sound of an approaching car. Glancing in the direction of the house, he saw a flash of scarlet through the fringe of bushes lining the drive. Calmly, he pulled off his blood-soaked overalls and gloves and bundled them into the holdall he'd brought with him. His jeans were clean, but his shirt collar showed a spattering of blood. Not to worry. That was fine.

He waited until the engine stopped and he heard a door slam, then he hurried towards the house. Halfway across the proposed pool area, he saw a smallish blonde woman come around the side of the house and walk towards him. He sprinted towards her. 'Mrs Naylor? Sandy?'

She stopped and looked at him, her head tilted to one side.

'Please! Don't go any further.' He held his arms wide, blocking her path.

'Who are you?' she demanded. 'Where's my Ritchie?'

'Please, Mrs Naylor. There's been a terrible accident.' He gripped her shoulders. 'You must not go over there. Let me get you indoors.'

'I don't understand. Where's Ritchie?'

'Mrs Naylor, your husband is dead. There's no easy way to tell you. I found him a few moments ago. I did what I could,' he indicated the blood on his shirt, 'but I was too late.'

Her scream rang in his ears. He held fast while she struggled to wrench herself away from him.

'Please, Mrs Naylor . . . do you have a phone? My battery is flat. We have to ring for an ambulance and the police.'

She sagged then, sobbing, heavy in his arms. After a moment, she dragged a phone from her bag and thrust it at him. He dialled 999, gave them his story and hung up. Sandy was too distraught to see him wipe the phone carefully before he handed it back.

He led Sandy inside the house, sat her down and got her a drink of water. 'You ring for someone to come and stay with you,' he said gently. 'I'll go back out and wait for the emergency services, but whatever you do, don't go out of the house. Promise me now.'

She gulped and said, 'I'll phone my dad.'

'Good girl. I'll see you in a minute. I'll wait for the ambulance and take them to where it happened. You ring your father.'

He handed her the phone and watched her dial. Then he left.

At a run, he crossed the drive and dove into the bushes, heading for the perimeter fence and the place where he had originally entered the garden. It was done.

CHAPTER SEVEN

Harry Byrd was waiting for them in the hotel reception. After Nikki had introduced Aiden, Harry suggested they go into the residents' lounge. Most visitors were either out or having an early lunch, so it was quiet.

The first thing Nikki did was give him a copy of the photofit image of his brother, Lucas.

He looked at it in silence. He cleared his throat. 'That's quite a shock. I've wondered for years what he would become, how he would look, but to actually see it.' He exhaled. Blinked.

'We know you haven't seen him, Harry, but would you say this image is probably true to life?' asked Nikki.

'Oh yes. My mother used to say that Lucas was like a little clone of me.' He looked up at them. 'You must have noticed the similarity. He looks like I did five years ago, except that I work indoors, whereas it seems my brother spends his days outside, so his skin is rougher.'

'We certainly commented on it, Harry,' said Nikki.

'I'm guessing you've tried to find him, Mr Byrd?' said Aiden. 'I don't mean originally — obviously there would have been a major search back then — but in later, more recent years.'

'I have.' Harry Byrd shook his head. 'I tried every avenue I could think of but had only one possible sighting. A friend of mine went on an adventure holiday with his kids — you know the kind, spending days in a woodland or forest environment, swimming, biking and walking. Well, while the kids were off with an instructor, he and his wife booked a spa massage, following a "forest-bathing" walk in the wilder part of the ancient woodland.'

'Forest-bathing?' asked Aiden.

For once Nikki actually knew about something esoteric. 'My mother told me about it. The Japanese have a name for it, but I've forgotten what it is. They believe that being in nature, and particularly among trees, can rejuvenate you — restore your energy and vitality. Nowadays you find places here where you can have a forest-bathing holiday, with a therapist and everything.'

'Exactly,' said Harry. 'Anyway, my friend told me about it when he got home. He said that this place had guides who took you to the best parts of the forest to practise this technique. He had a bit of a surprise when he saw me leading a group. He went up and spoke to "me" and only then realised his mistake. This guy was my double, apparently. Naturally, I chased halfway across the country, but when I got there, the people who ran the place said he'd left suddenly. They said they were sorry, because he was a brilliant forest therapist, the best they'd had. The manager told me his knowledge of trees was encyclopaedic.'

This smacked of advanced education. This man had studied somewhere and, to do that, he had to have had some sort of stable background, maybe even a "home" life. It affirmed her belief that when he ran away, Lucas had gone to a benefactor who cared for him. She said as much to Harry.

'I've wondered that, DI Galena,' he said thoughtfully. 'I've racked my brains but I can't think who it could be. After all, we were still teenagers — Lucas was only thirteen — and we were very close. Surely, I would have known if there was someone outside the family that he was attached to?'

'You can't recall anyone who paid particular attention to him,' asked Aiden, 'some relative, maybe, who had an interest in him?'

'No. I've thought about it constantly over the years and it's worried me. Was there someone, and I never made the connection? But,' he spread his hands, 'try as I might, I can't think of anyone at all.'

Nikki returned to the reason for their visit. 'Harry, we need to know more about Lucas's relationship with your father, particularly how he might have been affected, or encouraged, by your dad's particular, er, talents?'

'And maybe you could expand a little on your father's — if you'll excuse the term — peculiarities?' added Aiden.

'Where do I begin?' Harry scratched his head. 'The best way I can describe father and son is as the grand magician and the sorcerer's apprentice. Apart from Dad's eccentricities, which were many, he was first and foremost a scientist, and that meant conducting experiments, mainly on himself. He believed that it is possible to train the mind to have influence over matter.' He looked at them intently. 'And I don't mean "mind over matter" in the usual sense — taking control of one's emotions, rather than being controlled by them. Dad believed you could use the power of your mind to do far more than that.'

'Which is why he joined the CIA project,' said Aiden thoughtfully.

'Sadly and to his detriment, yes.' Harry sighed. 'But back to Lucas. My dad once told me that little Lucas was like an open book, waiting for Dad to write on the pages. As for me, he rather fondly said that my book was already written, too set in stone for him to edit. I didn't understand at the time, but I took it to mean that Lucas was like Dad, and I was like my mother.'

'Did you ever personally witness something that made you believe he had some kind of extrasensory talent?' asked Nikki, not for one moment thinking this to be the case.

'Oh yes! Regularly. He was capable of going into very deep, trance-like states that scared the shit out of me.'

Taken aback, Nikki said, 'Could you explain?'

'He believed that while he was in this state, he could travel to a different plane, in which time and distance didn't apply.' Harry shrugged. 'And unless he had some strange way of reading people, places and happenings, there had to be something in what he claimed. He once told Lucas and me that there had been an accident of some kind, and that someone we knew was mourning a terrible loss. We heard later that day that our teacher's son had been killed cycling along a main road. I think that particular incident cemented Lucas's belief that his father had what he called "magical powers."'

'So where did his belief in nature sprites come from?' asked Aiden.

'Father believed that all living things contained an energy force, something apparently proven by Kirlian photography, which shows auras or brilliant halos of light shining around plants, animate beings and objects.' He gave a little laugh. 'You can actually produce these photographs yourself. They're not supernatural at all, just a trick of the light. It's a natural reaction of photographic film to the corona effect of high voltage electrical energy. Great fun to produce and very beautiful, although not quite what my father believed. But Lucas began to "see" these energy forces in trees and plants. As he grew older, instead of shedding these beliefs like children shed a belief in Father Christmas, they escalated, probably due to his psychological problems, and he started to "see" them as actual spirits of nature.'

'And he still does,' said Nikki flatly.

'It would appear that way,' said Harry glumly. 'And I blame myself for it. If he'd remained as a therapist in the forest where he was so happy, he might never have taken this next step into, well, madness, I guess.'

'It would have happened at some point,' said Nikki. 'It's certainly not your fault. He's unstable, you know that.'

'Sir?' Aiden looked up from typing notes into his iPad. 'If it's not too painful, could I ask about the circumstances of your father's death? Were you ever told what happened?'

Harry looked into the distance. 'Being in that psychiatric secure unit broke my father, but he still had a considerable reputation among the other patients — or prisoners, whatever you want to call them. He spent most of his time in seclusion, but there was one man who was particularly aggressive towards him whenever they met out of lock-up. He swore that my father was trying to control his mind. One day he just flipped, and before anyone could get to him, he'd strangled my father to death with his bare hands.'

Aiden thanked him. 'I'm sorry to ask. But it's helpful to hear your side of the story too.'

The presence of Julian Hopwood-Byrd hovered over the rest of the discussion, and Nikki decided they'd get no more information on Lucas. She stood up to leave.

'I have to return home tomorrow for a few days,' Harry said. 'I have a carer with Mother while I am away, but I ought to get back and see how things are at home. If you wouldn't mind using my mobile to contact me, and I'll get back as quickly as I'm able.'

Nikki put his number into her phone and, just as she was saving it, a call came in. It was Joseph, so she excused herself and hurried outside to the foyer. 'Joseph? Has something happened?'

'Can you meet me at an address just outside Greenborough, close to the golf course?'

'Another one?'

'I'm afraid so, and it's not pleasant, Nikki. Prepare yourself.'

'Oh great!' She exhaled. 'Give me the address. We're finished here, so we'll be with you in fifteen.'

Nikki hung up. She decided not to say anything to Harry about Joseph's call, and they took their leave of him. As soon as they were in the car, she told Aiden.

'I wonder what he's done this time?' said Aiden grimly.

'Best not to speculate, we'll know soon enough. And from Joseph's tone, I'm glad we haven't had lunch yet.'

* * *

Joseph was discovering that it could be very difficult working so closely with someone you loved. This was an occasion where he would have done anything to spare Nikki the sight of this body. But although she was his partner, her role as the senior officer in charge of the case obliged her to see it, and there was nothing he could do.

He'd rung Rory the moment he reached the scene, even before calling Nikki, and he hoped that the pathologist would get there before her. His presence always helped alleviate a really harrowing situation. As a soldier, Joseph had seen some terrible things, but seeing them in the midst of a conflict or in a war zone was a very different experience to finding horror in a pretty, landscaped Lincolnshire garden. It had shocked him to the core that an apparently gentle, nature-loving man could have tortured another person so horribly. What he had done next seemed quite extraordinary.

Before he could ruminate further, he saw Professor Rory Wilkinson's vivid green Citroen pulling in behind a police vehicle. He hurried over to tell the pathologist what he had gathered from an initial look at the crime scene. 'It's, er, well, pretty grim, Rory,' he said, pulling a face. 'Even I felt sickened by it.'

Rory gave him a mock frown, 'Then thanks in advance, DS Easter, for not only interrupting a delicious late lunch, but for probably putting me off food for the rest of the day.' He shrugged, then smiled. 'There again, that's never happened before, so I'd better go and take a look.'

As Rory gathered up his pathologist's tools from the back of his car, Joseph saw Nikki and Aiden turn into the drive.

He went over to where they had parked.

'Okay, what's the state of play?' Nikki asked as she climbed out of the car.

'Well, we've got one dead male in the garden, a man called Ritchie Naylor. His devastated wife, Sandra, or Sandy, is in the kitchen with her father, who she called to be with her.' Joseph walked towards the house, with Nikki and Aiden close behind. 'Rory's at the site now, but you need to know something before you speak to anyone.' He stopped and explained what a sobbing Sandy had told him, about the very caring young man who had prevented her seeing her husband's body for fear of upsetting her further, and who had called the ambulance and police. She had no idea where he was now and suggested that maybe he didn't want to intrude on the family at such a terrible time.

'And you think it was Lucas?' exclaimed Nikki.

'Absolutely. The wife is very upset, but she described him clearly and told me that although she hadn't actually recognised him at the time, she remembered later that he was one of the woodsmen who worked with her husband's best mate at a private park close by.'

'Shelley House?'

He nodded. 'Her husband borrowed a digger from this other lad, name of Lance Smythe, who was on Arthur Morton's list of staff at the Arboretum. Ritchie was clearing the ground for a new swimming pool for his wife.'

Nikki's eyes narrowed. 'So, what you surmise is that this Ritchie was taking down bushes and trees, and our Nature Boy took umbrage and killed him?'

'Exactly.'

'Okay, I get that. It fits in with his last killing. But then to go to the wife and phone for emergency services? What's that all about?'

'I'm not sure,' Joseph said. 'And it makes even less sense when you see what he did to the poor guy. We thought the last one was bad, but this one is totally sickening.' His features crumpled momentarily, and then he gathered himself. 'So, what do you want to do first, boss? See the crime scene? Or the wife? My advice is talk to Sandy first, as she isn't aware yet of exactly what has happened to her husband, although after seeing a couple of green-faced coppers go past, she's starting to ask questions.'

Nikki puffed out her cheeks. 'I understand what you mean. I'd rather see what we're actually dealing with first, but maybe I should introduce myself. Okay, Joseph. Let's go and see the wife.'

She gave the older man and his daughter her condolences and promised to come and see them as soon as she'd had a chance to talk to her officers.

Soon, they were making their way towards the cordoned-off area, where Joseph could see a team working hard to secure the site and prepare it for Rory's team to start work. Ella Jarvis, Rory's forensics photographer, was there, already suited up and taking a video.

'We need some cover down here!' called out Rory. 'Rain is imminent according to the weather report, and this whole area has to be protected. A couple of tents and some ground sheets at the very least, and quickly, please.'

How complex the securing of a crime site was, thought Joseph. Gathering evidence was a laborious task, certainly nothing like as cool as it always looked on TV. Of paramount importance was that the chain of custody was never broken or compromised by contamination, from crime scene to courtroom.

On seeing them approach, Rory said, 'Perimeter's already established, log is set up and I've done my walk-around examination. Which was wholly unpleasant, thank *you*, dear Joseph. But I do have a pretty clear overview of what I believe happened.' He looked directly at Nikki. 'I'll take you through it, my dear detective inspector. Vomit bags are available on request — as you well know, I hate a mucky crime scene.'

Joseph couldn't hide the hint of a smile. Rory's dreadful black humour never ceased to lift his spirits at ghastly scenes such as this one, and he gave thanks for the quirky pathologist.

'Go for it, Rory, and you can keep your vomit bag, thank you. I've never needed one yet.' Nikki sounded quite blasé, but Joseph knew better by now and he continued to keep a watchful eye on her.

'There's no easy way to put this, my lovely friends. Our killer maimed the unfortunate gardener in the same manner as, according to him, the tree had been mutilated. As I see it, Mr Ritchie Naylor here was in the throes of a little tree felling.' He pointed from the body on the ground to the only tree still standing in the area and indicated some deep axe cuts in the trunk. 'Our killer emerged from the woodland behind the property, hopped over the low fence, came up behind Ritchie and swung into his lower back with this.' He pointed to where a long-handled heavy sledgehammer was lying on the recently raked soil nearby. 'The impact may have concussed his spinal cord, temporarily paralysing him, or it might have shattered the column and then the fractured bones severed it. The PM will tell us that. In either case, he was unable to move.' Rory looked down at the mutilated corpse and frowned. 'Our gentle tree hugger then clipped off his fingers with garden pruners and fed them into the crusher. I think he was mimicking the process used to take the tree down. The fingers were the fine branches. The arms, which he severed next, using the axe, were the thicker branches. I know this from the rather helpful evidence of one fingerless right arm still lying close to the shredder. Now, at this point I believe he stopped. Maybe he realised he was running out of time, maybe he saw the wife coming home, maybe that was as far as our tree hugger went before he was halted, and we won't know that until you catch him, and he tells you.' He looked from Joseph to Nikki. 'One thing is for certain . . .'

Joseph looked at him expectantly.

Rory pointed to the blood-soaked shredder. 'I'm afraid they won't get much for that on eBay. It's in a terrible state.'

Joseph groaned and Nikki asked if he'd ever considered a job as a stand-up comedian, as she wasn't certain pathology was really his forte.

'Oh no! I'd hate a live audience, dear heart. I'm much better off with the dead. And now, if you'll forgive me, I have a very unfortunate young man to deal with, as best I can.'

Joseph saw Spike and Cardiff approaching them, both carrying heavy metal cases of equipment.

'Ah good, reinforcements! It's all hands on deck for this one,' said Rory, then pulled a face and looked apologetically at the deceased, 'Oh dear, no pun intended, young fellow.'

Aiden, who had said nothing during the whole exchange, threw Joseph an anxious stare. "Is this guy for real?" his expression seemed to say.

'Take no notice, Aiden. Fortunately, the prof's one of a kind. But believe it or not, he's the best Home Office pathologist there is.'

On their way back to the house, Nikki said, 'He must have been covered in blood, Joseph. Did the wife mention that?'

'She said he had some blood on his shirt collar. He told her he'd tried to help Ritchie but was too late.'

'Then he was wearing some kind of coverall, so where is it?'

Joseph was pleased to see that she had slipped straight into work mode.

'Must have taken it with him,' said Aiden. 'One of the uniformed officers told me they have already checked the vicinity and there's nothing hidden there.'

Nikki's face was set like stone. 'There's so much here that I don't understand.' She rubbed at her forehead. 'Like why would a murderer call the police? Ambulance, yes. He'd already told the wife there'd been an accident, so that was understandable, but why call us too? And there was a chainsaw sitting there, but he never used it. I'm *very* relieved, believe me, but why not, as he was clearly set on dismembering the body? And why, oh why, be so solicitous to the wife? That I do *not* get.'

'There's a whole lot we're going to struggle with if we are to follow this man's thought patterns,' said Joseph darkly. He glanced at Aiden, who nodded resignedly.

'You can say that again.'

They stopped on the patio. 'The wife is going to want to see her husband,' said Joseph. 'If I have a word with her, maybe you could talk to the father alone, tell him it's not something that we can allow, for her own good.'

Nikki nodded. 'My thoughts too. She can see him at the mortuary when Rory has done his thing, but it's best to tell the father how it really is and get him on side.' She turned to Aiden. 'Would you liaise with both uniform and forensics to keep us updated on any further finds or developments, Aiden? Then, when we're through here, we'll get back to base and you can press on with your background research, okay?'

Aiden nodded and walked back to the crime site. Joseph noted the slightly hesitant gait. 'He's still in pain,' he said softly to Nikki. 'No wonder he's accepted a civilian post.'

She followed his gaze. 'I think his time with us might help him discover what he can and can't do regarding work, and just how much he can tackle.' She gave Joseph a smile. 'Don't worry, I'll keep an eye on him and not push him too hard.'

Joseph was struck by just how far Nikki had come since he first met her. Back then, she had been one of the spikiest, most irascible and outspoken officers he'd ever met. Her job had hung by a thread at that time, and if she hadn't had such a brilliant arrest rate as well as a superintendent who knew about her sad history and what drove her, she would have been long gone. Even in her foul moods, when he was lashed by her acid tongue, Joseph had seen what a brilliant detective she was and that, deep down, she was full of all the right things. He hoped that maybe he had had something to do with the metamorphosis that had occurred as they continued to work, and now live, together.

A crisp voice intruded on his thoughts. 'I'm hoping that faraway expression has something to do with this case, Sergeant?'

He grinned sheepishly. Maybe a little of the old Nikki still lurked in there, after all. 'Of course. What else?'

'Mmm. Well, I suggest that you rein in your thoughts, whatever they are, and let's go inside and do what we have to do — police work.'

Yes, he thought to himself, *she's still there*. And he was pleased. You would never cope with this job if you were a delicate, soft-petalled flower. A hard edge was a necessary survival tool.

He followed her in, the hint of a smile playing around his lips.

CHAPTER EIGHT

Nikki called another team meeting at four thirty that afternoon. She had updated the whiteboard with the new victim's name and a photograph provided by the grieving widow, Sandy Naylor.

'Her father is very down to earth and has been a great help with managing her. His name is Jason Hislop, and he owns Hislop Construction, based in one of the industrial estates in Greenborough. He's taking his daughter back with him until we've finished with the crime site, then he says they'll most likely sell the house. Sandy Naylor will never be able to live there again after this.'

Nikki then went on to explain how the killer had pretended to have been helping Ritchie after his accident and had dialled 999 for assistance.

'Did he use his own phone?' asked Ben.

'No, he said his battery was flat and he used the wife's. My concern is why ask for the police, thereby drawing attention to the fact that it wasn't an accident.'

'I've listened to the recording of his call,' added Joseph. 'He actually said he believed it had been a deliberate attack, not an accident. Oh, and Sandy was too distraught to hear what he said, other than that he was asking for an ambulance and that it was an emergency.'

'The wife also insisted that he had been very concerned that she didn't see her husband. Her words were, "He was anxious and very sincere when he said I mustn't go and look at what had happened to Ritchie. He made me promise to stay in the house."'

'We need Laura for that one,' said Cat. 'It's well beyond me.'

'He's way beyond all of us,' said Nikki. 'But I think we can now assume that our nature-loving boy is a serious threat to the safety of the whole community. He's not gone away. He's right here, somewhere in the Fens, most likely in the vicinity of Greenborough. I'm going to speak to the super and get him to ask uniform to step up the local search. I'll get Laura to suggest places that he might feel safe in, and we'll ramp up the whole investigation. We need to find him and quick. He's totally unstable and we are all very much aware — as you will be when you see forensics' photographs of our dismembered victim — of just what horrific acts he's capable of.' She looked around at the team. 'I realise you've had no real time to do any ferreting yet, but has anyone got anything to add, or to ask?'

Aiden stood up. 'One small thing and it's probably too early to mention, boss. Before we went to visit Harry Byrd, I did a swift search on Julian Hopwood-Byrd, with reference to his ideas and his later career. There was nothing at all, other than his early stuff on quantum biology and a bit about his college days. No mention of any of his later work and experiments or any of those papers that are purported to have brought him to the notice of the CIA.'

Nikki frowned. 'I'll mention that to Cam Walker. There's a chance the security services lifted everything when he joined that project. Keep looking, Aiden, but stop if you hit anything with warning signs on it. We were advised that his side of the investigation was a kid gloves affair, so it looks like Harry might be your best bet for info on our psychic scientist. Ring him before he leaves and ask him to let us know the moment he gets back, then go and visit him again.'

Aiden said he would and sat down.

'I'm trying to fathom where the kid Lucas disappeared to, boss, but I'm wading through treacle,' said Ben, sounding irritated. 'My next step was Harry Byrd, but you say he's leaving?'

'Only for a couple of days. He has an elderly mother being cared for at home, and he says he needs to check in on her. I suggest you keep at it, Ben, then, as soon as Aiden hears that Harry's back, both of you go and see him.' She could have done with having the man on hand at this early stage of the investigation, but she couldn't make him neglect his mother. 'To be honest, Ben, he's already told us that he has no idea who Lucas could have gone to. It's been bugging him for years, but he has no clue.'

'I still need to talk to him. Maybe I can pick up a thread that he's missed. When you are emotionally involved and very close to something, sometimes you do miss things.'

She nodded. Ben was right. A detached professional detective was best placed to see the whole picture. 'Anything else?'

Cat raised a hand. 'I've got the number Arthur Morton had for Luke Elmore, as he knew him, but it's no longer in service. If he has a phone, we have no details on it at all. But I have traced the volunteer woodland project that he was working on prior to the Arboretum. I'm going to see the ranger first thing tomorrow morning, if that's okay? It's in the Wolds, not far from Alford. I spoke to him, and he seemed to think Lucas had been to a horticultural college. He was going to try to hunt out the old files on volunteers — and he too knew our man as Luke Elmore.'

'Yes, go and see him, Cat. Has anyone had any luck with his car or a driving licence?'

Cat pulled a face. 'There's no record of any Luke Elmore, or Lucas Byrd, or Hopwood-Byrd or anything vaguely like that, boss, and no one ever took the registration number of his old car. Sean, the head gardener at Shelley House, said it was a bit of a rust bucket, an old, dark blue Vauxhall, but he didn't know the model. Cars aren't his thing, apparently. If Lucas has a driving licence, it's in a different name.'

'There's nothing at all listed on the PNC,' added Ben. 'He's never been in trouble under any of the names that we know him by.'

'I'll be interested to see which college he attended, Cat. He would have had to have given full details to enrol, so push on with that one.' Nikki looked around. 'Okay. If that's it, I'll go and see the super now. Joseph, come with me, please.'

When they walked into his office, Cam Walker was putting the telephone receiver down. He indicated two chairs and quickly scribbled a note before looking up at them. Nikki saw how tired his eyes were.

'So, we have another,' he said slowly.

'I'm afraid so, Cam. Not pretty either.'

'I heard. Are you two okay?'

'We had to be,' said Nikki, rather dismissively. 'No good going all lily-livered. It's a crime scene. It's what we deal with, isn't it?'

'You're not fooling anyone,' said Cam shrewdly.

'Okay.' She groaned. 'Frankly, Cam, it was horrible.'

'Made worse by the fact that everyone seems to think our killer is such a gentle soul, and ninety per cent of the time it seems he is,' added Joseph. 'But in that other ten per cent he is ruthless, quite inhuman.'

'And we have to get to him before every garden lover or old lady with green fingers is scared to go near a pair of shears or do a spot of pruning.' Cam shook his head. 'The way I'd have handled it would have been to emblazon his face across the front page of every newspaper and have live coverage on all the broadcast media telling the whole county to look out for this guy. But,' he opened a drawer and took out a sheet of paper, 'this arrived just before you did, followed by a confirmation call from somewhere so high up the ladder they probably need breathing apparatus to survive.' Nikki saw the official stamps when he turned it towards them.

'I'm not even allowed to make an announcement to the press,' Cam grumbled. 'It's being handled by someone else, and that faceless, nameless person is on his way here now from HQ. I'm afraid the whole station has to be made aware that, from now on, the man we are looking for is not to be named outside the station. As far as the world is concerned, we are hunting an unknown male believed to have psychological problems. We urge the public to report any suspicious incidents, and if they think they have seen such a person, they must not under any circumstances approach him.'

Nikki frowned. 'But you could have said that. Why send a muppet from HQ?'

'I'm clearly not trusted to do their bidding, or maybe they intend to say something very different when the cameras roll,' said Cam angrily.

'This is all because he's the son of Julian Hopwood-Byrd, isn't it?' said Joseph.

Cam nodded. 'Undoubtedly. Julian — a scientist, an eccentric, a psychic, a murderer and a victim. I wonder which one of those descriptions is causing all the flutter in the corridors of power?'

'Put all of them together and I'd say you had a very dangerous combination,' said Joseph seriously.

'But he's bloody dead!' said Nikki. 'So why all the cloak-and-dagger nonsense? It's all old history now, yesterday's news. What's the point?'

Cam shrugged. 'I've no idea, Nikki, unless things aren't quite as we are led to believe.'

'As in his history was doctored for the media?' asked Joseph.

'Things do get hushed up. Sadly, that's a fact,' said Cam. 'But this is all speculation. We may never know the truth of anything, we just have to catch a killer.'

'Yeah, not knowing half the facts and with one hand tied behind our backs,' muttered Nikki. 'I've already given the brother, Harry Byrd, one of the images, and I should think everyone within ten miles of Shelley House Arboretum knows we are looking for one of their employees, Luke Elmore. This is going to be Greenborough's worst-kept secret.'

'Then they should have acted earlier, told us from the word go that his identity was to be kept under wraps. My only directive was kid gloves, not Top Secret, For Your Eyes Only.'

'And talking about that, Aiden's finding that all info on dear Julian seems to have fallen into a black hole. There's a sad lack of anything of interest, unless you like quantum biology, whatever that is.'

'Why am I not surprised, Nikki?' Cam grumbled. 'Tell him to tread warily. There's probably nothing left to find, but just in case he digs a little too deep, make sure his enquiries don't ruffle too many feathers.'

'Already done, Cam. Will you let us know how you get on with this Man in Black after you've met him?' asked Nikki.

'Of course. He might even want to see you.'

Joseph snorted. 'Bad move on his part if he does, poor guy.'

At that moment Cam's phone rang and Nikki and Joseph slipped out of the office.

'All right,' said Nikki. 'We should all get home and rest while we can. Who knows what tomorrow will bring.' She grimaced. 'I keep seeing that chainsaw and thinking thank heaven for small mercies!'

'I know what you mean,' said Joseph, as they walked into the CID room. 'Oh, I'd booked tomorrow off, if you remember? I was going to give Vinnie a hand with a friend's houseboat engine. I'd better cancel—'

Nikki thought for a moment, then shook her head. 'No. We owe Vinnie, don't we? He's been there when we needed him in the past. You go help him. If it all goes totally tits up here, I can always ring you.'

He smiled. 'Good point, and it will be good to catch up.'

'Just get all the goss you can about him and that lovely Sheila Pearson. It's about time they tied the knot, and you can tell him that from me!'

Nikki disappeared into her office. She liked Vinnie. And she liked the fact that he and Joseph were still so close. They had been through such a lot together in Special Forces and, despite a few ups and downs, they were best friends as well as old army comrades. Yes, for Vinnie Silver's sake she'd cope without Joseph for one day.

* * *

Lucas basked in the warm, golden light from the trees around him. He could feel their gratitude seeping into him from every side. All the practical problems that his actions had caused him were suddenly worthwhile, and he knew he'd done the right thing. The only thing that irked him slightly was that he was deviating from his original path. He had to find the Elf King — after all, that's why he was here in Shrimptown.

He let out a long, slow breath and made his way to his temporary resting place. Evening was descending and he needed to pack up before darkness fell. Tomorrow, at first light, he'd move on to his next home and resume his quest. He hoped his brother would join him soon. From the day he left, all those many years ago, to go to his master's house, as he liked to call it, he had felt the pain of separation from the brother he loved. Of course, he had had no choice, or he would have remained in contact. Only once had his resolve wavered. He remembered the day as clearly as if it were yesterday. Harry, walking the old dog on the Heath, had been within shouting distance. Tears blurred his vision. It had broken his heart to see Harry and let him walk on alone.

Lucas cuffed away a tear. All that would change soon, and he and Harry would bring this dreadful business to a close.

He turned from the path, into the far reaches of the wood. Yes, brothers together. Forever!

CHAPTER NINE

Squinting into the morning sunlight, Vinnie greeted Joseph with a broad grin. 'Ready to become first mate?'

'More like un-able seaman, actually.' Joseph clasped his old army comrade in a bear hug. 'How are you doing, Vinnie?'

He didn't really need to ask. Vinnie Silver looked better than Joseph could ever remember. He had never seen the big man look so completely relaxed. His craggy, weathered face had lost its deep creases, and his eyes twinkled.

'I'm good, man. Really good.' He glanced behind him to where Sheila Pearson was emerging on to the stern deck of their narrowboat. 'And there's the reason.'

'As if I didn't know,' said Joseph, and called out a greeting to Sheila.

'We'll be back before you head off to work, sweetheart,' said Vinnie, jumping across on to the dock. 'Should take us a couple of hours, as long as we don't find any nasty surprises that Lenny hasn't mentioned!'

Sheila laughed. 'Right, well, knowing Lenny, I'll leave you both a cold lunch in the fridge and expect you when I see you!'

They strolled along the marina.

'It's working, then,' Joseph said, not needing to ask.

'It's working.'

Joseph felt about as close as he'd ever felt to warm and fuzzy. Vinnie had been a career soldier, a highly trained special-services operative and, when he left the army, built a very successful IT security-system business. But he became a loner and a rolling stone. All his life he'd loved the company of women but had never shown the slightest inclination to settle down, until he met Sheila.

Sheila was the owner of the Hanged Man public house in Greenborough and was a damned good publican. She was an independent and capable woman as well as being kind, totally genuine and very good-looking.

'You know what, mate, I never believed all that crap about love at first sight,' said Vinnie. 'But I was wrong. I just wish I'd met her earlier. We've wasted a lot of years.'

'The main thing is that you *have* met her, idiot! And it's the right time too. The old Vinnie might not have felt as you do now. Enjoy the present, don't dwell on what could have been.' Joseph punched his arm. 'Right, mate. Sermon over.'

'Thanks, Father Joseph, that's a relief!' Vinnie stopped. 'Before we get to Lenny's boat, there's something I want to ask you, private-like.'

'Yes?'

'We, that is, Sheila and I — well, we've decided to make it official.'

Joseph let out a whoop of delight. 'Brilliant! Best thing I've heard. Congratulations, Vinnie! When?'

'The week after next. It's just a registry-office do, nothing fancy, and we wondered if you and Nikki would be our witnesses. Then in the evening we'll have a slap-up dinner at Mario's, and I thought of asking Eve and Wendy and Lou and Rene, if they can make it. What do you think?'

'Perfect, mate, absolutely perfect.' And it was. Eve, Nikki's mother and her three old friends, all retired RAF officers, had become close friends of Vinnie's when they had inadvertently become involved in a hunt for a killer. Neither

Vinnie nor Sheila had any family and, as he and Joseph were closer than brothers, it would be perfect. 'I can't wait to tell Nikki. She'll be over the moon.'

'Do you think you'll both be able to get the time off?' Vinnie said anxiously.

'Try and stop us! For you, my friend, no question. Greenborough will have to cope without its A-team for a while. We'll be there, never fear.'

'Well, that's settled then. I'll give you the date and time and then I'll ring the Golden Girls and tell them.' He clapped Joseph on the shoulder. 'Let's fix Lenny's misbehaving engine, then we can go back for lunch and have a beer to toast the bride.'

* * *

It felt strange working without Joseph. DI Nikki Galena, the acerbic and bitter loner, driven to rid the streets of Greenborough of drug-dealing scum like those who had ended her darling daughter's life, had become a dedicated team player. Her team was her life now, with Joseph right up there as her ally and partner. Now, a simple day apart made her feel strangely vulnerable and rather cut adrift. There was no practical reason for it — she was unquestionably in charge whether he was there or not, but there it was.

The night had thankfully been quiet, with no reports of any untoward incidents. Uniform were extending their searches to every woodland, public and private, and were even finding their way into overgrown farmland copses. After a fairly recent case involving one of these tightly wooded areas left uncultivated for the sake of its wildlife and ecology, she was very anxious to rule those out. She knew from experience that such little overgrown patches could harbour all manner of secrets.

She was now waiting for their reports, if any, to come in. Outside, the main office was quieter than usual. Cat had gone straight from home to see the ranger who had taken on

Lucas as a volunteer in his woodland project. Aiden had his head down, researching. Ben was down in IT getting help accessing something that had beaten him. The place felt like a ghost town, not the hub of a murder inquiry. When she heard a knock on her door, she was pleased to see another face, no matter whose.

'Well, Sergeant Farrow! What brings you up to these heady heights?' She smiled broadly at him. 'Grab a pew, Niall, and sit down.'

Niall Farrow, married to Joseph's daughter Tamsin, was the nearest thing to a son-in-law Nikki would ever have. She adored them both and — off-duty — they considered her as family.

'I need your help.' He spoke in a low voice despite the closed door.

'Go on.'

'It's Yvonne Collins, ma'am.'

'Niall, we are on our own, so drop the ma'am, please, just for once. It makes me feel a hundred years old.'

He grinned at her. 'Sorry, but we did agree that at work we follow protocol. It's only right.'

She raised her eyebrows. 'Okay, Sergeant, tell me about our Vonnie.'

'Well, as you know, she's applied to work beyond her compulsory retirement age several times, and it's always been accepted. But I've just had a memo saying that by the end of the year, she has to go. They think she won't be able to continue to meet the necessary health criteria to cope with ordinary duties. I'm afraid her time is up.' He pulled a face. 'It won't be the same without Vonnie, honestly it won't. She taught me everything. She was the best mentor and crewmate a rookie could ever have. Now she has young PC Kyle Adams with her, and, in six months, she's made that kid into a first-rate copper with all the right values.' He sighed. 'She's got more local knowledge in her little finger than some of my guys have got in the whole of their bodies. She's going to be a massive loss to the team.'

'You don't have to tell me, my friend,' Nikki exclaimed. 'I know exactly the value of experience. We lost our Dave, didn't we? And lost something very valuable at the same time.'

'Well, that's what I was thinking, ma'am, er . . .' He looked at her ruefully. 'Is "boss" any better?'

'It'll do but go on.'

'Vonnie can't stay on in uniform, but she could come back as a civilian. Hell, half the station is manned by civilians these days. The thing is, she says the streets are her home, sitting in an office would kill her . . . but,' he looked hopefully at Nikki, 'she'd walk on hot coals for you and the sarge. Since you've lost Dave, what about trying to convince her to come back as a civilian interviewing officer with your team?'

Nikki whistled. 'Not that easy, Niall. Cutbacks? And I hate to use the B-word, but budget too. Dave's position has been terminated.'

Nikki found herself bathed in Niall's cheekiest and most boyish smile. 'Yes, but you are *the* DI Nikki Galena and the super knows our Vonnie's worth. If you tackled him, I'm betting he'd open a new position like a shot. And, hey, civilians are cheaper to run. What do you say?'

'I say, what is Vonnie's opinion on this clever and cunning scheme you've dreamed up, just because you can't bear to lose your old mentor?' She tried to look serious.

'Ah, well, that's another reason I'm here.' He looked at her hopefully. 'She doesn't actually know yet. I was rather thinking, if it came from you . . . ?'

She couldn't help but laugh at his cheek. 'You want the whole thing to come from me?'

'Er, in a nutshell, yes.'

'Niall!'

'Think about it! She'd fill the gap Dave's left — and all that local knowledge! We can't lose that, surely? She's been epic in her time, and she's got more arrests than half the station put together.'

His enthusiasm reminded her of his probationer days, when he was little more than a kid. Vonnie had practically had to have him in reins. 'Okay, okay. But let me sound out the super first, just to see if it's a possibility. And I have to be sure that Yvonne is fully on board and *wants* to be here, not because she feels a kind of obligation. Okay?'

She thought he was going to explode with delight.

'Oh yes! That's stellar! Thank you, ma—' The grin widened. 'Thank you, Nikki! You won't regret it.'

'I'd better not. I know I'd not regret Vonnie being here, but I could regret the earbashing I'm likely to get from the super. And if that's the case, I'll be certain to pass it down the ranks to you, Sergeant Farrow.'

He stood up, but she motioned him back into his seat. 'While I've got you here, is there anything filtering through from the officers on the ground regarding Lucas Byrd, or maybe his car?'

'I'm expecting some of them back,' he glanced at his watch, 'in the next half hour. I'll be sure to get anything of interest directly to you.' He was back in work mode in an instant. 'We're working in teams. I don't want anyone out there alone, knowing his tendency to assassinate people who injure nature. With their great feet, coppers can crush a whole load of bracken in one short search, let alone half a field of buttercups. No one is safe on their own and I've made a very strong point of that.'

'Sensible,' said Nikki. She smiled again. 'Okay, thanks for that and I'll keep you updated on Operation Keep-Our-Vonnie.'

This time he did leave. She hadn't told him, but it had been in her mind to approach Yvonne Collins anyway, when the time came for her to go. On several occasions, Vonnie had said she would welcome retirement, but on others she had admitted to being terrified of leaving what had been her whole life for thirty-five years. It could swing either way. Nikki just hoped that by the end of the year, there was a chance that Dave's desk would become Vonnie's, and that wealth of local knowledge would not be lost.

* * *

Cat enjoyed her drive to the Wolds. They were really very pretty. Some woods, rolling hills, and fields with hedgerow boundaries made a refreshing change from muddy watercourses and reed-lined ditches. As she pulled into the car park of Arlesmere Woods, where she had arranged to meet her ranger, she decided that she and Ben really ought to get out more. How long was it since they had just thrown some walking shoes in the back of the car and driven somewhere quiet, away from the station and all the crap they had to deal with day after day?

As she locked her vehicle, she determined that they would make some changes. They spent far too much downtime crashing in front of the TV with a pizza and a box set.

James Court was waiting for her, leaning against a mud-spattered Land Rover Discovery. He was a gangling, skinny man — in his mid-thirties, she guessed — with longish fair hair and a tanned face. He was wearing olive green cargo pants whose pockets were clearly stuffed with necessary items, workman's boots and a dark-green sweatshirt with a logo on it.

He seemed friendly enough, yet with an anxious air about him. After introducing himself and shaking Cat's hand, the worried look returned. 'I'm struggling to believe what you told me about Luke, DS Cullen. He was so passionate about ecology, one of the most dedicated volunteers we've ever had.'

'So you're a countryside ranger, is that right?' asked Cat.

'Yes. I started by volunteering with the National Trust, then went to college and obtained all the relevant qualifications. Now I cover three areas of woodland here and also liaise with local landowners and businesses whose activities might affect the environment.'

'And when did Lucas — sorry, you knew him as Luke — join you?' she asked.

James took a folded sheet of paper from one of his many pockets and handed it to her. 'This is all the information I could find on him, which isn't much. He joined as one of a group of regular volunteers. He'd already studied country-side management and dendrology — that's the science and study of wooded plants, like trees and shrubs.' He looked at her earnestly. 'He knew far more than any of us, including me, about trees and their history.' With a brief flash of humour, he added, 'A couple of his fellow workers called him an arbour-anorak.'

Cat looked at the paper. 'He's listed as having attended a university in Lancashire.'

'Yes, he said he had an undergraduate degree and I believed him. His knowledge of tree biomechanics could only have been gathered in an academic setting. He was purely volunteering and had obviously filled in a normal application form but we never checked up on the finer details. Most of what is on the list is what he told me when we were working together.' He frowned. 'I have to say, in retrospect, he was rather driven. I would think he didn't suffer fools gladly. He had rigid ideas, especially about the care and management of trees, and wasn't exactly open to other suggestions. Not that he argued. He just kind of dismissed them as irrelevant and carried on doing things his way.'

'That certainly fits in with what we've been told about him. Did he get on with the other helpers?'

'He was happier working alone, or with just one or two other dedicated souls, of which there were several. I mean, you don't do this just to get out of the house. You do it because you care and want to make a difference to the environment.'

'Did he have a particular friend?' she asked.

He frowned. 'You'll see a name at the bottom of that list, with an address and phone number. He's an older man who only gave up helping us quite recently, because of arthritis. His name is Ed Shipley. I wouldn't call him a friend exactly, but Luke liked to talk to Ed, because he was real old-school. His family lived for generations on the edge of some ancient woodlands somewhere, and his grandmother was a kind of natural healer, possibly a herbalist. Ed was very into the medicinal properties of plants, and this fascinated Luke, so I thought you might find Ed more useful to talk to than me.'

Cat thanked him for his help and headed for her car. She rang Nikki and told her she was going to try to speak to one of the other volunteers, who might know more about Lucas Hopwood-Byrd. On getting the okay, she rang Ed Shipley, who said he was free, and she was welcome to come over.

Ed lived in a small bungalow that had seen better days. However, the peeling paint and uncleaned windows faded into the background when she saw the picture-perfect cottage garden.

It looked like one of those "Olde Worlde" jigsaw puzzles that were a mass of impossibly colourful flowers. The only things missing were the thatched cottage and the wishing well.

Ed was a real old-timer, with a florid, chubby face and bright eyes. He wore a cloth cap and a short-sleeved check shirt, and his grubby gardener's trousers were held up with old-style braces.

'Kettle's on, me duck!' he called out, as she closed the gate behind her.

Eyeing the peeling paint, Cat wasn't too sure whether she wanted a drink, but it was impossible to refuse that wrinkled, winning smile. 'Smashing! Tea would be lovely.'

She was glad she had accepted. Inside, the tiny bungalow showed none of the neglect of the exterior. Cluttered, yes, but clean and tidy. The kitchen she entered was part food-preparation area and part horticultural office. Stacks of seed and plant catalogues teetered precariously on a chair. An open laptop still logged into a garden centre's website sat on one end of the wooden table, and in the corner of the room stood two tall stacks of unopened cardboard boxes labelled "New Seed Trays" and "10-cm flowerpots."

Ed poured boiling water into two spotless blue-and-white-striped mugs. 'Sorry it's only bags, duck, but I broke me teapot last week. It were me mam's too. Right upskittled I were.'

Cat loved hearing the local dialect, which was fast disappearing amid the influx of incomers. She knew it had become broader because he was upset by the breakage.

'I don't think I've ever seen a more colourful garden, Mr Shipley,' she said. 'It's beautiful!'

The old man was obviously pleased by her words of praise. 'It is, in't it? And it's Ed, by the way.'

'I'm puzzled, Ed. The ranger told me you came from some ancient woodland area somewhere, yet you've a broad Lincolnshire accent.'

He laughed. 'Me mam were from here and I was born here too. It were me dad's side that hailed from the Wychwood Forest. That's in Oxfordshire, ye know. I'd go for me holidays and spend time there wi' me gran. Happy days!'

Afraid he might start reminiscing, she moved on to Lucas Hopwood-Byrd. 'Ed, what can you tell me about the man you knew as Luke Elmore?'

His eyes twinkled. 'Luke? Clever as any professor, that one, but definitely not quite all there. Sweet lad though.'

Oh sure, thought Cat. 'You spent quite a bit of time with him, then?'

'Oh, aye, fair bit, an' 'e knew 'is trees an' all.' The way Ed slurped his tea reminded Cat of her grandfather. 'Better'n most.'

'So what makes you say he wasn't quite right?' Cat asked tentatively.

'Strange talk, me duck, strange talk. Made me think of times at me gran's place in the woods. Mayhap the oldens would talk like that, and it fair gave you the whim-whams, it did.' He sat back, holding his mug in both hands. 'He saw stuff. Stuff normal folk don't see. I reckoned that lad were two slices short of a picnic, lass. It was all in his head, I knows that well enough, but there were times I was afeared for 'im.'

'Where did he live, Ed, do you know?'

'Oh aye. He rented a room over a little village shop, halfway between here and Anderby Creek. When he wasn't working 'ere, he'd spend a lot of time on the beach and messing about at the creek. He knew quite a bit about boats. Said he had a friend had a boat down that way, but he never said where.'

'Did he ever talk about his family?' asked Cat.

'Nivver, duck, not once.' The old man shifted a little uncomfortably in his chair. 'Don't mind me asking, but what's the lad done to have the police asking about him?'

Cat knew it would be in the papers at some point, even if the name wasn't mentioned, but still she decided to be cautious. 'We aren't really at liberty to say yet, but we need to talk to him about a very serious crime.'

He shook his head rather sadly. 'Then it's a bad business, I'm sure. Mayhap his mind gave up on 'im. There were times he 'ad me right mizzled over the things 'e'd come out with, couldn't make 'im out at all. In the end, I gave up tryin' and accepted 'im for what I *could* understand. Thing was, no one loved nature more than 'e did!'

Cat nodded. The old guy was scarily close to the truth with that last comment. Lucas loved nature enough to kill for it. When she said she had to get back, the old man said, ''Ave a quick look at me garden afore 'e go?'

Cat said she'd love to.

'Me aud gran'd be tickety-boo about her grandson having a garden like this 'ere.' He waved an arm to indicate the sea of flowers. 'Most is good for medics, yer know.'

Cat knew that "medics" in the local dialect meant herbal cures. 'Luke was interested in that too, wasn't he, Ed?' she asked, looking at a glorious bed of purple and lilac lavender bushes.

'Couldn't get enough of it, me duck. Allus askin' summat about it. Reckons 'e knew as much as me when 'e left.'

As they wandered through the floral wonderland, Ed was picking little sprays of herbs and flowers. He rattled off some of the lovely local names for some of them, names like dick-a-dilver for periwinkle, herbigrass for rue and snowball for guelder-rose. When they finally returned to her car, he took a bit of gardener's raffia from his pocket and tied them into a bunch. 'Hang 'em up in yer airing cupboard, me duck, and they dries out. Smells so sweet and lifts the spirits and then yer can think o' this garden.'

Cat thanked him. All the way back to the station she breathed in the aromatic perfume. Murder or not, it made her smile.

CHAPTER TEN

Laura Archer often met up with her old mentor, Sam Page, who was in the habit of calling in to see her at her private consulting room. Today, however, after two cancelled appointments, she had decided to drive out to his lonely cottage on the edge of the bird reserve.

Sam met her at the door. 'Lovely day! Fancy a walk over to the lagoons? We've got some avocets there at the moment, along with redshanks and whimbrels.'

Laura pointed to her feet, which were clad in walking boots. 'All geared up. I know you very well, Sam Page.' She hugged him tightly. Sam was like a father to her. He was slowing up these days, but he still walked regularly, and his mind was sharp as a tack.

They walked towards the marsh, arm in arm. 'I've got an interesting one for you this time.' She told him about Lucas Hopwood-Byrd.

His eyes lit up. 'As you say, very interesting. And very dangerous, by the sound of it.'

'It's not something you hear of often, is it, Sam?'

He shook his head. 'I've had a few cases over the years, mostly military fantasists in my experience. All inadequate personalities with a desperate need to fabricate a much more powerful alter ego. The trouble is the kind of society we live in now is very conducive to fantasy. Films and TV all persuade us that we should be living lives of high drama and glamour.' He looked at her with interest. 'But your man doesn't sound like that at all.'

'He's not, Sam. My experience of that kind of thing has involved individuals who are experiencing delusions, mainly erotic ones. Stalkers who are convinced their victim is just playing hard to get and is really madly in love with them.' She stopped and watched a flight of swallows swoop in wide circles around them. 'Lucas doesn't really fit into any pattern that I know of. I did a paper on it a while ago, so I researched the syndrome extensively. The nearest I can come is people who been overly influenced by computer games and are acting out a revenge strategy in the form of an avatar—'

'—as the heroic human protector of the trees and forests,' finished Sam.

'More the earthly knight who protects the spirits who inhabit those trees.' Laura frowned. 'But it's not exactly that either. He's living in a parallel universe, his own little world, and we know what that could make him, don't we?'

'A schizophrenic?'

'Well, he sees things that don't exist outside his mind. His unusual beliefs aren't based on reality. It points to that, but even schizophrenia doesn't fit. He's sharp, bright, can communicate with others, especially people who share his passion for nature. He is extremely active too, known to be an exemplary worker with no lapses in concentration.'

'While schizophrenics can be confused, anxious, upset, angry or suspicious, but not seriously aggressive to others,' concluded Sam.

'And you don't get more aggressive than killing people.'

They walked on in silence, both pondering the enigma that was Lucas Hopwood-Byrd.

'Ever heard of a man called Julian Hopwood-Byrd, Sam?' Laura asked, after a while.

'The scientist who became a murderer, then was killed himself? Oh yes. I was fascinated when it finally hit the papers. What a drama!' He stopped and turned to her, his mouth slightly open. 'Byrd? Oh my! Really? They are related?'

'Lucas is Julian's son. There are two. The other son, Harry, is the one who brought the whole thing to our attention.'

'Well, I'll be damned! I never made the connection.' Sam stopped at a fork in the path and pointed across an area of boggy marsh to a lagoon. 'Look! Avocets. Aren't they beautiful?'

Laura smiled. There they were, the now-rare distinctively patterned black-and-white waders with the long, upturned bills, feeding in the shallow waters. 'Nikki rang me earlier, Sam. Whenever they try to look into Julian's background, they come up against a brick wall. They want to know if Lucas could have been affected, either by what happened to his father, or maybe his father's own peculiarities, but other than talking to Harry, they are pretty well snookered.'

'Somewhere I have a paper written by Julian Hopwood-Byrd, way back, long before he went to the States to work. He was a highly intelligent man, Laura, but drawn to ideas that most found preposterous.'

'So I hear. I'm told he went on to help the Americans with their remote viewing programme, but not just as a scientist, as a psychic too.'

Sam shrugged. 'Mmm, I read an internet article years ago about that, so it doesn't surprise me. As a matter of interest, many of those psychic volunteers, mainly soldiers, ended up in psychiatric hospitals, or else totally lost the plot and finished up chasing crop circles or claiming alien abduction.'

'And Julian killed a man.' A breeze rippled through her hair, and she brushed it from her eyes. 'Now his son has done the same.'

'In the name of nature.' Sam walked across to an old bird hide, climbed the steps and opened the door.

Inside it smelled of damp wood and something else that Laura didn't find particularly pleasant, but once they had opened up the big wooden viewing hatches, the view across the marsh and the water pools soon compensated for the dank odour.

'It's interesting, you know. Lucas kills for the love of nature and his father made a study of quantum biology, which they call the quirky nature of nature.'

'Not my field of study, Sam. I vaguely recall doing photosynthesis at school, but little more.'

'Oh, it's way beyond me, Laura. I just know that it's something to do with the application of quantum mechanics and theoretical chemistry to biological phenomena and problems.' Sam raised a shaggy eyebrow. 'You need a very different sort of brain than mine to get excited about that sort of thing.'

'So why on earth, if Julian was so highly intelligent, did he ditch all that and turn to such a contentious subject?' Laura wondered.

'Well, why not? After all, the paranormal has fascinated the greatest minds for centuries and as we psychologists say, "There's nowt so queer as folk!"' They both laughed.

'Isn't the human mind the most fascinating thing in the world?' Laura said.

'No doubt about it, but unfortunately, dear Laura, I'm going to be leaving you on your own with this little conundrum. You know my old friend Hugh Mackenzie? Well, he's going back up to his family home in Fortrose for a week and he's invited me to go with him for a bit of a holiday.'

'Oh, that's a lovely idea, Sam!' said Laura, squeezing his arm. 'You're not driving, surely?'

'No, we're flying up to Inverness airport, where his sister and her husband will collect us. We'll be staying with them. They've promised me bottlenose dolphins and more wildlife than I can shake a stick at. I'm taking my best binoculars. Oh, and apparently there's a very impressive craft beer at a local Cromarty brewery.'

'Sounds like heaven!' exclaimed Laura.

'That's exactly what I thought. But, Laura, if you need to talk over this new and very worrying case, I'll leave a contact number, just in case the mobile signal's not strong. Don't think I haven't got time for you.'

He meant it too. Well, she would certainly not be interrupting his well-earned break. Sam had been through a lot in the past year or so. Some fun, good company and good beer was just what he needed. 'When do you go?'

'In two days, so I'll search my files tonight and see if I have any old cases with a similar background.'

'Absolutely not! You concentrate on packing and polishing those binoculars. I'm pretty sure this man is a one-off, and if I can be of any help to the police, it's going to have to come from applying expertise and not case studies. Go toss a caber or something and forget about the Fens for a week!'

He gave a belly laugh. 'A caber! The heaviest thing I'll be lifting is a full pint glass!' He pointed out of the viewing hatch. 'Ah, look — whimbrels! How lovely!'

* * *

Nikki was down in the foyer, hoping to grab a word with Niall about Yvonne Collins, when she saw a man in a very expensive suit and shoes so shiny they looked glazed. He was wearing an official-looking identity card on a lanyard around his neck. She knew immediately that this was the man who had been sent to throw a fire blanket over the name of Lucas Hopwood-Byrd. Oddly, he also looked vaguely familiar. She watched as an officer was hurriedly dispatched to escort the man upstairs. He was clearly expected. Well, maybe she didn't know him at all, and he just resembled someone else. Whatever, it wasn't worth fretting over.

Niall was in his office, and he put the phone down as she entered. 'I was just ringing up to you, ma'am. We've found where he's been camped out, but he's moved on.'

'Where was he, Niall? Close by?' she asked.

'You know the Catterall Estate? It used to be a privately owned house with extensive grounds, then it became a conference centre, and then a property developer took it with a view to making it into a retirement village.'

Nikki nodded. 'They only started work a short while ago, didn't they?'

'Yes. They're rebuilding the whole place in a series of phases. Phase one is already under way and ground is being cleared for two and three. Stage five is a long way down the line, maybe two or three years, and it will require stripping out some overgrown woodland and the excavation of a small lake for some executive, lakeside, chalet homes for retired toffs.'

'Very nice. And he was there?'

'He'd built himself a sort of hide in the deepest part of the wood. My lot walked past it twice before they even knew it was there. Dead clever piece of woodcraft construction. Interwoven branches, and all lined with a thin tarpaulin. He didn't bother to take it down, must have decided to move on and just left it.' He looked at a scribbled memo. 'The team that found it also found blood-soaked coveralls, ma'am. He'd dug a hole and buried them, again not with any great intention to conceal — the freshly dug site was quite obvious. It looked like he was simply tidying up.'

'And how long ago do we think he vacated this hidey-hole?' she asked.

'Not very long. Around dawn, I'd say.'

It was now lunchtime. If he was staying in the area — and Nikki was sure that he was — he certainly wouldn't have gone far. 'Well, we have an idea now that he's going to stick to places he feels safe and comfortable, and that are surrounded by trees and woodland. Sadly, that means we have to start all over again with the search.'

Niall pulled a face. 'I've already ordered it. He might well think one of the best places to hide is somewhere we've already checked. So it's back to the starting block for my guys and gals, I'm afraid.'

'At least the Fens don't have that much woodland, and most of that is on private land, or on the perimeters of villages. It could have been much worse if we'd had to head north towards the Wolds.'

Niall began to sing quietly. '"Always look on the bright side of life."'

'Talking of the bright side,' Nikki said, 'I had a swift word with the super. If, and only if, our Vonnie is fully on board, Cam thinks he can reopen Dave's civilian interviewing-officer post and, between you and me, he welcomes it. He's of the same opinion as us: the force cannot afford to lose all that local and police procedural knowledge. Apart from which, Vonnie is a kind of matriarchal figure, someone the younger officers can go to for advice. Some of the more senior officers too, unless I'm very much mistaken.'

'I throw up my hands to that. Whenever I'm a bit out of my depth, she's the one I turn to.' His smile broadened. 'I appreciate it, really I do.'

'Hold up, we haven't got the lady herself on board yet!'

'I have every faith in you, ma'am,' said Niall, quite seriously.

Nikki wished that she felt the same. All of a sudden, she appreciated the breadth of the gap left by Dave's departure, which would only be made worse by the loss of Yvonne Collins. Their two heads contained knowledge and histories of criminals in Greenborough, and the crimes they had committed, that even she had never heard of. She prayed that Yvonne wasn't making plans to join the WI or the local rambling society, play bingo or knit blankets.

She made her way back upstairs, planning what to say to Vonnie, and then found her mind wandering back to the "Man in Black." Who *was* that guy?

* * *

Naturally there *were* some unforeseen problems with Lenny's engine, mainly due to lack of maintenance and timely repair.

But Vinnie had started his army life in the REME, the Royal Electrical and Mechanical Engineers, and he'd dealt with far bigger problems than an unloved narrowboat engine.

Lenny was a local character thereabouts, a bumbling, smiling, older man with little money, two cats and a rescue mutt, and a Micawber-ish view of the world that believed firmly in never worrying — something would always turn up. It certainly had this time, in the form of newbie narrowboat owner Vinnie Silver, and his valuable training, plus the close proximity of a marine-engine spares store and chandlery and Vinnie's God-given ability to talk people into giving him a good deal for the cash-strapped Lenny.

Wiping grease from his hands, Joseph decided it had been a good morning's work. He had thoroughly enjoyed doing something practical for a change, but more than that, he had loved working alongside his old buddy again. His memories of the old days were both good and bad, but the camaraderie they had shared made them all treasured. They had been a special team, and their rapport had been the saving of them on more than one occasion when they'd come under fire.

'Time for that beer.' Vinnie collected up his tools and grinned at Joseph's pensive face, 'Thinking about the old days, huh?'

'It was another world, but sometimes it feels like yesterday.' Joseph smiled. 'And look at us now! Who'd have thought it! Both settled down, and in a few days, you'll be even more settled than me. Now that's a turn-up for the books!'

'Yep, life still has a few surprises to throw at us, even at this stage in the game.' Vinnie let rip with a raucous laugh. 'Come on, soldier! That beer awaits.'

They found Sheila cleaning the narrowboat windows. 'He's told you our news?'

Joseph duly hugged her. 'Best thing I've heard in a long time!'

'And you'll both be able to be our witnesses? You didn't mind us asking?'

'We'd have been hurt if you'd asked anyone else, believe me. We'll be proud to be your witnesses, Sheila.' He took out his phone. 'Just in case she's tied up, I'll message Nikki now. Just you wait, I'll give it less than two minutes before this phone is ringing.'

He tapped in a quick text to Nikki. In less than *one* minute she rang, and they all went into fits of laughter.

Nikki was delighted, as he'd known she would be, and very happy to have been asked to be a witness at the wedding. 'Just tell them I don't do hats, okay? If I have to wear a hat, they're on their own!'

Joseph laughed. 'You're on loudspeaker, Nikki.'

'Good,' she said immediately. 'No misunderstanding then.'

'Received and understood,' called out Vinnie. 'Hats definitely not compulsory.'

After wishing them good luck, Nikki said she had to get back to work, while Joseph was ready for his beer.

They spent the next hour sitting on the little sun-drenched stern deck, each feeling relaxed and at peace. Joseph had escaped the chaos of the police station, Sheila the hubbub of her public house, and Vinnie had escaped a lonely existence haunted by long shadows from the past. Much later, when he thought back on it, Joseph believed that hour to be one of the most tranquil and companiable of his life. It was as if time had stopped for a while. The water lapped against the side of the boat, and in the distance the occasional engine chugged. He heard the call of waterfowl and once, a dog barked joyously. He took several deep breaths, another swig of beer and exhaled.

'I could stay here like this forever,' he said contentedly.

'Not quite,' said his friend. 'After lunch we need to take sweet *Ophelia* down to the boatyard for a pump-out.'

Sheila pulled a face. 'This life looks idyllic but it's damned hard work too. And sometimes rather smelly!'

'Oh, you love it really,' laughed Vinnie. 'And at least we do have a pump-out toilet, not a cassette that you empty yourself.'

'Small mercies,' returned Sheila, cuffing him playfully round the ear. 'And yes, I do love it, especially now I'm starting to get the hang of things.' She looked at Joseph. 'It's a different way of life altogether. I could never have done it without Vinnie being so practical. What with engines, generators, water pumps, bilge pumps, shower pumps, inverters and heaven knows what else!'

'We're lucky to have a permanent mooring. Most boats here are continuous cruisers, meaning they have to move their boat to another area every fourteen days. With Sheila still working part-time and generally looking after the Hanged Man, we'd never have been able to buy this baby if we'd had to keep on the move.'

It was plain to Joseph that Vinnie had taken to this life like a fish to water. He looked so happy here. It suited both of them, him and Sheila. It was a complete step to one side, away from what they both had known before, a new start together in a completely different environment. Joseph thought it was perfect for them.

'So, are you up for a short trip upriver?' asked Vinnie.

'Aye, Cap'n.' Joseph saluted smartly. 'So what's my role on this sturdy vessel? Cabin boy? Ship's cat? Please, anything but Master Bates!'

Their laughter could still be heard over the gentle chugging of the engine as they pulled out into the river.

* * *

As Joseph embarked on his short cruise, Dave Harris was making his way from his cottage in the grounds of Cressy Old Hall up to the main house to start work.

He strolled along with the sun on the back of his neck and a smile on his face. Life was good right now. Oh, he missed the team and the job he'd done for more years than he cared to remember, but after a very bad and very scary patch followed by the shock of retirement, he had landed on his feet.

He had recovered well from his sudden heart attack. Thank God it had been a fixable problem and, with a sensible diet and plenty of exercise, he now felt better than he had in years. He had a comfortable little cottage in a wooded area on the perimeter of the old estate, a job as security advisor for the beautiful property itself, and a new and very unlikely friend in the person of Clive Cressy-Lawson, the present lord of the manor.

For many years, Clive and the local police had conducted a running battle. Clive was not liked — more than that, practically every copper in the county considered him their enemy. That had been until tragedy, by way of a brutal murder, had struck Cressy Old Hall, and Dave had managed to restore Clive's faith in the "boys in blue." Now Dave worked for Clive and, despite their utterly different backgrounds, they had become firm friends.

As he approached the beautiful old house, Dave considered just how much had changed there in the past year. The entire workforce had been replaced or their jobs had been restructured, and new life had been breathed into the struggling old edifice. Grants had been obtained and now, instead of gates closed and secured against the public eye, the house and gardens were open, and visitors made welcome.

Dave walked into the estate office and was greeted by a bright and breezy 'Mornin'!' from Susie Wright, Clive's vivacious and extremely capable new housekeeper-cum-staff-manager.

'Just the man.' Susie picked up a couple of sheets of paper and passed them to Dave. 'Two new groundsmen starting today, Neil and Laurie. Nice chaps, both got very good references and grounding in woodland maintenance. I wondered if you had time to give them the guided tour and show them the ropes? You know the routine, a smiley-faced meet-and-greet, just a brief introduction to what we are all about, then Ken the head gardener can explain their actual duties afterwards.'

Dave took the papers. 'Of course, Susie. I'll check in with the boss, make sure all is well at the house, then I'm all yours.' He smiled at her, liking the fact that her businesslike attitude was nicely offset by enthusiasm and a sense of humour. There was something of his lovely Cat about her, although they were nothing like each other in looks, but having Susie around made missing his old team a little easier to cope with.

As he walked through the entrance hall, its walls lined with portraits of stately Cressy-Lawsons, he suppressed a chuckle as he recalled Cat's latest text.

Morning, you jammy old git! Hope that toffee-nosed twat is still treating you well. Miss you, Catkin xxx

The message had been followed by an emoji with a big tear running down its face.

He was going to meet her later in the week for lunch in town and a catch-up. Well, that had been the plan, but she had sent a quick message later saying they could be heading into another murder inquiry, so time yet to be advised. He wondered what would be coming their way this time. It felt strange to think that, for once, it would have nothing whatsoever to do with him.

CHAPTER ELEVEN

Spooky sat at her computer, hands flying over the keyboard, watching streams of letters, figures and symbols flow down one of the screens. Half her mind was following them intently, but another part was considering the Stargate Project and the British scientist who had been prepared to risk everything to prove that clairvoyance was real.

Spooky and her partner, Angie Blissett, known to everyone as Bliss, had a close friend who claimed to be clairvoyant. Bliss swore she possessed "an amazing and undeniable gift," but Spooky was not convinced. Gill Mason had a gift all right, but it was the ability to read people, not tarot cards. She believed Gill to be skilled in perceiving body language and the unconscious signals people gave off, rather than having any extrasensory powers. She liked Gill enormously and knew that she had a massive following of real believers. Sometimes she wished that she could believe too. After all, as Bliss often pointed out, she was open to other highly debatable phenomena, even the idea of life on other planets, so why not the possibility that some folk were born with a talent that enabled them to "see" things?

'Ah!' She stopped typing. 'Gotcher!' The fault she had been searching for suddenly showed itself. With a few more deft taps on the keyboard, she rectified the problem and reset the program. 'Job done,' she muttered. 'You're history, you pesky little gremlin.'

'I've heard that talking to inanimate objects could be a sign of madness.'

Aiden Gardner had come into the department without her noticing. She turned to look at him. 'I'm fully aware of that, thank you. When you've been here longer, you'll learn that pretty much everyone knows I'm barking mad.'

He grinned at her. 'Oh, right. That's okay then. Have you got a moment, Spooky?'

'Sure.' She pointed to an empty office chair. 'How can I help you? Another trip to Fairyland?'

'No. To be honest, I don't think it's even worth me going down that route at all. I mean, why bother when we all know Lucas is root-toot? It doesn't really matter what caused it. He was a troubled kid, his mental state has deteriorated as he's grown up, and now he's turned into this avenging-killer Nature God. We need to find him and stop him, not analyse him. Plenty of time for that when we have him locked up.'

'Oh dear, Aiden, you sound a tad disgruntled,' Spooky said.

He gave a little laugh. 'Not really. I just think I should prioritise. As a matter of fact, the one who really interests me is Julian, the scientist. If anyone wants to know about Lucas, they should look to his father first. He was not root-toot, I'm sure of it. Well, not when he went off to the States, at any rate. But my searches are throwing up nothing except some very basic and, I suspect, highly sanitised information released at the time of his death. Can you help me?'

'He puzzles me too, as it happens.' She opened a drawer and pulled out a sheaf of printouts. 'I'm ahead of you, actually. I've already started trawling.' She handed them to him. 'That should get you started. Meanwhile, I'll keep digging.' She stared at him. 'You met the brother, Harry, didn't you?'

Aiden nodded. 'And I'm pretty miffed that he's gone AWOL for a couple of days. He told us some weird stuff about Julian. Things that happened when they were young. And I'm sure he has a whole lot more to tell us if he thinks about it.' He leaned forward. 'Harry said his father really could do this remote viewing thing. He'd apparently told his sons that he'd seen a man they both knew mourning a sudden loss, and the next day they discovered it was true.'

'Bit tenuous, wouldn't you say? I mean, he could have heard about something happening to someone they knew in a dozen different ways.'

Aiden shrugged. 'Well, Harry was convinced, completely.'

'Those declassified CIA documents did say that "the Brit" had had a number of remarkable successes but,' Spooky shrugged, 'they were hardly going to say he was a washout, were they?'

'Harry also told me that his father went into trances. I'd dearly love to know what that was all about.' He looked puzzled suddenly. 'Do you know what Harry Byrd does for a living? He mentioned that, unlike his brother, he worked indoors, but I didn't press him at the time. It hasn't come up in any of Joseph's reports or memos.'

'No idea, but I can check if you like,' Spooky said.

'If you have time, I'd appreciate that.' Aiden stood up. 'And thanks for all this.' He waved the sheaf of papers. 'Can't wait to get into them.'

Frowning, Spooky watched him go. Besides being a whizz with technology, she was sensitive to people's emotions, and she was getting some unsettling vibes from Aiden Gardner. 'You are not a happy bunny, are you, my friend,' she whispered. 'I know an act when I see it. So, what is troubling you?'

Her question hung in the air. Apart from the soft hum as one of her computers updated a piece of software, all was silent.

* * *

Lucas felt unsettled. He was in a transient state, having left his last woodland home but not quite reaching his new one.

This in-between territory was a danger zone, in which he was completely vulnerable to the Elf King.

He told himself to be reasonable. Although the Elf King could be anywhere, he couldn't be *every*where, could he? Only another thirty minutes and he would be safe again. He quickened his pace. If only Harry would find him, it would be so much easier, the two of them together. He had never minded being a loner — he'd embraced his solitary state — but things had changed, and now he would feel much happier and safer with his beloved brother at his side.

He spent the next half hour recalling all those times when, as boys, they had spent whole days in his magic kingdom. Harry had created a whole new country for him out of the existing one. His own special world. Harry would find him. After all, Harry knew Shrimptown better than he did. And then they'd never be parted again. He'd make certain of it.

* * *

At four o'clock, Nikki received a phone call from Harry Byrd.

'DI Galena, things are okay here. I think I worry too much over Mother. She has assured me that she has all the help she needs at home, and her younger sister is arriving tomorrow morning to stay for a while. Corinne is one of those incredibly practical and well organised women, and I know my mother will be safe in her hands. Finding Lucas must take priority.'

'You're coming back, then?' asked Nikki hopefully.

'First thing in the morning, and I'll be bringing some things with me that might help us to locate my brother.'

Nikki perked up. This was good news. 'What sort of things, Harry?'

He gave an apologetic little laugh. 'Well, this will sound silly, but it's games we used to play as kids, a bit like an old-fashioned version of a computer game, but instead of technology, we used books, maps and plans to hunt for hidden treasure, and battle dragons, goblins and monsters.'

'Ah. And how will that help us exactly?'

'The games were set in the Fens — in Greenborough, or "Shrimptown" as we called it, in the county of Reedmire on the River Staghorn. I got Dad to buy us street and OS maps of the area. There's not an inch we didn't explore, despite never setting foot in the county.' Harry sounded positively excited. 'I kept them all, the maps and the notes we made recording our adventures. I'm betting he'll be in one of the places we used for hidey-holes and camps.'

Nikki nodded, her optimism returning. 'That sounds a real possibility. Could you bring them straight here as soon as you arrive, Harry? I'm very, very anxious to find him.'

'Of course. But would it be possible to copy them and let me have the originals back? If by any chance we don't find him, or, well, if something happens to him, they are pretty well all I have to remind me of a happy childhood.'

'Of course. In fact, I was going to suggest that anyway.'

'I should be with you at around nine thirty. I've kept my room at the hotel, so I'll go there, unload my things and come to the station. Is that okay, DI Galena?'

'We'll look forward to seeing you,' said Nikki. 'Drive carefully, Harry, you've got a lot on your mind.'

'You can say that again. Um, before I go, has — oh God — has Lucas done anything else while I was gone?'

'Not that we know of, Harry. We've heard nothing.'

Not that we know of. It hung in the air. But Harry wasn't stupid, he didn't need it spelled out for him.

She ended the call and sat back in her chair, tapping her fingers on the desk. Okay, it was something, but on second thoughts, not much to go on. A kids' game? A treasure-hunt map? Oh, please! She could hear it now: 'And how did you find your killer, Detective Inspector?' 'I rolled the dice, Superintendent, and landed on a magic portal in a briar patch in Shrimptown.' Shrimptown, of all the names! What about Prawnsville? Lobster City? Crab Valley? Jesus. She shook her head.

'Boss?' Cat stood in the doorway. 'Small thing, but we've ascertained how Lucas knew which of the boys had set

115

fire to the tree in the Arboretum. Those lads had been there before, and he and another gardener had seen them off, hence Lucas knew them by sight. We checked and discovered that the dead boy, Stuart Baker, and his best friend both worked at the supermarket Lucas shopped in, and we think he might have got talking to one or other of them and discovered what happened that way. The last part is conjecture, but we are going to double-check it with Stuart's friend. I'm pretty sure we're correct.'

'Good,' said Nikki. 'Knocks another small question mark off the list.'

Cat turned to go, but Nikki called her back. 'Heard from Dave recently?'

'All the time, boss.' Cat grinned. 'We text every day. I don't want him to feel that just because he's not here I don't love him anymore.'

'Quite right,' Nikki said. 'I was just wondering if we should let him know he'll be getting a visit from some of his old comrades. Cressy Old Hall grounds are on Niall's list of places to be searched first thing tomorrow morning. He was going to ring Cressy-Lawson but I said we'd contact Dave direct, and he can tell him.'

'I'll do it now, boss,' said Cat. 'The very least he can do is look out for them and have the kettle on.'

Nikki gave a little laugh, then a shadow crossed her face. 'Tread warily, Cat. That last dreadful incident at Cressy Old Hall nearly tipped him over the edge. He could well do without another evil bastard lurking in the bushes.'

'I understand, boss, don't worry. They've got a decent and knowledgeable team there who care about the gardens. As long as no idiot starts running wild with a machete in the shrubbery, they are probably safer than most. Leave it to me.'

Nikki was glad that Cat had kept in close contact with Dave. She herself made a point of talking to him every week, mainly because she was never quite sure that he'd made the right decision in moving on to the estate following that horrific murder. But it seemed she had been wrong to worry.

He was happy, contented and fully committed to his new life at Cressy Old Hall. The biggest surprise had been the friendship that had sprung up between him and its owner, a man she had once nearly taken a swing at. If ever there had been a metamorphosis, it was the one that had taken hold of Clive Cressy-Lawson. Oh, and Dave too, of course. She had come across him in town last week, and he'd looked younger and fitter than she'd ever seen him. He was even dressed differently and had totally lost that "worn-out old detective" appearance. He'd admitted to being relieved that the pressure of the job was finally off him, and to being happy to leave the house he had shared with his wife. He had suffered terribly during her illness and death, and his woodland cottage contained no painful memories.

'Good luck to you, old friend,' whispered Nikki to herself. 'I wonder if you realise how much you're missed?'

* * *

Cam Walker took an immediate dislike to Vernon Hackett, although the man had been nothing but polite and business-like towards him. He'd met his sort before. They weren't policemen — well, not proper ones. They had a specific job to carry out and they did it like automatons. People, and their emotions and feelings, didn't come into the equation. They never answered questions — were better than any politician at evading the direct answer. Worst of all was their disdain. They made you feel like an inferior and very ignorant species.

Cam sat at his desk, quietly fuming, while he was given instructions on how to react to questions about the murder suspect. Anything that concerned the media should be relayed immediately to Hackett himself. A mere temporary visitor, he nevertheless demanded an office — not a desk, not a workstation, but a private office — preferably close to what he called the "hub of activity." There was no use protesting that they didn't have a wealth of spare offices available on the off-chance that a passing autocrat might drop in. Finally, he decided to give Hackett the office of one of the other DIs who was off on leave for two weeks.

'I shall be giving an update to the press at five this afternoon on the station steps. You will be with me, of course.' Hackett glanced at an expensive gold wristwatch. 'In fifteen minutes' time. It will be brief, and I won't be taking questions.' He looked at Cam over a pair of heavy, dark-framed glasses that accentuated his heavy, dark eyes. 'It's unfortunate that the suspect's image was released. I'm assuming you have done all you can to retrieve the copies. And that you have also warned anyone who is aware of the suspect's identity that it goes no further.'

'As per your previous orders,' Cam muttered.

'Good.' He gave Cam a cold smile. 'Then all that's left is for you to show me to my office before we go downstairs.'

Hackett had said brief, and he'd meant it. The update, lasting mere minutes, told the clamouring mass of journalists and cameramen absolutely nothing they didn't know already, reiterating that they hadn't yet discovered the suspect's identity, and that they had no one in mind. More details would be released as and when appropriate. Cam had neither been introduced, nor asked to say anything. He felt like a stony-faced dummy, wheeled out to stand beside the mouthpiece so as to make it look more official.

The only thing he found interesting about the briefing was Nikki Galena's perplexed frown when she looked at Hackett. He reminded himself to ask her about it the next time he saw her.

Back in his office, he drenched it in room spray. Hackett had worn a cologne — no doubt desperately expensive — which, in more than one way, got up Cam's nose.

He wasn't aware of Nikki standing in the doorway until she said, 'Either someone has farted right royally, or you're trying to get rid of something, or someone, unpleasant.'

He smiled. 'The latter, as it happens. Come in and sit down, Nikki.'

'We are just off home, Cam, but I came to offer my commiserations on your having drawn the short straw and being obliged to accommodate the Man in Black. He's sitting downstairs in Colin's office watching the detectives in the CID room like some black-eyed venomous snake.'

'You've got the right word for him. My God, Nikki, he's a cold one.' Cam shuddered. 'Have you met him before somewhere? I saw that look you gave him during the press briefing.'

Nikki frowned. 'I'd swear I've come across him before, but I have no clue where or when.' She paused. 'Or why, for that matter. By the way, you know old Terry Seymour, don't you, the hack who works for the Greenborough rag? I heard him say, "Oh great! It's bloody Hackett. They only drag him out of his hole for something serious." So I went and had a quiet word with him. He reckons your Mr Hackett is, or was, from the Security Service.'

Cam frowned. 'MI5? Not what I was told, but then, nobody's told me much at all. I was led to believe that he was something to do with internal affairs.'

'I'm starting to think that there's a whole lot more to Julian Hopwood-Byrd than we've been told. This is no way to conduct a murder inquiry,' she said angrily. 'We have enough trouble trying to extricate the truth from the villains, let alone have our own people keeping us in the dark.'

He agreed with her wholeheartedly, but if the security people had closed ranks on them, they hadn't a snowball's chance in hell of finding a way through the barrier. 'If MI5 are involved — and I can't in a squillion years imagine why — the dark is exactly where we'll stay.'

'So what do we do, Cam?' asked Nikki.

'Find Lucas. It's all we can do. Just do our job, sticking to those parameters I told you about, and hunt down the killer. Keep it simple and try to blot out his father and his cranky escapades. It's a murder investigation, and we've handled those rather well in the past. Let's do it again.'

It was meant to be a rallying cry, but Cam wasn't deceiving himself. One look at Nikki told him that his friend wasn't fooled either. His words had no real enthusiasm behind them.

'Okay, Cam. It's just you and me and the end of the day. If we could slip back a decade or so, this is where you would open the top drawer of your desk and take out two glasses and a bottle of Scotch and we'd talk.' She looked him straight in the eye. 'I can still do the talking bit, even without the whisky. What's wrong?'

He screwed his eyes tight shut for a moment, then seemed to slump. 'It's Kaye, Nikki. She's not very well and she keeps putting off going to the doctor. It's become a really touchy subject. I'm worried sick, but she keeps brushing it off. It's not like her, Nikki.'

'What do you mean when you say not very well?' she asked.

'Tired to the point of lethargy, headaches and a lot of other symptoms she's not telling me about. Hell, Nikki, she's one of the fittest people I know! I hate to see her like this and frankly, I'm frightened.'

Nikki gave him a reassuring smile. 'Hey, it could be something as simple as overwork. I'm assuming she's still at the college? She could be really run down and maybe not sleeping properly.'

'True, she is very busy at the university. They're short-staffed and she's covering all manner of other jobs, but she's always thrived on her work. It's never affected her before.' He sighed. 'And she's never refused to listen to me either. We're a team, you know that, and we discuss things. Compromise. Normally if she thought it was worrying me, she'd go, just to put my mind at rest, but not this time.' Kaye was a wonderful woman, the best wife a man could have. Easy-going, very intelligent but with no side to her. Cam adored her, plain and simple. And he was hurting.

'Well, Cam, it sounds to me as if she's scared to go. If she's snappy about it, I'd be pretty certain that's what it is.' She looked at him. 'I'll ring her and suggest a coffee and a catch-up. We often do, so it's nothing out of the ordinary. She won't suspect we've talked, I promise.'

'Would you, Nikki?' He looked relieved. A problem shared and all that. 'And if you think I'm being an old woman, I'll drop it.'

'I'll text her tonight,' Nikki said. 'And if I'm worried too, I won't mess around. I'll tell you, Cam.'

'I appreciate that.'

'No problem, it's just a pity we couldn't have talked over a nice glass of malt. My, how the force has changed!'

* * *

That night after supper, Nikki and Joseph sat out in the garden of Cloud Cottage Farm and watched the sun go down — until the mosquitoes started to bite. Then they sat for another half hour in the kitchen, sipping brandy and telling each other about their respective days. It was rather nice, Nikki decided, having different stories to tell.

Joseph waxed lyrical about the trip on the narrowboat, even if it had just been to pump out a waste tank, but most of his talk concerned his old friend and the fact he was actually marrying and settling down.

Nikki told Joseph about Kaye being unwell and Cam's anxiety over it.

'I thought the excuses he gave us the other day were a bit lame,' Joseph said. 'So, you're going to talk to her?'

'Already arranged. I'm meeting her the day after tomorrow for a coffee. And I managed to do it without dropping Cam in it. Apparently, she's really touchy about the subject.' She grinned at him. 'This could be one of those occasions when being blunt actually helps. If I said, "Blimey, Kaye, you're looking a bit rough," it wouldn't exactly be out of character.'

'Very true.' Joseph rolled his eyes.

Then Nikki told him about Hackett and her feeling that she recognised him from somewhere. Cam disliked him so much, she said, that he'd actually fumigated his office after the man had left. 'And something else. I had a word with Spooky as I was getting ready to come home. She mentioned a few things that make me think Aiden might not be sticking to the agenda.'

Joseph looked concerned. 'As in?'

'He seems to be rather more interested in Julian than Lucas and his problems. Given the warnings we've been given and the sad lack of info about our mad scientist, I'm concerned he's going to wander into deep waters. I'd hate him to incur the wrath of Hackett and bring that man down on us.' She trusted Spooky to tread carefully when searching for information. She knew how to cover her digital footprints and had some very hi-tech equipment, but that wasn't the case with Aiden. 'Are you up to a friendly word to the wise tomorrow?'

Joseph nodded. 'Absolutely. First thing.'

Sleep proved elusive that night, and at two in the morning, those dark eyes still haunted her. If only she could recall where she'd seen him. She had considered doing a computer search but dismissed the notion. You couldn't google a man like that. No, she was going to have to rely on her memory, and, until it finally coughed up what it knew, those shiny shoes would just have to tail her.

* * *

As Nikki lay in bed craving sleep, Aiden Gardner was fighting it off. His wife Becca had turned in hours ago, but he sat up, reading over what Spooky had printed off for him. How had she managed to trace all this interesting stuff? He was no slouch when it came to computer searches, but she seemed to have used search engines he didn't even know existed.

Two hours into the sheaf of papers, it was clear that Julian Hopwood-Byrd had been a truly remarkable man, and Aiden was beginning to wish he hadn't died. Julian had written papers on controversial subjects that mainstream scientists considered spurious but had managed to sow seeds of doubt in the most sceptical. Most importantly, others had managed to replicate his experiments, empirical proof that "psi" phenomena — telepathy, precognition, clairvoyance and remote viewing — were real.

Aiden stretched — he needed sleep. Returning to work after such a long absence was draining him and, although he told no one, being on his feet for much longer than he was used to had intensified the pain in his legs and lower back. He had taken painkillers tonight, but he feared they'd wear off long before morning.

He picked up another printout. Just one more article, then he'd turn in.

Half an hour later, he returned them all to their folder, but the content of the last one was still going around in his head. Spooky had downloaded a fascinating and very up-to-date article from *Time* magazine in which the author found that the US military was accepting sailors and marines who possessed "Spidey-sense" — heightened powers of intuition that meant they could detect an impending attack or a dangerous situation before it happened. Julian had written about this years before, at a time when the technology was rudimentary compared to today's. Aiden believed that if the scientist were alive today, he could have blown much of modern scientific theory out of the water.

Aiden undressed, washed, brushed his teeth and slipped into bed. Becca murmured something, half asleep.

'Do you believe in ESP?' he asked her.

'In what?' She yawned.

'You know, clairvoyance.'

Becca groaned. 'What time is it, my darling? Well, whatever time it is, it's far too late at night for one of your big discussions.'

Her Greek accent always sounded more pronounced when she was sleepy. He never tired of listening to her. 'I suppose not. Sorry, babe. Night-night.' He kissed her hair, turned his back and closed his eyes.

'My great-grandmother had the gift, or so my parents told me,' she murmured, still half asleep. 'But then superstition abounded in our part of the country.'

'So, do you believe in it?' he asked again.

'No, I don't, now go to sleep.'

He turned to her and kissed her again. He was just slipping away when he heard her say, 'And you? Do you believe in it?'

Aiden pretended to be asleep. He really didn't know.

CHAPTER TWELVE

Lucas awoke before sunrise. He was calm and settled now, contented. He was warm, comfortable and, most of all, he felt safe.

There were different sights and sounds and smells around him now. With every move he made, different voices spoke softly to him, other faces swam in and out of his peripheral vision. Each time, it was like stepping into yet another world.

He watched the sky slowly turn grey until, suddenly, the rising sun split it asunder in a gash of fiery, scarlet light. There was something very special about the start of the day. It was all about new beginnings. He sprang to his feet.

Would it be today? Would Harry find him? He sensed his brother moving closer. He knew that Harry had been in Shrimptown — he would have come as soon as he received his letter. Then, for a day or so, his brother had seemed to be absent. Today he was back, Lucas knew it. This amazing sunrise spoke to him of hope.

He would have gone and found Harry himself — in any other place he would have done so, but not Shrimptown. Shrimptown was far too dangerous. This was the home of the Elf King and here, away from his safe places, he was in grave danger. The journey here had terrified him, but his nature-spirit friends had been with him every step of the way, guarding him, urging him on until he made it.

The first rays of the sun touched his bare chest. There was no warmth in the golden light yet, and in the slight breeze it felt crisp and chill, energising him, sending ripples of excitement through him.

Lucas looked around and liked what he saw. This place was very different from the Arboretum, but nevertheless, a good place to be. Apart from his adored trees, he missed only one other thing from Shelley House — and that was Karen Cotton.

He smiled. She was the nearest thing to a kindred spirit he had found in the whole of Reedmire. They could have been soulmates. He had felt it the moment they met — an affinity. He had reached out to her through meditation and felt how much they shared. If he had only had a little more time with her, they could have been inseparable. He could have shown her so much, among those majestic trees, under that starlit sky. Karen could have been a goddess. Ah, if only he had not had to leave so hastily.

He sat down on the dew-soaked grass, oblivious to the damp. If only those vile idiots hadn't injured and killed the robinia tree. It wasn't that he disliked Sean Cotton, in fact he liked him very much — the man cared deeply about the land and the trees — but he was on a different plane to Lucas and Karen, a more earthy, basic one. He was sure they were happy together in their way, but the thing was, Karen was like a royal princess who needed to be awakened to the powers she possessed. She was being held down by staying with a materially minded man like Sean. It was a waste.

Lucas lay back, his hands clasped behind his head. He shivered as his bare back met the wet grass. If he didn't have this important mission to fulfil, he would go back for her. Perhaps that was another reason to get this dreadful deed done as swiftly as possible. Then, with no Elf King to pursue him, he could go back and rescue his goddess. He imagined taking her by the hand and leading his auburn-haired beauty into the forest . . .

He leaped to his feet. This would not do. There would be time for that later, but not now. He slowed his breathing. He had much to do. First, he had to get some food. He needed to maintain his strength. His adversary was a powerful entity and Lucas had to meet him with equal strength.

The sun touched his face with a first hint of warmth. He called out to the sky, to the trees and the birds, 'I'm waiting, Harry! We have work to do. Your brother needs you!'

* * *

Nikki and Joseph were in early, and by eight thirty were on their second cup of coffee.

'I've been going over the same question half the bloody night,' said Nikki grumpily. 'Where did a thirteen-year-old boy go that he remained unfound for donkey's years, then turn up having acquired a wealth of horticultural knowledge? It beggars belief!'

Joseph pulled a face. 'He walks off into the night with a little rucksack of treasured possessions and disappears. He was going to someone, or someone was waiting with a car to take him away. It *has* to be that way. But who? And why can't Harry think of anyone, if they were so close? How could that kid have had someone who cared that much for him and his brother not know?'

'Harry will be here soon, Joseph. It's time to get him to dig deeper, if that's humanly possible.' Nikki stared into her coffee. 'I'm going to play devil's advocate here and be the distrusting police officer that I am. We only have Harry's word for all that went on in their childhood. I think it's time we went up to London and talked to a few people who knew the family. I'm not saying that Harry is necessarily lying, but he was part of a family that was disintegrating because of the father's mental-health collapse. He might not have seen things exactly as they were.'

Joseph nodded. 'Perhaps we should talk to the mother too. From the way Harry spoke, the old lady seemed very happy for him to try and find Lucas. Maybe she knows some-thing, something she's not shared with Harry.'

'Good point. However, we need to do it without upset-ting Harry. We need him on our side more than anyone at present. He's more or less all we have.'

'Other than Karen Cotton. She knows the adult Lucas, our killer. Harry only remembers his kid brother. I think she's very important,' Joseph said.

'You're right. But we still need to keep Harry sweet.' Nikki drained her coffee. 'As soon as Cam's free, I'm going to ask him what checks were carried out on Harry Byrd prior to the powers that be throwing this one at us. I'll feel happier in my mind if I know that Harry's recollections are all kosher.'

'And I'll check with Cat and Ben about how their look into Lucas's background is going. They were trying to corroborate what the countryside ranger said about Lucas attending a Lancashire university.'

'Yes, that's good,' Nikki said. 'I'm tempted to leave the hunt for our happy camper to Niall and his army of uniforms and throw everything we have into building a picture of him. If we can understand something of what was going on when he was younger, we might be able to anticipate what he's plan-ning and who this Elf King might be.' She looked at Joseph intently. 'I know I'm a pain in the arse when it comes to all this superstitious crap, but even I realise that Lucas is planning to kill someone in particular and, even if his deranged brain wants to turn his proposed victim into some faery freak, bot-tom line, he's still hunting a human being, so someone is in grave danger. We *have* to know who that person is.'

'Absolutely, Nikki.' Joseph nodded. 'And as you say, we'll only discover that if we go back into his past, because I'm certain it's to do with that and not someone who has upset him recently. If his latest behaviour is anything to go by, he acts very quickly when he perceives that someone has seriously transgressed the rules he believes in.'

'True, especially in the case of Ritchie Naylor. Lucas actually tried to prevent him touching that tree. He was only minutes too late.' Nikki picked up a report. 'Uniform have confirmed that the mate Ritchie borrowed that digger from, Lance Smythe, one of the groundsmen from Shelley House Arboretum, has confirmed that he did tell Lucas that he had loaned the equipment out to a friend and who he was. Apparently, Smythe used to be a self-employed garden landscaper, and now he's working for Arthur Morton, he hires out his old machinery rather than let it rot in his garage. He says his mini digger is well in demand.' She pushed the report away. 'We can guess that our Tree Avenger took a peek at exactly what area poor Ritchie was clearing and had no objection to a few shrubs and the grass where the pool was to go, but when he saw the fancy tree was going to have to come down, it was too much for him to take.'

'And Ritchie paid the price.' Joseph exhaled. 'So, we have to hope and pray that no one else upsets him and that he concentrates entirely on slaying the dragon. Meanwhile, we move heaven and earth to find out who that dragon is and get the poor bugger to safety.'

Nikki glanced at the wall clock and stood up. 'Half an hour before Harry gets here. I'm off to talk to Cam. You grab Cat and Ben and see if they've dredged up anything of use.' She stopped abruptly. 'Oh. Aiden. I forgot about him. Will you have a word with him first?'

'Already done it. He was in before us this morning. While you were checking the overnight reports, I had a fatherly chat and he said he's doing nothing other than use Spooky's info, which is far more in-depth than anything he could produce.'

She nodded. 'Okay, but watch him, Joseph.'

'Oh, I will, never fear.'

Too impatient to take the lift, Nikki ran up the stairs and found Cam already ensconced behind his desk, writing furiously. Nikki tapped lightly on the door and went in, closing it behind her.

'Before we get down to work, Cam, just in case Kaye didn't mention it, we're meeting up for a coffee tomorrow. She sounded really pleased about it. She didn't mention anything specific, but I got the feeling she might want to talk, so you hang on in there.'

He gave her a tired smile. 'I appreciate it, Nikki, very much.'

She tried to sound encouraging. 'It's nothing. We're all friends and if something's troubling her, Joseph and I want to know just as much as you. Leave it with me.' She dragged up a chair. 'Now, have you got a few minutes to answer a couple of questions?'

Cam Walker replaced the top on his precious fountain pen. 'Fire away.'

She explained her concerns about the veracity of everything Harry Byrd had told them.

Cam wrinkled his brow, then turned to his computer. After a while he said, 'Here we are. Well, he is who he says he is, no question. He does live in Highgate village and his mother is still alive, but it seems all further in-depth investigation was directed at the father, Julian. The whole security issue has come about because of him, and is why we have your Man in Black fixing his eagle eye on the CID room.'

Nikki gave Cam an irritated look. 'Oh yes, he's a right bundle of laughs, watching over us like a bleeding hungry vulture. Great for morale, he is.'

'And am I right in assuming you still can't recall where you know him from?' Cam raised an eyebrow at her.

She gave a grunt. 'I'm beginning to think I don't know him at all, and maybe I just saw something similar on a trip to the reptile house in the zoo when Hannah was a kid.'

Cam unsuccessfully suppressed a grin.

'That, or I watched some dark, dystopian film about Big Brother.'

'I didn't know you watched dark, dystopian films,' said Cam.

'I don't. I didn't even know what the word meant until Joseph explained it to me, but it sounded good, didn't it?'

'Very apt,' agreed Cam, smiling briefly. 'But going back to your question. When Harry brought the information about his brother to us, it flagged up immediate concern right across the board, which is what brought Hackett out of his tomb. Julian is basically Access Denied, except for what has been deemed sufficient information to satisfy the public. Go any further and alarm bells ring in some dusty office somewhere in the bowels of SIS.'

'And nothing exists about the Hopwood-Byrds as a family?' Nikki asked.

'Not a dicky bird,' confirmed Cam, 'if you'll forgive the pun.'

'Then that's where we need to go. We need to play happy families, although that's probably not what we'll find. It's the time when they arrived back from the States that interests me, just before Father murdered the gardener then died himself, and the boy Lucas walked away from his mother and brother.' Nikki paused, thinking hard. 'It's rather odd that the man Julian murdered was a gardener. It does smack of "like father like son," doesn't it? Yes, I'd really like to know more about that murder and Harry's claim that his brother caused an innocent man to die.'

Cam leaned back and steepled his fingers. 'I know why you have to do it, but do be careful, Nikki. We can't attack this investigation in the normal manner, so watch who you talk to and the questions you ask, okay?'

'Tough one if you have a gob like mine.' Nikki grimaced. 'But I do appreciate the situation and that my ground rules will need to be somewhat adapted. I'll be careful, don't worry.'

As she walked back downstairs, Nikki wondered how true that statement was.

'You look pensive, ma'am.'

She had been lost in thought and hadn't noticed Yvonne Collins approaching. 'Vonnie! Got a minute?' Busy or not, Nikki decided, it was time to talk. She had fifteen minutes before Harry was due to arrive — just nice time.

'Just popping a report in to the super, won't be a moment.'

Nikki waited in the stairwell until Yvonne came back down. 'Nothing wrong, is there?'

'Apart from a nature-loving killer, not a thing.' Nikki laughed. 'But I've got a little proposal for you. I don't want an answer immediately, okay? It's just something to consider.'

Inside her office, Nikki told Yvonne about her idea. Hoping she wasn't putting any pressure on her, she said, 'You're practically one of the team anyway. You've worked with us so often you know the dynamic and the people as well as I do. If you did decide you might like to join us, I'd suggest a decent holiday first, a proper break, just to make sure of your decision, but as I say, there is a job here with us, and only if you really want it.'

Yvonne said, 'I had thought it would be easier than this, ma'am. So many of my old colleagues have been counting the days until they can retire, can't wait to step back from all the pressure, but . . . the place has been more or less my whole life for more years than I can remember.'

'I can imagine,' said Nikki, meaning it. 'I think I'd be the same.'

'Well, I do appreciate the offer, and believe me, I'll give it serious thought.'

'No rush, honestly, but my door is open when you do decide.'

As Yvonne left, Nikki could almost hear the cogs turning over in her brain. Well, she had done what Niall had asked of her. Now back to Harry Byrd.

* * *

Joseph didn't have time to tell Nikki about Cat and Ben's progress before they were called to reception to meet Harry Byrd. 'They've made some headway, Nikki,' he whispered as they reached the foyer. 'I'll fill you in after this.'

Harry Byrd looked more relaxed this time and was dressed casually. 'I think I should get out into Greenborough and walk the streets, Detectives. I'm getting a strong feeling that my brother is actively looking for me, and he won't find me buried in a hotel lounge. I need to make myself conspicuous.'

'Let's talk about this, Harry,' said Nikki. 'We don't want you in danger too. I know he's your brother, but we have to weigh up what he's done. He's totally unstable and you haven't seen him in years. We can't risk you walking into trouble.' She opened the door to an interview room. 'Forgive the less than comfortable surroundings, but it's private and a lot quieter than upstairs, I promise you.'

And out of earshot of Hackett, thought Joseph. Cat and Ben had told him that no one was immune to the man's questions or that steely, unblinking gaze.

'We can offer tea or coffee, however,' Nikki said.

Harry asked for tea, and a uniformed officer hurried off to get it.

Once they were settled in the bare room, Harry opened the sports bag he'd been carrying and produced handfuls of books, drawings and maps. He piled them on the table and began to sort them out.

'I was surprised at how many there were,' he said. 'I found them in the attic.' He unfolded a large map of eastern England and pointed to what should have been Lincolnshire. 'The county of Reedmire.' He spoke almost reverently.

The map smelled musty, and it was a little faded, but legible enough.

'This was some labour of love,' exclaimed Joseph. 'It must have taken hours of work.'

'More like weeks, probably months to do the whole of England, but this was by far Lucas's favourite county.' Harry looked at it rather wistfully.

Joseph noted that the county borderlines, the positions of the cities, the towns, villages and other places of interest were all in the right positions, some even illustrated by sketchy drawings. Only the names were different.

'Why was Lucas attracted to this county in particular?' asked Nikki, staring at the town of Shrimptown — or as she knew it, Greenborough.

'Because it's the perfect place to access the faery realm.' Harry looked up. 'Sorry, but I have to explain this as my brother saw it. It will sound wacky to you, as it does to me, but it's the only way I can help you to understand him.'

He looked directly at Nikki, and Joseph was sure he saw the hint of an amused smile on his lips. Harry Byrd, it seemed, had correctly identified Nikki as a dyed-in-the-wool sceptic.

'Right, well, Lucas used visualisation to travel into his faery kingdom through doors, portals and gateways, as something like an avatar, an imaginary self. The portals he preferred were situated anywhere there was water — in marshes, a spring, a pool or the sea. And this county is a water world. Openings in old trees were good too, so I can understand why he went to the Arboretum.'

'Hold up,' said Nikki, frowning. 'We are talking about a little kid here, aren't we? A kid who can actually visualise a spirit self sauntering off into a magic kingdom? Is that possible?'

Harry looked at her patiently. 'Absolutely. His imagination was boundless. He had no human friends, DI Galena, so he built himself an entire world where his friends were of a different species. This started at a very early age.'

'And your father encouraged him,' Joseph said. It was not a question.

'I believe our father recognised all sorts of things in Lucas, both positive and negative. He knew the boy was destined to follow a less-trodden path, no matter what anyone said or did, so he guided him towards what he believed was at least a harmless one.' Harry gave a little laugh. 'One day, my little brother — completely seriously — described to me the "psychic protection" that he activated before travelling into the faery realm. He said that if he travelled there unprotected, he would be set on by mischievous tricksters who would threaten his safety.' He looked at Joseph. 'That could only have come from Father. He was always going on about protecting yourself when working with spirits.'

There was a pause as the constable entered with tea. Then Harry continued. 'He had rituals too, certain practices that he said built up trust with his faeries, and he once told me that the greatest thing he could do would be to dedicate himself to caring for trees. I had no idea that he would actually carry that ambition through to his adult years, although on reflection, perhaps I ought to have known him better. He wasn't ever going to grow out of his other-worldly beliefs.'

Joseph noticed that Nikki was getting impatient. She'd had enough of faery doorways and astral projections, so he decided to steer the conversation in another direction. 'Harry, you said there were some specific places that would have been of interest to Lucas. Can you point them out on your map?'

Over the next ten minutes, he identified around twenty of these places including, uncannily, the Arboretum at Shelley House. Lucas had called it "Oakengard," which reminded Joseph of *The Lord of the Rings*.

'Could we get this down to IT and ask Spooky to reproduce it for us?' said Nikki. 'Are you okay with that, Harry?'

He nodded. 'Just as long as I get it back. I have no idea if I'll ever see my brother again, other than in a dock, so this means a lot to me.' He pointed to the other maps. 'You can borrow them all if you think it will help. There might be a tiny seedling of a clue somewhere in our boyish adventures.'

Daunted by the number of maps and notebooks, Joseph asked if there were any that might be more helpful than others in finding Lucas.

'Not really. If you only had his diary, you'd be able to get right inside that troubled little head of his, but,' he gave Joseph a sad smile, 'that was the one thing he refused to be parted from. In fact, when you find him, I'm certain he'll still have it, including a record of what really happened to those poor people.' He let out a groan. 'God! It sounds like I want to see my brother found guilty of murder! I just want him found. Found and made safe — and those around him safe too.'

Nikki assured him he was doing the right thing by every-one. His help in the search for Lucas was invaluable.

'I really do think it might help if I walked around some of the places I've mentioned,' Harry said after a while. 'If Lucas is looking for me — and he did say to meet him here in that letter — he will undoubtedly expect me to go to those places we "travelled" to as youngsters.'

Nikki took her time to respond. Joseph knew what she was thinking — it was risky, but it made sense. Use Harry as willing bait to lure his brother out.

'If we agree, you cannot go alone, Harry, and that's final. We'll have plain-clothes officers watching your every step.' She stared at him. 'That's the deal, and it's not negotiable. And if he does show himself, Lucas won't notice our officers. They are very good at blending in, believe me.'

'I understand your reasoning, DI Galena, so okay, I'll work with you on this,' Harry said.

'Then I'll introduce you to Sergeant Niall Farrow, who heads up the uniformed section, and he'll suggest the best officers to go with you. Between us, we'll plan a route and a schedule and there will be one detective present at all times. We have to be very, very careful with you, but you have to appear quite natural. Do you think you can do that?'

'No matter who is around, I'll still be looking for Lucas, and that's exactly what I'll do,' he said. 'I'll probably forget about your people.'

'Just don't forget to stick to the route and the timetable. They are crucial. We need to ensure we have eyes on you at every moment,' Nikki said. 'Now, I suggest you go back to the hotel. I'll need to get this okayed, but if all is well, I'll ring you the moment we have a green light.'

After Harry had left with an escorting officer, Nikki looked at Joseph. 'What do you think?'

'He'll go anyway, we both know that. This way, if our killer makes a move, we have a chance of catching him. I'm with you and I think Cam will be too.'

'Let's hope that's the case. I'll go right now, then I'll meet you in my office and you can bring me up to speed on Cat and Ben's progress.'

Joseph remained behind, collecting up the books, note-pads and maps, pausing every now and then to skim through one of them. They were almost works of art. He must ask Harry, he thought to himself, which one of the two brothers was the artist. He opened one notebook and found a beautifully decorated description of the life and times of a woodland sprite. With the maps, it would have made a superb illustrated children's book. Considering that it had been created by a couple of youngsters, it was most impressive.

He took them all back to his office and rang the IT department to say he was bringing them down.

'Actually, Sarge,' Spooky replied, 'I've got to come up to the back office and check on a glitchy IT connection. I'll call in on my way and collect them.'

A few minutes later she was perusing the maps and the history of Lucas's faery kingdom. She laughed. 'I must say, this makes a refreshing change from mugshots and crime-scene photos. And this is the work of a kid! I wish I could draw like that now.'

'One or two are very dark and sinister, which shows another side to his vivid imagination,' said Joseph. 'It's the main map that we'll be needing ASAP, Spooks. It's pretty big, but can you sort us some copies?'

'No problem, Sarge. I've got a smashing wide-format printer–scanner that will deal with that easy-peasy.' She grinned at him. 'Hell, I could even produce it on canvas if you want to frame it and hang it on the wall.'

'Just a couple of copies will be fine, thanks,' Joseph grinned.

'What about the rest of the stuff?' She frowned at the books heaped on the table.

'Skip all that for now. I'll sort through it, and if anything seems relevant, I'll pop it down to you.'

After Spooky had left, Joseph opened another book and turned to a page with a strange pencil drawing that reminded him of woodcut pictures from old books. It was simply a tree, with a sturdy, straight trunk. Within the deep grooves of its bark, you could make out a hidden figure. Its arms were raised and travelled the route of the lower branches, making it seem like an integral part of the tree itself. It appeared to be a woman, possibly wearing a flowing gown, or maybe nothing — it was hard to make out from her diaphanous, cobweb-like appearance. 'A dryad?' he whispered to himself. 'Is this what you see, Lucas? A tree spirit?' He pictured an axe hacking its way into the trunk. It would have severed that almost transparent figure in two. For a brief moment, he felt the pain of hard steel on flesh.

Joseph shut the book, feeling oddly uncomfortable. He had caught a glimpse, had a flash of understanding of what Lucas felt when Ritchie Naylor took an axe to that tree.

He was quite relieved when he heard Cat's voice. He looked up and saw her standing in his doorway.

'You look like you've seen a bloody ghost, Sarge.'

'A spirit, actually, Cat, but let's not go there right now. What can I do for you?'

CHAPTER THIRTEEN

Aiden Gardner didn't appreciate Hawkeye Hackett watching his every move. In fact, he resented it. He was certain that Hackett was paying more attention to him than anyone else. He suspected that the Man in Black was using his very high-spec computer to track and monitor every site he accessed. Aiden was beginning to feel paranoid. He had some interesting contacts lined up but couldn't decide whether to risk speaking to or even emailing them in case Hackett swooped in and pulled the plug on him.

He glanced up and saw Hackett checking his watch, getting to his feet and leaving his office.

The moment the door closed behind him, Aiden picked up the phone. 'Mr Paine? Steven Paine?'

Aiden quickly explained the reason for his call.

'I'm trying to build up a picture of Julian Hopwood-Byrd, sir, from before he left to work in the States.'

'Let me just stop you there, young man,' Steven Paine said. 'You're some journalist trying to rake up old history, aren't you? Well, I have nothing to say about Julian.'

'Sir! Please ring the number I gave you. It's the Greenborough Police Station switchboard, who will put you through to CID where I work. It's important. And, sir? I'm very much interested in Julian's work and I'm no sceptic, I promise.' Aiden waited, praying the man wouldn't hang up on him.

'How did you get my name?'

'From a paper that he wrote, sir: *Illusion, Trickery or the Real Thing?* On psychokinesis. He credited you for your assistance, and then I traced you through your college.'

Aiden heard a laugh. 'My goodness, that old thing! It's still available? I thought it had been lifted with everything el—'

He stopped abruptly.

'Sir, I'd dearly love to talk to you. Could you possibly spare me half an hour of your time?'

'Can you tell me why you want to know about Julian?' asked Steven Paine cautiously.

Aiden decided to go out on a limb. 'His son is in serious trouble, and I have to get to the truth. To do that, I need to know more about Julian. But please, don't tell anyone I told you that.'

'I moved from London to Ely after I retired. I suppose I'm about two or three hours from you. Can you come this afternoon?'

Aiden silently cheered. *Result!* 'Certainly, Mr Paine. If you could just give me your address?'

Pleased with himself for having made a big step forward — and without Hackett knowing — he just had to get the okay from Nikki, but he doubted that she'd object. It would cripple his injured leg, driving for over two hours, but damn it, what were painkillers for? He had a good feeling about this man. He'd seen several mentions of him in Spooky's printouts, checked him out and discovered that he was a friend of Julian's from their college days. He'd liked the way the man had jumped to Julian's defence when he believed Aiden to be a journalist. That spoke of loyalty. To be loyal to someone, you had to know them well, or admire them.

Nikki was not in her office, so he approached Joseph and told him what had happened. Initially the sergeant had looked unsure, asking if he thought spending so much time on the father's somewhat bizarre beliefs was going to help them find Lucas.

Aiden thought fast. 'Actually, I wasn't thinking so much about his work, Sarge, more about whether this old friend knew the family, especially the two boys. Paine seems very loyal to Julian and that does point to a close friendship, what do you think?'

'Put like that, I doubt the boss will object. We're trying to chase up people who might have known the family on their return from America. She'll be here shortly, so run it past her.'

Despite what he'd said, Aiden did want to know about Julian's work. It fascinated him. He was even beginning to wonder if there really could be something behind what most of the world considered nothing but bunkum. According to Spooky's reports, Steven Paine had been a regular and enthusiastic assistant to Julian in his experiments, so who better to talk to?

He returned to his workstation, hoping that Nikki would get back before Hackett. When, a few minutes later, she hurried in, he leaped to his feet and caught her before she'd opened the door to her office.

'DI Galena! I've found a man who might have known Harry and Lucas as boys. Is it okay to drive to Ely after lunch and speak to him? He's an old friend of the family, and perfectly happy to talk.'

'Certainly,' Nikki began, then stopped and frowned. 'Ely's a bit of a drive, Aiden. Are you sure you're up to it?'

'Oh, it will smart a bit.' He laughed, brushing it aside. 'But I've got a small pharmacy at my disposal. I'll cope, never fear.'

'When are you planning on leaving?'

'Around half twelve, maybe one o'clock?' he said.

'I could try and get you a driver. Niall might have an officer who could go with you,' she offered.

He shook his head. He didn't want anyone with him. They'd be sure to come in too, which would put paid to the kind of questions he intended to ask. 'Thank you, boss, but I'll be fine, honest. It's time I tested my strengths and weaknesses. I need to know what I'm capable of for when I'm back full-time.' He looked at her appealingly. 'And uniform have got their work cut out hunting for Lucas without providing a taxi service for a half-lame ex-detective!'

Just two minutes before Hackett returned, Aiden had his green light. He glanced up at the vulture's office and thought, *Up yours, sucker!*

* * *

Nikki closed the office door behind Joseph. 'Cam has said we can go ahead, but only with maximum covert cover at all times. He doesn't want Harry out of our sight for one minute, not even at the hotel. I've already seen Niall, and two officers have been deployed to Corley Grange. They'll book in as a married couple and monitor his every move.'

Joseph nodded. 'Cam believes that Lucas will seek him out?'

'He's sure of it. After all those years, he invited his brother here to complete a lethal task. He will have to find Harry, or he might not be able to finish his mission. He'll make contact at some point soon and we'll be watching and waiting.' But Nikki was concerned that Harry Byrd might not comply. His desperate need to find his long-lost brother could easily make him forget the police investigation and the fact that his little brother had already killed twice.

'I'm totally with you there,' Joseph said. 'The slightest hint of where Lucas is and he'll be off. He won't be deliberately avoiding us, rather the urge to find his brother will kick in and he'll forget everything else.'

'Niall is fully aware of the situation and is already arranging a couple of teams of plain-clothes officers ready to instruct as soon as we've planned out Harry's route. Uniformed backup will be available in the area whenever Harry is on the move.' She paced around her office. 'That's all we can do for now, but we mustn't give up on getting to grips with the family history. There's always a chance that Lucas will go it alone and try to murder the Elf King without his brother's help. So, we need to find out who that is, and fast.'

'Which brings us to Cat and Ben,' said Joseph. 'They might need to take off to London, to visit the Hopwood-Byrd house.'

'Okay, fill me in.' Nikki flopped down in her chair facing Joseph.

'First, the university Lucas said he attended. Cat believes he was telling the truth when he said Lancashire. The courses he mentioned to the countryside ranger are held at Myerscough College, in Preston. Cat has spoken to them several times and, although there was never any Lucas Byrd or Luke Elmore registered with them, she has found a member of staff who is prepared to do a little delving for her. This man remembers people talking about a very unusual young man at about the time Lucas would have been the right age. Apparently, this student was very much a loner, but was known to be an extremely clever arboriculturist. This tutor's subject was actually equine studies, so Lucas would not have been one of his students, but he thinks he knows who we mean and is going to make inquiries for Cat.'

Nikki felt a glimmer of hope. 'If we can just get the name he used as a young man, we might discover where he went and who he was with.'

'Exactly. Cat's going to let us know the minute she hears from the college.' Joseph leaned forward. 'Now for their reason for wanting to go to the Smoke. Ben has located someone who claims to have spent time with Lucas not long before he ran away. This older lady fostered problem children and used to live in the same road, right opposite the Hopwood-Byrds. She said that young Luke was fascinated by a particular tree that she had in her garden, and she would allow him to go in to see it up close. She said the questions he asked about it were very advanced for his years, and they struck up something of a tentative friendship.'

'How did Ben find this woman?' asked Nikki.

'Through a local residents' group online. He went on to their Facebook page and asked for anyone who had lived in the same road at the time the family returned to England. Someone came up with this woman, Mrs Delia Cleghorne, and he rang her. Ben reckons she sounds like a bit of a diamond. The thing is, she mentioned a disabled daughter who liked Luke and shared his passion for wildlife. She was possibly a bit strange too, although naturally the mother didn't admit that bit. The two youngsters talked a lot. Apparently, Mrs Cleghorne and her daughter felt desperately sorry for him and were worried about how his father's murder had affected him.'

'Does he know if the daughter is still living with the mother?' asked Nikki.

'Oh yes. It sounds like they kind of care for each other now the old lady is getting on a bit.' Joseph looked at her. 'So what do you think? Should they go?'

'Well, now we're planning to tail Harry Byrd through the streets of Shrimptown, I'm guessing that lets you and me out of a trip to London, so why not? Sooner rather than later, I'd say. And while they're there, they can do a few discreet enquiries into whether Harry's mother is interviewable.' She thought for a moment, then added, 'Without talking to Harry. I think it's time to have a heart-to-heart with Mother while her son's not there.'

Joseph stood up. 'I'll go tell them.'

'And you can also tell them that I'm sorry, but it's not an excuse to drive into the West End, take in a show and go for a meal in Chinatown either. Talk to both old ladies and get back here pronto.' She gave Joseph a half-smile. 'If they get anything that leads to us finding Nature Boy, I'll treat them to a proper night out on the town when this is all over.'

Joseph grinned back. 'London! Maybe we could join them?'

'Why not? If you're paying.'

'Deal!'

Joseph had barely left the office when Nikki had another, rather more unwelcome visitor.

'I'd like a progress report if you have the time, DI Galena.'

She bit back a retort, smiled coldly and said, 'Come in, Mr Hackett, but it won't take long, I'm afraid. Progress isn't exactly happening right now, especially as we can't release the e-fit likeness or tell the public who we are looking for in connection with the two murders.'

Hackett sat himself down in the chair that Joseph had just vacated. 'A necessary evil, I'm afraid.' His smile was even colder than hers. 'And something that good policing will overcome, I'm sure.'

Nikki felt her anger rising but didn't want to cause trouble for Cameron Walker. With great difficulty, she kept her reply fairly polite: 'I'm sure you can't blame us for feeling a little as if our hands are being tied, Mr Hackett, and that feeling is exacerbated by the fact that we have no idea why. We understand that it seems to revolve around our killer's father, but surely that dreadful incident is so far in the past that it shouldn't interfere with a present-day investigation.'

Hackett regarded her for a while, his gaze unblinking. 'We've met before, DI Galena.'

'I did recognise you, Mr Hackett, but the name didn't register.'

'Not surprising. We were never formally introduced. It was a fleeting and very swift incident, not a time for pleasantries.'

Of course! She saw again the doors of the CID room fly open and a troop of plain-clothed strangers march in, accompanied by a chief superintendent. They were made to step away from their computers and told to leave the office. They had trodden on some toes in high places and had been closed down. 'I'm guessing you've had a promotion since we met last?' she said, with a slightly bored air. 'You were one of the foot soldiers back then.'

'I'm good at my job,' he stated flatly. 'It's been recognised.'

'I hope you aren't planning on a rerun of that "incident," as you put it. We're desperately trying to catch a killer here. Whatever weird stuff is going on in some other department shouldn't hinder a murder investigation.'

Hackett sat back and continued to stare at her. 'Despite what you think, I have no wish to hinder you, DI Galena, but there are lines in this case that must not be crossed. I'm only here to put the brakes on should you inadvertently wander into a danger zone.' His glacial expression melted very slightly. 'I'm afraid I'm not at liberty to give you any details, but believe me, it's in both our interests to get this man caught as quickly as possible, and not just before another victim dies. Lucas Hopwood-Byrd needs to be neutralised and this whole affair satisfactorily closed, as expeditiously as possible.'

Nikki frowned. Had there been a hint of genuine concern? 'If we knew where the line was, we might be able to comply a little more easily,' she said evenly.

After a moment or two's consideration, he said, 'Keep the inquiry away from Julian Hopwood-Byrd and confine it to Lucas. That's your red line.'

'Mr Hackett, I assure you our inquiries are directed at the two sons. Finding Lucas and keeping Harry safe, that's my priority.'

'I'm sure it is *your* priority. Just make sure it's that of your whole team.' Hackett stood up. 'Thank you for your time, DI Galena. I'm glad we understand each other.'

Nikki was left staring at an empty chair.

* * *

Joseph had passed on the message about London to Cat and Ben, and they were now checking with Mrs Cleghorne about when they might visit. It was midday. If they left almost immediately, they could be there by around half past two.

Joseph went to tell Nikki that they were losing no time and would be heading off as soon as they had contacted the old lady.

'Before they go, Joseph, tell them to be wary of asking direct questions about Julian, the father. And,' the worry lines on her face deepened, 'get them to make sure that anyone they talk to understands the importance of keeping our investigation a secret. We don't want this Cleghorne woman telling the entire community about it.'

Joseph didn't ask why. He didn't need to. He'd seen Hackett leaving her office a few moments before. He did as she said, then hurried back into her office and closed the door.

She told him exactly what Hackett had said.

'So he implied, but never actually said, that we're not all singing from the same hymn sheet?' he asked.

'Exactly. Now, I know we originally believed that we had to understand Julian in order to see the extent of his influence on his young son, but his brother Harry has pretty well filled in the gaps about that, so we really need to focus entirely on Lucas. Our new directive, should we wish to hold this case together and not get shut down — as we were once before, if you remember — *has* to be to find Lucas and identify this bloody Elf King of his, hopefully getting to him before Lucas does.'

Joseph nodded solemnly. 'I'll never forget that case. Being told to step away from your computer and leave your office and knowing it was all totally out of your hands was just . . . an experience I don't want to replicate.'

'Well, it could happen. Joseph, you know we could have a weak link, don't you?'

'Aiden?'

'Aiden. And I hold myself entirely to blame. I told him to look into the spooky side of the case, and they don't come much spookier than Julian. We have to get him to back off from the father.'

'Spooky, too. She's provided him with all manner of stuff. I'm sure she's used untraceable pathways, she's no fool, but she's very interested. She knows quite a bit about Stargate and the rest of it. I'd better go warn her.'

'I'll speak to Spooky. Joseph, you go and talk to Aiden before he heads off to Ely and inadvertently opens a can of worms.'

Nikki was already on her feet.

Cat and Ben were just leaving. 'The old lady will be there, so will the daughter, so we're going to hit the road, Sarge,' called out Ben.

'One thing before you go.' Joseph hurried across and told them what Nikki had said. Cat looked dubious. 'But his name will come up, Sarge. It's bound to. You can't talk to someone about an old neighbour and not even mention his name.'

'Just steer it towards the two brothers as far as possible and don't ask about the father. And hammer home that it's to go no further. Do your best.' Joseph looked around. 'Where's Aiden?'

'Oh, he left early, Sarge,' said Cat. 'He said to tell you he didn't want the boss to change her mind and take a valuable officer off the hunt. He said he'd take it steady, and he'll be fine on his own.'

Joseph cursed inwardly. 'You two take care, all right? Ring us if there's anything of note to report, otherwise we'll see you tomorrow.'

He watched them go, then got his phone out and called Aiden. There was no reply. The phone rang — it wasn't switched off, he just didn't answer. Joseph cursed again, this time out loud. Okay, maybe he was driving and couldn't answer. Or he just didn't want to talk to them.

Joseph had a feeling he knew which was the truth. Well, there was more than one way to get hold of him. He went to Aiden's desk and looked for his memo pad. He would have scribbled down the address of where he was going.

Aiden's desk was clear and very tidy, unlike his own, which was overflowing with paperwork. Joseph opened a drawer and raised his eyebrows. Even the batch of printouts he had been given by Spooky had gone. He'd taken all his notes with him.

Joseph frowned and gritted his teeth. He'd mentioned Ely. As that meant nothing to Joseph, Aiden had to have picked it up from Spooky's documentation. And she would have kept copies.

He left the CID room and ran down the stairs to the IT department, glad to see that Nikki was still there.

'Aiden has already left, boss,' he said.

'Shit! Then ring him, Joseph, and explain.'

'Sorry, he's just not answering.'

'Bugger! Keep trying. And text him too.'

'I will, but right now I need Spooky's help.' He turned to the IT chief. 'A man resident in Ely in Cambridgeshire, Spooky, an old family friend of Julian's. Aiden must have got his name from your research. Can you locate him for me? Then I can ring Aiden and talk to him there, or failing that, at least put the fear of God into his interviewee.'

'Did he give you a name, Sarge?' Spooky asked.

'Oh. Give me a minute.' Had he mentioned a name? Joseph closed his eyes and tried to remember. 'Yes! Not a full name, just the surname. It was Pain, although I've no idea how you spell it.'

'That's enough for me.' Spooky pulled a face. 'I do recall it, but unless my memory fails me, he was no family friend. I'm pretty sure he was a colleague, working alongside your scientist on his experiments.'

'Damn and blast! Track this guy, Spooks, fast as you can, or I can see Aiden Gardner sending this investigation directly to hell in a handcart!'

CHAPTER FOURTEEN

Lucas still had some supplies with him, but he was an experienced forager and enjoyed finding and gathering wild foods. When he worked in the Wolds, he had taught youngsters the ethics of foraging — never take unless there is a plentiful supply, and only ever take enough for your personal use. It was good to see those children learning to respect and connect with nature. His face darkened. Of course, kids weren't always respectful. Just this morning he had heard some of them screaming around on bikes, yelling and shouting and disturbing the tranquil atmosphere.

He tried to put them out of his mind, wanting to retain the mellow feeling that the woods were bestowing on him as he passed between the trees. His basket contained a few delicious-looking mushrooms, some wood sorrel, chickweed and a few sprigs of other edible wild greens, along with a handful of wild strawberries. For some reason he always felt healthier and happier when he ate these gifts from nature. He could hardly wait to share what he'd learned with his brother. It would be such a delight to cook for him and present him with a meal full of natural goodness. He shivered in anticipation at the thought of finally seeing Harry again.

Reunited. What a wonderful word! Harry was close now. He didn't know why or how he knew but he was certain that his brother was moving ever nearer. Now, did he just wait — after all, Harry would remember this place — or should he actively go and seek him out? He could do that now he was in this particular area. Here, there were safe pathways linking all their "special" places, protected from the Elf King. Lucas could move undetected between them, and as long as he didn't stray from those set paths, he would remain safe.

Lucas walked slowly back towards his temporary home, resolving to cook his lunch and then decide.

The boys came out of nowhere. Three of them on mountain bikes.

The first sped past Lucas and was gone almost before he noticed him. The second boy managed to catch Lucas's basket as he passed, scattering his precious harvest.

Lucas yelled at them, and the third boy careered off the path, falling into a patch of bracken. He laughed loudly at Lucas, who was desperately trying to salvage his lunch, hauled up his bike and sped off.

Lucas heard them shouting to each other as they rode away. 'Feral scum,' he muttered. He checked to see if he had lost any of his precious food, then hurried off towards home. On entering a small clearing a couple of hundred yards from his home, he found the three boys standing in a semicircle, bikes on stands, waiting for him.

He stopped and stared at them, his lip curled. They were the worst kind. He could not see one single redeeming feature in any of them.

The ringleader of the group stood slightly in front of the others, idly snapping the leaves and twigs off the overhanging branch of a beautiful horse chestnut tree.

Lucas's jaw tensed, and his eyes narrowed. He felt a little jolt of pain each twig broke. 'Stop it! Leave that tree alone!'

A chorus of derisive laughs filled the clearing.

'Oh ho, we've got ourselves a nutter, lads! He wants us to leave the tree alone!' The older boy was grinning evilly at Lucas. 'Maybe we don't want to! Do we, lads?' He grabbed the graceful branch and snapped it in two.

The other two joined in, as if on cue.

Lucas screamed. The boys laughed and started to dance around him, taunting him and waving the damaged branches in front of his face.

Cold and very, very angry, Lucas placed his basket carefully on the ground and lunged at the first boy.

The speed and sudden aggression of his action took them all by surprise. Lucas grasped the boy's right arm, held it straight and smashed it down across the handlebars of his bike. The bones in the elbow shattered audibly and an agonised scream rent the air. He pushed the boy to the floor and hissed, 'So how do you like it?'

The boy screamed, begging Lucas to leave him alone and not kill him.

Lucas picked up his basket. 'Get him out of here and never, ever do anything like that again.' He took a step towards the two others and yelled, 'Go! Take him and go!'

Leaving their bikes, they half-carried their friend away from the clearing. Lucas was mildly impressed by the way the broken arm dangled at an angle that closely resembled the broken branch of the tree. Karma was a beautiful thing.

The boy's screams gradually died away into the distance. Lucas made his way home. He couldn't stay here now, but he had his safe pathways, and he knew exactly where he would go next. It was always prudent to have a Plan B, in case of small, unexpected and annoying occurrences.

* * *

Aiden was in agony by the time he reached Ely. He had expected to ache, but now he was really paying the price. He stopped in a lay-by, found some more painkillers in his glove compartment and washed them down with water he'd brought with him. He sat for a few moments, wondering sadly if he would ever get his fitness back, then shook himself and returned his thoughts to his mission. All this pain had to be worthwhile. Aiden took his phone from his pocket, saw three missed calls and a message. He was to back off asking any questions whatsoever about Julian Hopwood-Byrd or his work. Aiden turned his phone off.

He located Paine's home easily, a simple, white-rendered cottage among a small cluster of houses around a tree-lined green. This was a far prettier part of the Fens than Greenborough, but for some reason, he preferred the rough edges of his county. Perhaps it was the bleakness of it that always drew him back.

Steven Paine met him at the door and invited him in. The man was probably in his late sixties, but it was difficult to judge his exact age. He had thin, receding grey hair, was a little overweight and wore rather old-fashioned clothes in the form of beige jumbo-cord trousers, a dull-green, corduroy, long-sleeved shirt and a knitted Fair Isle tank-top.

He led Aiden through to the lounge and offered him a hot drink, which Aiden accepted gratefully. The strong tablets had left him with a bad taste in his mouth and a slight dizziness.

Drinks served, Steven sat opposite him on a well-worn sofa. 'So, how can I help? *If* I can. I might not know the kind of things you are looking for.' Steven had a London accent, an educated one.

'You were associated with Julian for some time, sir, so I assume you were an advocate of his work?' Aiden said.

Steven puffed out his cheeks and lounged back on the sofa. 'I was in awe of the man, Mr Gardner, and I'm not ashamed to say it. He had a kind of wild charisma, and the intensity with which he pursued his theories was intoxicating. To be frank, his brain worked on a different plane to everyone else's. It was not only a privilege to work with him, but assisting him with his experiments was, well, almost addictive.' He let out a painful sigh. 'It still hurts when I remember what happened to him. If only he had taken a different path, we would all be celebrating his life and work, instead of trying to bury it. He was a very great man.'

Aiden sipped the hot tea thirstily. He had been right to visit Steven Paine. Steven would be the lodestar on which he would build his profile of the real Julian. 'You clearly knew him very well, sir. As a matter of interest, how did he, as a committed and passionate scientist, take to family life with two young boys, one of whom had certain learning difficulties?'

Steven laughed. 'Oh, Julian adored them. He quite simply had the ability to compartmentalise. He was like a house with many rooms and, once he was through the door of one room, all the others were firmly closed. He lived fully in whatever room he was in, and when it came to his family, he was absolutely one of them. And by the way, in Julian's eyes the child was gifted, not challenged.'

Aiden nodded. 'We've been told that he encouraged the child in his fantasies.'

Steven looked at him shrewdly. 'But were they fantasies? What if they were a gift? The father was gifted, why not the son?'

Aiden was taken aback. 'Well, it's been said that the boy saw faeries. Surely, sir, that can't be factual.'

Steven shrugged. 'Faery was just a word, a child's description of what he perceived. What if the things he saw were beyond a child's ability to understand or explain? What if he could actually see energy sources emitting from living things?'

'His brother told the police that was what Julian thought. And parts of his studies concerned energy sources, didn't they?'

Steven nodded. 'I worked extensively with him on the question of the scientific explanation versus the acceptance of auras as a natural occurrence.' He pulled a face. 'But even if you were interested, which I very much doubt, the papers no longer exist.'

'What happened, sir? Why was everything wiped?'

Steven gave a humourless laugh. 'You'd have to ask the Americans *and* our own security services about that, young man. And they won't tell you, that's for sure.'

Aiden believed him on that score. Hackett's beady eyes on him earlier that day were proof enough. He was suddenly reminded of Joseph Easter's text. 'Sir, if you should be asked, would you mind not mentioning that I enquired about Julian or his work? My questions are supposed to centre entirely on the boys.'

'Makes no difference to me, Mr Gardner. I've already been warned off more times than I can count. If this visit is noticed, then just talking to you will probably constitute hard labour. But fear not, I don't talk to anyone these days. Except the cat.' His eyes moved to a grey ball of fur curled up in a tight ball on a window seat. 'And by the look of it, even she's had enough of my conversation.'

'Before I ask a few questions that I've prepared, can I ask you candidly, between you and me, if you believe in clairvoyance? Do you believe that Julian was a real clairvoyant and truly managed to access data through remote viewing?'

Steven didn't hesitate. 'Of course I believe it. Julian Hopwood-Byrd was the most powerful clairvoyant I've ever met, or ever will. And I personally witnessed his abilities in the field of remote viewing. Why on earth do you think the Americans wanted him so bloody badly?'

Aiden concentrated on his tea and tried to calm his excited mind. Here was an extremely well-educated man and a scientist, extolling the virtues of a subject that DI Nikki Galena would undoubtedly call a load of bollocks. It was all very confusing.

'Listen to me,' said Steven patiently. 'The Americans were very anxious that the Soviets didn't get ahead of them with their so-called psychic spying. They believed that with the right training anyone could be taught to use their mind to that end, so they drew on soldiers from the US Army to be their guinea pigs. When one of their scientists chanced on a paper written by Julian and further investigation revealed that he did indeed possess some kind of "talent," they suddenly realised the huge advantage of using a real clairvoyant.'

Before he could say more, Steven Paine's home phone rang.

Aiden was pretty sure who the caller was going to be. He looked almost beseechingly at Steven. 'If that should be my boss . . .'

Steven Paine went to answer it. After a few moments he said, 'Ah, yes, I do understand, Sergeant Easter, but I can assure you that your very pleasant officer here and I are having an interesting conversation about faeries. Would you like to speak to him?'

He passed the phone to Aiden.

'What the hell's the matter with your mobile, Aiden? We've been trying to get you for hours!'

'I'm sorry, Sarge, really I am. I put my phone in my grab bag in the boot when I picked up some sandwiches and forgot it was there until I arrived. I did read your message, though, and have complied fully.' He hoped he sounded contrite enough.

Joseph didn't sound convinced. 'Just leave Julian out of whatever you are saying, got it? It's vital you don't ruffle feathers, or we could *all* finish up looking for new jobs.'

Aiden assured him that he understood the situation, then handed the phone back to Steven. 'Thank you, sir. I'm apparently treading on rather dangerous ground here.'

Steven stared at him with an expression that Aiden found hard to decipher. 'Oh yes, Mr Gardner, you certainly are.'

They talked for another half an hour, until it was time for Aiden to leave. He walked down the path without noticing the figure observing him from a short distance away. Neither did he hear the click of a camera shutter.

* * *

PC Yvonne Collins and her young crewmate PC Kyle Adams hurried into the A & E department at Greenborough

Hospital, wondering what they would find. All they knew was that there'd been an attack on some boys in a wood. Boys and woods were not a good combination, and they were already mentally ticking off the likely perverts in the area.

Inside, they found one of their colleagues, a newbie called PC Johnnie Little, two anxious-looking adults and two boys of around ten years old.

'What have we got?' asked Yvonne.

Johnnie Little rattled off what he knew so far. 'The boys, three of them, were playing on their bikes in the wood when a man came out of the bushes and viciously attacked the eldest boy. He broke the boy's arm, Vonnie, really severely.'

'What? For no reason?' Yvonne looked from one child to the other. Since neither boy could meet her gaze, she guessed there was more to it than that.

'And these people?' She nodded to the couple sitting with the boys.

'Mr Andrew Tompkins, Jimmy Tompkins's father.' The young policeman pointed at the smaller of the two lads. 'And this is Lucy Brown, Kieran, the other boy's mother.'

'And the injured lad, how is he?' Yvonne asked.

'The doctor will come and talk to you shortly, Vonnie. Both his parents are with him. It's not life-threatening, but it could be life-changing.' He looked at his notepad. 'Name is Harley—'

'Don't tell me. Harley Courtney, of Bellhouse Buildings, the Carborough Estate,' Yvonne said. 'I've felt that lad's collar more times than I've had hot dinners.'

'Well, by the sounds of it, he's going to be out of action for some time to come,' said Johnnie.

She returned her gaze to the other boys, neither of whom had crossed her path before — though if they stayed friendly with Harley that might not last long. 'Okay, lads, this is no time to be lying to the police. That, my little friends, can have some very nasty consequences.'

Both boys looked frightened, and the one called Kieran started to cry.

Yvonne threw them what she hoped was a motherly smile. 'Tell the truth, and all will be well.'

'He was weird, that man, really weird. He was picking weeds and putting them in a basket,' Kieran burst out. His mother quietly passed him a tissue. 'And he yelled at Harley for hurting a tree! How weird is that!'

Kyle and Vonnie stiffened, and Kyle leaned towards the boy.

'What exactly was Harley doing to the tree, Kieran?'

Kieran sniffed louder. 'Nuffin! Just breaking the branches.'

'And pulling off the leaves,' added Jimmy. He stared at his feet and mumbled, 'And so did we.'

His father grunted. 'Not exactly a crime, Officer, is it? And they're just youngsters after all.'

'Would you excuse us for a minute?' Yvonne grabbed Kyle's arm and led him out of earshot. 'Quick! Go ring this in. Notify Sergeant Farrow that our man was in Campmarsh Woods around lunchtime today. We need a team down there straight away. And tell him to pass that on to DI Galena. I'll get a description off the kids, but I'm certain it was Lucas Byrd who injured that lad.'

'Yeah, a broken arm for a broken branch. Sounds like him, doesn't it?' Kyle hurried out of the department, while Vonnie returned to the waiting room.

It didn't take long to verify her suspicion. The description fitted perfectly. When she showed them the e-fit likeness, they both nodded frantically. Yes, they said, that was the "weirdo."

Having confirmed that neither boy had been harmed, she asked if they would be willing to take the police to the exact spot where it had happened. Both agreed to go back to the woods.

'I need to stay here and see the doctor about Harley, but I'll arrange a car to come and get you,' Yvonne said.

'With blue lights and sirens?' asked Jimmy, earning himself a cuff around the ear from his dad.

'Maybe. We'll see,' whispered Yvonne, hopeful of keeping the boys on side.

She radioed in a request for a car to be dispatched urgently. The faster they could discover where the attack had occurred and which way Lucas was heading, the better their chance of apprehending him. This was important. A confirmed sighting, and only a short time ago!

Kyle returned just as the orthopaedic doctor arrived. He took her aside. 'I've never seen such injuries,' he said. 'There are multiple fractures and a lot of tissue and nerve damage. I've got a top orthopaedic surgeon coming in from another hospital to operate on him.'

'Will he regain the use of that arm?' Vonnie asked. The kid was a bad one and probably heading for a life of crime, but he was only eleven, and he didn't deserve this.

'That will depend on what we find when we get in there. It'll come down to the surgeon's skills. He may get considerable movement back or,' he pulled a face, 'very little. There's no guarantee.'

'Can we talk to him yet?' Yvonne asked.

'Sure. Just for a bit. He's been given very strong pain relief and he's pretty woozy, but he is conscious. I'll just go and inform the parents that you'll be talking to their son.'

'I know them, I'm afraid.' Now Vonnie pulled a face. 'I've had some arguments with them in the past over Harley's conduct. Mr Courtney isn't fond of coppers and can be a little, er, colourful in his language. I'll try to keep it low-key.'

The doctor raised an eyebrow. 'He's already slagged off the doctors and nursing staff, along with the whole NHS in general, so do what you will with him. My priority is the injured boy, as his father's should be.'

She followed the doctor into the cubicle and took a deep breath. 'Ah, Mr and Mrs Courtney. You remember me, I'm sure . . .'

CHAPTER FIFTEEN

'Oh, just great! No one in the office and we get a bloody sighting.' Nikki threw her arms up in the air. 'What a bummer!'

'It doesn't need both of us out in that wood, Nikki,' said Joseph, reading the memo. 'You stay here. I'll go and tramp the woods and I'll ring you if there's any indication as to where he is now.'

Nikki hesitated but then acquiesced. 'You're right. I'd rather stay here in case there's a more up-to-date sighting, and you're better at field work. Zena and I will keep everything ticking over here.' She looked at him anxiously. 'Go carefully, Joseph. He could still be out there, hiding.'

He smiled at her. 'Of course, and don't worry, he's probably miles away by now.'

Twenty minutes later, he was at the exact spot in Campmarsh Woods where the incident had occurred, thanks to a message from Niall and the what3words app.

'The story so far . . .' said Niall, 'I'll give you the brief version. Kids taunt this guy they suspect to be a weirdo. Harley breaks a tree branch, and he yells at them. Then the others follow suit and start waving the broken branches at him. At that, the man goes apeshit, smashes Harley's arm across the handlebars of his mountain bike and shouts, "So how do you like it?" Harley begs for mercy and the guy cools it a bit, tells the kids to get their mate out of there, and they help him to get away. They leave the bikes and run. Once away from the mad guy, they call Jimmy's father, who comes out to rescue them.'

Joseph gazed at the scene with its recently broken branches and litter of twigs and leaves. He looked up to see two white-faced boys with a man and a woman and a uniformed constable beside them, all watching the police carefully search the area.

The bikes were still there, two on their stands and one on the ground, which had splashes of blood on it. Seeing the blood, Joseph understood how much force had been used to break the boy's arm badly enough that the shattered bone penetrated the skin. 'Did the boys see which way he went? Or did he remain here?' he asked.

'The one called Kieran said he saw the man watch them trying to get the injured boy away, then walked off down that path there.' Niall pointed to a narrow track. 'I've had a team follow it, but there was no sign of him.'

'This isn't a part I know at all,' said Joseph, looking around.

'Me neither. It's a kind of go-nowhere place. Most of the paths lead in a circle back to the road you came in on, or to the creek or the river.'

'So what was Lucas doing here?' ruminated Joseph. 'There's no sign of another of his hidden camps, is there? It is kind of wild and overgrown in places.'

'We haven't been here that long,' Niall said, 'but my guys know what to look for after seeing the last place he hid out in, and there's nothing so far. I was just going to follow the path that Kieran said he took myself. Want to come?'

'I was going to suggest that,' said Joseph.

As they went, Joseph turned a sharp eye on the surroundings, taking everything in, looking for anything out of the ordinary. He had automatically reverted to soldier mode — alert, watching for snipers, checking the ground for IEDs.

He shook his head to rid his mind of the memory of a patrol he had been on, long ago in a very hot country. Few men had made it back to base that day.

Soon the wood thinned out and they came to a fork. In one direction he could see a tree-lined path to the river and the other, a much less used track, had to be the way to the creek.

Niall looked from one to the other. 'Which one? The creek?'

Joseph nodded. 'Yes, we'll check that way first.'

Niall was tapping on his phone as he walked. 'I'm just checking a satellite view of the wood. The creek meanders down and feeds into the river a little way along, but this path seems to be a dead end.'

And it was. The track petered out into a clearing, and in front of them lay Campmarsh Creek, a minor tributary of the river.

'I'd say someone has been here recently,' said Joseph, 'but whether it was Lucas or the boys, it's impossible to tell.'

They turned around and made their way to the second path and the river.

Again, there were signs that people had walked that way, but according to Niall, the place was frequented by the more intrepid dog walkers. There were a couple of old and disintegrating moorings and little else. Joseph calculated that it would be a good three or four miles upriver before you reached the stretch of water where Vinnie and Sheila had their mooring. In the opposite direction, salt marsh and then the Wash, with little else in between.

'I'm beginning to think he pretended to walk in this direction just to misdirect the boys,' Niall said dejectedly. 'He has no camp or hidey-hole around here.'

Joseph agreed, although he couldn't help but think that they'd missed something. He decided that he'd been correct when he told Nikki that Lucas would be long gone. There was no trace of him.

'Niall, I suggest you leave a crew concealed somewhere where they can watch the road entrance to the wood — just in case I'm wrong. But other than that, I'd clear the area and send everyone home. We know it was Lucas. He's an experienced woodsman, so he won't be leaving us any clues, and in all honesty, we don't need them. Lucas Byrd injured that boy and disappeared again. I'm not even calling forensics, it would be a total waste of time, money and resources.'

'You're right,' Niall said. 'I'd do better to deploy officers further out and see if anyone matching his description has been seen leaving the area.'

'Good idea. Well, I'm going back to base. We're thin on the ground this afternoon and right now Nikki's flying solo.'

Niall grinned. 'What? No one to yell at? She'll have some catching up to do when everyone gets back.'

'You're so right, son. I can hardly wait.'

* * *

Their trip had been remarkably easy, until they hit the M25.

'The satnav says twenty-nine minutes,' said Cat. 'We take the M1 and the Barnet bypass, then the Bishops Avenue and Hampstead Lane.'

'With this traffic we can double that,' said Ben gloomily. 'Now I know why I love the Fens.'

As it happened, it took exactly half an hour, plus another five minutes to locate the house they were looking for.

'So, this is where the Hopwood-Byrds live,' said Cat, slightly in awe.

'Very nice!' breathed Ben. 'There's money in this road, isn't there?'

Cat looked again. 'Maybe there used to be, but I think that's changed. I'm betting most of these lovely old houses are split up into flats and bedsits by now.'

'I guess. Easy access to the City and the West End. Yeah, and a snobby address in a nice area. I think you're right.'

Cat undid her seat belt. 'Right. Let's go and see what Mrs Delia Cleghorne's like, shall we?'

'Could we just take a peep at her neighbours' house first?'

The Hopwood-Byrd residence, called "Arcadia," was a genteel and elegant house, if somewhat tired. 'It seems that house maintenance isn't very high on Harry's list of priorities,' commented Ben. 'It's not exactly a ruin, but it's crying out for a lick of paint.'

'Maybe having to have a carer for his mother and the overheads on a big London property like this are draining him. We have no idea of his circumstances, do we?' Cat stared at the house, wondering what it would be like to have more than two bedrooms. 'And I keep forgetting to ask what he does for a living.'

Ben narrowed his eyes. 'I reckon he's loaded. And you know what? I don't think he works at all.'

'Okay, Detective, how do you work that out?' asked Cat.

'I'll tell you on the drive home. Right now, we should look up our old lady and I hope she has the kettle on.'

The Cleghorne property was very different. There was no name, just the number — twenty-one. It was smaller than Arcadia and semi-detached, with a black-and-white gable and a front door with the shiniest brass knocker and letterbox Cat had ever seen.

Inside it was just as well cared-for. The black-and-white Victorian tiles on the hall floor gleamed, and the walls were unmarked. Unlike Arcadia, this house was loved.

Mrs Cleghorne, who insisted on being called Delia, was not quite what Cat had expected. She was a willowy, tall woman with weathered skin and a mop of curly iron-grey hair, and she was wearing a bright-blue polo top, faded denim jeans and blue-and-white sports shoes. Cat calculated that she must be in her mid- to late seventies, but in those modern clothes she could have been any age. She smiled at them warmly.

'Come and meet my daughter, my dears, and then I'll make some tea. You must be gasping after that trip.' She spoke in a strong London accent. 'This is my Mandy,' she said proudly, ushering them into a light, airy conservatory.

The doors opened on to a colourful and generously planted patio, where a woman sat in a wheelchair. She smiled and, laughing, said, 'Hello! Forgive me for not getting up.'

Cat liked her immediately. She and Ben shook her hand.

'Let's sit out here. It's still lovely and warm.' Mandy pointed to two garden chairs with thick padded cushions.

Some of Mandy's movements and her speech reminded Cat of the sister of an old friend from school. She wondered if Mandy, too, had cerebral palsy.

'Mum makes good tea, and I'm betting there'll be warm scones too. She likes to make visitors welcome.'

When the promised scones arrived, Cat eyed them with relish. 'You really shouldn't have gone to so much trouble,' she said, 'but I'm glad you did!'

'You want to know about little Lucas, don't you?' asked Delia, when everyone had been served. She pointed. 'Well, that's what first attracted the lad into the garden.'

Cat and Ben saw a massive and very odd-looking tree towering over the garden.

'It's a monkey puzzle tree,' said Delia with a smile.

'Araucaria araucana,' added Mandy smoothly.

'It's said that these trees can live for a thousand years and were around at the time of the dinosaurs, two hundred million years ago. People call them living fossils.' Delia smiled at them. 'So you can see why our little Lucas was fascinated by it, can't you?'

'I liked Lucas very much,' said Mandy wistfully. 'I think I understood him.'

Ben flashed Cat a look that said, *Maybe back then you did, but you wouldn't now.*

Cat sipped her tea. 'Can you tell us when you first met Lucas and something about how he got on with his family?'

Delia looked at them thoughtfully. 'Well, now, I knew the Hopwood-Byrds before they left to go abroad. They had no children then, of course. They didn't mix socially, but they were polite, whenever we saw them in their garden or out in the village. I think the fact that my husband and I fostered children back then didn't help. It didn't make us very popular with the neighbours. Some of my foster children were a little wild, I'm afraid, and we did take a lot of problem kids, bless them. We never had too much bother from any of them, but some folk only see poor unfortunate children like them as trouble.' Her ready smile faded, but soon returned. 'Little Lucas was a very unusual boy indeed. He was very intelligent, which I suppose came from the father, but distinctly, well, other-worldly.'

'He saw faeries,' said Mandy, matter-of-factly. 'He saw them everywhere in the garden. He even described the custodian of the monkey puzzle tree. And sometimes . . .' She stared at the ancient tree with a faraway expression. 'Sometimes I think I see it too.'

Though not contradicting her daughter, Delia raised an eyebrow. 'As I said, other-worldly. And that probably came from the father too.' She stared into her tea. 'I suspected that Lucas's home life wasn't terribly satisfactory, Officers. It was far from stable, what with the father so deeply into whatever he was studying — something metaphysical, I believe. And I'm not sure that the mother was aware that her son Lucas was quite severely impaired in some areas.'

'And Harry? The other son?' asked Ben.

'Never saw much of him, dear, but Lucas loved him, as he did his eccentric father. He worshipped his dad, was always quoting strange facts about the natural world that could only have come from Julian.' She heaved a big sigh. 'I'm afraid the Hopwood-Byrds had a bit of a reputation around here. People even called them cranks and nutcases. And they had some very odd visitors, coming and going at all hours of the day and night. No wonder they were considered strange.'

'And now?' asked Ben.

'Now? Well, that terrible business with the gardener put the fear of God into people and everyone kept well away.

Then, when he was put into that hospital or prison, or whatever it was, people still kept their distance. That kind of thing hangs over a neighbourhood. It taints it, sometimes makes it notorious. Some folk moved away after it happened, and house prices dropped for a while. It's all right again now and we do see Harry occasionally, but he's as private as his parents were.'

'And the mother? I understand she's disabled,' said Cat. Mother and daughter exchanged a glance.

'She doesn't come out at all now,' Delia said. 'Anita never even sits in the garden anymore. People, whom we assume are carers, come and go every day. Personally, I think Julian's death finished her off and she took to her bed.'

'There's a lady staying there now,' added Mandy. 'She's got funny hair. I saw her taking cases from her car. And then Harry went off with bags and stuff.'

Delia looked between them. 'What's happened, Officers? Why are you so interested in a boy who ran away so long ago?'

Before either detective could answer, Mandy swung her chair around to face her mother and said, 'Because he's killed someone, just like his dad.'

Cat and Ben had no idea what to say to this. Delia, however, made up for it.

'Amanda! What on earth do you mean by saying something dreadful like that? Lucas would no more kill someone than fly to the moon.'

Mandy shrugged. 'Oh, Mum, it's obvious. CID detectives don't drive all this way for a nice chat about the neighbours. And I saw the news last night. There have been two murders in Lincolnshire, where these police officers come from, so it stands to reason.'

Delia looked at them helplessly, clearly waiting for them to deny what her daughter had just said.

Ben chose his words carefully. 'We need to find Lucas, Delia. He's missing, and Mandy is right, inasmuch as there have been two deaths and we need to talk to him.'

'Oh my God,' Delia whispered. 'Whatever happened?'

'We aren't at liberty to say at present, I'm afraid, but we do think Lucas can help us,' Cat said. She turned to Mandy. 'Aside from that very smart piece of deduction, why do you accept so readily the fact that Lucas is capable of killing someone?'

Mandy didn't answer immediately. 'He believed that he had inherited many of his father's abilities. He tried to be like him. He told me he wanted to be the living embodiment of Julian after he was gone. Of course, then he was talking about the future, his father dying of old age. When Julian was killed, Lucas was devastated. He never got over it.'

'What we really want to know is where he went, or more importantly, who he went to when he ran away.'

Delia shook her head. 'It was a terrible shock when it happened. At the time I racked my brains to think where that lad could have gone. I would have helped him if I could, but I didn't have a clue.' She looked across to Mandy. 'He never even told you, did he, my darling?'

As before, Mandy took her time to answer. 'I never saw him again. He promised to always be my friend and perhaps he is, somewhere, but I don't know where he went.'

Cat and Ben stayed talking about the young Lucas for another thirty minutes. They gave mother and daughter their cards, asking them to call if they thought of or heard anything that might assist them.

'We're just going to call in on the off-chance that Mrs Hopwood-Byrd might be up to talking to us,' said Cat on their way out.

'Good luck with that,' said Delia flatly. 'Don't be surprised if you get turned away at the door. I haven't seen her let anyone in for a long time.'

They went round to Arcadia and rang the doorbell. A couple of minutes later, the door was opened by an older, very heavily built woman, who did, as Mandy had said, have very strange hair — a wild mane reaching to her shoulders and hanging round her face, a strange cross between strawberry and tangerine in colour. Cat had to make a concerted effort not to stare.

The two detectives showed her their warrant cards and asked if they could have a few words with Mrs Hopwood-Byrd.

The woman looked vexed. 'Well, since you're the police, I shall go and ask, of course, but Anita is not a well woman, Officers. Normally I'd say no straight away. Harry — that's her son — has said that's all right. Please, step inside. If you'll just wait a moment, I'll go and speak to Anita.'

They watched as she hurried up a wide flight of stairs. Cat noted that she was remarkably agile for someone of her size.

She wasn't away long. 'I'm so sorry. I feared as much, but she's just not up to it.' She turned on a smile. 'But can I offer you tea or coffee? I'm Corinne Blake, Anita's sister.'

They didn't need more tea, but they accepted in order to buy a little time in the house and find out what the sister remembered.

The lounge had a slightly musty smell to it, as if it went mostly unused. Like the house's exterior, it was in dire need of freshening up. Cat didn't want to spend more time than necessary in the place, which reminded her of the old people's home her gran had ended up in.

'Your sister is disabled, we understand,' Ben said.

Corinne Blake sighed. 'I suppose you could call it that. It's not a disabling medical condition, although she does suffer badly with arthritis. It's her mental state, a sort of terminal apathy.'

Cat wondered if her tone was due to desolation at her sister's plight, or maybe she suspected her of malingering.

'Harry's tried everything. She's been seen by all sorts of specialists, but Julian's death was the finishing of the Anita we all knew.'

'Do you live close by, Mrs Blake?' asked Cat. 'It's very good of you to look after her while Harry is helping the police.'

'I live in Scotland. This is a mercy mission and probably the last I'll make, I'm afraid. My husband needs me too, so

I'm torn. I've told Harry that this is the last time, and he understands.'

'So you weren't around when they came home from the States?' Ben asked.

'Actually, I was. We only moved back to Scotland a few years ago. It's my husband's home. We used to live about five miles from here.' She pushed a swathe of tangerine hair away from her pale face and looked solemnly at them. 'In all my life I had never seen such a change in a man. He was a husk of his original self. It was a horrible shock, I can tell you.' She exhaled. 'Talk about a bittersweet reunion. I met my nephews for the first time, which was magical, but I had to come to terms with the fact that my brother-in-law was no longer the person who'd set off so full of excitement and anticipation.' Corinne Blake shook her head, as if still trying to come to terms with it.

'And would you blame that dreadful incident involving the gardener for this terrible change in him?' asked Cat.

The strangest expression came over the woman's face. Cat, who was usually very good at reading people, was mystified.

After a while, Corinne said, 'I'm afraid I can't answer that. It's not that I won't, you understand. I simply cannot. It was too out of character. I still can't believe that Julian had it in him to kill, even after all he'd been through.'

'And the gardener? We heard that he acted inappropriately with one of the boys,' said Cat cautiously.

Corinne made a loud harrumphing noise. 'Another thing I'd never believe! Not in a month of Sundays. But,' she drew her big frame up in a shrug, 'like it or not, it happened, so what do I know?'

The tea actually wasn't too bad, and when Corinne slipped out for a few moments to check on her sister, Cat whispered to Ben, 'Is it me, or do you get the feeling that nothing here is quite as it seems?'

He nodded. 'I think so too.'

Corinne returned, looking somewhat unsettled. 'I'm afraid I'm going to have to ask you to leave shortly, Detectives.

Your unexpected visit has agitated Anita. She gets distressed very easily. Even having a new carer upsets her.' She grunted. 'I'll be relieved when Harry's back and I can go home. I know that sounds callous, but you just cannot help some people.'

Cat stood up. 'Thank you for the tea, Mrs Blake. Just one last question before we go. Do you know who Lucas went to when he ran away?'

Corinne looked even more sombre. 'No, I don't. But he went to someone all right, and it had to be a very special person. Lucas had a single-track mind. He saw everything in black and white, and ignored or dismissed anyone who thought differently to him. Whoever helped him was on his wavelength, but as to who it was, I have no idea. I'm sorry.'

Those words were Cat and Ben's signal to leave.

They drove to the nearest service station, filled up the car, used the facilities and grabbed a takeaway. They were on the M1 before they'd relaxed enough to discuss the three extraordinary women they had just met.

'And what about your theory that Harry is loaded?' Cat said. 'Nothing in that house shouted wealth or pots of wonga.'

'I'm still sure of it.' Ben stared ahead, his eyes on the traffic and the road snaking ahead of them. 'And I'd still swear he doesn't work either. Regarding money, think about what happened, Cat. I reckon that if we get Spooky to do a bit of careful sleuthing, we'll find that the US government paid Julian a massive amount of compensation, and possibly even hush money as well, for the damage that project did to him. Lucas is long gone, Mother is incapable of making decisions, so he'll have power of attorney. So, who holds the purse strings now?'

'Harry,' murmured Cat.

'You know what, I'd go as far as to say he doesn't even live in that Arcadia place.'

'But what about Mother?' Cat said. 'She's bedridden.'

'Is she, though? We never saw her. According to Harry she categorically stated that finding Lucas was their number-one priority. Does that sound like the woman Mrs Blake described?'

'Oh my! It wasn't that she couldn't, she just didn't want to talk to us, did she? The sister is covering for her.' Cat frowned. 'And if her loving son is with her all the time, why have carers in and out so regularly? It sounds like he lives locally and does spend time here with her, or he wouldn't have called the sister in to help out, but the carers look after her needs, and he actually lives elsewhere.'

'Luckily that can be checked out, and it's the first thing I'm going to do when we're back in the office.' Ben changed lanes and accelerated. 'A little bit of proof for you. Sniff your clothes. What do you smell?'

Cat answered immediately. 'They're all musty, from that house. It's horrible.'

'Harry's clothes are smart, well-pressed and have no smell. I met him on his way out of the station. I've got a very keen sense of smell. I'd have noticed it immediately.'

They were losing the light now as dusk approached. Cat began to feel sleepy, but her mind was still trying to make sense of it all. 'I'm wondering,' she said thoughtfully, 'if our friend Mandy knows more about Lucas's disappearance than she's saying.'

'I feel the same,' said Ben. 'And she never really answered that question properly, did she? She said she never saw him again and then all that stuff about him always being her friend, but she never said straight out that she didn't know who he went to. I wondered at the time whether she did know but had maybe promised never to tell. They were close, that's obvious.'

Leaning back in her seat, Cat closed her eyes. There was so much more to this than they were seeing, oh, so much more . . . And with that thought, she drifted off to sleep.

CHAPTER SIXTEEN

Nikki and Joseph arrived home late that evening. Nikki had felt guilty about not having seen her mother for weeks, so they drove home via Beech Lacey and called in for a coffee and a quick catch-up with Eve and Wendy in Monks Lantern, their converted chapel home.

Now it was almost nine o'clock. Joseph was preparing a late supper and Nikki was talking on the phone. There had been two earlier calls, one from Cat, who told her that their visit to London had thrown up more questions than answers, and the other from an apologetic Aiden, more or less to assure her that he hadn't stepped out of line, something she felt far from certain about. Now she was talking to Laura Archer.

'I've been run off my feet with emergency calls,' said Laura. 'Hence not calling in to see you. Is tomorrow morning okay to drop by? Not that I've got too much to offer.'

'Fine,' said Nikki. 'As we've had a new development, I'd be glad of it.' She went on to tell Laura about Lucas's attack on the boy in the woods. 'He could have killed him, couldn't he?'

'Oh yes, quite easily, I'm sure,' said Laura. 'I guess the boy's age, or something either he or one of the other boys said, stopped him.' She thought for a moment. 'Actually, it was quite risky for him to let them go. He had no idea where those boys lived. If it had been close by, or if someone had been able to respond to a phone call for help very quickly, he could have been caught before he had a chance to decamp.'

'I thought that too,' said Nikki. 'As it was, he had to have moved very smartly to completely disappear before our people moved in on that wood. Joseph went out there himself and said there was no sign anywhere of an old camp, or even the slightest indication of where he went.'

'It's his territory, isn't it?' Laura mused aloud. 'He's highly skilled in woodlore. He reminds me of those scouts you used to see in cowboy films, who could cover their tracks or hunt others undetected through wild country. Or maybe he's more of a survivalist.'

'Whatever he is, he's a killer, and right now, he's way ahead of us,' said Nikki gloomily. She looked up and saw Joseph indicating that supper was ready. 'Better go, Laura. We haven't eaten yet. I'll see you in the morning.'

Over supper the conversation rather predictably turned to their resident Man in Black and his talk with Nikki.

'You realise that takes him into a different league,' said Joseph, tearing off a piece of hot focaccia bread. 'He's government security rather than one of our own.'

'We suspected that anyway, didn't we? He's no copper, Joseph. He gives me the heebie-jeebies, sitting in that office with a face like a slapped arse.' She ate a forkful of delicious pasta and sighed. 'Okay, it's a relief to finally remember where I've seen him before, but I hate knowing that from day one on the force our every move has been monitored. Those people know everything about all of us.'

'Probably a lot more than we would like them to,' Joseph agreed grimly. 'Like our living arrangements, for starters.'

Nikki groaned. 'I hadn't thought of that. I was thinking along the lines of our work records.'

'Well, it could be our success rate that means they leave us alone,' Joseph said. 'Our relationship might not be of too much concern to them as long as our department continues to achieve on a high level, and we certainly don't flaunt what we are to each other.' He smiled at her a little sadly. 'Even if I'd love to.'

She laid her fork down, reached across and touched his hand. 'Me too, Joseph, me too.'

They ate in silence for a while. When the meal was over, Joseph brewed a pot of coffee and opened a tin of her favourite amaretti biscuits, which he'd made for her a few days ago.

'It's odd,' said Nikki, savouring the almond flavour. 'I find Lucas Byrd far more disturbing than almost all of the other dangerous psychopaths we've come across in our time.'

Joseph stirred his coffee. 'It's because of his other side, I suppose, the side that Karen Cotton knew. And he isn't without the capacity for love. He certainly loves nature, to the point of killing to protect it. Karen saw a gentle, if rather deluded soul. Hell, she taught him to meditate, for heaven's sake! She cared about him. As did his employers and that old local guy, Ed Shipley, from the woodland volunteer group. They liked him a lot and admired his passion and his knowledge, and it's pretty clear that Lucas wasn't putting on some cunning act to deceive them. He *was* that nature-loving person.'

'Oh yes, *they* got the caring Dr Jekyll, and we are left with Mr Hyde. Oh, joy! And not only that, because he had a mad scientist for a father, we have also attracted the attention of the security services. Aren't we the lucky ones?' She bit down angrily on her biscuit.

'Excuse me, but they are meant to be savoured, not annihilated,' admonished Joseph with a grin.

She smiled back. 'Sorry, Joseph. They are delicious, honestly, and you're an angel to make them for me. I don't deserve it.'

'You certainly don't, but there you go.' He winked at her. 'Now, let's put murder on the back-burner for a while and talk about something nice, like Vinnie and Sheila's wedding. And maybe . . . why you won't wear a hat?'

'Because I look a right tosser, that's why! Hats and I just don't get on. Remember the uniform bowlers? Well, most of the other PCs looked great in them. I looked like Charlie bloody Chaplin! All I needed was the moustache and the cane.'

'Ah, I'm beginning to get the picture, but as it's a wedding, I thought maybe something pretty and flowery would be more fitting?'

Nikki threw him a withering look. 'Joseph Easter! Do I look like the pretty, flowery type?'

'I just thought . . .'

'No hats! Got it?'

'Er, how are the biscuits?'

'I thought you'd see reason.' She smiled benignly. 'Lovely, thank you.'

* * *

Not so very far away, Lucas crawled into bed and closed his eyes. He had followed the safe pathway and moved on to his next special place. He was disappointed that another day had passed without seeing his brother, but those wicked boys had upset his plans with their malicious actions. He would have preferred to stay where he was, just to give Harry time to find him, because he was certain he would be following the old map. Still, this place was just as good and probably even more powerful than the wood by the creek. He hoped he'd dream about meeting Harry again, but his dreams hadn't been good ones of late. He feared that although he was safe from physical harm, the Elf King might be causing bad energies to seep into his sleeping mind. It was possible. The Elf King was very powerful.

Lucas turned over on to his side. For the first time since he'd left his master's house, he felt lonely. Lonely for a brother he hadn't seen since he was a boy, the brother who had built him a kingdom of his own, in which he now lived.

Sounds from outside floated into his shelter and soothed him. He loved what he called the night music, the sounds of nature, a reassuring unseen presence, although it was also a time for mischief and dark forces to be abroad. But tonight Lucas felt safe.

He thought about tomorrow. Maybe Harry would come. Maybe.

* * *

Karen Cotton struggled to sleep. It was now almost two o'clock and all she had achieved was a few minutes of restless dozing. Next to her, Sean slept soundly. His breathing, not quite a snore but almost, was usually soporific, but still sleep would not come.

She felt restless and a little anxious. She knew the reason for it, but that didn't make it any better.

Luke Elmore was the problem. She felt confused and not a little guilty. She had given the police his likeness, and in doing so had handed him to them on a plate. She should have felt good about it, but she didn't. She had liked him, felt they shared something, a spiritual quality. She had come across this kind of affinity in the past, but usually with healers or other teachers like herself, not someone with no prior knowledge of meditation or mindfulness. She had been sure that, although his beliefs were not hers, they had been genuine — which, of course, left him open to being labelled as delusional.

Trying not to disturb her husband, she eased herself into a more comfortable position. What chance did Luke have of growing up to be a Mr Average? From what the police had told her, none at all. So he saw spirits — well, so did good Christians, many of whom saw angels. What were they if not beautiful winged creatures?

She was drawn to him, too, by his belief in powerful spiritual energies. Through her work with yoga, meditation and other healing techniques, she had come to believe that positive energy and a hopeful outlook aided the healing process more than any medicine. She understood his belief that being surrounded by nature and allowing it to flow into you like warm sunshine empowered you. It was a simple and proven fact that most people felt happier and more peaceful in nature. Why else would we flock to the sea, the mountains, the lakes and the forests for our holidays? Luke had just taken it to another level — and a tiny bit of her envied him that.

Karen moved closer to Sean and the comforting warmth of his body.

Coming from the Carborough Estate to this beautiful place had been the making of them both. For Sean, it was like coming home. He was at his best working in the gardens, nurturing and maintaining them. And for her, it had been a revelation. Her career as a holistic teacher had blossomed, for here she had found an inner peace that she wanted to share with others, bringing balance to their lives. Negative energy was a destroyer, she firmly believed. When you hate, the person who most suffers is you. It always turns inwards in the end.

Karen finally understood why she had been watching the night hours pass so slowly. It was Luke's capacity to do terrible damage in a moment of hate that was frightening her. He should have been a shining light, a beacon of calm and tranquillity. He should have risen above anger at what he saw happening and seen it as an opportunity for change, an opening to bring enlightenment to others. He could have been an example, but he had become a destroyer. It just didn't fit with what she had seen in Luke Elmore.

She experienced a sudden urge to get up and go and look for him. He needed to know this, to understand that he was so much more than these flashes of negative energy that caused him to do terrible harm. To know he had the power to stop it if he chose.

She closed her eyes, then opened them wide. She had just visualised him in a prison cell, his bright light fading, his energy depleting. He would die in there. She couldn't allow that to happen — but oh, the things he had done! How could she condone murder? It went against nature, everything good that both she and he cared for. If only she could find him, speak to him, maybe she could stop him committing more terrible acts . . .

It was all too much to consider at half past two in the morning and at last Karen Cotton fell asleep. It wasn't peaceful or restful, but it was oblivion of a kind.

CHAPTER SEVENTEEN

The next day, they hit the ground running. Nikki needed to debrief Cat and Ben, and also Aiden, but before that she wanted to liaise with Niall. It was to be the first of Harry's visits to some of the places on his brother's old map. Between CID and Niall's team from uniform, they had managed to organise it like a military exercise — they just needed Harry to comply. In Nikki's eyes that was the only weak point, not because she believed he wanted to go it alone, but purely because in his desperation to find his brother he might forget about his minders. They would need to keep a very close eye on him.

'I've arranged to speak to him on a video link at his hotel,' she told Niall. 'Just in case Lucas has discovered where his brother is staying, I don't want him seeing Harry coming into the police station to get his orders. And I don't want our guys turning up there en masse either. We have your two plain-clothes officers undercover there, we all have a copy of the map, and I'm going to talk Harry through exactly where to go and when. He will leave the hotel on his own and take his car to the first of the "special places," which is St Saviour's Church — or to be precise, the graveyard. There are some ancient yew trees there, which is what made it important to Lucas.'

'I was wondering if you'd considered fitting him with a wire, ma'am?' said Niall. 'We could keep in closer contact then.'

Nikki pulled a face. 'I decided against it. He's never used one before and I want him to appear perfectly normal. Wire him up and he might start to feel like something out of *Spooks* and decide to give a running commentary on everything he sees or thinks. If he has no sightings today, maybe I'll reconsider, but let's rely on constant observation to start with.'

Niall agreed. They double-checked their timings and Nikki returned to her office to link in with Harry Byrd at the Corley Grange Hotel.

It didn't take long and, when she ended the video call, Nikki was sure that, if nothing else, Harry knew exactly where he was going and when, and what to do if he should have a sighting. They did not expect direct contact, but made provision for it, just in case. Harry would be under surveillance every step of the way, with a series of undercover officers frequently swapping positions as Harry moved around, so as not to attract attention to one particular man or woman. It was all they could do. By using Lucas's map and his brother as bait, they hoped to draw him out.

As she walked through the CID room on the way to the debriefings, she saw that Aiden's desk was empty. She glanced at Cat, busy hammering furiously on her keyboard, and said, 'Aiden?'

Cat shrugged. 'No idea, boss. He was here earlier but I never saw the going of him.'

'Well, I'll see you and Ben first, then. Five minutes in my office.'

'Okay, boss,' Cat said. 'Ben's in IT with Spooky but he'll be back any minute.'

Nikki went to grab a quick cup of coffee. Joseph had beaten her to the vending machine and had already got drinks for them both.

'Seen Aiden?' she asked, taking a beaker from him.

He frowned. 'No, not for half an hour, and the worrying thing is that Hackett isn't in his lair — sorry, his office — either.'

'Oh shit!' muttered Nikki. 'If he's collared Aiden . . .'

'Let's not panic yet. Could be a coincidence.'

Nikki had her doubts about that but supposed he could be right. Hackett could easily be with the super, and Aiden could be anywhere in the building. She had too much to think about as it was without adding suppositions about the Man in Black to her concerns. 'Joseph, I know we are up to our necks in all this, but I promised to meet Kaye for a coffee this morning and I really must go. Cam is worried sick about her, and I can't let him down. Will you hold the fort?'

'Of course,' said Joseph immediately. 'We aren't expecting Lucas to show on Harry's first day out, and if anything major happens, I can always ring you. You go. Cam's been damned good to us.'

'Exactly, and I hate to see him so anxious. Let's talk to the others, then I'll get off.'

It took around fifteen minutes for Cat and Ben to explain what they believed was happening in the Highgate house. They told Nikki and Joseph that they suspected Mandy, Delia Cleghorne's daughter, knew more than she was prepared to share about where Lucas had gone when he left home.

'The mother is straight as a die, I'd put money on that, but I'm wondering if her daughter might open up more if we made our inquiries more official, rather than over tea and scones,' said Ben. 'We could bring them here. It might make Mandy think again about being so loyal. Seeing the inside of an interview room could change her mind.'

Nikki frowned. 'She's disabled, you said?'

'I think it's cerebral palsy,' said Cat. 'She had the occasional spasm, and some of her movements and her speech put me in mind of an old friend's sister. She had it, too, poor thing.'

'Wheelchair?'

'Yes, but they have a specially modified vehicle. I saw it parked outside,' answered Ben. 'Or if Delia didn't want to drive this far, we have a vehicle here that can accommodate a wheelchair. I'd be happy to collect her.'

'You're really sure she knows something?' queried Nikki. They both nodded. 'Convinced,' said Cat.

'Then ring her. See what reaction you get. Oh, and try to talk to the mother alone. If she's being straight with you, she might suspect the same thing.'

'Will do, boss,' said Ben.

'Now, you also got odd feelings about Mrs Hopwood-Byrd, didn't you? You thought she was avoiding seeing you?' Nikki frowned. 'If she was so insistent that Harry make it his priority to help us find Lucas, why wouldn't she be willing to assist us herself? Doesn't make sense.'

Joseph looked pensive. 'I'd say either she wasn't as amenable as Harry said, which means Harry lied to us, or something's going on in that house that we don't know about.'

'Or both,' added Ben. 'We got the strangest feeling about that house and its occupants. I went to see Spooky earlier, and she showed me something interesting. Look.' He handed round a printout. 'The only photograph on record of Mrs Anita Hopwood-Byrd, apparently taken by a press photographer during all the furore over her husband's conviction for murder.'

Nikki found herself staring at a petite, raven-haired woman, with delicate, fragile features and an expression of utter desolation.

'We met the sister yesterday. Her name is Corinne Blake. I've confirmed the name is correct, and the information she gave us checks out, but . . .' He exhaled. 'Initially, we believed that this sister was covering for Anita because she didn't want to talk to us, but now we feel there's something even odder about her, although we aren't sure what it is.'

'Explain,' said Nikki, suddenly getting bad vibes about the whole thing.

'Okay, I know siblings can be very different physically, but this Corinne was the complete opposite of the woman in this picture. She also stated that she was from London and had only moved to Scotland a short while back.'

'Right. So?' Nikki urged him on.

'She had a Scottish accent, I swear. As you know, boss, I'm fascinated by accents and dialects, and that lady definitely flagged up concern.'

Nikki turned to Cat. 'Do you agree?'

Cat nodded. 'I do, and another thing, she was quite dramatic. It's hard to explain, but she was quite opinionated about some of the things we asked about. She made quite a meal out of Lucas being tunnel-visioned and a couple of other things were sort of embellished by her personal opinions. She has to be family, boss, because she knew so much about all their dark secrets, but something didn't ring true.'

'So what the hell is going on in that house?' barked Nikki with a glance at Joseph.

'Maybe another trip is in order, this time with a warrant,' he offered.

'We'd never get one. Not on such a flimsy basis. No offence, Ben, but we don't suspect an offence has been committed and we don't know about any evidence that could be found there to benefit a trial.' Her frown had deepened. 'We need a lot more than that, I'm afraid.'

Her biggest worry was Harry Byrd. He had been prepared to do anything to find his brother. Was there another very different reason for his needing to locate Lucas, other than helping him? And at home — could there also be a very different scenario there to the one he had described?

Nikki's head was spinning. 'Are we being used?' she murmured and turned to the others. 'If nothing adds up at Arcadia, then I cannot help but wonder if Harry is playing an elaborate game with us. Perhaps he can't achieve his goal alone and needs us to make it happen.' After a few moments' consideration, they all concurred.

'So how do we play this?' asked Joseph.

'I need to think that over,' Nikki said. 'Meanwhile, we maintain the status quo, let him go out — after all, we are watching him like hawks anyway. And whatever happens, we don't let on that we have doubts about his honesty. If there is some alternative motive for Harry's presence here, it has to be very important to him. He had no idea we were going to Highgate village yesterday, yet the elaborate cover was already in place. If he *is* covering up something shady, he's done a whole lot of preparation.' She shrugged. 'And you could be wrong, of course. Corinne could easily be chalk and cheese to her sister, and she could have picked up the accent from her Scottish husband. It has been known to happen. Until we know more, say nothing, but keep digging, and start with ringing Mrs Cleghorne. It would be interesting to hear how long it's been since she saw Anita Hopwood-Byrd in person, wouldn't it?'

'And finally,' added Ben, 'do you think you might be able to find out what Harry Byrd does, or did, for a living? We suspect the family received a lot of money from the US government in the aftermath of the trials the father took part in, and that Harry is the sole beneficiary via a power of attorney. Spooky is checking that out — very, very delicately, I promise. We all know that Big Brother is watching us. And although we have no proof, I've asked Spooky to see if Harry owns any other property, because we have reason to suspect that he doesn't actually live in the family home.'

Which made Harry an even bigger liar. Nikki was loath to believe that, but she was forced to consider it. Her detectives weren't fanciful, far from it. If someone registered concern, it must be followed up. A good police officer learned to listen to those inner voices, for they were rarely wrong. Nikki cleared her throat. 'Definitely get hold of that old neighbour as soon as possible. You two aren't required for the observation exercise on Harry. Joseph and I have that in hand, so make finding the truth about the Highgate set-up your main priority.'

Nikki knew that if there was some sinister mystery in Highgate village, Cat and Ben would uncover it. She moved on. 'Now, where the hell is Aiden?' Automatically, she glanced from Aiden's workspace to Hackett's office. Both were still empty.

'Shall I go and look for him?' asked Joseph.

'Yes, please. If he was here earlier, he has to be somewhere in the station.' She frowned and lowered her voice, 'And keep an eye out for Hackett, Joseph. If they are huddled together somewhere, with Aiden receiving a bollocking from our resident cuckoo in the nest, I'd very much like to know.'

'He's more like a vulture than a cuckoo,' muttered Joseph, as he headed for the door.

As it turned out, he returned a couple of minutes later with an anxious-looking Aiden Gardner.

'I apologise, boss,' he said. 'I've got a slow puncture in a front tyre of my car, and I was trying to get someone to sort it for me. I should have said, but the garage that deals with the traffic vehicles said that if I got it there straight away, they'd fix it and pop it back later.'

Nikki hated not believing him, but the fact was, she had serious reservations about Aiden Gardner. Surely he wouldn't lie about something like that — he could so easily be found out! Reluctantly, she gave him the benefit of the doubt. 'A word to one of the team would have been appreciated,' she said. 'I'm very anxious to crack on this morning, and I need to talk to you.'

She told him to close the door and indicated a chair. There were several ways she could deal with this, but she chose to be candid and, for once in her life, decided against going in with all guns blazing. 'Okay, Aiden, I'm going to be perfectly honest with you and I expect your full cooperation. It's absolutely vital that we all work together, or this case is going to be shut down faster than you'd believe possible.'

Aiden exhaled. 'I'm starting to understand that it's much bigger than it appeared.'

'Bigger and darker, unless I'm horribly wrong, and that doesn't happen often.' She stared at him. 'Bottom line, Hackett has you in his sights and by visiting Steven Paine yesterday, you made sure he marked your card.' Aiden went to speak, but she held up her hand. 'I know we sanctioned it, but don't give me any more bullshit. You knew damned well you weren't visiting that man as a family friend of the Hopwood-Byrds. You went because you knew Paine had worked closely with Julian.' She adopted a gentler tone. 'It's my fault. I'm fully aware of that. We asked you when you started to check out his background and all the weird stuff he was researching, but now I'm asking you to drop everything that relates to Julian. It's been made very clear to me that Julian is a red line. If we cross it, it's over. Finito.' She stared at him.

A whole range of emotions crossed his face, and then he sighed. 'I'm sorry, boss. I got fascinated by the man. I believed, and still do, that he was extraordinarily talented. Maybe if he had never joined Stargate and simply kept on with his own research, he would have been acknowledged as one of the greatest scientists of our time. That's what Paine believes, I know.' He looked down at his hands. 'I believed that discovering more about Julian would help us understand his son, Lucas. I thought that was the route to take and I'm sorry I overstepped the mark, but when you discover a complex and exciting man like Julian, you want to know everything about him. The research becomes a compulsion.'

Nikki contemplated him thoughtfully. 'So can you, in all honesty, drop this like I ask? Or will the detective in you be like a dog with a bone? Because unless I have your assurance that you can toe the line, I have to take you off the case.'

He looked up and met her gaze. 'I won't let you down again. If you think it's appropriate, I can work with Laura on what makes Lucas tick, his fantasy prone personality disorder and how that could affect his future behaviour. I promise to stick to the faery kingdom and abandon Stargate for good.'

Nikki wanted to believe him. Hell, she needed all the help she could get to catch this deluded killer. But the slightest niggle remained. 'Hackett is not one of us, Aiden. And now he's watching your every move. If the damage isn't already done — and I pray it isn't — we need to make him believe that our only aim is catching Lucas and that we are all completely committed to that end, and that end only.' She paused. 'With that in mind, I'm going to talk to him. I'm going to tell him you were following a bona fide lead with a man you believed to be a close friend of the family and therefore someone who might give us an insight into Lucas's history, but,' she looked at him long and hard, 'that you soon realised this strand of the inquiry was taking you dangerously close to Julian's past, so you've reported this to me and are backing off. I want you to corroborate this if questioned and show no further interest in Paine, okay?'

Had there been a moment of hesitation? She hoped she'd imagined it.

'Absolutely, boss. It's Fairyland all the way from now on.' He smiled apologetically. 'And thank you. I swear I never meant to jeopardise the investigation.'

After he'd left, Nikki drew in a long breath and sat for a few moments in silence. Her idea of openly admitting that Aiden's trip had been a mistake seemed the only way to move forward. She stood up. If she could pull this off with the Man in Black, she deserved a bloody damehood for services to the acting profession. That, and maybe a fresh coffee and a Danish.

* * *

Harry Byrd kept a constant eye on his phone. At an allotted time, he would receive a text, after which he was to leave his room and venture out on his first sortie in search of his brother. He was impatient but also a little apprehensive. It had been so long since they had seen each other, he had no idea what their reunion would be like. He'd played out scenario after scenario in his head but could never decide how Lucas would react when he saw him for the first time after so many years. Lucas had always been an enigma, and there was no reason to believe that he'd be any different now. The fact was, he didn't even know what his own reaction would be. Finding his brother had been his raison d'être from the moment Lucas disappeared, and now his long crusade was nearing its end.

He looked again at his messages. It was far too early, but he didn't want to miss any change in the schedule.

He had not wanted his visit to Shrimptown to be like this. It had become grotesquely reminiscent of some bad spy novel. Nevertheless, it was a means to an end. Lucas was no fool. He could never have evaded discovery for so long if he hadn't been absolutely alert. By now, Lucas must have developed the keen senses of a hunted wild animal, or more aptly, the qualities of one of his ethereal beings, simply melting away before they could be captured.

Harry knew that by his mere presence in Shrimptown, by walking the streets and alleyways, visiting those precious "safe places" on their map, he was doing the right thing. Lucas would be watching and waiting for him. That was all he had to do, simply be visible. Lucas would do the rest.

Not long now. He paced the hotel room, chest tight with anticipation. Would it, could it be today? He stared at his phone.

* * *

Hackett was nowhere to be found. Nikki cursed under her breath. It was bad enough with him in his lair, staring out at them all with that vulpine gaze, but it was even more disconcerting not to know where the hell he was. She paid a flying visit to Cam's office, briefly updated him on the day's plans for Harry Byrd's walkabout and, having been assured that Cam had no idea where Hackett was, hurried back down to the CID room.

Joseph was preparing to join the team on the streets, ensconced in the back of a specially equipped van from which he would observe Niall's officers as they tailed Harry. She felt bad about slipping out for half an hour, but she knew Joseph would ring if there was even the slightest hint of a sighting of Lucas Hopwood-Byrd. Cam Walker had been a friend for a long, long time. More than that, he was the glue that held her precious job and her relationship with Joseph together. If she owed anyone anything, it was Cam. She had come late to the realisation that there had to be a balance between dedicated police work and being a decent human being outside the force as well as in it. Friends and family were important too, and Cam's wife Kaye was a good friend. Kaye managed to balance her career at the university with being a supportive and loving police wife, which was no mean feat in anyone's book. Nikki had always had a soft spot for her, and it was nothing out of the ordinary for them to grab a coffee or a lunch together when their respective jobs allowed. It was unusual for Kaye to keep anything from her soulmate, Cam, and Nikki was worried.

Nikki strode briskly towards the Café Printemps but then her pace slowed. She felt almost frightened to hear her friend's secret. And what would she say to Cam if Kaye had really bad news? Nikki wondered if she was really cut out for dealing with this kind of problem. Give her a villain or some devious lying individual any day, but not delicate matters of the heart. Well, she was here now.

Kaye was already seated at a table for two by the window of the small café. Her smile was warm, and she was clearly happy to see Nikki, but there was a haunted look on her face and a slight hollowness beneath her cheekbones. She was either extremely tired or ill. Nikki had told Joseph that she would be direct, but on seeing Kaye looking so washed out, she faltered. Instead, she flopped down and grinned.

'Okay, lady, give me the ticking off I deserve! It's been far too long and all my fault. Well, that and the famous "job."' She widened her smile. 'Have you ordered?'

They always had the same thing when they met in this particular café. The chocolate eclairs were to die for, and they both loved strong coffee, rather than the milky, frothy things most people seemed to drink these days.

'I've only just arrived,' said Kaye. 'And knowing that you've got a serious case on, I wasn't sure you'd make it.'

'Half an hour's catch-up with you is the perfect antidote to murder, my friend.' She turned to the counter. 'The usual, please, Danny.'

The young man nodded.

Nikki turned back to Kaye and made up her mind. She sat back and looked intently at her friend. 'Now, please tell me that those dark shadows under your eyes aren't some new fashion statement. And remember that you're talking to Nikki Galena, so whitewash won't work, okay?'

Kaye pulled a face. 'Guilty as charged,' she said softly. 'I knew I could neither hide it, nor fob you off, Nikki. In fact, it's a relief to finally talk to someone I can trust.' She looked down. 'The fact is, I'm running on empty, but I'm scared to stop, in case I don't start again.'

'Is it work?'

'Partly,' said Kaye. 'It's been tough for a month or two now. Shortage of staff, trying to cover for each other so that the students still get the best education possible, and we've had a couple of difficult— well, troubled kids, so it's been time-consuming and stressful, to say the least.'

'And the main issue?' Nikki asked softly.

'I blame my mother.' Kaye gave a bitter little laugh. 'Mum was a nursing sister for as long as I can remember. She said you should never go to the doctor unless you absolutely had to because if they looked hard enough, they'd always find something.'

So Kaye *was* frightened over a health problem.

Kaye continued. 'I've been lucky, really. I've always had very good health and I do my best to make sure that Cam and I eat well and get some exercise, but just recently . . .'

'Something's wrong and you're scared of knowing what it might be?' prompted Nikki.

'Scared? I'm terrified!'

Danny arrived with the drinks, then Kaye resumed, 'It's not just Mum's warning, Nikki. You see, she finally had to see a doctor herself and found she had cancer. She died shortly afterwards.'

Oh bugger, thought Nikki. The mother had probably left it far too long before seeking help and, if she wasn't careful, Kaye could do the same. But if she was that anxious, it could be a problem. 'You know what I'm going to say, don't you, Kaye?'

'Oh yes, and I know that's what I should do. I just can't cope with actually doing it.' She stared down into her coffee cup. 'And I can't cope with seeing Cam all stressed out either but,' she shook her head sadly, 'I just can't talk to him about it. It's not logical. I love him dearly and I'd never intentionally hurt him, but . . . I just can't bring myself to tell him.'

'Because it would make it real?'

She nodded. 'And then I would be forced to act, wouldn't I?'

Nikki sipped the hot coffee. 'I have noticed a change in him at work, Kaye. He says it's pressure from management and that we have a complex case running, which is true, but I know you both better than that. I know it won't help you if I say he looks worried sick, but it's a fact. It's affecting his work.' She knew that Kaye took Cam's work very seriously and hoped this could make her realise that the time was coming when she had no choice but to face her demons.

'Did he ask you to speak to me, Nikki?' Kaye was still staring into her drink.

'No, he didn't, I promise. But I do throw my hands up to wanting to ask you what's wrong — as a dear friend.' She reached across and touched Kaye's hand. 'So, what's been happening with you?'

Kaye looked thoroughly miserable. 'Mainly it's that I'm so tired all the time, Nikki. I mean exhausted, really fatigued, not like when you've overdone it, more a real, sick exhaustion. And dizziness too, and sometimes a nagging pain in my upper back and across my shoulders.' She shrugged. 'To be honest, I feel awful all over and I'm starting to recognise the same symptoms as my mother had, and that is really scary.'

Nikki frowned. 'Kaye, those symptoms could indicate a dozen different illnesses, some probably really easily sorted. You have to speak to your doctor, you really do.' She sat back and smiled at her friend. 'You know, a little while ago, my mum admitted to being terrified that something terrible was wrong with her, and it turned out to be anaemia. Now she takes iron tablets and she's fit as a fiddle again. It could be something as simple as that, but you need to know.'

Nikki could see that Kaye was struggling. She obviously knew exactly what she should be doing, but her fear was stopping her in her tracks. Nikki drank her coffee and waited, but still Kaye said nothing. 'I'll go with you, if that would help?' Nikki asked. 'You don't have to go alone.'

'You must think I'm such an idiot, acting like this, but I loved my mother so much and it was such a shock when she died. I don't think I've seen a doctor since.'

'All the more reason to go,' urged Nikki. 'At least he or she'll know that you're not a hypochondriac.' She stared at Kaye. 'And you do have Cam to consider. Can you imagine what's going through his mind?'

Kaye looked up. 'You're right, Nikki. I love my husband dearly. I really can't do this to him.' She picked up her phone. 'I'm not even sure if I've got the doctor's number . . . I think I put it in when Cam was poorly at some point. Ah, yes.' She heaved in a breath. 'Here goes nothing.'

As Kaye waited to be put through, Nikki noticed that her hands were shaking. This was no easy thing for her to do.

Kaye was saying, 'Oh, right, well, yes, that's fine, thank you. See you then.'

'Well done you!'

'They have a cancellation for this afternoon at four, with a Dr Groves, a woman apparently.' Kaye stared at her phone, as if only half believing that she'd made the call. 'Do you know, when I said I'd meet you this morning, I think I knew that this would happen. I just needed a kick up the backside.'

'And who better to do it?' Nikki beamed at her. 'And I'm happy to go with you, even if just to make sure you don't chicken out.'

'No, Nikki. Now I've made that appointment, I will go, I promise, and I'll let you know what this Doctor Groves says.'

'You'd better!' She didn't want to rush off immediately, but Nikki was starting to get anxious about Harry Byrd walking the streets of Greenborough, hunting for his killer brother. Or was the killer brother hunting for him?

Kaye must have sensed her impatience, for she said, 'I'm holding you up. You must get away, Nikki. I really appreciate you coming, but you'll be needed at the station. You have a very dangerous man out there.' She smiled warmly at Nikki. 'You get off. I'll settle up here. This is my treat.'

'So it's mine next time.' Nikki stood up. 'Ring me later? Without fail?'

'Guide's honour.'

They hugged. Nikki hurried back through the side streets to the station. At the main door, she noticed a familiar figure talking to two others in a car parked in the visitor's bay, a man and a woman, both looking severe. So Hackett wasn't working alone in Greenborough. The visitors had "official" stamped all over them. Well, at least he was on-site now, and she would collar him the moment he set foot back in his lair. She wanted him to hear what she had to say before he could bring the subject up himself.

As they had agreed that Kaye would ring Cam and tell him about her appointment herself, she hurried into the CID room and pitched straight back into work. 'Okay, everyone. Anything happen while I was out?' When no one spoke up, she added, 'Well, don't all answer at once, will you?'

CHAPTER EIGHTEEN

Joseph watched Harry Byrd on the monitor inside the back of the recon vehicle. He wore earphones through which he received reports from the officers on the streets who were observing Harry and anyone else in the vicinity. Harry had been out there for over an hour, and so far, no one even vaguely resembling Lucas had been seen. Not that they expected anything to happen today. Lucas was unhinged but no fool. Even if he did manage to locate his brother, which was unlikely on his first trip out, it was doubtful that he would make a move immediately.

Joseph had received a message from Nikki, saying she was back at the station, so he decided to contact her with an update.

'Nothing to report, as expected.'

'Bored yet?' asked Nikki.

'Not yet, but it'll come,' he replied dryly.

'And Harry? How is our human magnet shaping up as a lure?'

Joseph thought for a moment. 'He's either taken to it like a duck to water, or . . . or he's so committed to finding his brother that he's forgotten about us altogether. His every move is that of someone looking for a lost loved one. He's observant and has an air of expectancy, tinged with desperate hope and a sort of sadness, as if he realises that his search could be fruitless.'

'Blimey, Joseph! You can tell all that from a figure on a computer screen? That's impressive! And I have to say, pretty deep.'

'It's not me, Nikki, it's him. He's a deep person and not one to underestimate. I'm certain Harry Byrd has his own agenda. I'm just hoping Cat and Ben can shine a bit more light on him.'

'Me too. And his weird family.' She paused. 'Ring me back in ten, Joseph. I have to go. I've just seen Hackett come in.'

Joseph ended the call and returned to Harry Byrd. Now he was sitting on a memorial bench in the grounds of St Saviour's Church, gazing across at the old yew trees, as if remembering when he and his little brother had played there as children, constructing their imaginary place. Joseph wished he could feel sorry for this lonely-looking man, but there were so many unanswered questions about him and what Nikki described as his weird family that it was hard to sympathise. The truth was, he wasn't quite sure how he felt about Harry Byrd.

'Sir?' The IT technician sitting next to him pointed to another screen. 'I've linked into a CCTV camera at the church, and we have a possible sighting! Look.'

Joseph spun around and stared in the direction the man was pointing. A slim figure, partially obscured by trees, was standing in the shadows and apparently watching Harry. Joseph grabbed his microphone and spoke to two of the officers on the street. 'Jim! Karen! Inside St Saviour's churchyard, one hundred metres from the main gate to the right, beneath a cluster of trees. Male suspect. Investigate and report please, and softly, softly!'

'Damn it, he's gone,' cursed the IT operator. 'And there isn't another camera in that area, Sarge.'

'Larry? Anyone exiting the churchyard from the west gate?'

'No one, Sarge.'

'Negative result, Sarge.' PC Jim Price's voice echoed in Joseph's ear. 'Just some kid taking a leak in the shrubbery. He's not the target.'

With a sigh, Joseph told the others to stand down and resume observation. It would have been ridiculously lucky to have got a sighting this early. He rubbed his eyes. It was going to be a very long morning, but at least Harry had stuck to the prescribed route and timetable. The next part of the walk would take him along a couple of cobbled alleyways that led to the river. There were very few cameras there, so Joseph would have to rely on the plain-clothes team for updates until he could pick him up again on the screen.

Harry stood up, looked around and began to walk slowly out of the churchyard.

'Bang on time, Harry,' Joseph murmured to himself, and he passed on the information to the others. 'On the move again, going west towards Blackman's Alley and out of camera coverage. He's all yours, guys.'

* * *

The moment Hackett set foot inside the CID room, Nikki accosted him.

'Mr Hackett, sir, I need a word, please.'

He looked mildly irritated, but nodded and walked ahead of her towards his temporary office. He indicated a seat, but Nikki chose to stand.

'It won't take long, Mr Hackett. It's something I'd like you to be aware of. It occurred yesterday and I nipped it in the bud the moment I heard about it.' She explained that an interview had been held on the erroneous belief that a man, Mr Steven Paine, was a friend of the Hopwood-Byrd family and therefore might have been able to shine some light on Lucas's background and possibly even his disappearance.

'It soon transpired that this was not the case, and that Paine was actually a colleague of Julian Hopwood-Byrd's, not

197

a family friend. Naturally, my officer aborted the interview and immediately reported this to me.' She raised an eyebrow. 'And I thought it prudent to let you know too.'

Hackett gave her a long and oddly blank stare, as if he were unsuccessfully trying to calculate something. 'And which of your officers was this?'

You know bloody well which one it was, she thought, *you little rat!* 'Aiden Gardner. But you have no need to worry, he's dropped that line of inquiry completely and moved to a different area, that of Lucas's mental health issues.'

Again she was treated to that enigmatic stare. She swallowed and went on. 'This case is complex enough, Mr Hackett, and, as it involves a family, there will be times when there is a crossover between family members. It's inevitable. The best I can do is steer us away from Julian and his work or his history every time this happens and let you know that I'm aware of it and have prevented any further inquiries in that particular direction.'

'I think it would be even more prudent if you make sure that all your officers look a little more closely into the backgrounds of those people they intend to interview *before* they do so, don't you?' Hackett gave her a cold smile. 'I know all about Paine, DI Galena, and it should have been plainly obvious to Gardner that the man was a work colleague, not a family friend.'

'Sorry, but we don't have the wealth of background knowledge that you seem to have, Mr Hackett, and as no one is being exactly forthcoming, we are left scratching about in the dark. That, and we don't have the luxury of time. We have a cold-blooded killer out there, so we aren't holding a moratorium on every man jack we want to interview!' *Calm down, Nikki. You're going to lose it with this shit if you aren't careful.* She took a deep breath. 'It's frustrating when there are restrictions on you, and you know lives are at risk. I hope you understand that.'

'Actually, I do.' She detected a hint of apology, or maybe it was empathy in his words. 'It's not my intention to obstruct, I've told you that before, but sadly it's not in my remit to explain anything to you either. I have no choice in the matter.' His eyes narrowed. 'But a word of warning, DI Galena. Rein in Gardner and keep him in check. Watch him carefully, as I will continue to do. He's your weak link. One wrong move and he's out, with the possibility of serious repercussions for your whole investigation. Understand?'

Any sign of softening, if it had indeed been there in the first place, had gone.

Nikki feared he was right, but she wasn't going to admit it. 'Understood, although you are talking about an excellent detective with a flawless career behind him.'

'*Ex*-detective, DI Galena. And, as you say, that career is behind him. I hope he doesn't blot his copybook and blight any future opportunity to work within the police force as a civilian.'

This sounded like a threat. Nikki decided to leave before she said something she'd regret. 'That won't happen,' she said instead.

As she closed the door behind her, she wished she could be sure of that final statement, but she wasn't. So she was going to do exactly as Hackett had said and watch Aiden Gardner like a hawk.

* * *

Ben asked Delia Cleghorne if she and her daughter could possibly come to Greenborough to speak to them again. She received his words in silence, and then he heard her sigh. Perhaps she found the prospect of the trip daunting, or the thought of being part of a major investigation had upset her. He was about to say as much when he heard her give a completely unexpected response.

'Of course I'll bring my daughter to see you — and as soon as you like. We have little by way of prior engagements at present. But the thing is, I'm not sure how much help she'll be. To be frank, she's always been rather secretive about her friendship with Lucas, and if Mandy clams up, it's the devil's own job to get anything out of her.'

'We have to try, Mrs Cleghorne,' said Ben. 'Can I ask, have you ever suspected that Mandy might know more about Lucas than she admits?'

'Oh yes.' She gave a little humourless laugh. 'I'll be honest with you, Detective. If his disappearance hadn't been so sudden, so dramatic, and I hadn't been concerned about how it would affect my daughter, I would have been relieved to see him gone. Not that I didn't worry about the lad, but . . .' Another pause. 'You see, I never felt that their friendship was a particularly healthy one. It was too odd, too other-worldly, too secretive.'

This made holding the interview all the more imperative for Ben. 'We really do need to talk to Mandy. It seems to me that she may be the key to understanding more about Lucas Hopwood-Byrd.'

'Don't get your hopes up. She's a stubborn one,' Delia Cleghorne said. 'But we'll be with you tomorrow morning at around eleven o'clock, and I'll do all I can to convince Mandy that she has to be open with you. We'll probably book in somewhere and stay the night, or even a couple of days. We used to often take little trips out and we've never been to the Fens, so I'll treat it as a mini holiday.'

Ben was relieved that she was so willing to come. He liked Delia Cleghorne. He believed she was a sensible woman and pretty astute where her daughter was concerned. 'One last thing.' Ben had been going to leave this until he saw her but decided to ask now. 'Would you think it possible that Harry Byrd doesn't actually live with his mother?'

'Oh my! Well, I'd never considered that. But he does come and go a lot and there are times when we don't see him at all for a while, so I suppose it's possible. But if that's the case and Anita is unwell . . . Oh my God, that's awful!'

'Please, Delia, it's only a supposition on our part. But I just wanted your thoughts on it.'

Delia exhaled. 'Now you've put the thought into my mind, I'd say it's more than possible. Come to think of it, Mandy said something to rather the same effect the other day. She wondered why Anita needed a night carer when she had Harry there.'

Ben thanked her and hung up.

'I gather she's happy to drive?' asked Cat.

'She's fine. They're going to do a trip around the Fens while they're here.' He grinned at Cat. 'And guess who's already asking why Mrs Hopwood-Byrd needs the night carers?'

'Our razor-sharp friend Amanda Cleghorne?'

He laughed. 'The same.'

'This could be an interesting interview, couldn't it?' Cat looked thoughtful. 'Any ideas on how best to tackle her? Should we do it as we originally decided?'

'Doing the good-cop-bad-cop bit?' He pulled a face. 'You know, in retrospect, I don't think that'll work. Mandy's too smart to be taken in by such a ruse, and ten to one it wouldn't intimidate her one iota. I can see her smiling enigmatically at me and saying sod all.'

'What I'd like to do is let her see the evidence on the whiteboard and then tell it how it is,' Cat said.

'Good idea, but we daren't, what with data protection and all that.' He paused, thinking. 'Although we could doctor the board, take away all names and places, just leaving the photos. They alone would make her realise just what her childhood friend has done.'

Cat grinned. 'Then we have a plan. What time will they be here?'

He told her, then asked, 'Any luck on tracing other properties?'

'Zilch, but he could be renting, which would be almost impossible to check. I even asked at a couple of local residential hotels, but again, nothing.' Cat pulled a face.

'Then it's the sister with the hair, Corinne Blake. Let's see what we can dig up about her, shall we?'

'I thought I might also make a few inquiries into Anita Hopwood-Byrd's carers, although that could be tricky. We don't want Harry finding out that we're asking questions about his mother's situation.' Cat hesitated. 'Actually, I'll shelve that for now and stick to Corinne.'

'Sensible.' They were having to walk on eggshells where Julian Hopwood-Byrd and his wife were concerned.

With that thought in mind, he looked over to Dave's old desk, where Aiden Gardner was talking on the phone. Aiden was a good bloke with an exemplary record, and it had been a stroke of serious bad luck to get injured the way he had, but there was something about the man that unsettled Ben. He was just too intense. Ben wondered if it was a need to prove that he could still do the job. Or maybe being in pain all the time and having to take analgesics like sweeties didn't help. He'd seen him swill down those tablets and feared he was suffering more than he admitted. Ben couldn't even begin to think how he would react if his precious job were taken away from him. He'd feel as if a part of him had been stolen and he'd become less than whole. He grunted. Worrying about a guy who was probably just trying to make the best of a piss-poor situation shouldn't be his concern right now. With Lucas Hopwood-Byrd waiting in the shadows of his beloved trees, there was no time to waste in idle conjecture.

* * *

Nikki had contacted Joseph and told him about her visit to Hackett. Now she was trying to decide whether she should go to Cam and suggest that, in the interests of the investigation, Aiden should be moved to something else. She had the feeling that Hackett would be down on Aiden even if he touched on the forbidden subject unintentionally.

It wasn't an easy decision. Her main priority was finding Lucas and making him safe, but even though she knew it could jeopardise the whole case, she still felt compassion for the man who had been such a dedicated detective. If she dropped him now, she could be doing him further damage. She smiled a little sadly to herself. Even she, blunt, plain-spoken Nikki, could see the hurt in his eyes. Did she really want to give him another kick in the teeth?

'Bugger! I'm getting soft in my old age,' Nikki muttered to herself. 'But I'm watching you, my friend. One teeny-weeny step out of line and I'll get to you before bloody Hackett does.'

There was a knock on her door. Yvonne Collins was looking amused — she had heard. Nikki smiled at her. 'It's all right. It's safe to come in, I'm quite harmless really.'

'Not what the criminal fraternity around here think,' said Yvonne, returning the grin.

'Ah well, that's as it should be. Come in, Vonnie, and grab a seat,' said Nikki, silently hoping Yvonne had had a chance to consider her offer.

'I went out to Cressy Old Hall early this morning, ma'am. Dave had notified Niall that there were two new woodsmen starting there and was worried in case one of them turned out to be Lucas Byrd. He'd said one of them had been held up and was arriving late last night, so I called in on my way to work.'

'And all's well?'

'Nothing like the e-fit photo, ma'am. Dave said he's a big lad, going on six foot and built like a championship boxer. Thank heavens. Dave and Mr Cressy-Lawson have had enough trouble out there to last them a lifetime.'

She seemed to be about to say more, so Nikki waited.

'Er, while I was there, I grabbed a few words with Dave about your offer of the civilian post here. Dave's old job, to be precise.' She took a deep breath. 'He asked how I felt about it. I said I'd been in two minds — there were things I'd been planning to do. He laughed at that and said they were the same things he had been thinking of and now he was beginning to achieve them. But he reckons that if I'm even *considering* accepting the post, I'm not ready to jack everything in just yet, and that when the day comes to walk away, I'll know for sure. He said that making the transition from active copper through the civilian posting is the perfect way to ease yourself into a totally new way of life and mitigates the culture shock of just stopping after a whole life in the force.'

'Our Dave should take a job as a counsellor for retiring bobbies,' said Nikki, her hopes rising. 'So, are you taking his sage and friendly advice?'

Yvonne's grin broadened. 'If you'll have me, ma'am, and if that offer of a few weeks' holiday before I start still stands? Then I'd love to join you.'

'Best news I've had for a long time,' Nikki said, 'and Niall will be dancing with joy. That lad's been worried sick about you leaving. You are his lodestar, Vonnie, always have been and always will be.'

She laughed. 'That "lad," as you put it, is a damned good policeman in his own right. He doesn't need me anymore. But as I consider him to be the son I never had, I still need to keep tabs on him and tick him off when appropriate.'

So Niall had two surrogate mothers, because Nikki felt very much the same about him, especially as he was practically her son-in-law anyway.

'The one who worries me most is young Kyle Adams. I'm anxious that when I leave uniform, he gets a really good crewmate. That young man could go far, but he needs someone to encourage and teach him, not a jobsworth.' She pulled a face. 'And there are a few of them, unfortunately. The ones that have all the excuses to get themselves out of actually working.'

'Sadly every station has some of those,' said Nikki. 'But a word in the right ear will ensure that a promising young officer doesn't get shafted with a Bongo.' Nikki liked that term. It meant Books On, Never Goes Out and was wholly appropriate for a lazy copper.

As Yvonne left, Nikki felt as if she had been given two gifts in one. Yvonne Collins had more local knowledge of the area and its inhabitants than anyone in Greenborough, which was a mammoth advantage for their investigations.

And because of her manner and her age, she would also help to fill the gaping hole left by Dave Harris. There wasn't a day went by when Nikki didn't miss that man.

She noticed there was a lump in her throat and once again shook her head. 'Oh hell! I really am getting bloody soft in my old age.'

CHAPTER NINETEEN

Quite content and feeling safe from the Elf King in his new "home," Lucas grew more confident. He finally got out his copies of the old maps and began to work out a plan of action. He didn't know why, but since early that morning he'd been calm, able to think more clearly than he had in a long time, possibly not since the days he'd spent with Karen, his beautiful kindred spirit.

With a little grunt, Lucas pushed all thoughts of Karen away. She was a distraction — a lovely one, admittedly — but he needed to focus on his goal, the one that would lead him to his Holy Grail: the death of the Elf King.

Lucas shivered with excitement. He was so very close. After all these years, almost close enough to touch him. He closed his eyes. He could hear water trickling and knew that was why he felt so at one with himself. He belonged beside water, which was why he loved this place, his glorious Shrimptown, with its rivers and drains, ditches and dykes, the marsh and the sea. He sighed in delight. The perfect, perfect place for the final chapter. And freedom.

If only he hadn't had to delay his plan while he dealt with those transgressions against the faery kingdom. He had had no choice in the matter. Those terrible people had to be punished, but he wished they hadn't disrupted his search for his beloved brother. But thoughts of Harry soon caused him to forget them. He was back on track now. Just as long as no other wicked destroyer crossed his path from now on.

His finger traced the walks they had shared, the lanes where they had played. Their names all evoked fond memories, prepared him for his planned walk along one of those hallowed paths. He wondered if Harry would be doing the same. The thought was almost intoxicating.

The loud roar of an engine brought him to his feet. Wound up to full throttle, it screamed, shattering the peace of his refuge. He heard shouting. A white-hot anger overcame him, and he seethed with rage. Yet again he had been diverted from his work.

Lucas left the shelter and ran towards the source of the commotion. He watched in horror as a black-clad youth rode a quad bike through the meadow that flanked the lane he was standing on.

With a whoop, the driver flung his bike about, cutting a swathe through the wild flowers and green pasture of the field, sending great clods of earth and grass high into the air.

Lucas could barely breathe in his fury. Then, before he could even move, a big, tall man raced past him and into the field.

'Sod off, you arsehole! This is private land, and you're wrecking it! Fuck off out of here!'

The bike coughed, then stalled, and Lucas heard the youth curse loudly as he tried desperately to start it again.

The tall man didn't break his stride. Just before he got to the bike, the engine caught, and the kid gunned it and roared off, waving two fingers as he went.

Lucas stood transfixed in anguish at the screams of pain coming from the depths of the soil, from every crushed blade of grass and every broken petal.

'Second time this week. Last time he was racing along the towpath and nearly hit my friend's dog. Little bastard!'

The cries of agony still resounding in his head, Lucas tried to focus his attention on the big man who was now standing next to him.

'I wish I'd got my hands on him. But then again, perhaps it's best I didn't.' The statement was followed by a harsh, humourless laugh.

If only he had, Lucas thought. A big fellow like this one could have done some serious damage. 'Who is he?' he croaked. 'Where does he come from, do you know?'

'I've seen that quad bike in the garden of one of the cottages on the far side of the lock-keeper's lodge, down near the crossroads into town. Know it?'

Lucas nodded. He didn't, but he wasn't going to let on.

'The wretched kid is called Craig. That other time, he had another boy riding with him, and I heard him call out his name. Well, better get back, I suppose. Things to do, and he'll no doubt live to come back and annoy us all another day. See you!' He strode off back down the path.

Now, ice-cold and determined, Lucas repeated the directions the man had given. The cottages on the far side of the lock-keeper's lodge. Shouldn't be hard to find.

* * *

Spooky sat staring at her screen and feeling guilty. Nikki had just left the IT department, having expressed her concern about Aiden and his intense interest in the Stargate Project. Spooky felt it was her fault for giving him so much material on the subject. The fact was, she had always been fascinated by the topic, and finding a police investigation running that had a connection to it had been really exciting. She sipped at a half-cold cup of coffee and frowned, remembering the uncomfortable feeling Aiden had given her when he spoke about Julian Hopwood-Byrd. She wished she had left her folder of information firmly locked in her desk drawer.

Now that she knew exactly who Vernon Hackett was, Spooky had erased all trace of her research on Julian and his connections with the CIA, not that she'd left any in the first place. Even so, she had removed even peripheral and perfectly legitimate studies that contained any reference to the man or the project. This wasn't to say that she didn't have a wealth of knowledge already in hard copy or lodged firmly in her brain, and one or two questions continued to nag away at her.

She stood up and went out into the corridor for a refill of bad machine-coffee. As she waited for it to pour, a young woman with long, dark hair caught back into a ponytail approached her down the corridor. Tiffany Cookson was simply beautiful. In her late twenties, she had a clear, fresh complexion with expressive brown eyes and a ready smile. She wouldn't have looked out of place on the red carpet at a BAFTA award ceremony, but in fact Tiffany Cookson was just about the best Greenborough IT operator that Spooky had ever had the pleasure to work with.

'What'll you have, Tiff?' Spooky asked. 'Bad black coffee, grim white, vile tea or a passable chocolate?'

'Put like that, the chocolate sounds the least unbearable, thank you, Spooks.' They exchanged smiles.

She handed Tiffany the drink and started to move back to her station.

'You look a bit tense, Spooks, if you don't mind me saying.' Tiffany was staring after her thoughtfully. 'Despite that ever-present grin.'

Spooky shrugged. 'Oh, I'm just processing a bit of a conundrum and not quite coming up with a satisfactory answer.'

'Can I help? Sometimes a different viewpoint makes things clearer.'

'Wish I could, Tiff, but it's a sticky one, wrapped up in red tape.'

'Oh, one of those. Well, we're all on the same team here. You know where I am if you need a sounding board.'

Spooky thanked her and went back to her computer. It was frustrating, not being able to talk to Tiffany or anyone else about this case. She sat and stared at her screensaver, an image of some far-off nebula that usually soothed her and helped her concentrate. Today, it reminded her of Stargate. She swore softly and replaced it with a photograph of her dog, Fox, occupying the entire length of the sofa and sleeping soundly with his tongue hanging out.

Of course, there was someone she could talk to, but Nikki had a massive weight on her shoulders with the murders, and Spooky had no intention of adding to her burden. Meanwhile, she would keep scratching away at those nagging irritations, because she had a feeling they were important and, if ignored, they might have dire consequences somewhere along the line. She would have to find a way to do it that even Hackett's eagle eyes wouldn't spot.

Spooky took out her mobile phone. 'Hey, Kurt! Long time no see. I think it's time we met up for a drink.' After chatting for a while, she said casually, 'Remember you still owe me one? Yeah, well, guess what, it's payback time.' She listened. 'Oh yes, it's tasty all right, but more what I'd call, well, forbidden fruit. How about a lunchtime beer in the Hanged Man?'

After she ended the call, she felt a whole lot better. Kurt was one of the few computer nerds who was actually cleverer than she was. Even better, they went back a long way and she trusted him completely. She was not about to contravene any laws or break any oaths because what was bothering her was kind of outside the investigation, more of a separate thread altogether. Plus, to her knowledge, Kurt had more official clearance than anyone on the planet. Her secrets would be safe with him, no matter what.

* * *

Cam listened intently to what his wife was telling him. Somewhat disjointed, her utterances lurched between apologies, declarations of love and admissions about the anxiety that had kept her from speaking to him before now. When it came out that she was seeing a doctor that afternoon, he could have jumped for joy. He hadn't seen Nikki after her "coffee and a chat" with Kaye, but whatever she'd said seemed to have worked.

'I'll get out for half an hour and go with you. No arguments, the station can cope without me for once.' He hoped he sounded sufficiently forceful.

Kaye, however, insisted on going alone. She wouldn't hear of him taking time off when they had such a serious case running. She promised to ring the moment she got back and assured him that since this was a first consultation, he wasn't needed. 'They'll suggest blood tests, darling, that's all. I'm not going to get a diagnosis today. If it goes further, then yes, I'd love you to go with me, but not today. I've got this covered, honestly.'

Kaye was adamant. Well, at least she had made the decision to go, so he would have to accept that. He told her again how relieved he was and, after a few more words, they ended the call.

He wanted to rush downstairs and talk to Nikki but knew she'd be busy. This was a personal matter, and right now they had serious police business to be getting on with. He made a mental note to buy a bottle of single malt to keep in his desk drawer for her next end-of-day visit.

* * *

Over the phone later that morning, Laura Archer and Aiden Gardner discussed fantasy prone personality disorder at some length. The psychologist confessed that Lucas's particular fantasy was very unusual. She sensed that he was distracted, not fully concentrating on this aspect of the inquiry, and that worried her. She'd been seeing him professionally since his accident and, although he had made a remarkable recovery from his physical injuries, the loss of his job as a serving police officer weighed more heavily on him than most people knew. She had hoped that taking the civilian post in Durham would be the making of him, giving him a fresh start in a new location and with new colleagues. Now she wasn't so sure. Working with Nikki and her team had been a good idea, a kind of stepping stone from the old into the new, but Laura was seeing a considerable change in Aiden, and it wasn't for the better.

'Listen, Aiden, I put out a few feelers asking for help from other professionals, and I've got an appointment booked this afternoon with a woman who might just help to shed some light on Lucas's condition. I don't know her well, but I have met her and heard her lecture once or twice. She has some very unconventional beliefs, but she's no fool. She's studied certain aspects of folklore that deal with traditions and beliefs associated with trees and the natural landscape. I was going to take Sam, but he's cavorting around the lochs and glens of Scotland, so do you want to come along?'

He agreed, but without enthusiasm, which left Laura anxious to get him alone and talk to him in earnest. She had a very bad feeling about Aiden's own mental health, let alone that of their Fairyland killer. 'I'll pick you up at two, Aiden. We are driving down to a place called Anderby Manor, not far from Bourne. It should only take about forty-five minutes. The woman's name is Elvinia Torres, and she's quite an interesting character.'

He said he would look forward to meeting her, and that he'd always liked quirky women, but his attempt at lightness was unconvincing.

'I wonder what's going on in that head of yours?' Laura murmured to herself when the call had ended.

* * *

Ben was frustrated at how little information he could find about Harry's aunt, the wild-haired Corinne Blake. The more he thought about the woman, the stronger the feeling of something not being right in that old house became. He was looking forward to seeing Delia Cleghorne and her daughter Mandy again because, although the daughter was clearly secretive about her childhood friend, Delia brought a little bit of sanity to a bizarrely weird situation.

His desk phone rang. 'Spooky here, Ben. I've been doing a bit of searching into your Mr Harry Byrd's occupation, and I'm afraid I can't find much.'

Why was he not surprised? 'Give me what you have, Spooks. Whatever it is, it's going to be more than I've managed to come up with.'

'He went to university at Teesside but didn't achieve much. His undergrad course was Human Resource Management, which he was supremely unsuited to, apparently. He just scraped through his degree, but never went any further. He left uni and took an HRM post in a large distribution business operating out of Brent Cross but didn't stay long. He must have realised that he had taken a wrong career path, because the next thing I've found him doing is working on a daily paper as some kind of researcher. He stayed there for practically three years, after which it all gets murky. He seems to have dropped out of the system, probably doing cash-in-hand jobs, or maybe he just gave up work and looked after his mother.'

'That rather confirms our suspicion that he isn't working,' said Ben. 'We're desperate to know more about Harry's personal life and that of his mother and aunt, but the restrictions regarding the father have made it almost impossible.'

'Nikki gave me the lowdown earlier, and the fact that we're all sailing dangerously close to the wind regarding Hackett,' Spooky said. 'We have to be mega careful that we don't cross lines.' She paused. 'Stay where you are, Ben. I'm coming up to the CID room, okay?'

Ben stared at the phone. Spooky was clearly not happy about talking on the phone. Surely they weren't being tapped? Right here in the police station? My God, if they were, then Julian Hopwood-Byrd was even more of a hot potato than they'd thought. What the hell had that man done to warrant this kind of cover-up?

He was still hypothesising when Spooky hurried into the room. She pulled up a vacant chair and plonked herself down. 'Okay, what specific area are you wanting information on?' she said in a low voice.

Almost under his breath, he said, 'We need to find out whether the US government made a settlement on Julian when he was, er, "retired" from their services. Plus, the mother, Anita, is something of an enigma. Is she physically disabled? Mentally damaged? Both? And if so, does Harry hold power of attorney over her property and financial affairs?'

She looked at him with interest. 'How come this brother Harry, who is ostensibly your ally and who came to you first, is of such interest to you?'

'We've visited the house, Spooks, and nothing adds up. Without a clear picture of the people involved, we'll never unravel the truth about Lucas Byrd. We have to get some actual facts.' He quickly lowered his voice.

'I see,' said Spooky pensively.

'We even have their neighbours, a mother and daughter who actually knew Lucas as a little lad, driving up tomorrow to try to fill in some gaps.'

Spooky gazed around the office. 'I see the Prison Governor is in residence.'

'He misses nothing, Spooks. He's giving us all the creeps. It's like being in one of those diving cages and being circled by a great white shark.' Ben had a look of distaste on his face. 'You can't work properly, and you're frightened to even do your job, what with him ready to pounce at any moment. We all just want Lucas found before he kills again, so that justice can take its course.'

'I wouldn't be too sure about that, Ben,' said Spooky seriously. 'I'd say there's a damned good chance of the whole thing either flaring up at that point or being magically whipped out of your hands and never seen again.'

She was probably right. 'We're being used, aren't we? Little foot soldiers sent into battle without knowing what the war is all about.'

'Absolutely. This is serious, Ben, and not something security services are ever going to share with the likes of us plebs.' Then she grinned mischievously. 'But maybe they underestimate us.' She stood up. 'And now I have to go, but I think I can provide you with the info you need, although you'll have to keep it hidden from the shark. I'll be in touch, and I'll let you know how I'll get this info to you. It won't be in your inbox, that's for sure.'

After she had gone, Ben sat looking at his hands, struck by the magnitude of it all. He'd never dealt with anything remotely like this before. Hell, they were the good guys, weren't they? Why were they having to behave like naughty school kids keeping stuff from teacher? Thank goodness they had Spooky. He knew her reputation and he was pretty certain that she wouldn't be averse to taking the odd trip into the dark web. He just prayed that she wasn't up against an even more powerful adversary than she imagined.

* * *

Nikki had been listening to the latest update from Joseph. She was just ending the call when there was a loud knock on her office door. Having expected Cam to walk in, she was startled to see the ice-blue eyes and shoulder-length dark hair of the DI from Intelligence.

'Morgan Flint! What are you doing here?' Nikki exclaimed.

'Just a courtesy call, Nikki.' Morgan smiled at her. 'Connor and I need to interview a Greenborough resident, and rather than phone and explain, we thought we'd call by and say hello.'

'And maybe grab a cup of coffee?' DS Connor Hale flashed her a dazzling smile. 'And also say hi to my old mate Yvonne Collins, if she's on shift today?'

'Of course, on both counts!' Nikki jumped up, went to the door and called out to anyone who was free to do a drinks run to the café round the corner. She turned back to Morgan.

'I won't insult you with machine crap. I'll send someone to dig out Yvonne. She'll be delighted to see you both again.'

A while back, Morgan and Connor had been seconded to Greenborough to assist in a complex case. Their help had been invaluable. Nikki knew few powerful women detectives and got on with even fewer, but Morgan — the Ice Queen as her team called her — was an exception. Connor had teamed up with Yvonne, who had acted as a local liaison, and together, they had worked wonders.

Someone was sent to get Yvonne, and they all sat down.

'I hate to say this, Nikki, but you look wrung out.' Morgan stared at her. 'And where's the lovely Joseph Easter?'

'Sitting on his arse in the back of a van, eyes glued to CCTV coverage of a bloke walking the streets of Greenborough, and probably bored to death by now,' she said.

Morgan laughed. 'Copped the short straw, huh?'

'Something like that, although as this bloke is acting as bait to catch a killer, it's pretty vital stuff.'

'Which answers my question about being wrung out,' stated Morgan. 'Another tough case?'

Nikki groaned. 'It's not the case itself, although that's certainly bad enough. There's an element about it that has attracted the Men in Black.'

Morgan Flint's face darkened. 'It's not us, I can assure you.'

'Oh, we know it's nothing to do with our own Intelligence. It's a very different kind of security, and it seems we are treading where we shouldn't.'

'That's sincerely bad news, Nikki. Those guys are everyone's worst nightmare. So, you are trying to run a case with your hands tied behind your back?'

'And don't forget the blindfold,' Nikki added gloomily. 'How can you investigate a member of a family — and it's a family with problems that you just would never believe — when one of them is totally off limits? And I mean off limits to the point of one wrong word in a certain area and they'll pull the plug on us.'

'Bloody impossible! How on earth can you work like that?' Morgan shook her head angrily. She lowered her voice. 'Can we help in any way? I mean, off the record?' She smiled innocently. 'Like, today's interview should wrap up the investigation we have running, so we'd be happy to do a bit of undercover sleuthing for you.'

'We suspect that our every move is being scrutinised, Morgan, every phone call and every email. I'd dearly love to say yes to your offer, but I don't know how we can.'

'There are ways,' Connor said quietly. 'And we have been involved with these people before, so we know how they work.'

At that moment, Yvonne knocked on the door. 'You wanted to see me, ma'am? Oh! Connor! And DI Flint! This is unexpected. How lovely to see you again.'

'Leave the door open, Vonnie,' said Nikki softly. 'I'd like Eagle-Eye to witness this joyful reunion.'

A few minutes later, the coffees arrived. To anyone who happened to glance through the open door it must have looked very casual and unplanned, as of course it was. Or had been. Now Nikki saw an avenue opening up, a lifeline being thrown her way. Morgan Flint had more resources at her fingertips than the whole of the Fenland Constabulary put together. 'So, how do we do this?' she began.

* * *

Hackett knocked on Cameron Walker's door and marched straight in, rattling Cam intensely. 'Yes?'

'There are two officers downstairs from Intelligence. Exactly why are they here?'

Cam narrowed his eyes, picked up a memo and thrust it at Hackett. 'A courtesy call, actually. Detective Inspector Morgan Flint and DS Connor Hale are interviewing a witness for a high-profile case they are working on, and this witness happens to reside in Greenborough. That,' he pointed to the memo, 'is the case number and the witness's name and address. Having helped us on a serious case early last year, they've taken the opportunity to call in and speak to the officers they worked alongside. Satisfied?'

Hackett read the memo, then pushed it into his pocket.

'Check it out, please do. It's kosher, I assure you,' added Cam sourly.

'I don't like coincidences,' Hackett said flatly. 'And in my book Intel officers turning up in DI Galena's office constitutes an unlikely coincidence.'

'Think what you like,' growled Cam, 'but it's exactly what it seems — a courtesy call as they are working on our patch. It's called good manners. It's what we do. Now, if that's all, I have work to get on with.'

Hackett seemed on the verge of replying, then he tightened his lips, turned on his heel and left.

Cam reached into a drawer for the can of air freshener.

CHAPTER TWENTY

Karen Cotton took a walk out to where her husband Sean was working. She called out to him, and he waved back.

'You left your lunch behind, sweetheart.' She sat down on a carved wooden seat that looked out across Sean's Pinetum.

'It's supposed to rain this afternoon and I'd really like to get this area finished.' He sat down beside her. 'I know I shouldn't say it, but I miss Luke. I know he's not the man we thought he was — there's little doubt that he did the terrible things they said — but, hell, Karen, he was a grafter! He did so much of the hard work here and he really loved this place.'

'I know he did,' she said sadly. 'But it's the depth of that love that has driven him to kill.' She missed him too. Luke had seemed to belong here, among the trees and the wildlife, as if he were an integral part of it. Now, looking around at all the various shades of green, it seemed as if something was missing. 'What a strange young man he was.'

'Well, chances are we'll never get another worker like him, so I'd better get on.' Sean stood up. 'Thanks for bringing the sandwiches. I'll eat them as soon as I finish clearing this patch.'

He kissed her lightly and returned to his work. She sat for a minute or two more, then wandered back towards their cottage. There were no more classes today, so she had some time to herself.

She walked slowly, enjoying the warm breeze on her bare arms. She was really blessed to live in such a lovely setting, and never ceased to marvel at how she got here — from the Carborough Estate to heaven.

Karen paused at the entrance to the glade where the boy had set fire to the robinia tree and set Luke off on his killing spree. Where was Luke now? Despite herself, she couldn't help feeling guilty for enabling the police to produce his likeness. It felt like she had betrayed his trust. They had been friends of sorts, and even now, whenever she thought of him, she didn't see a monster but the other-worldly young man who seemed to embody the whole of nature.

Back home, she made a drink, sat at the kitchen table and opened a notebook. She wasn't sure if she was doing it to help the police or herself, but she had decided to try to recall anything Luke had told her that might point to where he was now.

She took a few deep breaths, closed her eyes, straightened her back, emptied her mind and concentrated entirely upon the time she had spent with Luke.

It was a kind of meditation, and through it, she was able to direct herself back to some of their conversations. She wrote down anything that came into her mind that seemed relevant. She had done this before. You didn't look at your hand as it wrote but simply allowed the pen to flow over the page and record whatever thoughts arose. Reading it afterwards it often came as a surprise to see both what you had written and how.

Karen's mind drifted to a particular conversation they had had concerning relaxation techniques and places you could go to in your mind to feel safe and at peace.

'Mine is a beach,' she'd said dreamily, 'white sand fringed with palm trees. I lie in this lovely canopy tent filled with soft cushions and watch the sea, listening to the waves breaking on the shore, or watching the stars over the water.

A friend of mine has a magnificent waterfall with a cavern behind it as her safe place. Where would yours be, Luke?'

'I already have one,' he said surprisingly quickly. 'But it's a real place that I went to once, a long time ago. Now I go there in my mind.'

'Where is it? Where do you go for peace?'

'Inside the oldest oak tree in England. It's hollow. You can sit inside it. It's over a thousand years old, and its spirit is the wisest I've ever met.' He whispered the last few words.

'The Bowthorpe Oak.' She smiled. 'That's here in Lincolnshire, out near Bourne. I've visited it too.'

He clearly liked the thought that she knew the place and said he felt happy that he could share it with her.

Her mind moved to another conversation, this one about putting down roots, and places you'd choose to live if money were no object. She'd admitted that she was exactly where she wanted to be and would change nothing, until old age made it difficult to continue.

Luke, however, listed various locations — names and places she'd never heard of. He said he would be happy living anywhere where the nature spirits were safe and happy. He would need somewhere close to a portal to the faery kingdom, so that, with their permission, he could go through and spend time with them.

'Where are these portals, Luke? And how do you get in?' she'd asked.

'Oh, just doors,' he said quite casually. Then he talked about something called "pathworking" — a means by which your spirit self enters through the gateways. It seemed to her that he was talking about visualisation and imagery, but not as she knew it. He hadn't learned it as a form of therapy, it was natural to him.

'You learn very quickly to spot them — a circle of mushrooms, an opening in a rock or a tree, sunlight forming an archway through the branches of trees — they are endless.' He sighed. 'But the best of all, and where I love to be more than anywhere, even more than here, are watery places. They are the

magic ones — marshes, lakes, rivers, a pool, or even the sea.'
He smiled at her gently. 'I can teach you, just as you taught me
to meditate. You could come with me, and do you know the
most wonderful thing? Most people can only allow their spirit
selves to venture through the portals, but I can actually travel
there physically — as a man. You could too, but as a goddess.'

Karen raised her head and glanced around her kitchen,
glad to find that she was alone, and that Luke was not there
with her. She had forgotten that exact conversation and the
discomfort she had felt when she realised the depth of his
obsession with his imaginary faery world. That and the way
he had declared her a goddess. Then she had felt more than
just discomfort. She had felt fear.

* * *

Lucas's other world, the one he saw and others didn't, was
becoming more real with every moment, and "normal" life,
whatever that was, was slipping further and further away. It
scared him a little, but he didn't struggle against it. He knew
he had to find Harry, but he also had to do what the nature
spirits could not do for themselves — take revenge on their
enemies.

He had gone to the lock with the meadow's cries of pain
still ringing in his ears. The spirits' anguish was unbearable,
forcing him to act before it overwhelmed him.

He'd needed to ask for directions, but he didn't care
who remembered him. When this was done, he'd melt away
again, to another safe place. They must know what he looked
like in any case, so it really didn't matter. Just as long as they
didn't catch him, and that wasn't going to happen while he
had his safe places to hide in.

He approached the cottages, the heavy cosh tucked down
one of his trouser legs, trying to ignore the clamour of voices
in his head and concentrate on what he had to do. There
must be no witnesses and, so far, he'd seen no one. There
were only two cottages, one of which looked dilapidated and

unlived-in. A weathered *For Sale* sign had been hammered into the ground next to the front gate, and all the windows were closed, despite the heat.

Lucas took a deep breath and held it. He had just spotted the mud-covered ATV parked up next to a ramshackle shed in a field beside the second cottage. He murmured a prayer to all the nature spirits who could hear him, calling on them to help him in his act of retribution. Their tiny voices urged him on.

Lucas walked into the field and stood next to the quad bike. He knew a lot about these things. He'd used one all the time in his work in the forest. The difference was, he used the vehicle as a tool to assist in the maintenance and care of the forest. This machine had been abused, turned into a plaything — a lethal one.

'Oi! Get away from that!'

It was the voice he had heard earlier, whooping and yelling as the quad bike churned up the meadow.

Lucas smiled and held his hands up. 'It's all right, mate, I'm not gonna touch it. Great machine, isn't it? I'm looking at getting one myself. Got any tips?'

Craig stared at him suspiciously, appeared to decide he posed no threat and sauntered over. 'I've 'ad a couple before this, but this beast is fuckin' wicked.'

What's wicked is you, idiot, thought Lucas. But he nodded in admiration. 'Looks it.' He gave the teen a big, wide-eyed grin and asked, 'You wouldn't start it up, would you, so's I could hear the engine? Bet it sounds awesome. And you clearly know how to handle it.'

The idiot almost swelled with pride. 'Sure. Dad's at work, so we can really let rip.' He gave Lucas a conspiratorial smile. 'My old man gets dead stroppy if I rev her up when he's around, but he's an arsehole anyway.'

He's not the only one, thought Lucas.

Whatever Craig believed would happen next, as he produced the ignition key and leaned across the handlebars, it was not the vicious blow across the back of his neck.

Lucas watched dispassionately as the teenager's eyes bulged with shock and pain and his legs buckled under him. He suspected that the damage the heavily weighted cosh had done to the cervical area of the spinal column was far greater than that inflicted on the man who had destroyed the Indian bean tree.

Craig lay beside the mud-caked quad bike with only his eyes showing any sign of life.

'It's time for your last lesson on this earth, and it's all about biology.' Lucas squatted down next to him and picked up the fallen key. 'It's a valuable lesson. Pity you'll have learned it too late. Root systems are amazing things, you know. The root of a plant takes up life-giving water and valuable nutrients that abide in the soil in which it grows. They also anchor it to the ground in order to keep it steady, which of course is absolutely necessary for it to survive, but . . . if you had a brain, young Craig, you would probably see where this is going.' He glowered at the paralysed young man. 'Their roots also make them prisoners. They have no way of escaping danger. They're helpless, unable to move. Sound familiar, Craig?'

He stood up. 'And so the punishment should fit the crime, don't you think? This is for all the beautiful things you destroyed in the meadow down by the river.'

Lucas climbed on to the quad bike and started it up. 'Do as you would be done by would have been a more sensible creed to live by, Craig. Then this would never have had to happen.'

He spun the bike away from the helpless boy, then turned it round to face him. The powerful machine leaped forward.

* * *

When Harry returned to his hotel for lunch, Joseph told the team to stand down until early afternoon, when he would resume his trip around the mythical Shrimptown. There had been no more possible sightings and Joseph was beginning to remember just how mind-numbingly boring being on observation really was.

When he walked into the CID room, he heard Nikki calling out to him from her open office door.

'Joseph! Just had a shout! Ring Niall and get him to reorganise your afternoon. Second thoughts, tell him to pull the plug on the whole show. Tell him to make sure Harry stays put at the hotel until further notice. Now, with me, please!'

All thoughts of lunch left him. 'Is it Lucas again?'

'Got his hallmark all over it. Let's go.' Nikki waved her car keys at him. 'We'll take my car.'

'Where?'

'A lock-keeper's cottage at Turner's Lock, just out of town, on the river. A teenage boy has been fatally injured in a paddock next to his home.'

Joseph rang Niall on their way out of the station. 'He's got it covered, Nikki. He said he's got all available officers heading to the crime scene. Coincidentally, I was close to Turner's Lock when I went upriver with Vinnie and Sheila. It's nice there, really peaceful.'

'Not anymore,' Nikki said grimly. 'They'll be playing host to the usual circus of police vehicles, forensics and before too long, the inevitable media vans will be rolling in.' She left the car park at speed.

'What actual details do we have?' asked Joseph.

'Very little yet, but the sergeant told me it's a bloody mess down there, and he meant it quite literally. He used the term "carnage." Had lunch yet?'

'No, I came straight back to the nick.'

'Just as well.'

Usually, nothing put Joseph off his food. In the course of his previous career as a special ops soldier, he'd seen more dead bodies than he cared to remember. Now he considered what Lucas had done to the unfortunate Ritchie Naylor and decided there was a first time for everything. 'No chance this was a freak accident, I suppose?'

'Absolutely none, according to the report.' Nikki sighed. 'If this is Lucas — and ten to one it is — he's completely out of control, Joseph. We have to find him! Hell, he's somewhere right under our noses, isn't he? This place is only ten minutes from the bloody police station.'

'He's like one of his own spirit wraiths — in plain sight but no one sees him.'

'Sounds like someone saw him this time. Only they didn't know he was a killer hunting his prey. Uniform are chasing that up already. A local said a pleasant young man asked directions to the cottages, a guy who sounded a lot like Lucas Byrd.' Nikki slowed down and turned into the side road that ran down to the river. 'I wonder what on earth this victim did to get himself slaughtered?'

'I dread to think.' Joseph meant it. 'But I'm guessing we are soon going to find out.'

'Well, we have one thing in our favour,' said Nikki. 'This only happened a very short time ago, so he can't have got far, and uniform will have officers all over the area in no time. It's the best chance we've had of picking him up.'

'So, who discovered the, er, carnage so quickly?' asked Joseph.

'Amazon delivery driver, delivering a parcel to the bloke's address. Unfortunately there was no one able to sign for it.' She threw him a sidelong glance. 'Sorry, bad taste, but I need something to help me cope with what I think we're going to find in that pasture.'

Joseph understood that completely.

They were there in under ten minutes. Already cars and vans and men and women were everywhere.

'Here we go again,' muttered Nikki. 'Deep breath.'

There hadn't been sufficient time to erect a screen or a cover to prevent prying eyes from seeing the victim, but three uniformed officers were attending to that as Nikki and Joseph approached.

'They look a little green around the gills,' commented Joseph darkly. 'I reckon your sergeant was right about the bloody mess.'

He was.

Joseph had seen this kind of thing in war zones, but in the peaceful Lincolnshire countryside, it jarred even his battle-scarred senses. He closed his eyes for a moment and gathered himself. If he felt this way, how did Nikki feel?

He glanced across at her. She had pulled on her professional mask and looked totally impassive. Whatever she really felt inside, it did not show. She was looking backwards and forwards, from the blood-spattered ATV to the crushed and torn flesh and bone that had once been a human being, and trying to calculate exactly what had happened.

'I've seen some things since I first started in this job,' she said slowly, 'but this one takes a bit of beating.'

'If it helps, it equals anything I've come across, and that really is saying something,' he breathed.

'How many times do you think he ran over the victim?' she asked.

'That's one for Rory to answer. I couldn't begin to guess.' This went so much further than premeditated murder. It was destruction on a grand scale. The mere thought of the rage that had made an apparently gentle, nature-loving man carry out such an appalling and devastating act was incomprehensible.

Nikki shook her head. 'And somehow forensics have to deal with this. I wouldn't know where to begin.'

'It's no worse than some train or air crashes, I guess, but even so, I'm not sure how Rory copes.' He paused. 'I think I'm getting too old for this.' He used to just slip into a different gear and deal with things. Now Joseph realised that he internalised much more, considered emotions and feelings rather than the practical.

He looked up and saw Nikki giving him a small smile. 'It's not that. We aren't the people we used to be. We are older, yes, but also a little bit wiser and a lot more human. I used to think that because of what we deal with, this job hardened us, but I don't think that way anymore. I think it gives us understanding. We are not just growing older, Joseph, we are growing up.'

He stared at her. He'd never heard the irascible Nikki Galena speak with such gentleness and insight.

'I know that's not the case for everyone,' she added, 'but it is for me. And you too, I believe.'

Before he could reply, the old Nikki was back. 'Right. Ramblings over. We'll do what they pay us for and get our arses into gear and stop this crazy psycho from massacring half the population of Greenborough. Come on, this one is way past anything we can do for him, poor sod.' She turned away from the gruesome scene and shouted to the uniforms, 'Quick as you can, please! Get an awning over the area. I don't want one single member of the public seeing this. Understand?'

Forensics arrived fifteen minutes later, and, after a swift appraisal, Nikki decided to leave them to their unpleasant task. Even Rory seemed unable to muster more than a few words, so after making sure that all the crime-scene protection and health-and-safety measures were in place, Nikki liaised with the crime-scene manager and decided to return to the station.

They found Cam in the car park in deep conversation with his uniformed counterpart. He called them over when he saw them and asked for a brief update. Nikki was remarkably succinct.

'It's a manhunt now, but not like any we've had to organise before.' Cam looked very angry. 'Mainly because of the bloody directive from about as high up as it gets that we cannot, under any circumstances, allow our killer to be named.'

Superintendent Mike Forshaw shook his head and growled, 'It's madness! We know who he is, and we have a very good likeness of him, but we have to damn well sit on it!'

'Or they shut us down,' concluded Nikki.

Before she could say more, a civilian who worked on the front desk approached them. 'DI Galena, there's a lady in reception to see you. She asked for you by name, said you know her. She's a Mrs Karen Cotton.'

Joseph glanced at Nikki, interested. Now there was someone who really knew the killer, and better than most. 'Shall I go and get her, boss?'

'Yes, and take her up to my office, not an interview room, okay? I'll be there in five.' She suddenly reached out and touched his arm. 'Cancel my last, Joseph. I don't want Hackett jumping to the wrong conclusion if he sees her in my office. Go grab an interview room after all.'

He hurried off, leaving Nikki with Cam and Mike. He was very anxious indeed to hear what had brought the gardener's wife down from her little piece of heaven.

CHAPTER TWENTY-ONE

Karen Cotton looked as immaculate and beautiful as ever, making Nikki feel like a total ragbag. Then she reminded herself of how she spent her days. She didn't need to look like a movie star, just a dedicated copper.

'This could be a waste of time, but I don't think so.' Karen looked from Nikki to Joseph. 'If you can make any sense of it, that is.'

She unfolded two sheets of A4 notepaper covered in spidery handwriting and pushed them across the table. 'I used a technique we sometimes use in meditation to clear my mind and focus entirely on conversations that I had with—' She stopped abruptly, looking helplessly at them. 'I was warned, along with everyone else at Shelley House, never to mention his name. What shall I call him, DI Galena?'

Nikki had heard that Hackett, or some of his cronies, had swarmed all over the Arboretum, issuing what amounted to threats. 'In this room, Karen, you can call him Lucas. Outside, he has no name.'

She nodded. 'Well, I used a kind of automatic writing to invoke names of places that Lucas mentioned when we talked, and I was amazed at what my subconscious mind had retained. I know my memory is accurate, and I've remembered those names just as he pronounced them, but I don't recognise any of them. I wondered if they mean anything to you. Why I wanted to do this is because I'm sure they're what he used to refer to as "safe places," so he could be hiding in one of them now.' She shrugged. 'I wish I'd questioned him further, but I didn't. He could be unnerving sometimes.'

Nikki noticed how she shivered slightly when she used the word *unnerving*. She picked up one sheet, Joseph the other. She stared at the writing, wondering why some of the names sounded vaguely familiar, but while she pondered, Joseph was on his feet.

'Excuse me. Be right back.' And he was out of the door.

Karen looked mildly surprised, so Nikki said, 'I could be wrong, but I think Joseph could be on to something.' She eyed Karen thoughtfully. 'Tell me, how do you feel about those long talks you and Lucas had now you know what he's capable of?'

Karen looked at her lap. 'I have mixed feelings. Part of me still finds it hard to believe, but now I'm also starting to see other meanings in the things he said to me. I don't know why I didn't worry more at the time, but I saw him as just a simple soul, not a deranged psychopath.' She raised her eyes to Nikki's. 'Now I'm frightened.'

At that moment, Joseph returned, a look of triumph on his face. 'Thought so! Look!'

Nikki saw that he was carrying one of Harry's and Lucas's childhood maps of Shrimptown. So that was why the names were vaguely familiar to her!

Joseph laid it out on the table, then pointed to some of the names on Karen's papers. 'See here. He mentions Merlin's Marsh Path, and it's right here on their map. And this one, Heron's Hideaway — it's marked on the map as being down by the estuary. He was talking about the names that he and his brother invented for real places in and around Greenborough.'

It didn't take them long to link the names that Lucas had mentioned to Karen with the ones Harry had painstakingly superimposed on Lincolnshire.

'So, let me get this right. These are what he believes are his safe places, his favourite ones?' Nikki asked.

'That's right,' Joseph said. 'Remember where uniform found that camouflaged tent that he left behind? It's called the Catterall Estate. Well, that area was once Catterall Woods, and if you look on the map, it's the place the boys called Creepy Hollow.'

She frowned. 'So he actually pitched his camp in one of his safe places?'

'He did. And he did it again by hanging out in Campmarsh Woods, where he broke that boy's arm.' Joseph stuck his finger on the map. 'Their name for it was Campfire Corner.'

Nikki smiled up at him. For once something was looking promising. 'This will narrow down the search no end. We no longer have to scour the entire damned county, just the places he talked about to you, Karen. Thank you so much for bringing this in.'

Karen smiled weakly. 'I had a feeling these strange places would be important. And I also think you should pay careful attention to this.' She pointed to the second sheet of paper. At the bottom, she had scrawled a couple of lines. 'I have no memory of writing this, Officers, but it has to be something that surfaced while I was meditating on our talks. I think it's crucial to where he will be hiding now.'

Joseph took it from her and read it out loud. *'I am drawn again and again to the most powerful portal of all — the water. It is the very essence of the faery kingdom, the place where time and space merge. There I can reach a deeper level than anywhere on Earth. It is my utopia.'*

Nikki sniffed. 'Very profound, I'm sure, but what the dickens is he going on about?'

'I think he's telling you that you can disregard all the places on the map that aren't close to water,' said Karen. 'I'm certain that's where you'll find him, Detective Inspector.'

It was another step forward, she supposed, but in this particular county? The whole frigging place was close to water! Nikki kept her mouth closed. It would still narrow the search down, if only a little. 'We need to take this to the super,' she said finally. 'Can we keep these, Karen?' She pointed to the papers.

'Of course. I did them for you.'

'You've been a diamond, Karen, and we appreciate it,' Nikki said.

She meant it. First the ID picture, now this. Karen Cotton truly was a star in her book. She frowned as a sudden thought hit her. It was a remote chance, but if Lucas Hopwood-Byrd suspected that Karen had been helping them, she could be in grave danger. Nikki then considered the location of the Cottons' cottage, which was isolated, in the middle of a wood. Karen had already admitted to being frightened of Lucas, and from what they had been told, he had been very attached to her.

She noticed Joseph staring at her. She urgently needed to talk to him but didn't want to cause Karen any distress. She smiled at her. 'Before you go, Karen, would you mind giving us a few minutes to run this past our superintendent? It won't take longer than that. He might have some more questions for you.'

'No problem. I'm in no hurry to get back.'

Nikki gestured to Joseph to follow her. As they hurried down the corridor, she told him of her fears.

'Mmm, it did cross my mind as well. But I really don't know how Lucas could be aware of the help that she has given us. Unless . . .' He scratched his chin thoughtfully. 'If he really was out on the streets of Greenborough looking for Harry, he could have seen her come in here to help us with the e-fit and put two and two together. It's a real long shot and very doubtful, but still a vague possibility.'

'I don't want to scare her further, Joseph. She's already starting to feel very uncomfortable about the time they spent alone together, now she knows he's a killer. I'm wondering about speaking to her husband, Sean. What do you think?'

He nodded. 'I agree, I think we should. Karen's no fool, Nikki. I also believe you should tell her to be wary before she leaves here today. Play it down by all means, but she should be told.'

'Okay, let's throw what we have at Cam, then go back and let her know what we think.'

As they approached the exit to the car park, where Cam and Mike were still discussing the search strategy, Joseph pointed to the door of the back office. 'I'll just pop in here and get a couple of photocopies of Karen's place names run off, so Cam can have his own copies.'

He was back in moments. 'I want to really digest some of the other scribbles on these papers. They look like random thoughts, but there might just be a nugget of gold hidden in all the crap.'

'Over to you, my friend,' said Nikki, raising her eyebrows. 'I'm not sure automatic writing, whatever the hell that is, is in my remit. I'd certainly never see the nugget in the crap and that's for sure.'

Joseph chuckled. 'Good point. Leave it to me.'

The two superintendents were visibly relieved to hear their news and Cam flashed Nikki a thankful smile. 'I'll get someone on to converting these made-up names into real places immediately.'

'Then we'll hit each of the target areas simultaneously. Since this last killing we have the promise of officers coming in from other divisions, so we'll hit hard and fast,' said Mike animatedly.

'Don't forget to prioritise all the locations that are close to water, Super,' said Joseph. 'Karen is certain that's where we'll find him.'

Cam nodded. 'Okay, leave it to us.'

Nikki and Joseph were soon back in the interview room with Karen. They passed on the superintendent's thanks for all her help.

'This probably goes without saying, but be careful, Karen.' Nikki tried to keep it as light as she could. 'We have to admit to being a bit concerned for your safety, simply because Lucas was very fond of you, and if he's in a state of

234

confusion, or maybe frightened, he could just turn to his old mentor for help.'

Karen Cotton exhaled. 'Believe me, Inspector, I'd thought of that already, and not without considerable anxiety.'

'It's an unlikely scenario,' said Joseph softly. 'He apparently has two main objectives now — to find his long-lost brother and to rid the world of some unknown person, possibly a faery entity, whom he refers to as the Elf King. These two undertakings will be paramount in his mind, plus he knows there is a major police hunt in progress. I don't think he'll have the time or inclination to look you up for a chat.' He gave her a reassuring smile. 'But, just in case I'm wrong, please stay vigilant, won't you?'

'Until we catch him — and with all the assistance you've given us, that should be very soon — don't go anywhere alone.' Nikki looked at her with understanding. 'You're obviously an independent woman, as are most of us, but just for a while, keep close to other people, okay? Especially your husband.'

Karen nodded. 'You don't need to tell me, Officers. It's really sunk in since I read through what I wrote.' She gave a little laugh. 'And to think, just a few days ago I was actually considering actively looking for him. Knowing that he liked and trusted me, I thought I could find him and make him understand that he had to give himself up before more people died.'

Nikki swallowed. 'You are joking, aren't you? Lucas Byrd is an out-of-control, murdering psychopath.'

Karen rubbed absent-mindedly at a biro mark on the tabletop. 'I honestly believed I could help.'

Joseph butted in before Nikki could say any more. 'I'm sure you had everyone's best interests at heart, Karen, but you must assure us that you don't still intend to look for him. You don't, do you? It could be fatal.'

She looked up, somewhat sheepishly. 'It's all right. I promise I don't. And before you call me all the idiots on earth, you must remember that I only saw the best of that young man. I often heard my husband say what an exceptionally hard worker Luke was, and that he'd never known anyone more in tune with nature and the trees in his care. Luke never showed the slightest sign of aggression, Detectives, and his strange fey beliefs always came across as gentle and beautiful, with nothing dangerous or harmful in them. I hope you can understand how difficult it's been to be told what Luke has become.' She pointed to the two pieces of paper. 'It was only that last meditation and seeing the things I wrote down that made me realise that that other side of him had always been there, just well cloaked from sight.' She shook her head slowly from side to side, as if still not quite believing this apparent truth. 'If it means anything, I still don't think he would want to hurt me.'

'Why?' asked Joseph.

'Because he considered me as a kind of equal, a kindred soul. He said I could join him in the faery kingdom and become a goddess.'

Nikki closed her eyes and counted to ten. She tried hard not to express her impatience but failed. 'Faery kingdom? Goddesses? Jesus H. Christ on a bike! Have I slipped into some parallel universe?'

There was a long and painful silence. Then, to her utter amazement, the two other occupants of the room broke into peals of laughter.

'Well,' Joseph said to Karen, 'I think my boss has just brought the whole thing back down to earth rather well.'

'Maybe that's for the best,' Karen said. 'I know how that sounded, especially to a practical woman like you, Detective Inspector Galena, but remember, they weren't my words, they were Luke's, and he meant them most sincerely.'

Nikki muttered her apologies. Cam Walker's advice to stick to the science was all very well, but they kept coming back to avenging murdered dryads and nature spirits. Now it was goddesses and faery pathways to another realm. What total, utter bullshit! How the hell Joseph Easter could so easily combine good solid policing with an understand-ing of this garbage was beyond her comprehension. Maybe she should go and live in an ashram for a year? Maybe she should take off to foreign lands to find herself? She groaned inwardly. And maybe she should get a bloody grip and catch Lucas Hopwood-Byrd!

'Okay, feet back on the ground. Karen, you take great care of yourself. I'm going to get someone to follow you home right now. No protestations. The more I think about sweet Lucas and his warped mind, the twitchier I get. I hadn't wanted to frighten you, but I'm sorry, I'm taking no chances. Where is your husband working today?'

'In the Pinetum, at the far end of the gardens, but I can ring him. He can meet me at the gates.'

'Do that and don't make light of it to Sean. Tell it like it is. Lucas, or Luke as you knew him, is barking bloody mad and I want your husband to watch you very closely indeed.'

* * *

Rain beat down as they pulled out of the police station car park. When Aiden saw all the marked vehicles and the crowds of officers wearing protective vests, he felt very lonely. In his time in uniform, he had loved the buzz of a big shout — pull-ing on his stabby and getting tooled up with as many gizmos as he could stuff into his equipment belt, just in case. That feeling of excitement continued after he became a detective. He still relished every case, every investigation, and being an integral part of a team. Now the only part he played was a spare one. When he'd first set foot inside Greenborough CID room, he'd believed he could do it — work happily as a civilian officer. Now he had begun to doubt it.

'You're quiet, Aiden,' remarked Laura, as they pulled on to the main road out of town.

'Sorry. Bad night. I think the leg is trying to tell me it's not used to working full-time yet.'

Laura nodded.

Aiden began to regret having agreed to visit this woman. He was conscious that Laura seemed to have her psychologist's hat on today, and the last thing he needed right now was a professional consultation. He decided to try to steer the conversation away from himself. 'So, tell me about this quirky character we're going to see.'

'Elvinia Torres,' Laura said, 'is actually a well-respected author on esoteric and obscure subjects. She is also an expert on earth-centred religions.'

'And how can she help us?' asked Aiden, wondering if he was wasting his time on a wild goose chase.

'I'm treating the conversation with her as a tool to assist me in building a psychological profile of Lucas Byrd. Earth-centred religion is also called nature worship, and I reckon our Lucas fits into that rather well.'

'You said she knew about folklore that concerns trees. Now that sounds very much more to the point.' Aiden tried to sound bright, but he was struggling to concentrate. Sure, he'd taken some heavy-duty painkillers to cope with the drive, but it wasn't that. His mind seemed to swing constantly back to Julian Hopwood-Byrd.

Laura was talking again, but he was only half listening. His heart sank when he heard her say, 'Right, Aiden Gardner. I want to know what's troubling you. Whatever you tell me won't go any further. There are only the two of us in this car and I'm not taking notes. So talk to me.'

He started to deny having any problems, then he let out a long, exasperated sigh. 'It's this case. Well, sort of. It's him. The man who must not be named. The Voldemort of Highgate village.'

'Ah, I see,' breathed Laura. 'And you can't cope with being told to walk away from your line of inquiry.'

Aiden massaged his aching leg. 'It's much more than that. I *have* to know everything I possibly can about Julian, and the only person who can help me is strictly off limits. He was a colleague of Julian's called Steven Paine. I believe I was getting somewhere with him but if I even pick up a phone,

Hackett will close the whole thing down in the blink of an eye. That man has got me in his crosshairs.'

'And if he pulls the plug on her, DI Nikki Galena will be a very unhappy bunny,' Laura concluded.

'She'd be incandescent, and I wouldn't blame her. Laura, I swear Julian is at the heart of this mystery but we daren't even speak his name, let alone investigate him.'

Laura glanced at him. 'What is it about Julian that has you so intrigued?'

What was it? He wasn't sure he could explain. 'I believe he really did have a talent, some unusual and very special gift.' He tried to formulate his feelings. 'I think I'm angry about the way he was treated. People pushed him too hard down the wrong paths and ended up destroying him. He could have become one of the greatest minds of our time.'

Laura frowned. 'This talent that you speak of, it's not the kind of thing I would expect a rational, unsentimental policeman to embrace so enthusiastically. How come you became so fascinated?'

'Well, I've read some of his papers and they make sense. Just imagine if that talent could have been channelled into, I don't know, crime-fighting for instance, how much difference it would have made.' He shook his head. 'Talking to Steven Paine was another revelation. He had worked closely with Julian, and he swore the man was for real. He still does, after all those years.'

'Forgive me, Aiden,' Laura slowed down to negotiate a sharp corner, 'but all this sounds rather personal, outside of the investigation. It's as if you're challenging what happened when Julian went to the States, not trying to find out about his son, Lucas.'

'They were very close. Harry has admitted that. I wanted to know the man, thereby seeing what Lucas saw. I wanted to know how that strange gift affected the possibly already-disturbed mind of the son.' He lowered his voice. 'But I admit that I've become sidetracked into finding what really happened to that brilliant scientist.' He looked at Laura. 'And the biggest question, the one that gives me sleepless nights, is why the hell have Hackett and his shady mates been posted to Greenborough to make sure that Julian Hopwood-Byrd doesn't rise from the grave? Why would a long-dead, burned-out scientist-turned-murderer-turned-murder-victim be of the slightest interest to anyone? Answer me that, Laura, and I'll be a happy man.'

CHAPTER TWENTY-TWO

Knowing that her hands were tied with regards to her usual methods of investigation, Spooky was grateful that for the cost of a lunch and a pint of beer, she could gain access to some very valuable information and the promise of help whenever she needed it. Kurt was a handy man to know, and the fact that he lived and worked in Greenborough made her life even easier. He was what is known as an ethical hacker, contracted by several large companies to hunt for vulnerabilities in their systems. What he did for a living was completely legal, but he was not averse to wandering from the straight and narrow on occasions and donning a grey, or even a black hat instead of his usual white one.

'This is going to require kid gloves, my friend,' warned Spooky, sipping her beer. 'We have a government agent camped out in our CID office and Big Brother is monitoring every site we access on our computers and every call we make. We are wrapped up tighter than Tutankhamun's mummy. Even I dare not access too much.'

Kurt raised an eyebrow. 'That's saying something, Spooks. Unless you've lost your touch, you have always been considered seriously hot shit in the cybersecurity industry — second only to my good self, of course.' He grinned broadly.

Spooky inclined her head. 'Thank you, kind sir. What an accolade! Oh, I've still got the edge all right. I could easily hide my activities from these guys, but I have to think of the serious case CID has running. I can't afford for anyone to even suspect that I'm looking at things I shouldn't. It's more a case of damage limitation.'

'So, how can I help?'

'Well, I know this is going to look like something out of an old spy movie, but when I've finished my drink, I'll get up and go to the loo. I'll be leaving a copy of the local paper on the seat. There's a list inside. When we leave, take the paper with you, okay?'

Kurt's expression made her want to laugh. He changed instantly from a somewhat nerdy professional into a naughty schoolboy. 'Oh cool!' he whispered, 'but how do I get the info back to you?'

'I've got a burner phone in my pocket. The number is on the sheet. Text me, but only on that number, not my usual mobile or work ones. Just on the throwaway, okay?'

'Better and better! Love it.' He became serious again. 'And have no fear of your spooks gaining access to my system. They'd have more chance of hacking into the Kremlin.'

'I believe you, Kurt.' She returned his gaze. 'And I don't have to tell you that I need all this yesterday.'

'As soon as I get back, I'll get to work. I'm my own boss, Spooky, and I'm thoroughly intrigued. I can't wait to see what on earth you're so worried about.'

'Worried doesn't even begin to describe it, mate. We're shitting hot bricks over this one.'

Kurt downed his beer and pushed his empty plate away from him. 'Then bugger off to the ladies' and let the maestro do what he does best.'

* * *

At just after three that afternoon, Nikki had a call from Rory, who seemed to have reverted to his usual, black-humoured self. Yet again she marvelled at his ability to rise above the horrors of his job.

'Now, before we get down to practicalities, dear lady, I'm forced to ask — no, forced to *insist*, beg even, that you please refrain from calling me out to situations that would be better dealt with using a large shovel and a bucket rather than all my expensive forensics equipment.' He made a retching sound. 'What I mean to say is, you have more officers roaming the Fens than the Queen has soldiers, so will you please catch this maniac and give me a break?'

'Uh, sorry, Rory, but we're doing our best, honestly.' She would have liked to reply in kind, but recalling the scene in that field, she was unable to muster the proper tone.

Rory stopped trying. 'It does make you wonder, doesn't it? The human being is capable of so much that is marvellous — courage, compassion, the ability to love unconditionally. Then you get someone like your rogue tree-lover. The sheer ferocity he showed in that attack is terrifying, Nikki. And I hate to say this, but so little was left of the victim that any post-mortem will take a month of Sundays to produce a conclusion. I'll do my best for you, of course, but . . . exactly how your assailant immobilised his target might never be known. What is clear is the fact that he deliberately drove the quad bike over the body at speed. The tyre marks in the surrounding ground show the number of times the bike braked and swung around, indicating — at the very least — twenty deliberate hits.'

'As soon as we saw the crime site, we knew that would be the case, Rory. Did you find anything at all in the area that might have belonged to the victim, so we can identify him?'

'We retrieved a number of items from among the remains. A smartwatch, for starters. Completely shattered, of course, but the purple strap and its design made it easy to identify. A debit card inside the back pocket of what was left of his jeans and also a set of imitation military dog tags. My lovely assistant, Cardiff, has traced it to an online company. I'll send you the details shortly. From what we've got, I'd guess your victim is a male teenager.'

'Do any of them indicate that they belonged to a Craig Steadman?' she asked, knowing that to be the name on the Amazon parcel that the unfortunate driver had delivered not long after the murder.

'Absolutely. That's the name on the card and the tags.'

'Then we'll go ahead and contact the family.' It was a task she wasn't relishing in the slightest. The body couldn't be identified in the usual way, meaning that the nearest and dearest would be unable to say goodbye to their loved one. They would never have closure. Nikki couldn't imagine how she would have coped if she hadn't been able to make that last gesture after Hannah died.

'I'll keep in touch, dear heart,' Rory was saying. 'And I'll email you the few details that we do have.'

She thanked him and hung up. Now she had a name — albeit not yet forensically confirmed — she could begin inquiries. Since the punishments Lucas meted out always reflected the crime, she was pretty sure what the teenager had done, but she needed a lot more than a hunch. She stood up.

* * *

As Ben waited for the coffee machine to cough up his change, he saw Spooky walking down the corridor, searching through her pockets for some coins.

'It's on a go-slow today,' he muttered, giving the over-worked machine a hearty thump.

'Nothing new there, then,' said Spooky, and lowered her voice. 'I should have some news for you before end of play today, but one thing is certain, Julian H.-B. did get a payout — a massive one. That's all I know at present, but check your jacket pocket when you get home tonight. If the criminals can use burner phones, why not us? Now, what shall I have — tea or coffee?'

Smiling at her, Ben retrieved his change. 'I'd go with the coffee, and thanks, Spooky, for everything.' He walked slowly back to the CID room. Compensation on a massive scale, Spooky had said. Exactly how massive? He pictured the old house in Highgate. Well, they certainly hadn't put any of Julian's payout into the property. It had looked way beyond tired. 'So where is all that money?' whispered Ben to himself.

He wandered casually up to Cat's workstation. 'You look pensive,' she said.

He leaned against her desk, conscious of Hackett watching. 'Keep it to yourself, but our Lucas's father did get a payout from the US government, and it was a big one. I'm wondering where it is now.'

Cat lounged back in her seat. 'Well, fuck my old boots, and how did you find that out, my little cherub?'

He went back to his desk. 'I've joined the underworld for starters — more to follow. Now, what are you on at present, Catkin?'

'Pondering the still-unresolved mystery of where the hell Lucas went when he left home, and how the devil he got to become such an expert on trees.' She let out a long, low sigh. 'And I'm getting bloody nowhere, as usual.' She stopped talking, seeing Nikki and Joseph heading their way.

'Will you two hold the fort here, please?' Nikki asked. 'We need to get back out to Turner's Lock and find out what provoked Lucas into carrying out his last vicious attack.'

Ben and Cat nodded. 'No problem, boss,' said Ben. 'We'll get in touch if anything important comes in.'

'Is there anything you need to update me with before we head off?' asked Nikki.

Ben decided not to mention what Spooky had discovered until he knew more, so he shook his head. 'Until we get to talk to Delia and Mandy tomorrow, we're hitting our heads against brick walls.'

Nikki pulled a face. 'Aren't we all? But do me a favour, give Harry Byrd a ring, will you? Don't give him any details, just say we believe that his brother has committed another crime and we might have to reschedule his walks.'

'I'll do that now, boss,' Cat said. 'But we can't really let him go out again, can we? It's just too risky now that Lucas has upped the ante.'

'Of course not,' said Nikki, 'but I don't want Harry to know that we've pulled the plug just yet. I don't trust him not to go it alone, and that could be disastrous. Keep him onside, Cat. Make him think the delay is simple logistics and tell him to wait for another call from me on my return.'

'Shall I alert the team at his hotel, boss? Make sure they keep a close eye on him?' asked Ben.

'Certainly, and tell them to be extra vigilant. It could be my nasty suspicious nature, but I suspect Harry could well give them the slip if left to his own devices.'

Ben watched them go, almost aching with the desire to know the real story behind that very strange family from Highgate.

* * *

Things were no longer so clear to Lucas, and it made him angry and upset. He couldn't afford to lose focus, yet there were all these people harming the spirits. Why did they do it? He knew that others were unable to see what he did in the natural world, but even if the faery beings were invisible to them, there was still the beauty of nature. Why destroy it?

He collected himself. It didn't matter. People like that would never change, but at least he had been given the power to show them the error of their ways. It was an inconvenience and it delayed his mission, but this was a cross he'd have to bear. What he needed to do now was regain that wonderful clarity. If only Karen was here. She would help him free his mind and restore his sense of purpose. But she wasn't, was she? So he would just have to cope alone. At least he was in a safe place. He relaxed just a little. Despite the police swarming over half the county, they would not find him here. He was protected.

* * *

246

The drive leading up to Anderby Manor was lined with huge rhododendrons. Aiden was impressed.

'It's not quite as it appears,' said Laura. 'I've never been here before, but Elvinia told me that the cost of the upkeep to her family home made it impossible to keep it on. She compromised by having it split into apartments, and she retained the top floor.'

'Even so, what a glorious setting. My wife would love it here. She loves older properties. I think she must have been a lady of the manor in some previous life.'

They walked up the steps to the porticoed front entrance. The door stood open.

'Laura! And you must be Aiden. Lovely to meet you. Come in!'

Elvinia Torres was an imposing figure — tall, heavy but not quite overweight, with wavy shoulder-length salt-and-pepper hair and strong, well-defined features. She had to be in her late sixties, maybe older, and she wore navy linen cargo pants, scoop-necked white T-shirt and loose open-fronted shirt with the sleeves rolled up.

Aiden was a little taken aback, having imagined some fey little thing with flowing, colourful skirts and strings of beads.

She led the way up two wide flights of stairs to her apartment where, once again, Aiden had made the wrong assumption. Having been told that her interests lay in folklore and unusual belief systems, and then seeing her grand old house, he had imagined her rooms to be full of olde-worlde charm, stuffed to the gunwales with memorabilia and quaint artefacts. It proved to be elegant, light and airy, designed in a contemporary style that did nothing to detract from the original building's charm. Aiden looked around in awe. In fact, he saw, the modern furniture and carefully chosen decorations actually enhanced the space.

'Let's go to my study,' said Elvinia. 'Actually, it's not really a study, just my favourite room, the place I spend most of my time in.' She strode off ahead of them.

It was easy to see why she loved it. They found big French doors opening on to a balcony with a view across the gardens to a lake, and trees and fields beyond. It was quite beautiful.

'Now, how can I help you?' Elvinia said.

'I've been consulted regarding a man suffering from fantasy prone personality disorder, Elvinia. I'm pretty au fait with it in general, but this particular case is unusual. His fantasy world is inhabited by nature spirits, and he refers to it as the faery kingdom.'

'Are you sure this is actually a disorder and not a deep, honest belief in the world of faery?'

'It's not just a belief,' Laura said. 'He also exhibits very disturbed and dangerous behaviour.'

'Which leads me to believe that we are talking about the murders in Greenborough, right?' Shrewdly, she looked from one to the other of them.

Aiden decided there was little point in denying something that was so obvious to this highly intelligent woman. 'As you will understand, we cannot discuss our investigation at present, but yes, we believe that our killer is the man in question.'

'Mmm. It's very rare for someone who loves the natural world to act so brutally. They're usually gentle, loving souls.' She looked to Laura. 'So, you are obviously right about a mental breakdown. Tell me, do you know if this fantasy world is something new, or has it been with him since childhood?'

'According to his brother, he has always been this way,' said Laura. 'And it would appear that he was encouraged by one of his parents, who saw the son's differences as more of a gift than a problem.'

Elvinia raised an eyebrow. Was that surprise he saw, or was it excitement? Aiden wasn't sure.

'Okay, give me some of his background and then tell me what form this fantasy takes. Is this faery kingdom of his a happy place, or is it threatening?'

Between them they told Elvinia as much as they knew about his upbringing, followed by his mysterious disappearance, the career he chose after university and finally what the people he worked with thought of him. They were both very careful to avoid mentioning Julian Hopwood-Byrd by name.

'It would appear that he sees both sides of the coin regarding his nature spirits,' Laura said. 'We have pictures he drew when he was younger which are quite beautiful, especially those depicting tree dryads and flower sprites. But a couple of our detectives interviewed someone who told them that his sprites were a long way from Cicely Mary Barker's and much more sinister.'

Elvinia was silent for a while. 'I can only explain beliefs of this kind as a form of religion, like nature worship. Nature is at the very heart of our spirituality and forms the keystone of so many religious beliefs, like paganism and shamanism, Gaia philosophy among others. This man's love of trees is nothing unusual. It is far more common than you would believe. Hindus, Buddhists, Jains, all venerate trees — like the banyan and the sacred fig.' She smiled at Aiden. 'I realise that this is a long way from crime-fighting and policing, but it may help you to realise that tree deities are present in many, many cultures, and tree spirits abound in folklore. Read up on Celtic tree lore sometime. It's fascinating. And, as with everything, there is good and bad, so your man seeing both beautiful creatures and malevolent tricksters is perfectly understandable.'

'You sound as if you accept his beliefs,' said Aiden incredulously.

'I do,' she said, 'but that doesn't mean I accept what his damaged mind has done to them. To take a precious, sacred life is unthinkable. I don't know any of the circumstances surrounding his crimes, but from what the media *didn't* say, I can guess that what he has done is absolutely beyond the pale.'

'You can say that again,' murmured Aiden.

'The police are desperate to find him,' said Laura, 'and I'm trying to build a profile of him, using my knowledge of his particular personality disorder, so that they may under-stand what this crusade of his is all about and, hopefully, locate his hiding place.' She frowned. 'The thing is, we only have one indicator, which is the fact that he told a woman who befriended him that he needs to be close to water. Would that seem possible to you?'

'Without a doubt,' said Elvinia. 'If his beliefs are as strong as you say, he will want to access a faery portal, join his spirits in their realm and leave this world behind. I gather that he is devolving, becoming increasingly out of touch with reality.'

'Oh, I believe so,' said Laura.

'Then, when he's finished with his crusade, whatever that is, he'll seek to escape. The most powerful portals are to be found in water. That's where he'll be, no question about it.' Elvinia looked down at a notepad on which she had been scribbling notes as they spoke. After a while she said, 'His younger life. It seems very disordered, is that right?'

They nodded.

'His parents? You mentioned that one of them encour-aged his fantasies? Was it the father or the mother?'

Aiden wondered what to say. They were straying into dangerous waters here. 'We understand it was the father.'

'Interesting.' Elvinia looked thoughtful. 'And when would this have been?'

Now Aiden was really worried. He gave a vague indication. 'I see.'

A silence hung over the room. Elvinia abruptly closed the notebook. 'Please do keep me updated on how the case is going. If I can help in any other way, feel free to ring me, but for now, I'm afraid there is little more I can add.'

Laura thanked her and assured her that they would be in touch, hopefully to say that he had been caught, and Elvinia walked them back to their car. Her thoughtful look wasn't lost on Aiden.

As they drove back beneath the rhododendrons, all he could think of was that interested gleam in Elvinia Torres's eyes. She knew exactly who they were talking about. He had no idea how, but he was certain of it.

His first impulse was to ask Laura if she had picked up on it too, but then he stopped himself. Steven Paine was forbidden to him, but if he was right, Elvinia Torres could be his new source of information on Julian and his work. She would certainly not be on Hackett's radar, and since she was an expert on tree folklore, he could visit her quite legitimately.

Their trip to Anderby Manor had been worthwhile after all.

CHAPTER TWENTY-THREE

After spending an hour talking to the people who lived in and around Turner's Lock, Nikki and Joseph were now sitting in their vehicle outside the crime scene, waiting for Craig's father to return home. From the people they had spoken to, they had formed a rather unpleasant impression of young Craig. It appeared he was a tearaway with little or no regard for other people or their property.

'Not a single person has had a good word to say about him,' sighed Joseph. He found that rather sad. A kid was dead, murdered in a horrific way, but once the furore had died down, he very much doubted that Craig would be missed at all. More likely everyone would be relieved at his absence.

'Maybe we'll get a different side to him from his dad,' said Nikki, sounding doubtful. 'He must have had some redeeming features.'

Joseph wondered. He wasn't too hopeful on that score. They had been told by people who knew the family that the father–son relationship was strained at best. Now it was down to Nikki to tell Bryan Steadman what they believed had happened to his son.

Knowing she was dreading it, Joseph would have done anything to relieve her of the unpleasant duty, but she was the SIO and took her responsibilities very seriously. All he could do was be there to support her and do what he could to ease the situation.

'There doesn't seem to be a mother on the scene,' said Nikki, looking out of the car window. 'Maybe that's why Craig was such problem.'

'Well, we'll soon know.' Joseph pointed to a car being driven at a little more speed than was necessary along the narrow lane. 'Bryan Steadman, if I'm not mistaken.'

Steadman had the haggard appearance of a man who had suffered hardship of one sort or another for a very long time. The worry lines were too deep-set to be because of the recent news. He unlocked the front door and pushed it open for them. The inside of the house was a shambles, and as they all went inside, its owner seemed to see it for the first time. He stared around with a slack, empty expression on his face. 'I'm sorry. I do my best. But . . .'

'It's all right, Mr Steadman,' Nikki said. 'We aren't here to judge you. Things can't be easy for you. Can we make you a cup of tea?'

Again, Joseph marvelled at how unlike the old Nikki she had become. She spoke so gently.

'No, no, I'm fine.' Steadman swallowed and gathered himself. 'Just tell me what happened. Are you sure it's really my son? The boy who has been found — is it *definitely* Craig?'

So intense was the man's gaze that it could have sliced through a block of ice.

'Although we don't have actual proof as yet, we believe it is, sir,' Nikki said.

'He was wearing dog tags with his name engraved on them,' added Joseph.

'Ah yes, his "hard-man" jewellery.' Steadman grunted.

'And a debit card, sir, in—'

'The back pocket of his jeans.'

They nodded.

'Then as you say, little doubt.' He sank on to a hard kitchen chair. 'They said he was too badly injured for me to identify him.'

Joseph moved some things from two other chairs, and they sat down together. 'I'm afraid that's true,' he said. 'He was very badly hurt, so a visual identification isn't considered appropriate.' He tried to steer the conversation away from the details of the injuries. 'Can you tell us a bit about Craig, sir? We need to find out what precipitated such a violent attack.'

Bryan Steadman gave a bitter laugh. 'I reckon he finally upset the wrong person. After years of being a nuisance, a thug and a bully, someone saw the red mist. I've been waiting for something to happen for a long time, but I thought it would be just a right going-over, not this.' He groaned. 'Sounds awful, doesn't it, coming from a parent, but he was out of control, Officers. I needed help but I didn't know where to go for it. It seemed like I'd failed him. It still does, but it's worse now.'

They talked for a while, and although he seemed something of a loner, they managed to convince him to accept help from their Family Liaison Officer. When they finally left, they took with them a long list of names and addresses of people who had been seriously upset by young Craig's unacceptable behaviour.

'Poor guy,' muttered Nikki as they drove away. 'Sounds like Craig was a bad seed, if there is such a thing. Been that way since early childhood. *He* was the reason his mother left home, so I got that all wrong. I thought it would have been the other way around.'

'Sounds more like an undiagnosed behavioural problem that escalated,' said Joseph. He glanced down the list of names and let out a slow whistle. 'And these are just the ones that he pushed to the limit. How many more people did he piss off?' He stopped and read one of the names again. 'Hey, I know one of these people, Nikki. He's the old guy whose houseboat engine Vinnie and I practically rebuilt. He's a really laid-back character. I can't see him getting rattled by a kid.'

'Want to go and visit him? It's not far. Maybe it will help to speak to someone who was on the receiving end of Craig's bad behaviour.' Nikki glanced across at him.

'Sure. Hang a right at the crossroads and I'll direct you to the towpath car park.'

Lenny Smithers welcomed Joseph like a long-lost friend and insisted that they join him for tea. 'Come aboard! The kettle's on — as always.' He gave a raucous laugh.

The interior of Lenny's narrowboat was like something from an old film. Mementos of a lifetime spent on the stage were crammed into the tiny living space, leaving little room to move. Joseph almost laughed when he saw Nikki's expression of amazement.

Suddenly, to his surprise, she gasped and said, 'Good Lord! You're Arnie Ledbetter, aren't you?'

Lenny gave a little bow. 'None other, dear lady. Ah, those were the days!'

'My daughter adored you! She never missed an instalment. It was her favourite programme.'

'A girl of exceedingly good taste. Give her my very best, won't you?' He beamed at Nikki.

Joseph's heart sank, but Nikki said quite calmly, 'Of course I will. She'll be thrilled to know I've met you.'

As Lenny busied himself in the galley making the tea, Joseph whispered, 'Who's Arnie Ledbetter?'

'An absolute rogue of a tramp in a kids' TV series called *Arnie Bends the Rules*.' She smiled. 'It was so politically incorrect and anti-establishment that I'm surprised it wasn't banned. Talk about setting a bad example for little kids!'

'But they loved it?'

'Oh yes. It had a massive following. It was very funny, even I found it so, and it was worth it to see Hannah giggling away at Arnie's antics.'

'I guess that was in the days when I was a different person in another country,' Joseph said a little flatly. 'I've never heard of it.'

Lenny returned with the tea and, aware of the limited time they had, they asked him straight away to tell them about Craig Steadman.

'Oh dear, the angry young man on that horrid, noisy machine of his. Not one of my favourites, I must admit. I'm guessing he's gone a bit too far this time and actually hurt someone?' Lenny looked from one to the other enquiringly.

'Er, not exactly,' said Nikki. 'As a matter of fact, he's been murdered.'

Lenny raised an eyebrow. 'That's bad, very bad. But the boy was angry and bitter. He seemed to enjoy hurting or upsetting people. I always thought he had no conscience at all. I was sure that he would have felt no compassion even if he'd seriously injured another human being — or a defence-less animal.' He glanced at a dog sleeping peacefully in a corner. 'He's deaf, bless him, that's why he isn't sitting on your lap by now. He doesn't even know you're here.'

'We heard you had words with Craig's father about him, Lenny. Why was that?' asked Joseph.

He looked again at his dog. 'If it hadn't been for your good mate Vinnie Silver, that lovely old mutt would be dead by now, not deaf! That boy drove his damned quad bike down the towpath and deliberately tried to run my Murphy over. If Vinnie hadn't snatched him out of harm's way, well . . . it doesn't bear thinking about. So, yes, I spoke to the father.' He shook his head. 'And to be honest, I felt sorry for the man. I was one of many to complain, I'm afraid.' He sipped his tea and looked at Joseph. 'Go and talk to your friend. I believe he had another run-in with the unfortunate young Craig quite recently.'

'We certainly will, Mr Smithers,' Nikki said. 'And the tea was great, but unfortunately we have to press on.'

'Lenny, dear lady, just call me Lenny. Call by any time you like, you'll be very welcome, *and* that discerning daughter of yours.'

Nikki smiled and thanked him for his help.

Back on dry land, Joseph decided not to mention it. It was the first time he had ever seen Nikki talk happily about Hannah and not have a look of intense pain in her eyes.

'So, Vinnie has crossed swords with our murder victim too,' she said, as they walked down to where the *Ophelia* was moored. 'And Lenny said it was recent, so this could be interesting.'

Vinnie was surprised and delighted to see them. He told them that Sheila had gone over to the Hanged Man to do a stock inventory and wouldn't be back for hours. 'She'll be pig-sick that she's missed you.' He eyed them both. 'But this isn't a social visit, is it?'

When they told him what had happened, Vinnie's face turned pale. 'My God! I could be in the line-up for that. I've threatened him on more than one occasion, especially after he tried to mow down Lenny's dog, Murphy. I could cheerfully have flung the little sod in the river and prayed he couldn't swim. The nearby river folk all heard me tell him what I'd do to him if I got hold of him. And then earlier today, I almost dragged him off that bloody bike after he stalled it while he was in the middle of chewing up that meadow over there.' He pointed across the towpath. 'In front of a witness, too. I could be in serious trouble.'

'Relax, soldier,' said Joseph. 'We've already got a suspect. We're just trying to get a picture of what the dead boy was really like.' Then, he suddenly stopped speaking. He glanced at Nikki, who appeared deep in thought, and said, 'Vinnie, can we run this back a bit? You said that Craig took his quad bike into that meadow over there?'

'And used it like a dirt track, yeah. It was like a demolition derby. Still is, mate, go and look for yourselves.'

They walked down the towpath and across to the meadow.

'Hellfire! What a mess,' exclaimed Nikki. 'But I think we might have our motive, don't you, Joseph?'

Vinnie looked at them, uncomprehending. 'Motive? This ploughed-up meadow?'

Joseph looked hard at his friend. 'Vinnie, this is important. You said you had a witness. Was it a woman? A man? A child?'

'A man.'

Joseph hurriedly pulled one of the e-fit pictures from his inside pocket. 'Is this him?'

Vinnie stared down at it and nodded. 'That's him all right.'

'Do you know him?' asked Nikki urgently.

'I don't know his name, but I've seen him around a bit. We just acknowledge each other, like all the neighbours on the water.'

'Where? Here?' asked Joseph.

'Not here exactly, just on the waterways. He's got a small cabin cruiser. Nice little craft.'

Nikki gasped. 'He has a boat! Of course. He told Karen he was happiest by water. Vinnie, do you know where he moors it?'

'He doesn't have a permanent mooring — well, not around here. I think he's from out of the area and just enjoying the Fens.' He frowned. 'Come on, guys, please don't tell me this is the lunatic who has been murdering people.'

Neither Joseph nor Nikki answered.

Joseph said, 'How did he react when he saw the kid on the bike wrecking that meadow?'

Vinnie frowned. 'He was silent, Joseph. He didn't say anything, but he looked as if he was in shock — no, more like he was in pain, if that makes any sense. And . . .' Vinnie blanched. 'Oh my God!'

'What? Come on, Vinnie. What?' demanded Nikki.

'When he did speak, he asked if I knew who the boy was. And I told him his name was Craig and how he had caused havoc on the towpath. I even told him where I thought Craig lived. I thought he was going to visit the family and complain.' Vinnie swallowed. 'I condemned that kid to death, didn't I?'

'Forget it, Vinnie,' said Joseph. 'He'd have found him with or without your help. The moment he tore up that meadow, Craig's days were numbered. It's not your fault, man.'

But Vinnie still looked devastated.

'We mean it, Vinnie,' added Nikki firmly. 'So no guilt trips. This killer takes no prisoners. He metes out justice on an eye-for-an-eye basis and wastes no time. A whole load of people around here knew Craig, so I absolutely guarantee that he would have found him and killed him before many hours had passed, no matter who answered his questions. Now, let's change tack. This is big. You're the first person to have given us a lead. The boat — would you recognise it again?'

Vinnie took a breath. 'Of course. It was a Sea Ray. I'm not sure of the model, but it was white. Unfortunately I never noticed a name on it, but I'd know it if I saw it again.'

'When you spoke to him, Vinnie, did you see where it was moored?' asked Joseph, suddenly realising that they were standing close to where their killer had stood, and not so long ago.

'No. I was so incensed by Craig and his antics that I never looked.' Vinnie was obviously annoyed with himself. 'But I saw it on the water when I went for an early morning run yesterday. Actually, I wondered where he was heading, or perhaps returning from, as it's not a popular area. It's down near Burtons Gowt. There's a lot of little backwater tributaries that kind of go nowhere until you get back on to the main drain and into the river.'

Joseph took out his phone and found a map of the area. 'That's how he got away from Campmarsh Woods so quickly after he broke that boy's arm, Nikki! He didn't use the roads at all. He used the waterways! And after about a mile they connect with Burtons Gowt.' It was a lead, the best yet, but searching those waters would be like looking for a needle in a haystack.

'I'll ring this in,' said Nikki. 'Vinnie, you are a star!'

Vinnie smiled at her then turned to Joseph. 'That man, your killer. He seemed so ordinary, so pleasant. He clearly loved the water, and he handled that boat really well. I'd say he was no newbie like me, mate. He's well experienced.'

Joseph immediately recalled something Cat had said after she'd interviewed an old boy who had worked with Lucas as a woodland volunteer. Lucas 'knew a bit about boats' and had a friend with one moored somewhere at Anderby Creek, so he used to go and mess about down there on his days off. It wasn't a friend's boat at all, it was his! Joseph's mind went into overdrive. Now they had a description of the craft, they could get the Anderby Creek boys to make inquiries of people moored in the area at the time when Lucas's movements indicated that he had gone there. They might even be able to get the cruiser's name as well as the name the boat was registered under.

He smiled at his anxious-looking comrade. 'Hey you! You have no idea what this means. You've just answered many of the questions that have been holding this investigation up. We finally know where to look! We'll get him, Vinnie, and it'll be down to you.'

'I'm not sure about that, Joseph, but what I will do is ask around and see if anyone knows more about that cruiser than I do, like where it was moored up earlier today. I share a motor dinghy with a couple of the others here. I'll take her down to where I saw him and check out that area. No way can I get the *Ophelia* into some of those tributaries, and she doesn't exactly fly along, but the dinghy will be perfect.' He looked at Joseph. 'I want to help, make amends for opening my big gob to a psycho.'

'Then use that big gob to ask around by all means, and keep in touch, but don't go out hunting, Vinnie. I mean it. We're going to have our teams all over that area, on and off the water, and I don't want you getting caught up in it. Now, if you can just give me in a description of what matey-boy was wearing, we need to get back to base.'

'Cargo pants, er, they were a kind of putty colour and a plain polo shirt in navy, I think. Didn't notice his shoes, I'm afraid, but his hair was different to that picture you showed me. Closer cropped, much shorter, and he had a shadow of a beard, as if he hadn't shaved for a few days.'

'Perfect,' said Joseph. 'Something recent at last.' He looked across to Nikki, who was pushing her phone back into her pocket. 'Back to the factory, boss?'

'Yes, and fast. I've just been on to the super. He's well pleased and is putting things into motion as we speak. But . . . but something's wrong there. I need to get back straight away.' She turned to Vinnie. 'Thanks again. We really appreciate everything you've told us. Keep your eyes peeled out here, won't you? See him again, you get on that phone direct to us, okay? Love to Sheila.'

Joseph clapped his friend on the back. 'I'll see you very soon, mate.'

Vinnie's face was serious. 'Just catch him, Joseph.'

* * *

As soon as Nikki entered Cam Walker's office, she knew that something was seriously wrong.

'Good work out there with the houseboat owners, Nikki. I've already deployed teams into that area and now we know he possibly owns a cabin cruiser moored in or around Anderby, we have requested that division to make enquiries in boatyards and chandlers located in that area.'

'And we have an updated description,' added Nikki. She had already got Spooky to generate a few changes to the original picture and had texted it to Vinnie, who gave it the thumbs up. So now they knew exactly who they were looking for. She handed him a copy.

'Excellent, if only we could use the damned thing! We should be saturating the area with this picture, not sitting on it. I really don't take kindly to having my hands tied.'

'Neither do we, Cam, believe me,' said Nikki. 'But has something else occurred while we've been out? You look worried as hell.'

'Two things, actually. One, Harry rang in from the hotel. He has a bee in his bonnet about checking out a certain place, just out of town. He said he'd been going over their old maps and remembered that it had special significance for his brother. He knows we can't do another walk round today but wants— no, insists that we allow him and a team to go and visit this particular spot. He has a feeling that Lucas might have left him some kind of message or sign there, and he says he has to be with them as only he would recognise it.'

It was almost five o'clock by now, and Nikki didn't like the thought of having to do this so late in the day. Greenborough wasn't exactly the busiest town in the world, but it wasn't a good time. 'I wouldn't recommend it, Cam. Tomorrow, maybe, if he thinks it's vital, but not today.'

'My thoughts precisely, but he's insistent, and I get the feeling that if we refuse, he'll throw his teddy out of the pram and go it alone. We can't afford that,' Cam said.

'Okay, but not like his observed walks. He can go with two officers, and it'll be there and back, no messing. Where is this "special place" anyway?'

'A ruined chapel on the edge of Fenny Bridge village, about two miles outside Greenborough,' Cam said, reading the directions from a memo.

'Any water close by?'

'Not that I can recall.' Cam scratched his head. 'It's in the middle of some fields and was part of old Fenny Bridge Manor before they turned it into a nursing home.'

Nikki shrugged. 'Then I doubt he'll find anything. Our Lucas is sticking to water at present.'

'Can I leave that with you then, Nikki?' Cam still looked worried.

'Of course, but tell me, what is the thing that's really worrying you?' She regarded him shrewdly.

'It's Kaye.' He swallowed. 'She saw her GP, who insisted that they do an ECG straight away. It wasn't right, Nikki. They've sent her out wired up to a twenty-four-hour heart monitor.'

'How is she about that, Cam?' Nikki said.

'Strangely okay. She's shocked, but said that she'd been so dreading the cancer that killed her mother that this was something out of the blue. She never suspected her heart. She sounded almost relieved.' He shook his head. 'It's me that's bricking it. This could be really serious, Nikki.'

'One step at a time, Cam. Don't get ahead of yourself. Wait to hear what the monitor comes up with and take it from there. At least her doc was on it immediately, and that's what you want. A few tests and then, if there's a problem, it'll be dealt with early.' She groaned. 'Listen to me! What a load of platitudes. You know all that and you don't want me rabbiting on like an idiot. Why don't you get home? I'll sort out Harry, and Superintendent Mike Forshaw will have the search in hand. We'll ring if anything comes of it, I promise.'

Cam gave her a tired smile. 'Know what, Nikki? I'm going to do just that. I want to be with my wife.'

* * *

Yvonne and Kyle knew the old chapel well and when they heard that DI Galena was asking for volunteers, they immediately offered to go with Harry.

Now they were walking along the path to the deserted old building.

'This is weird,' whispered Harry. 'To see this place for real is bizarre. It's just a tiny disused chapel, but my brother's vivid imagination turned it into something sinister and Gothic. His name for it was Casper's Crypt.'

'Well, it is supposed to be haunted,' said Kyle.

Yvonne threw him a warning look.

Kyle shut up, but Harry didn't seem to have heard anyway. He looked oddly distracted.

Yvonne led the way into the old building. They didn't need to worry about it being locked, as the door had long gone. In fact, apart from the way it was structured, there was little left to show its original usage.

'What do you know about this place?' asked Harry, looking around him.

Yvonne shrugged. 'Little to tell, sir. It was once part of a landowner's estate, then as the family fell on hard times and the land was sold off in parcels, the chapel became a place of worship for the villagers, who had no local church of their own.' She stared at an old carved memorial plaque on the wall and tried to make out the name. 'Sadly there wasn't the money to warrant a regular vicar, and services dwindled. Eventually it was deconsecrated and fell into ruin.'

Harry looked at her, finally registering interest. 'For a town bobby you know a lot about it — if you don't mind me saying.'

'My grandmother lived in the village. She recalled coming here as a child. She said it was a pretty place and she and her sisters would sometimes play in the tiny graveyard that surrounds it. They used to make up stories from the names on the gravestones.' Yvonne, who had loved her gran, smiled at the memory. 'She said they gave the long-dead people exciting adventures in wonderful exotic locations that they had only ever read about in books.'

'A different world,' murmured Harry.

'What are we looking for, sir?' asked Kyle, nudging a pile of dusty, crumbling stones with the toe of his boot.

'Anything by way of a sign to let me know that he has been here.' Harry scanned the walls. 'I don't know what. I just know that if I see something, I'll recognise it.' He frowned. 'No graffiti. That's odd, isn't it?'

'Not really,' said Yvonne. 'The village, such as it was, doesn't exist anymore. As Greenborough expanded, it ate up the surrounding villages and this part was taken over for arable farming. This chapel is one of those places you just glance at as you drive past on your way to somewhere else. Not even homeless people or tramps bed down here for the night.'

They began to walk around, looking for anything recent that could have significance for Harry. Personally, Yvonne doubted that they'd find anything. There seemed to be no other footprints on the floor and, in the places where the roof had gone completely, there was nothing but piles of rubble.

After a quarter of an hour, she could sense disappointment coming off Harry in waves. 'Why is this place so important to your brother, sir?' she asked.

Harry sighed. 'He said it had very powerful spirit protectors. That as a shrine, it was both a portal into another world and very special in its own right.' He gave a humourless laugh. 'I know. It's total crap, but it's what he believed and that's why I feel he would have had to visit here when he came to Shrimptown.'

'If he did, he must have been disappointed,' said Kyle grimly. 'There's nothing vaguely special about this place. It's just a ruin.'

Harry's laugh echoed off the stone walls. 'What you don't appreciate, young man, is that Lucas wouldn't see this as you do. He lives in an imaginary world and to him, this dreary and broken place would probably glow with a magical aura, as if every block of stone had diamonds in it.'

They continued to search for another ten minutes, then Kyle called out, 'Sir! Could this be what you're looking for?'

He was staring at the floor, and when she followed his gaze, Yvonne saw an old memorial stone set into the floor close to where the altar rail would have been. It seemed to have been cleared of dirt. In the middle of it, some pebbles had been arranged in the shape of a triangle with a single stone at its centre.

Harry Byrd let out a gasp. 'Yes. He was here. Lucas was here.'

Yvonne squinted at the crude symbol. 'What does it mean, sir?'

'That he is safe.' Harry didn't elucidate, just nodded with satisfaction. He shuffled from foot to foot, almost dancing with excitement. 'Thank you, Officers. We can go now.'

They drove back to the Corley Grange Hotel in silence.

Yvonne gripped the steering wheel, her face set in determination. So Lucas Hopwood-Byrd believed he was safe, did he? The teams combing the waterways would have to withdraw as they lost the light, but the night shift would still be out there. The fey Mr H.-B. had reckoned without the Fenland Constabulary with its DI, Nikki Galena, and the team she was soon to join.

Don't bank on being safe for long, sunshine. We will find you.

CHAPTER TWENTY-FOUR

'How do you hide a boat?' asked Cat, dipping a digestive biscuit into her tea.

'Either in plain sight, like down at the marina where it might get missed among all the others, or you could get into one of the tiny inlets off the main river, or one of the drains. And of course, he could have found a boathouse or a mooring on private land, and then we'd really be scuppered.' Ben helped himself to a biscuit from the open packet on Cat's desk. 'My money is on him being holed up somewhere off the main waterways.'

'I was hoping they'd have spotted him overnight,' Cat said. 'Or at least have had a sighting to follow up. And since we can't put out his description and ask the public for their help, we are really handicapped.' She glared in the direction of Hackett's office. 'Thanks to him. Damn it, I'd love to know what he knows that we don't.'

That morning, they had been in a good hour before the others to clear their desks before working out what to ask Delia Cleghorne and her daughter. So much rested on this interview. It was going to take all their combined skills to get the enigmatic Mandy to open up to them about her old friend, but somehow they had to make it work. They weren't getting the true picture about the residents of the Hopwood-Byrd establishment, and in the absence of a search warrant, their only hope was this girl who watched it from her window.

Ben looked at his watch. 'Half an hour and they should be here. Better go and see the boss to find out if there's anything in particular she wants us to ask about.' He stood up. 'Coming?'

Accompanied by Joseph, they went into Nikki's office. 'So,' she began, 'nothing new came in overnight from uniform, but this morning Joseph spoke to Vinnie Silver, who's given us a more detailed description of the craft we believe Lucas is using. It's a white Sea Ray 245 Weekender two-berth cruiser. Several boaters have recognised his craft, but no one seems to know anything about the man himself. It doesn't seem to have a name, as no one has noticed one.'

'Vinnie's still out talking to people,' added Joseph. 'He's hoping to find someone who might know of a mooring he uses, or a particular area where he's been seen more than once.'

'Yvonne Collins sent me a report of something they found with Harry Byrd yesterday, a kind of sign. I've been over to Harry's hotel and spoken with him.' Nikki looked directly at Ben. 'I cannot stress firmly enough how important it is that you try to elicit some more information about him and his mother from the Cleghornes. I'd like to know if the daughter, Amanda, knew where Lucas went when he ran away. Those missing years could be invaluable in trying to identify who Lucas wants to kill — which is his reason for being here. Harry swears he has no idea, but I'm not totally convinced of that.'

'We're well aware that this interview is crucial, boss,' said Ben, with a glance at Cat. 'We'll do our very best, I promise.'

Cat nodded. 'I second that, boss. If anyone can make that girl talk, it's going to be us. Even if we have to use unconventional interview techniques.'

'Oh, I believe you.' Nikki gave them a half-smile. 'Now, listen to this. I mentioned something they saw in the chapel. Harry believes it was a message from his brother. It was a symbol, a pyramid shape made of stones with a single pebble in the centre. He said it meant that Lucas was safe. The thing is, Yvonne was watching him carefully when he looked at it, and she was bothered by a strange expression on his face. She's been thinking about it all night. Now she's wondering if maybe the message meant more than he was telling them.' Nikki sat back in her chair. 'On the strength of that, I rang him, but I picked up nothing. He just kept going on about how he desperately wanted to go back out today. I refused to allow it, saying that apart from being too dangerous, his brother was now thought to have abandoned his beloved trees and was using waterways to get around, so it was very unlikely that he would come into the town. Then Harry insisted that he should go to some of the other "special places," closer to water. No way do I want him sodding well wandering around and getting in the way of the search parties. He was getting pretty het up, so I offered to go over his old map with him to see if there are any of these special safe places close to where Vinnie saw him.' She exhaled. 'And that was a wasted trip, as he could only identify one area, and uniform had already thoroughly checked it out yesterday evening. He says he's frustrated. He wants to be out there looking for his brother, not shut in a bloody hotel, and while I do understand that, I got the same vibes off him that our Yvonne did. Some very odd expressions crossed his face as we looked at that map together.' Her gaze travelled from Ben to Cat. 'He's not telling us everything, I'm certain of it.'

'We think he's getting more and more desperate to find Lucas, and we're terrified that he might try to go it alone,' added Joseph. 'We've doubled the number of officers watching him at the hotel. As the boss says, we can't have him going solo. We have absolutely no way of knowing if the letter Lucas sent to Harry asking him to join him here was a lure. Lucas is psychotic and truly dangerous. Harry could walk into a trap and finish up dead.'

'That's a good point,' said Cat sombrely. 'Harry's been searching for so many years and to be this close but forced to remain inactive must be torture. In his determination to find Lucas he could have forgotten what Little Bro has become — a dangerous psycho.'

Ben nodded. 'If, in his mission to find Lucas, he's gone to the trouble of setting up a whole network of lies regarding their mysterious family history, he's going to be climbing the walls of that hotel room.'

They sat in silence for a while, absorbing all this. It made their talk with Mandy even more crucial. It was bad enough having to chase a killer with Hackett and his invisible cohorts looming over them, but add a loose cannon to the mix and the situation could become a powder keg.

Ben decided it was time to let Nikki in on Spooky's information. 'Boss, there's something else you need to know. And before you think the worst, let me assure you that this information has been accessed absolutely securely and well away from our systems.'

Nikki's eyes narrowed, but she nodded.

'Spooky passed this on to me without Hackett's knowledge. She got it from a trusted source.' He paused. 'The father received a massive payout from the US. Following his mother's breakdown, Harry acquired power of attorney over both her finances and decisions regarding her health. The thing is, we have no idea where that money is. Spooky also said that the timeline between a certain person returning to the UK and his violent death doesn't add up. It's being investigated covertly by the very best in the business. She said to say please just trust her, this is Hackett-proof. She'll update us as and when info becomes available.'

Nikki sat impassive as a statue. Then she abruptly said, 'You need to get yourselves downstairs. The Cleghornes will be here any minute. Do your best.'

Ben drew in a deep breath and stood up. 'We will, boss. Come on, Catkin, let's do this.'

* * *

Initially, Nikki had been horrified that Spooky was continuing to work on Julian. It was far too risky. No matter what secure route she took, they were up against a government department with more resources than anything she could even dream of. Then she became a little calmer. Ben had said her information came from outside the system. Nikki trusted Spooky. No way would she wilfully endanger an investigation. She thought for a moment and recalled a comment that Cam Walker had made at the very start of it all. Referring to the dossier on Stargate, he had mentioned a clause in the agreement all "volunteers" joining the project had to sign. It warned them that they could suffer harm in the course of the experiments. Obviously, this was to let the US government out of being held responsible. Yet they had paid Julian a huge sum in compensation. Why? And if they had, where the dickens was it?

'Curiouser and curiouser,' murmured Joseph thoughtfully, evidently thinking along the same lines.

'Oh, Joseph! I wish this bloody case was over. I never thought I'd have to say it, but this one is way beyond my capabilities. It's not a job for a local CID at all, is it? We shouldn't be handling something like this.'

'My thoughts precisely,' Joseph whispered. 'Why hasn't this been whisked away to some special unit by now? Why aren't the spooks handling it in-house? Or even Morgan Flint and her elite team? She offered to help, unofficially, but we've heard nothing more. Has she been warned off too?'

'I suspect you're right. I also suspect that we're being used, maybe as scapegoats. We take the flak if everything goes to hell in a handcart. Or maybe we're a kind of cover, to make the whole thing appear like a normal police manhunt when in fact it's something far deeper.'

It made her blood boil. Being used, no matter by whom or what for, was unacceptable in her book. 'Do you know, Joseph, I'm beginning to think that if the faceless ones are using us, then maybe the usual rules don't apply. It kind of changes my outlook on correct procedure, if you get my meaning.'

A slow smile spread over his face. 'You mean anything goes? Old-style policing, even?'

She smiled back. 'I think I do, Joseph. Because we are going to crack this case. We are going to find Lucas, and if in the process we stumble on something nasty hiding in the shadows, I'm going to make it public, as long as it's appropriate and endangers no one. I'm not going to stand by and let them yank our strings and make us dance, then shove us back in a box with tape across our mouths.'

Joseph's eyes sparkled. 'I think I like the sound of this new directive. But we have to be very, very careful, don't we? I mean, downright devious.'

'I don't think Hackett believes we are anything more than a bunch of carrot-crunching local yokels with warrant cards. I suggest we allow him to think that way. Meanwhile, we work our fucking socks off and blast this case right out of the water.'

'And drown the bastard in the process,' concluded Joseph happily.

It was a kind of relief to come to that conclusion. Nikki couldn't wait to find out whether Ben and Cat had managed to extract anything tasty from Mandy Cleghorne. She had very much wanted to be in on the interview, but she knew that Cat and Ben had built up a rapport with the two women, especially the mother, Delia. She trusted her detectives' ability. Even so, it wasn't easy to stand back when she had so many questions hurtling around in her mind.

'I've told Cat that when they're through, you and I will go down and introduce ourselves, just to be polite and to get a look at who we are dealing with.'

'Okay, that's good. In the meantime, what do you want me to press on with?' asked Joseph.

'Check in with everyone for updates on their statuses, Joseph, mainly uniform and Vinnie. I'm off to see Cam Walker, but for the time being I'll omit to mention our new thoughts on how we are going to handle things. I also want to know how Kaye got on at the doctor's. She was going to ring me, but she hasn't, so I'm a tad worried to say the least.'

Nikki hesitated outside the superintendent's office door, wondering what he was going to say. When she finally mustered the courage to go in, she knew from Cam's expression that it was not good news.

'She didn't tell me everything on the phone yesterday. Apparently, they've told her that depending on the result of the twenty-four-hour monitor, she must be prepared for several other tests and will most likely be referred to a specialist heart hospital, probably Leicester.' He gave Nikki a weak smile. 'She apologised for not ringing you, but she's still trying to get her head around it.'

'Tell her I'm here whenever she wants to talk, Cam, but no pressure. Just give her my love and say I'm so very pleased she found the courage to go.' She looked at her friend. 'And I don't have to ask how you are. It's all over your face.'

'I always think of heart problems as being something that affects the elderly or men like me who are a bit overweight, spend half their lives behind a desk and have stressful jobs, not someone as apparently fit and healthy as my Kaye. And she's no age either, not in the grand scheme of things.' He sank further into his chair. 'Silly, really. After all the hassle of her not daring to see a doctor, she's handling it far better than I am.' He straightened up. 'But right now, I have to try and get my brain into work mode. What do you have for me?'

Nikki brought him up to speed without mentioning Spooky and her outside "secure source". She'd keep that one to herself, at least until they had garnered all they could from the Hopwood-Byrds' old neighbours. 'And I'm seeing Laura Archer shortly. She and Aiden visited some expert on folklore and stuff with a view to understanding Lucas's specific type of fantasy prone personality disorder. I'm not sure if it will help, but any port in a storm, as they say.'

'And Aiden?'

'He's backed right off and is keeping his head down. I think he really understands the situation at last, but I must admit I'll be rather glad when this is all wrapped up and he takes up his new post. I could be wrong, but I think he's struggling with pain, and his intensity about certain areas of this investigation does worry me.' She hated admitting to having concerns about a fellow officer, but it was the truth and Cam deserved that.

'If it gets too much, just say. I can take him off this case in the blink of an eye, you know.' Cam stared at her. 'I trust your judgement, but if you get a whiff of the slightest problem, come to me. There's too much at stake to jeopardise the case for the sake of an old colleague who isn't even a serving police officer anymore.'

'That's one of the reasons I want him to have every chance, Cam. He's been dealt a shitty blow getting injured like that. I can't kick him when he's down, but I am watching him, I promise.'

'Then we'll leave it there for now.'

As Nikki stood up to go, Cam said, 'I'm getting away early today. I've insisted on going with Kaye when she has the box taken off. Her doc has said that although she'll have to have confirmation from a consultant, she'll be able to give us an idea of whether there are any serious anomalies in the readings. I'm not leaving her to hear that alone.'

'Of course not.' Nikki felt so sorry for this big strong man, eaten up with anxiety for his wife while trying to keep a murder investigation rolling. 'I'll let you know if anything big goes down here, and you keep me informed about Kaye.'

'I'm here until four o'clock. Who knows, we may just have him in the bag by then.'

'That's the spirit, sir! Glass half-full.'

'And pigs might fly, but we can always hope.'

CHAPTER TWENTY-FIVE

After careful consideration, Cat and Ben had decided not to take Delia and Mandy Cleghorne into one of the usual interview rooms. Delia had been accommodating enough to bring her disabled daughter on a considerably lengthy trip in order to help them, so they thought the least they could do would be to make things as pleasant as possible. They opted for a quiet room generally used to interview people considered vulnerable, such as possible rape victims and children. It still had recording equipment but was much more comfortable and not nearly as bleak as a formal interview room. They also had another reason. To reach it, you could take a shortcut, bypass the main corridor and walk through the CID room straight past the whiteboards.

As agreed, Ben stopped when they reached the boards. 'Cat, maybe we should inform the DI that Delia and her daughter have arrived? I know that she wants to introduce herself at some point.'

Cat nodded, and went off in the direction of Nikki's office. A few moments later she returned. 'She's with the psychologist at present, but she'll be along as soon as she's finished.'

They continued to the quiet room, having given the inquisitive Mandy plenty of time to take in the images of what her dear old friend Lucas had been up to since she saw him last.

Once they were settled, Cat organised drinks for them all. Ben thanked them for coming and told them he had arranged for the police to cover their expenses.

Saying that wasn't necessary, Delia produced a large plastic lunch box. 'For your tea break, my dears, just some chocolate brownies. Now, how can we help you?'

This wasn't quite the start they had planned. The idea was to keep it factual and focussed, though already Cat was wondering if the chocolate brownies would be as good as Delia's homemade scones.

Mandy rolled her eyes. 'She's baked enough for the whole station. I told her this wasn't going to be a tea-and-cakes kind of chat, but she cooked them anyway.'

Cat immediately saw her way in. 'So, what sort of meeting did you think this would be, Mandy?'

Mandy gave them an amused smile. 'Well, I wondered if you might try the good-cop–bad-cop routine, but then I thought that wouldn't really work, as neither of you are hard enough to play a convincing bad cop. So then I thought, well, they must be pretty desperate to drag us all the way up here, so maybe—'

'Amanda! Please!' Delia Cleghorne said. 'For heaven's sake, take this seriously. You saw the photographs in that other room. The little boy that we both liked and cared about has gone. This new Lucas is killing and maiming people. If you know anything that can help these people, damned well tell them, girl!'

Even Mandy looked taken aback at this uncharacteristic outburst. The whiteboard trick had been for Mandy's benefit, but it seemed to have galvanised Delia on a grand scale.

Mandy said, rather sullenly, 'You do know we were *meant* to see those pictures, Mother? It's all part of the strategy.'

Ben smiled. 'Not a word of a lie, Mandy. You are one of the sharpest women I've ever met. In case your suspicious mind is thinking this is some other sneaky tactic, it isn't. It's a simple observation. You think like a detective.

You cut through the crap and see things for how they are. Just one thing doesn't add up.' He regarded her quizzically. 'And that's why you are so blinkered when it comes to Lucas Hopwood-Byrd. Were you in love with him, even way back then as a young teenager?'

Mandy spluttered out a denial. 'He was my best friend! Of course I didn't love him! We were children!'

'But for some reason you're refusing to admit that he has evolved into a dangerous killer.' Ben looked straight at her. 'You're stuck in the past, with a little boy who saw tree spirits and shared secrets. That's really strange for someone who is so clued-up and observant.'

Mandy said nothing.

'The thing is, Mandy,' said Cat calmly, 'you were quite correct when you said we were making sure you saw those pictures. Well, we did it because we are, as you rightly said, pretty desperate. Otherwise we wouldn't have dreamed of it.' She picked up her beaker of coffee and took a sip. 'And now we're going to do something else that we wouldn't dream of doing under normal circumstances. We're going to tell you some things about this case that no one — and I really mean no one — knows.' She glanced at Ben.

'One small thing before we start,' he said. 'Some of forensics' photos aren't yet on the board. Yesterday, Lucas murdered a teenage boy. He mutilated his body so badly that he wasn't recognisable. His father asked to see him, but . . .' Ben sighed. 'There'll be no closure for that grieving parent, I'm afraid. If you feel it would help you to understand the kind of devastation that Lucas is causing right now, I'm prepared to show them to you.'

Mandy shifted uncomfortably in her chair, then nibbled on her thumbnail. After a while she asked, 'What were you going to tell me? That no one else knows?'

Ben drew in a breath. 'We think that everything we've been told about the Hopwood-Byrd family members and their weird history is what, in police speak, is known as a crock of shit.'

'A web of lies,' added Cat, looking rather apologetically at Delia. She returned her gaze to Mandy. 'And we believe that you are the only person who might know the truth.'

'You actually knew Lucas as a boy and a young teen,' Ben continued. 'He confided in you and, to our knowledge, no one else.'

'And because of your situation, in terms of both your location and your personal life, you see what goes on in Arcadia. You might not even be aware of just how important your observations on the comings and goings there could be to us.' Cat's look was unblinking. 'You can help us stop this carnage, Mandy. So far, we are losing the battle, and only you can help us. Are you willing to do so?'

Mandy looked at each of them in turn. 'What do you want to know?'

Cat heard Delia sigh.

Ben said, 'We are looking at two avenues. One concerns the present situation at Arcadia and the other is Lucas and his missing years.'

'I never lied to you,' said Mandy flatly.

'But you didn't tell us everything,' Cat said softly. 'Did you?'

'I never saw Lucas again, and I never knew where he went but,' she rubbed one wrist against the other in a strange twisting motion, 'I do know why he went and who helped him.'

Cat heard the Hallelujah Chorus ring out in her head. At last!

Mandy was now looking at her mother. 'Sorry, Mum, but a promise is a promise, and I swore I'd never tell.' She stared into her lap. 'So I never even told you.'

Delia smiled gently. 'It doesn't matter, sweetheart. What matters is that you speak out now. And you're not breaking your promise to Lucas. He forfeited the right to your loyalty when he started taking innocent lives.'

'Whoever he killed wouldn't have been innocent, Mum — well, not to him. They'll have breached the laws he lives by and harmed the nature spirits.' She drew in a breath. 'But even so, I see that he can't go on like this. He has to be made safe, for his own sake as well as everyone else's.'

Cat was struck by this young woman's insight. She'd be an asset to any CID team. Even though she hadn't been upfront with them, Cat had liked her from the moment they first met.

Mandy settled her gaze on Ben. 'Lucas told me that he feared for his life if he stayed at home. He was thirteen years old and terrified. He told me that his dead father, his mother and brother were not as people believed them to be, and although he loved them dearly, he had to get away. He said he would always be my friend and that one day he'd explain.' Her face clouded. 'But I doubt that will happen now.'

'Who was he scared of?' asked Cat.

'He refused to say, just that something had happened to put him in danger. He left very quickly after that conversation, and I never saw him again.' Mandy swallowed. 'I wondered if it was another fantasy of his, but I had the feeling it was for real. I was pleased that he had someone to go to, but now I'm beginning to wonder if even that had been a terrible mistake. He hasn't exactly become a model citizen, has he?'

'Who helped him, Mandy?'

'Mr Dawson,'

It meant nothing to Cat. 'Who is Mr Dawson?'

'His old teacher. His own son was killed in a bicycle accident, after which Mr Dawson retired. I think he had always had a soft spot for Lucas, and maybe he saw him as a kind of substitute son. Lucas would sneak off and visit him without anyone knowing. He told me that Mr Dawson was very kind to him. When he ran away, he went to him.'

It made sense. The name Dawson had never been mentioned, but Harry had spoken of a teacher, although only in connection with his father's supposed clairvoyant powers. Things clicked into place. If Lucas had become a surrogate son, then the teacher would naturally have been mindful of his education and seen him through college.

'Do you know if this man lived, or lives near you?' asked Ben.

She shook her head. 'Lucas said they were going away, but that's all. He didn't say where.'

Cat's mind was racing ahead. He could be traced. And they'd start with the school where Dawson had taught. She asked Mandy where it was, and was given the name and location.

When there was no more to be gleaned from Mandy about the disappearance, they moved on to the family and the possibility that Harry didn't actually live in Arcadia. Here things became less clear.

'We've been over and over this, Officers,' said Delia, frowning. 'We think you're right about him living somewhere else, but short of following him, we couldn't be sure. However, there's something else that Mandy noticed, about the carers.' She looked at her daughter.

'I've had plenty of carers in my time,' Mandy said, 'so I know many of them quite well. The people who call at Arcadia are definitely not from the local services. They're all private. *And* they changed to a different company the day before Harry left to come here. The new people have a tiny logo on their uniforms. It's a shame, really, because I was hoping to have a friendly chat with one of them and do a little digging about Anita.'

'Anita is a puzzle,' said Ben. 'Harry makes her out to be all sweetness and light, urging him to help the police to find Lucas, yet she wouldn't even speak to us. Her sister said she'd had a panic attack or something, and we had to leave.'

'Sister? Her sister is in Highgate?' Delia looked confused.

'Yes. Remember the woman with the weird tangerine-coloured hair, Mandy? You said you saw her arrive just before Harry left to come here,' Ben said.

'That woman is not Anita's sister, Detective,' Delia said. 'I met the sister many years ago, at around the time of the murder. Corinne looks very much like Anita, petite and dark, nothing like the woman Mandy saw.'

So who the devil had they spoken to? Who was this woman claiming to be Corinne Blake? This interview was bringing a whole lot more to light than she'd expected. She and Ben had had their doubts about the woman with the tangerine hair, but it came as quite a shock to hear that she was definitely an impostor.

'Is Corinne Scottish?' asked Ben.

'Corinne? No way. She's a Londoner through and through, like me.' Delia smiled. 'She married a Scot, though — Duncan Blake — and I understand that they moved back across the border to his family home a few years back. That's why I was surprised to hear that she was back in London.'

Cat looked at Ben. 'Our Tangerine Dream had done her homework, then. That's exactly what she told us. So, who is she?'

'I wondered that,' said Mandy thoughtfully. 'She reminds me of someone, although I can't think who.' She took out her phone and started scrolling through the gallery. 'Ah, found it. This might help to trace her. My phone has a very good camera.' She passed the mobile to Cat.

'Blimey, Mandy. You should become a PI. This is very good for a covert shot.' She handed the phone to Ben.

The image showed the woman coming out of the front door of Arcadia. It was surprisingly clear.

'I took a few, but that one is full-face and a good likeness.' She looked a little sheepish. 'I know I shouldn't do it — Mum's always telling me off — but people fascinate me.' Her eyes narrowed. 'Especially people like the wild-hair lady.'

'Can we download these?' asked Ben.

'Of course, go ahead. And while you are about it, there's a shot of one of the carers walking back to her car. I zoomed in on that logo I was telling you about. It could tell you which company they work for.'

Mandy was certainly making amends for her earlier reticence. What she had told them had answered a lot of their questions, but also opened up others. Now there was the question of the woman posing as Anita's sister.

While Ben downloaded the photos from Mandy's phone, Cat began to tie up a few loose ends. 'Can you recall what Anita looked like when you saw her last, Delia? You said she used to sit in the garden sometimes.'

'It must have been six weeks ago, maybe longer. They have an arbour with a seat underneath, and Anita was sitting there, all alone and very still. I waved as I passed, but she hardly responded. She looked poorly, really poorly. And old.' Delia shrugged. 'I'm not exactly in the bloom of youth myself but I still look as if I have a pulse.'

'On a good day,' said Mandy with a grin.

Cat was relieved that the two women were themselves again. 'Look, I'm just going to organise some more drinks and see if our boss is free yet.' She looked from one to the other of them. 'I know this wasn't easy, but it's been of immense help to us. We've ticked more boxes in the last hour than we have in days.'

Cat hurried off to Nikki's office with the feeling that they were finally making progress.

CHAPTER TWENTY-SIX

The usually serene Laura Archer seemed tense, and Nikki wondered what she was about to hear.

'Apart from confirming that Lucas will very likely be found close to water and that when he has finished his business here, he will want to try to find a route into his faery kingdom and disappear for ever, I'm afraid our trip to see Elvinia Torres didn't throw up much. I now know rather more about earth-centred religions than I did before, and that venerating trees is common practice everywhere, but really, I could just as well have picked up the phone and saved on fuel.' She looked rather glumly at Nikki. 'Sorry.'

'Don't apologise. That's the way it goes, Laura. But you expected more?'

'Actually, Nikki, I got a lot more than I bargained for.' Her face darkened. 'You know I took Aiden with me?'

Nikki nodded, now feeling edgy herself. 'Yes, I was pleased. At least it made him drop his other line of inquiry.'

'Well, I hope I'm wrong, but I'm thinking it was a bad move.'

'You're worrying me, Laura.'

'The thing is, Elvinia is a very intelligent woman indeed and, having heard about the Fens murders in the media and finding me accompanied by someone attached to CID, she rightly deduced that we were trying to profile our suspect murderer. Nothing was given away that shouldn't have been, certainly no names. Naturally, she asked a lot of questions in order to help us, but she seemed to be showing a bit too much interest in our subject's childhood. Towards the end of our chat, she seemed suddenly to withdraw and become distracted.' Laura gave a little laugh. 'Her body language was screaming that she wanted us gone. I knew we'd get nothing more from her, so we took our leave.'

'And what did you deduce from that?' asked Nikki, not yet seeing a problem.

'Aiden was quiet on the journey home and I'm absolutely certain that he'd picked up on the same thing I had, that Elvinia Torres actually knew who we were talking about.'

Nikki sat bolt upright. 'She *knew* Lucas? Are you sure?'

'Even more so now.' Laura took a couple of printouts from her case. 'When I got back, I looked up everything I could find on Elvinia Torres. And guess what? She's a contemporary of Julian Hopwood-Byrd. Same university and the same year. And considering that her interest was in religious metaphysics, amongst other things, I decided they probably knew each other.' She pushed a copy of a photograph across the desk to Nikki. 'And I was right. This is one picture that slipped through the net when the powers that be tried to eradicate Julian from the internet. Probably because his full name isn't on it, only hers, and it's her maiden name, Elvinia Carr.'

Nikki stared at the black-and-white image of a group of students sitting on the grass. They had glasses in their hands and were toasting someone. In the background was the university. The caption read, *Sarah Beany and Elvinia Carr celebrate with J.H.-B. and two other friends.* 'So which one is Julian?'

'I've been told that Harry and Lucas favoured their father in appearance, so I'm guessing he's the tall one with his arm around Elvinia. I'd say they were a couple, wouldn't you?'

Nikki thought that she was most likely right, but frowned. 'That's odd. Apparently, Julian hated photographs. He refused to have any taken of him or his family, not even school ones.'

'Oh,' said Laura, 'then I'd say it started later in life, perhaps after the kids were born, because he's smiling for the camera in that picture.'

Nikki considered that, then added, 'Or maybe something occurred that made him fearful of people taking pictures of him or the boys and being recognised. Perhaps at that point he was becoming unhinged, if you'll excuse the rather unprofessional description of his mental condition.'

'That's very possible, Nikki. But listen, something else that bothers me is the fact that I didn't contact Elvinia. *She* rang *me* and offered her expertise. I'd put feelers out to some of my colleagues, so I wasn't surprised, but thinking about it, could she have been using me to get inside info on the investigation?' Laura bit her lip. 'If that's the case, then I'm really sorry. It's my fault entirely. And not only that, but I'll bet a pound to a penny that Aiden Gardner searched Google, just like I did, the moment his backside hit his office chair.'

Laura looked thoroughly miserable, and Nikki wasn't sure what to say to make her feel any better. Being used by other people seemed to be the order of the day with this case. Worse than that, if Aiden had used a police computer, had Hackett also made the connection? And if so, would she be able to explain that one away to their eagle-eyed observer?

'Obviously I can't tell you what Aiden said to me on the drive down,' continued Laura, 'because of professional ethics, but suffice it to say that I don't think he is able to let go of Julian and his work. It's not his intention to jeopardise the case or anything like that, and he's fully aware that Hackett is watching his every move, but if he's dug up the same information that I have, he could just see Elvinia as a new and quite legitimate contact to discuss Julian with.'

Nikki thought about that. 'That could be very risky, as we have no idea what Elvinia Torres's agenda is — if she has one.'

'Exactly. And I'm sure she has an agenda, Nikki. I'm trained to read people. Her whole demeanour changed at one specific point in the conversation, as if something had suddenly fallen into place. As if her suspicions had been confirmed.'

Nikki stood up. 'I'll call Aiden in here. Are you up for a bit of acting, Laura?'

'I don't think Kenneth Branagh would recommend me for RADA, but I'll give it a try.' Laura attempted a smile. 'What are you thinking of?'

'Follow my lead, that's all,' said Nikki. 'When required, I can act for England.'

She went out into the CID room and called for Aiden to come to her office.

'He left the room a few minutes ago, ma'am,' the office manager said. 'Shall I go and look for him?'

'Ring his mobile, Zena, and ask him to come straight back.' Her nerves jangled in irritation and concern. *Not again, Aiden, because this will be the last time.* Nikki gritted her teeth, then saw Joseph walk through the door. She beckoned to him. 'Got a few minutes?'

He hurried over to her. 'Problem? You look harassed.'

'I'm not sure. Come in and I'll give you a brief rundown on what Laura's just told me.'

'Damn this constraint that's hanging over our inquiries!' Joseph said, when he had been put in the picture. 'Otherwise I'd be out there like a shot demanding to know why the hell she's interested in our investigation. She might even know something that could be of real help to us, instead of palming us off with a load of guff about tree-lovers and nature worship.' He looked anxiously at Nikki. 'And where the hell is Aiden? I've been downstairs for half an hour, and he was nowhere to be seen. If he's buggered off again, I'll not be responsib—'

Zena appeared in the doorway. 'He's on his way up, ma'am. He said he missed breakfast and popped out to grab something to eat.'

Nikki thanked her, and she withdrew.

'Do we believe him?' Nikki said.

'Yes, and we should give him the benefit of the doubt,' said Laura, looking out of the door, 'because he's coming back into the CID room with a bag from the deli. Of course, it's debatable whether he went out of hunger or the need to make a private phone call.'

'Okay, Joseph, relax and try not to growl,' said Nikki softly. 'I'm not going to nail him to the wall and cross-examine him. Well, not yet. I want to see his reaction to what we have to say about Elvinia.' She looked at Laura. 'Surely that's not her real name? Elvinia sounds a bit like something out of her own flaming faery kingdom.'

Laura did smile at that. 'That's something else I checked out and yes, it's her real name all right. It means Queen of the Elves — an old Irish name, I believe. Rather appropriate, don't you think?'

Nikki raised her eyebrows.

'You wanted me, boss?' Aiden Gardner stood in the doorway.

'Ah, Aiden, good. Go and get another chair, then come on in. We just want your opinion on something.' Even Nikki thought she sounded calm and relaxed.

When he was seated, she said, 'It's regarding your trip to see the folklore expert yesterday, Aiden. Laura might have picked up on something and we wondered if you, as a detective, noticed the same thing.'

His face registered nothing other than mild interest.

'Did Elvinia Torres give you cause for concern regarding anything you spoke to her about, Aiden?'

His brow furrowed. 'Not that I can recall. She is a very interesting lady and clearly very knowledgeable, although I struggle to understand how someone with her academic background can so readily believe in all that fanciful, mystical stuff.' He turned to Laura. 'What was it that bothered you about her, Laura?'

'Just her mood change towards the end of our conversation,' said Laura dismissively. 'It's probably the psychologist in me, analysing everyone and everything. If you didn't notice anything, then I'm probably mistaken.'

Aiden shook his head. 'Sorry if I missed something. She did look at her watch a few times, so maybe she had another appointment.'

'Maybe.' Laura looked at Nikki.

'So, you didn't notice that Elvinia was paying a lot of attention to our killer's past history, and in particular his childhood and his relationship with his parents,' Nikki said evenly.

'Surely that was because she was trying to build a picture of a boy who became a murderer, and what drew him to be so interested in nature spirits in the first place.' His reply was quick and reasonable. 'It didn't seem to be of much concern.'

'So, if we checked the search history on your computer or your phone, we'd find nothing about Elvinia Torres,' Joseph said coldly.

The look that flashed across Aiden's face told Nikki all she wanted to know.

'I . . . I, well, yes, I did look her up. She seemed an interesting person, that's all.' He looked around at their grave faces. 'What is this? A bloody inquisition?'

'No! It's three people trying to stop a murder investigation from going to rat shit because of one man's obsession with a dead scientist,' hissed Nikki. 'Aiden, are you totally incapable of telling the truth? You were such a damned good detective, why are you hell-bent on ruining everything, past, present *and* future?'

Aiden put his head in his hands. 'I'm sorry, I'm sorry.' He swallowed loudly, then looked up. 'Yes, I caught on immediately that she was too damned interested in Lucas as a kid. By the time we left I was convinced that she knew exactly who our killer was. I wanted to talk to Laura about it, but something stopped me.' He grimaced. 'From her age, I guessed that Elvinia must have known Julian from somewhere and yes, I googled her.'

'And found the same things Laura did and decided that she could replace Steven Paine as your go-to person for more info on Julian,' Nikki said. 'The big question is, have you contacted her yet? And I want the truth this time.'

He said nothing for a while, then, 'There was no answer. I never got through. And that's a fact.'

Nikki exhaled. 'Well, that's something.' She looked at Aiden. 'Do *not* contact her again. Didn't it occur to you to wonder why Elvinia is so interested in this case? Or were you so blinkered by your own obsession with Julian that you didn't think in that direction?'

He looked perplexed. 'You think she had some sort of underhand reason for talking to us?'

'Sure of it,' said Laura. 'The question is, what is it?'

'And because of Hackett, we dare not ask,' grumbled Joseph. 'So, as we have no idea what her agenda is, do as the DI says, Aiden. No more contact. None at all. You're just lucky that Julian's name never came up in those searches, or Hackett's early warning system would have picked it up and he'd have marched you out of that door before you could draw breath.'

Aiden sighed. He looked rather forlornly at Nikki. 'I think you should take me off this case, boss. I'm messing up all along the line. Perhaps I was wrong in thinking that I could still do the job without a warrant card. I just don't feel like I'm part of anything anymore and, if I'm honest, this thing about Julian has got me totally hooked. It's in my head that he is at the heart of this case, and I cannot shake it off. And not being able to investigate properly seems to have magnified it.'

'I can understand that last part,' said Nikki. 'Every avenue that looks hopeful gets closed down if the slightest hint of Julian's name shows itself. It's intolerable.' She paused, aware that Aiden's whole future career with the force, even as a civilian, rested on the outcome of this interview. 'I have to tell you that I was going to have you taken off the case the moment I realised that you were going it alone again, but I think losing an officer in the middle of a murder inquiry would be counterproductive. But can you work as a team member, Aiden?

Really? Because if I have to watch you, then I'm not watching the bad guys, and that's not going to happen. Your choice.' Yet again, she'd flung him a line, and she sincerely hoped she hadn't made a glorious cock-up in doing so.

Aiden seemed to struggle with himself. Then he looked directly at her. 'Thank you, ma'am. I won't let you down this time, I swear.'

'Right, then I suggest you and Laura put your heads together and compare notes. I'm sure you have *lots* to talk about. Now bugger off and do some work.'

Alone again, Nikki saw Cat approaching with a definite spring in her step. She told Nikki everything that Mandy had said. Nikki was delighted. 'Cat Cullen, I could hug you! Well done! Now, get on to chasing up this Dawson as fast as you can. We want him here, pronto, or if that's not possible, you and Ben go to him. He's the key to everything!'

Ben came and joined them. 'Mandy's camera is a little gold mine. We need to find out who this woman is.' He handed her a printout.

'Nice mullet!' snorted Nikki, then stopped and looked closer. 'Whoa! That face is vaguely familiar, but I have no idea where from.' She hated that feeling. 'Anyway, I can find out by making another trip to Corley Grange Hotel. It's time Harry Byrd started telling the truth, or he'll be swapping that nice comfy hotel for the custody suite on a charge of wasting police time and perverting the course of justice.' She stopped talking and frowned, her eyes drawn back to the image of the woman with the mane of wild hair. 'Actually, I won't visit Harry. I'm fed up with trailing round the Fen after him, I'm going to have uniform bring him to me. And you, Joseph, are going to pay a call on Vinnie Silver's friend, Lenny Smithers. Take him a copy of this picture and ask him if he can identify this woman.'

Joseph looked confused. 'Why Lenny?'

'Just do it, Joseph, and as quickly as possible!'

* * *

Twenty minutes later, Lenny Smithers was pointing at the picture and laughing raucously.

'Oh deary me! The passage of time hasn't done much for our Suzie, has it?'

'You know this woman?'

'Suzie Melrose. She played the part of Mrs Chippy in *Arnie Bends the Rules*. Wasn't a major role, but she was a regular. She had a small part in one of the long-running soaps after that and finished up doing voice-overs for commercials. Haven't seen her in anything for yonks, dear boy.' He was still chuckling to himself. 'Hasn't worn too well, I must say, unless it's make-up and this is a clip from a part she was playing.'

'Kind of,' said Joseph thoughtfully. So she was an actress. His brow furrowed. But why would Harry use an actress to help care for his mother? Obviously, she wasn't doing anything of the sort. But what was she doing there, then? Maybe it was time to get that warrant and take a look inside Arcadia.

He thanked Lenny for his help and raced back to his car. Before he could even start the engine, his phone rang. He heard Nikki's angry voice saying, 'Sodding bloody Harry has done a runner! So much for doubling up on the crews watching him, he's vanished without trace. He even left me a note in his room! *"So sorry. I appreciate everything you've done, DI Galena, but I need to find my brother before it's too late, Harry."* Damn it, damn it!'

'Shit!' Joseph hissed, 'And there's definitely something going on in Highgate. That woman is an actress, but you knew that already, didn't you?'

'I wasn't sure, but she looked like an older, bulkier version of a woman from Hannah's favourite show. So I was right?'

'Yes, and I've got a name for her — Suzie Melrose.'

'Okay, get yourself back here, Joseph. We need to know more about the set-up in Arcadia.'

As soon as he set foot back in her office, Joseph realised that something else was bothering her.

'I've been played for a fool, Joseph.' Nikki was pacing her office. 'And I walked right into it! What an arse!'

'Explain?'

'All that fuss about his needing to get back out there on the streets was a load of cobblers. All along he was planning to go it alone, but he needed to know exactly where to look — and who told him the places the police search was concentrating on and where his brother was last seen? Yours bloody truly! And who said that Lucas was using the waterways and had forsaken the woods? The same idiot. I practically handed him map references! I was asking for his help, Joseph, or so I thought, whereas in reality I was just feeding him the info he needed.' She stopped pacing and sank down in her chair. 'I cannot believe I was so gullible!'

'But that also means he's walking into an area that's saturated with our uniforms. No matter what, he won't find it easy. Have you already notified Niall and the officers in charge of the search?'

'Done. The minute I realised what a prat I'd been.'

'Come on, Nikki,' he said gently. 'We all thought we were working with him, not *for* him. He brought this whole thing to our notice in the first place, provided all that info, those maps, everything, so it was logical to enlist his help in this last push to find Lucas. We'd have all done the same, so let's move on. He has clearly spun some complex story and even backed it up with a bogus relative who'll confirm all he's told us. That's where we need to be looking. We can do nothing more to assist the search, so let's try to unravel the lies and see what we are really dealing with.'

Joseph saw the old steeliness come back into Nikki's eyes.

'Okay.' She took a deep breath. 'Now, if Cat and Ben can track Dawson and we discover why Lucas fled his home and never went back, it will be a major move ahead.'

'And it's linked specifically to Lucas, so hopefully it won't be stymied by Hackett.' Joseph flashed a glance across the CID room to where the man sat working on his computer — but looking in their direction.

Nikki's phone rang.

'DI Galena,' she snapped.

'Ma'am, just an update from the search teams. Nothing exciting. In fact, it's a bit worrying.'

As Niall's voice echoed around the office, Joseph hurriedly shut the door, and Nikki lowered the volume on the speaker. Neither of them wanted whatever this was to be broadcast just yet.

'Go ahead, Niall.'

'I've had several reports coming in that our guys aren't alone out there. They suspect — well, actually they are certain — that operatives from Hackett's department are shadowing them.'

'Oh perfect!' murmured Nikki through gritted teeth. 'Thanks for the heads-up, Niall. I guess we should have expected it. We know fuck all about what's going on but whatever it is, they are certain to want to be in at the kill, so to speak.'

'That's what I thought,' said Niall glumly. 'Pretty well word for word. I'll keep you updated, ma'am.'

Nikki hung up and looked at Joseph. 'Listen and tell me what you think. Time is not on our side. I wanted to go to Highgate myself but it's not an option. I'm going to get Cam to ask the Met to help us. I want a team around to Arcadia with a warrant and, as I fear for the life of Anita Hopwood-Byrd, it's kosher. I want that Suzie woman picked up and taken to the nearest Met station, and I want to interview her via video link. It will cut time down to a minimum, as long as Cam can set it in motion fast. Do you agree?'

Joseph nodded emphatically. 'Go! Do it now. But look casual when you leave the office. Our Man in Black is paying us a lot of attention right now.'

'If he asks anything, Joseph, make him believe that we are all pretty hyped up because we are getting closer to finding Lucas, nothing else.'

'It would make sense. Let's just hope Cam can cut through all the red tape without attracting Hackett's attention.'

Nikki was only gone for ten minutes. She returned wearing a look of satisfaction. 'He's on it,' she whispered. 'And we've had a stroke of luck. An old friend of his is a superintendent in the Highgate area *and* she's affiliated with DI Morgan Flint in some way, which is a massive bonus. Cam said he and the Met super go back a long way, and she'll pull out all the stops to help.'

Was the tide turning? Joseph felt a surge of adrenalin. He believed it was. And about time too!

* * *

Lucas was struggling. The difference between reality and fantasy was no longer clear, and increasingly his world was becoming home to the uglier side of nature. He was seeing the darker creatures, the ones that inhabited the shadows, that slithered from under rocks and out of decaying tree stumps and crawled through stagnant, slimy pools. Their faces were ugly, their bodies twisted, their movements distorted and unpredictable. His lovely spirits were still there but they were distant, almost transparent, and their beautiful inner light was nothing but a dim glow.

A part of him, the part that still reasoned, knew he needed medication. His body craved the relief that only the hated chemicals could provide. But there were none, not anymore, and as the journey was almost at an end, he would have to manage without them. Somehow, he would need to summon the strength — and sanity — to make it through. One single thing spurred him on and gave him strength. He believed that he had seen the Elf King again. And he was close by. Very close.

Lucas forced the trolls and goblins back into the shadows and stagnant pools, called on the higher beings to help him succeed, and stared unblinking into a cloudless blue sky at last.

Harry was almost here. Then he could slay the Elf King and he and his brother would be together for ever, as they had been all those years ago, before darkness enshrouded their world.

* * *

In a lovely old house some twenty miles from Greenborough, a woman sat in her favourite chair and stared out over the gardens. She hoped that her emotions hadn't given her away, but she had a feeling they had. What she feared had been confirmed. The question now was what to do about it?

Thirty minutes later, Elvinia was still no closer to an answer.

CHAPTER TWENTY-SEVEN

Just after midday, Ben felt a tremor in his pocket. His secret Spooky phone. He stood up. 'Nature calls,' he said to Cat.

'Well, hurry up. I've got a call coming in any minute from Lucas's old school, hopefully with a forwarding address for Mr Dawson. And it's Eric Dawson, by the way.'

'Great! Won't be a tick.' He hurried off to the men's room and, making sure he was alone, went into a cubicle and opened the message from Spooky.

Nothing adds up, Ben. There are firewalls around things that should be common knowledge and access denied and blocks if you try to check out regular stuff that was reported in the media at the time. My friend says this will take a lot longer than he thought. He can do it, but it's very tricky. And that payout cleared a cool million.

He blinked a couple of times and reread it. He had the sudden feeling that they were all perched on the red-hot rim of a volcano that was ready to erupt. What the hell had Julian done to warrant such a high-level cover-up?

Finding no answers, he flushed the toilet and washed his hands, just in case anyone wondered what he was up to, and hurried back to the office.

Cat was seated with her arms crossed, staring at the phone. He went over to her desk. 'Spooky's hit firewalls that would keep the flames of hell out,' he whispered. 'And the payout exceeded a million. What on earth are we involved in?'

She puffed out her cheeks. 'I don't even want to know. I just wish it was over and we could go back to chasing villains and closing down wacky-baccy factories. I can't help thinking that someone is going to get hurt, working in the dark like this.'

He nodded. 'I'm going to update the boss.'

Before he was two paces from her desk, her phone rang. He stopped and waited.

Cat answered, scribbled madly on a memo sheet and thanked the caller profusely. 'Got it! Dawson's place is less than an hour away, a village this side of Rutland Water. Tell the boss we've got this. We'll go as soon as I've rung the number they gave me.'

In less than five minutes he was back and grabbing his jacket from the back of his chair. 'All set?'

Cat looked pensive. 'Um. This isn't quite what I'd hoped, Ben,' she said flatly.

'Why? What's the problem?'

'Mr Eric Dawson is dead. Died a couple of weeks ago.'

'Oh fuck!' Unlike most coppers, Ben rarely swore, but in this case, he felt perfectly justified.

'However, we are still going. I've just spoken to his daughter, Alyson. She's willing to talk to us. She says she has something of her father's that could be of assistance to us, and she'll explain when we get there.'

'Then let's go.' He held the door open for her. 'By the way, Delia and Mandy are staying at the Fisherman's Hotel on the river, not far from the marina. Delia has left us the numbers of the hotel and their mobiles. I've told them to ring either of us if anything else comes to mind. Meanwhile, let's go and try to see if we can fill in those gaping holes in Lucas's past, shall we?'

* * *

Joseph felt as if he had suddenly been thrown into limbo. Things were happening around him, but he wasn't a part of them. The man of action was doing nothing but wait. Waiting for the Met to report on whatever they found at Arcadia. For Cat and Ben to hopefully bring back some missing pieces from the puzzle that was Lucas Hopwood-Byrd. Waiting for that all-important call from Niall to tell them there'd been a sighting of their quarry.

Nikki was fielding calls in her office, while he had shut himself in his "cupboard" and closed the door. Piled on his desk in untidy heaps were all the musty-smelling books, diaries and maps that Harry had brought with him, as well as the scribblings of Karen Cotton with her recollections of her conversations with the man she had known as Luke. He'd skimmed through some of them, but the sheer volume had put him off an in-depth reading. Now he needed a distraction, and as there might just be some tiny nugget of information leading to Lucas's whereabouts hiding somewhere in those fading, dusty pages, he could put it off no longer.

He dispensed with the ones that he had already looked through and concentrated on the others. It was soon obvious that Lucas really did see two different kinds of nature spirits. Some of his sketches, especially in his diaries, were ethereal and quite beautiful, whereas others made Joseph shudder. If he really "saw" all this, it must have been terrifying for him. How would you live with it? He could have been medicated, of course. But without the name he'd adopted after he left home, they could check nothing.

After half an hour he went to get a coffee, then returned to his work. So far, he had found nothing that would help them, but he persevered. The notebook he was looking at now had no illustrations. It seemed to consist of random thoughts and comments. Some he had to read more than once to make sense of them. Towards the end of the entries, Joseph began to feel slightly uncomfortable. Some of the statements expressed extreme agitation, and the ramblings grew more disjointed and chaotic, indicating mistrust, suspicion and fear. Although no name was mentioned, Joseph was certain that whatever had gone wrong concerned Harry.

He stared for a long time at the scrawl on the last page. It was a riot of unconnected thoughts, random words and strange manic sketches etched in thick black pen. He'd seen that kind of thing before — they were the work of a seriously sick mind. Then a thought occurred to him. He swallowed. He could be terribly wrong, but there was a twisted kind of sense to it, and if he was right . . .

Joseph hurried into Nikki's office.

She looked up. 'Okay, Joseph. Tell me.'

'I think I might know who the Elf King is.'

'And?'

'I've been going through Lucas's writings, and I think it's Harry. Something happened between them that we're not aware of, a terrible event that precipitated Lucas's flight. If his diaries are anything to go by, I think he wants things back as they were when they were children, but to do that he needs to kill whatever Harry had become. He needs to eradicate the evil side, to release the brother that he loves.'

'The Elf King,' said Nikki, and exhaled. 'So he sends that note to bring Harry to Shrimptown so that he can kill him?'

'It's possible. And since Harry is so desperate to find his little brother, he comes willingly, setting up a plausible cover at home and then manipulating the police force into helping him in his search.'

'But he has no idea that he is walking straight into a trap. Oh shit! This could be a nightmare, Joseph. Now we have two Byrd brothers to find!'

'In a very big, watery county.' The enormity of the challenge washed over him like the incoming tide crashing on to the beach. It also washed away his earlier feeling that they were finally getting somewhere. 'I'm willing to bet that whatever "safe place" he's hiding in, it's not on that damned map and we don't know about it, because Harry purposely didn't mention it.' He strode over to the window and stared out. 'How did Harry get past four officers, Nikki? Do we know?'

She gave a long sigh. 'I've just had a call from our guys at the hotel. It looks like he planned it ages ago, probably when he first arrived at the hotel. It has a spa and a plunge pool. The changing rooms have a storage area next to them with an exit out to a yard where there are some refuse bins and a walkway to the car park. Apparently, he used the sauna and pool regularly, always following exactly the same routine. This time he went to the spa but only showered and dressed again. He must have had a complete change of clothes stashed in the locker. He slipped unnoticed out of the staff exit and into a waiting taxi. They're checking all the cab companies to try and find the driver,' she shrugged, 'but he had it all planned so well that we'll not find him that way. He's long gone, Joseph. It's a waiting game for us, I'm afraid.'

'Then I'll grab us a couple of sandwiches for lunch and get back to those disturbed and frightening ramblings. There may be something, some tiny clue that Harry didn't eradicate if, as I suspect, he doctored his little brother's notes before handing them over.'

Fifteen minutes later, having deposited Nikki's snack on her desk, Joseph returned to his office and once again closed the door.

* * *

Nikki ate her sandwich without tasting it. As she sipped her coffee, her phone vibrated with a message.

Warrant obtained. Search begins fourteen hundred hours. Pulling out all stops available. Morgan.
We owe you one! Nikki.
You certainly do! Morgan.

Nikki was surprised at the speedy reaction to Cam's request and could only think that his friend and Morgan Flint had even more clout than she'd believed. She glanced at the clock. In twenty minutes, the Met officers would be entering Arcadia. What in hell would they find there? Something? Nothing? Or more than they bargained for?

Nikki sipped her coffee thoughtfully. One thing was for sure, it wouldn't be bloody faeries!

* * *

'Oh my!' said Cat. 'This is a far cry from the Fen villages, isn't it?'

Ben looked at the pretty stone cottages and their colourful gardens. 'And twice the price, if not more.'

The address they had been given was Compton Acre, Quarry Lane, Reddington, the second-to-last property on the left-hand side. Even the satnav worked here, which was a pleasant change from many Fenland locations, and they found it easily.

Alyson Dawson was older than Ben had envisaged, smartly dressed in dark clothing, and wore a serious expression that spoke of both grief and anxiety. *She's probably dealing with enough right now*, Ben thought, *without having us barging into her life*. He gave her his best smile, said they were very sorry to intrude at such a difficult time, but they were investigating a number of serious crimes and had no option.

'The funeral is the day after tomorrow, Officers. I shall be going home shortly afterwards, so I'll help you all I can while I'm here.'

She ushered them into a combined kitchen, diner and sunroom. It was homely and comfortable, filled with photographs and overflowing bookcases. She indicated a sofa, whipping away a large multicoloured crocheted blanket before they sat down. 'Dad had a cat and a dog. My partner collected the dog yesterday — we are taking him — but I'm still looking for a home for the cat. Poor thing has been here all her life. I wouldn't have split them up, but my partner is allergic to cat fur.'

Ben glanced at Cat and gave her a rueful smile. They had come by their own British Blue, a cat called Byron, when it

301

had become "orphaned" in another case. Now Byron owned the house.

'How can I help?'

'We understand your father took in a teenage boy not long after your brother Josh was killed. Is that correct?'

Alyson nodded. 'He did, although I'm not aware of the full circumstances. My parents split up a while before Josh died. He stayed with Dad, and I went with my mother. It was as amicable as these things can be — for our sakes, I suspect — and I visited regularly. I loved them both dearly, but when Mum and Dad were together, they just fought all the time. The house was a war zone. So I guess it was for the best. Anyway, when Josh was killed, Mum blamed Dad, even though it was no more his fault than hers. I suppose she just needed someone to hit out at. And Dad, well, he was devastated. Within a month, the house was on the market. Dad swore he couldn't stay there without Josh.' She looked at them intently. 'Then Dad became obsessed with helping someone. He said he had lost one boy but could save another. I didn't understand what he meant, and when I asked him, he said I was too young. He said that one day he'd explain it all, but he never did.' She stood up, went to a Welsh dresser and opened one of the drawers. 'This might be the explanation, Officers. It's not been opened, and you can see why.'

Ben took the proffered envelope. On the front was written, *For your safekeeping, my dearest Alyson. Should the police contact you on my death, please hand this to them unopened. Your ever-loving father, Eric.*

'You will get this back, Alyson,' said Cat, 'but we might need it as evidence. It depends on the contents.'

Ben pulled on a pair of nitrile gloves and opened it. He read the long letter in silence, then passed it across to Cat.

'Did you ever meet the boy your father took in?' he asked Alyson.

'Oh yes, although I didn't visit Dad often after he moved here from London. I saw Marcus no more than three or four times, I should think. He seemed very shy. He always seemed to be in the garden, or out walking in the countryside. I never once saw him inside the cottage. Dad told me later that he went to university and excelled in his subject but struggled to socialise. When he graduated, he went to work in woodland reserves, using his skills in arboriculture, I believe.' She smiled sadly. 'I thought it rather fitting that his name was Marcus — it was Josh's middle name too.'

Ben wasn't surprised that Alyson knew Lucas by a different name. Dawson would hardly use the real one. 'Did he stay in touch with your father after leaving home?'

'Yes, for a long time. Then once, when I visited Dad, he seemed agitated. He said that he was very concerned about Marcus's health. I took that to mean mental health and I was right. Then, for the first time, Dad told me that Marcus had been badly damaged in his childhood, but he had managed to get him on to a drug regime that suited him, and he was optimistic about his future life.'

'But Marcus came off his meds,' prompted Ben.

She nodded. 'Dad said Marcus hated chemicals. He tried course after course of natural medicines, but his impairment was far too advanced by then, and it seems he spiralled out of control. As far as I know, Dad never saw him again.' Alyson looked even sadder than before. 'He was almost as distraught as when our Josh died, and he went downhill not long after.'

Cat looked up from the letter. 'Did you ever wonder how your father came to be Marcus's guardian, Alyson?'

'Not really. Well, not when I was younger. Don't forget, Officer, my family had been shattered — fragmented by the divorce and then Josh's death. It was a horrible time. Much later, after I became an adult, it did seem a little odd to me that a single man like him had been allowed to foster a teenager. I even mentioned it once, but Dad shrugged it off, saying that Marcus's circumstances were special, that he was deemed a suitable, responsible adult, and that having known him for years through school, he was probably the most appropriate and qualified person available. I never took it further.'

'It will come out, Alyson, and maybe it's best that you hear it from us, but the boy's name was Lucas Hopwood-Byrd, not Marcus, and it is believed that he ran away from home specifically so that your father could get him out of the area.' Cat spoke softly. 'And please don't read anything inappropriate into that. Your father took him in because the boy feared for his life.'

'And for what it's worth,' added Ben, 'we think that might have been true. He could well have been in grave danger and your father, heartbroken over Josh, "adopted" him without going through the official procedures and then passed him off as his own son.'

A long silence followed. Suddenly Alyson said, 'Can I get anyone tea? Coffee?'

Ben understood that she needed to be alone for a while, to distance herself from the thought that her father had, in essence, abducted the boy. He said that tea would be lovely.

While Alyson made the tea, Ben, speaking in a low voice, said, 'He put him through uni and anything else official under the name Josh Marcus Dawson, his son's name.'

'I'll call the uni as soon as we get back, but I'm guessing that'll be the case.' Cat put the letter back in the envelope. 'I bet we'll find a driving licence under that name too.'

'And maybe a boat licence for the waterways? I think I'll ring this straight in to the boss. She can get the ball rolling.' He pulled out his phone. 'Ma'am? We have a name for you. Lucas went through his late teens and young adult life as Josh Marcus Dawson.'

Nikki asked if he could speak freely and he said not, but that they would be leaving in about twenty minutes. 'Eric Dawson left an explanatory letter, and it makes for very disturbing reading. If it ties in with whatever you discover in Highgate, it could turn the whole case on its head. I'll ring as soon as we're back in the car.'

Cat tapped the envelope. 'This is scary stuff, Ben. Do you think it's true, or is it another story that Lucas dreamed up and then managed to sell to Dawson?'

'I think it's true.'

Alyson came in with the drinks, which she set down on a low coffee table in front of them. 'I have to ask. You mentioned serious crimes. What has Marcus done? Sorry, I still think of him as Marcus. It's the name I know him by.'

'We understand,' Ben said. 'He has used a lot of different names. But in answer to your question, we are looking for him in connection with three deaths and one serious assault. He's a very sick man, Alyson, who suffers from a personality disorder that makes him very dangerous indeed.'

She stiffened, clearly badly shocked. 'I would never have dreamed it. Him, of all people. He was so timid and so at one with nature.' She sat down heavily. 'Actually, there's someone else you should talk to, my uncle Terry. He's my father's younger brother. He knew Marcus. In fact, I think he spent quite a bit of time with him at one point. I seem to remember Dad telling me that Terry taught Marcus to handle a boat. I know that Uncle Terry loved sailing and boating and apparently Marcus took to it like a natural. Terry would know a lot more about him than I do.'

Boats. Cat flashed Ben an excited look.

'Can you give us his contact details, please?' Ben asked.

'Of course. Right now, he's staying at the Premier Inn on the main road into town. He's come up a few days before the funeral to help me sort out some of Dad's things.' Alyson glanced at her watch. 'I was going down there to collect him after you'd gone. Would you like to talk to him now? I can show you where it is and introduce you.'

They readily agreed, and in around twenty minutes were sitting at a table in the bar area of the hotel.

Terry Dawson was a broad, ruddy-faced man with bushy grey eyebrows and a shock of thick iron-grey hair. When he was told the reason for their visit, he stared at them incredulously.

'Surely there has to be some mistake, Officers. That can't be true. I mean, I know he had a strange side to him and a vivid imagination, but young Marcus wouldn't hurt a fly!'

305

Ben thought he was probably right — flies were quite safe, but human beings were a different matter. 'No mistake, sir. And it's absolutely crucial that we find him before there are more deaths.'

'We understand he has a cabin cruiser, sir,' said Cat, 'and we are anxious to locate it. It was last seen on the River Westland and in the drains and waterways between Greenborough and the estuary to the Wash.'

'The River Westland? Really?' Terry sounded surprised.

'Does that mean something to you, sir?' she asked.

'It certainly does. We used to go there together when I was teaching Marcus the ropes. I had a nice little Freeman 22 cruiser back then, lovely little river boat she was, the *Beautiful Alice*. Sold her to a friend and she's still going strong. Should have kept her.'

'Sir,' Ben said, bringing him back on track, 'we think he's hiding out somewhere he considers special and safe. Is there a part of the river you think could fit the bill?'

Terry Dawson's brow creased into furrows. 'Oh my! That area is a mass of waterways. I wouldn't know where to start.'

You are not alone there, thought Ben grimly.

'Can you give me a little more time, Officers? To be honest, my mind is occupied with my brother's death right now, and in any case, I haven't even thought about Marcus for years. We lost touch when he got a job working in a forest somewhere further north.'

'I'm afraid time isn't on our side, Mr Dawson,' said Cat. 'We're sorry to have to ask all this at such a sad and difficult time, but would you give it some serious thought? It is important.'

'Of course I will. I'll put my mind to it, I promise. Can I have your numbers? I'll ring immediately if I think of anywhere that might be of use to you.'

They thanked him and prepared to leave. 'Before we go, Mr Dawson,' added Ben, 'did your brother tell you anything about Marcus's background?'

'Only that it was imperative that his real family never found him. He made it sound as if social services had taken him away from the family for his own safety. Eric said he was special in some way.' Terry pulled a face. 'Believe me, I almost got out the thumbscrews to find out why, but Eric clammed up and there was no budging him. I admit to stooping to ask the lad himself the odd question about his past, but all he ever said was that Eric was now his father and he was happy in his father's house. He wouldn't say any more than that and I didn't dare push him.'

They thanked him again, offered him and Alyson their condolences and walked back to the car.

'So near and yet so far a-bloody-way!' cursed Cat.

'I know,' Ben said, 'but Terry might just come up trumps. He obviously loved messing around on the river with the lad.' They had achieved a lot on this trip, thanks to a dead man who'd thought to write them a letter. If Terry could just recall some place where Lucas might go, they would have him. 'You drive, Cat. I'd better ring the boss.'

CHAPTER TWENTY-EIGHT

'We've got your bogus "sister," Nikki. She's enjoying the comforts of the custody suite after being processed. I can get you a video call with her in about fifteen minutes. I've emailed a link.' Morgan Flint sounded unusually excited.

'And Anita? The mother?' Nikki asked.

'No sign, Nikki. Suzie Melrose was alone in the house.'

Somehow that didn't come as a surprise. Every word that had come out of Harry's mouth had been a lie, or so it would seem, so why not lie about his mother too? 'Do we know where she is?'

'Not yet. We are checking that out now. Suzie has given us the name of the nursing home that Harry Byrd said she'd been taken to, but we can find no record of it anywhere. Our Suzie is singing like a bird, you'll be pleased to hear. Reckons that no matter how much she's being paid, it's not worth this.' She chuckled. 'I'm inclined to agree with her.'

'Do we know if Suzie ever actually saw Anita Hopwood-Byrd?' asked Nikki, beginning to imagine some rather darker scenarios.

'Oh yes, she did meet her. She described her as being a pathetic shell of a woman.'

Well, that was something, Nikki supposed. But where was she now? God. How she'd like to get her hands on Harry! Things were bad enough having to hunt for a psycho killer without his brother lying through his teeth and sending them on a wild goose chase.

'I'll leave the rest for Suzie to tell you, Nikki.'

'One last thing, then, what was the impression your guys got of the house itself when they went in?'

'The senior officer told me that for a posh drum in a nice location it looked pretty rubbish. He reckoned that no one had done any updating or even given it a lick of paint for years. He said it was as if some old person lived there and had totally lost interest in the home. It wasn't full of clutter or even really dirty, just unloved and uncared for.'

Well, that tallied with Ben's and Cat's descriptions. Nikki thanked Morgan, then called for Joseph. She definitely wanted him present for the interview with Suzie Melrose.

'I've checked out the name Josh Marcus Dawson, boss, and yes, we have a vehicle registered to him, a Vauxhall Astra, and the cabin cruiser, the Sea Ray. The name of the craft is, rather appropriately, *Clear Vision*.' Joseph rolled his eyes. 'Clairvoyance. So he still had fond thoughts of his real father and his strange talent, even after all those years of living as Dawson's son.'

'Have you spoken to Niall recently?' she asked.

'He's up to his ears fielding reports from the teams on the ground and on the water, but there's nothing as yet, not a single sighting of man, boat or brother.'

'He's holed up somewhere, isn't he?' She sighed. 'Is he waiting for Harry to join him somewhere they both know and we don't, or is he just lying low until the heat is off?'

'Whichever it is, Harry is very likely in grave danger,' Joseph said. 'Having lied until he's blue in the face to try to locate his brother, he might find that the outcome isn't quite as he'd hoped.'

'I know,' Nikki said. 'I could personally wring his sodding neck. He obviously believes that brotherly love will overcome the fact that Little Bro is off the wall and just as likely to top him for bad-mouthing a dandelion as look at him!'

Joseph tried not to smile but failed dismally. 'Nikki Galena, your way with words never ceases to delight me.'

She smiled back at him ruefully. 'Well, honestly. You've got to admit it's exasperating. What more proof does he need? We have three dead bodies and an injured boy! There's no telling some people, is there?' She looked up at the clock. 'Time to log in and meet Suzie Melrose.'

* * *

Joseph decided that the ageing actress was either playing the part of her life — that of an innocent, deceived victim — or she was terrified and telling the truth. He soon settled on the latter.

It took a while to calm the histrionics, but eventually the story started to unfold. Suzie had known Harry Byrd for years — he was a friend of a friend. It had taken a bit of cajoling to get her to admit that Harry was the secret partner of a well-known actor called Tim Reagan and had been for some time. Well, thought Joseph, they had guessed that Harry didn't always live at the family home, but this answered why they could find no other property listed to his name. He was staying with a *secret partner*.

'He asked me if I'd consider helping him out in a sort of acting role, pretending to be his aunt.' Suzie started to get agitated at this point. 'Look, Detectives, you have to understand, I've had no work for months. For ages I've taken anything I've been offered to keep my head above water, but the work had just dried up. Even the voice-overs had run out. I was desperate and Harry offered me a life-saving figure if I'd help him.'

'Did he explain why he was doing this?' asked Nikki. 'What did he tell you was going on exactly?'

Suzie looked away from the camera, then they saw her shifting in her chair. 'Not in detail, just that he would give

310

me some things to say that must be learned like lines from a script, and which I must forget forever when the job was done. He said it was desperately complicated, that his family had secrets that must never come out. It sounds overdramatic and ridiculous now, but he made it sound so plausible.' She drew in a breath. 'He said he had to go away for a while because his brother was in terrible trouble, and only he could sort it out. The problem was the police had the wrong end of the stick about the situation and he was desperate to contain the whole thing. In the past, his aunt had stayed with his mother, but she'd moved away, plus she couldn't be trusted to say the right thing if anyone came asking questions.'

'So you agreed. And he told you what?' asked Nikki, impatiently staring at her monitor.

'He gave me a whole lot of history about his aunt and his family. Told me to swot this up for the part. He gave me answers to questions that people might ask and said that if I got it right and fooled everyone, he would give me considerably more than we had agreed.' Suzie began to look really uncomfortable. 'But he never said that some of those people would be the police!'

'But you kept up the pretence, didn't you? Lying to our officers and obstructing the course of justice.' Nikki kept on relentlessly. 'Just how gullible are you, Suzie? Or more to the point, how much did he give you to obstruct our enquiries?'

'I didn't think I was obstructing anything! I thought I was helping a friend in trouble!'

'Yes, and for a considerable payment! Come on. You had to suspect that something dodgy was going on when you read your lines. Didn't it worry you when you read about the incident with the father and the gardener? Just how much did he give you to do this and keep quiet about it?' Nikki glared at the monitor screen.

'Five thousand pounds,' Suzie whispered.

'Nice work if you can get it!' Nikki sat back and shook her head incredulously. 'Now tell us what else you had to do to earn all that.'

Suzie dabbed at her eyes with a tissue. 'Harry's mother was getting worse, slipping further and further into her own world. He decided that a home was the only answer. She would be too much for me and the carers to cope with while he was away. But he didn't want anyone to know that anything was going on, not until he returned. So he arranged for Anita to go into a private clinic — he took her himself — then he cancelled the carers.'

Joseph began to understand the change of nursing care companies. 'You took Mother's place. Pretended, sorry, *acted* the part of Mother and when the new carers came in, they knew no different?'

'It was only supposed to be for a few days. They came in twice a day, and I'd always find some way to dismiss them. Then, as soon as they were gone, I became Corinne again,' admitted Suzie.

'Why in heaven's name go through such an elaborate rigmarole? What did it matter if Mother was in a home, or if carers came or didn't?' He was totally nonplussed.

Suzie sighed. 'I don't know, but Harry was adamant that there must be no change in the normal routine. He wanted no attention paid to the house.'

'And when this was over,' asked Nikki, 'what were his plans, for himself and his mother? Did he say?'

'DI Galena, please believe that Harry adores his mum, but he told me he couldn't cope any longer, or give her all the care and attention that she needed. He was going to find her the very best place to end her days, and then he and Tim were going abroad to live, far from those terrible family secrets that he mentioned.'

'But no mention of his little brother joining them,' whispered Joseph to Nikki.

'My thoughts precisely,' she returned. 'He told us he wanted Lucas back in his life, but if he's buggering off to Tenerife or somewhere hot and sweaty, it's going to be a long journey if Lucas sends him a visiting order from Rampton, or Broadmoor, or whichever high-security hospital he ends up in.' Nikki looked at Joseph. 'I've heard enough, what say you?'

Joseph agreed. This was not moving the hunt for Lucas ahead. It was certainly interesting and posed lots of questions about Harry but wasn't helping them in their main objective.

Nikki ended the meeting by discussing with one of the Met officers how they might transfer Suzie Melrose to the Fens for further questioning. They also wanted the "script" that Harry had prepared, as well as any further information on where the mother had been taken.

'Anita's sudden move to a home is beginning to worry me,' said Nikki. 'Did he give Suzie the name of some bogus nursing home to stop her knowing too much, or getting in touch, or is it something more sinister?'

'I'm as worried as you over that one,' said Joseph.

Nikki's mobile rang. 'Morgan Flint,' she said, putting it on loudspeaker.

'What did you think of all that?' asked Morgan.

'Bizarre,' said Nikki. 'Why go to all that trouble — and cost, for that matter — when he could have parked Mother in a home and gone after Lucas anyway?'

Morgan laughed. 'Our thoughts precisely. But I've phoned to ask if you'd like us to continue checking the nursing homes, or would you prefer we dig up the back garden?'

'Well, we'd be really grateful if you'd try and find her, Morgan. We are run ragged hunting for our killer and his idiot brother.'

Nikki sounded as fraught as she looked.

'Happily,' came Morgan's strong voice, 'and I'm going to go and take a look at that house for myself. I'll do a walk round with my phone and send you a video of anything interesting. Meanwhile, my colleagues here are packing up your out-of-work actress ready for dispatch to your tender loving care. Speak later and good hunting.' She ended the call.

'What now?' asked Joseph.

'Wait for Cat and Ben to get back and have a look at this letter of Eric Dawson's.'

'I keep thinking back to the start of the case and how fascinating I thought it all was. The father being headhunted for the Stargate Project, then all the drama that occurred when he returned home — a murder followed by his own violent death. Then his strange, disturbed son's disappearance and finally the older brother's years of searching. It felt like the plot of some thriller. Now all I can see is the madness. There's probably not one sane member in that family, and innocent people have died because of them.' Joseph shook his head.

'You forgot to throw in Hackett and his spooks,' added Nikki.

'Oh yeah, that too.'

'All in all and flaming faeries apart, this is the investigation from hell.' She opened her mouth to speak then stood up. 'I need to go and have a quick word with Cameron before he leaves. He's off early to go to the doctor with Kaye.'

'Oh, right. Tell him we'll be thinking of them. And while you're away, I'll try to track down the real Corinne Blake and get her take on the goings-on at Arcadia.' He saw the look that passed across Nikki's face and said, 'Don't worry, I won't mention that her nephew has magicked her sister away.'

He returned to his office. Cat had had no luck tracking Corinne Blake when she'd tried before, but knowing the husband's name changed everything. In under ten minutes, he'd located Duncan Blake and discovered that he and his wife Corinne lived in a place called Crossbannock in Kirkcudbrightshire. It took a little longer to get their number, but very soon the phone was ringing. Duncan answered and Joseph introduced himself, asking if it was possible to have a word with his wife. While he waited, he wondered what he was going to say to the woman. He'd have to tread carefully. He didn't want to scare her.

'Corinne Blake here, how can I help you, Sergeant Easter?'

He took a deep breath. 'Good afternoon, Mrs Blake. I'm very sorry to bother you, but we need your help with a serious case that we are investigating. It involves your nephews, Lucas and Harry Hopwood-Byrd.'

He heard a loud exhalation, then, 'Oh God! Not again.'

There was a long silence. 'Mrs Blake? Are you still there?'

'Yes, I'm still here.' She sounded wearily resigned. 'Tell me it has nothing to do with the deaths that we've read about in the papers, please.'

'I wish I could, Mrs Blake, but I'm afraid we are very anxious to talk to Lucas and he cannot be found. And Harry . . . well, he's been helping us to find his brother, but he hasn't been totally truthful and now he's gone off alone.'

'Marrying Julian was the worst thing my sister could have done. Her life was blighted from the moment she said "I do." And it seems he's still wreaking havoc, even from beyond the grave.'

'But she did love him?' questioned Joseph gently.

'Oh, she loved him all right, Sergeant. To distraction. Followed him halfway across the world, only to see him destroyed by his own experiments and his willingness always to go that one step further.'

There was bitterness and pain in her words, but Joseph detected something else too. 'One step further?'

Corinne Blake sighed. 'I have no proof, Sergeant. What I know came from my sister, and she told me that she had been warned never to speak to anyone about what happened to Julian. She was afraid of some sort of retribution. But I don't think I can stay quiet forever, and as the whole family seems to have disintegrated, does it even matter anymore?'

'Mrs Blake, whatever you tell me will remain confidential between me and my team. We have more constraints on us than you would think possible for a police force. Even this call could be terminated at any moment.' It sounded somewhat melodramatic but with Hackett, anything was possible.

'You won't be able to prove anything either, sad to say,' Corinne went on, 'but you'll know I'm telling the truth when you consider one little-known fact. My brother-in-law signed a waiver when he went to the States. He readily accepted that the project he was to work on was risky, so why did the government pay out a fortune to him when they shipped him home?'

'Do you have any idea why, Mrs Blake?'

'I do. Anita told me at a very low point in her life. He was so bloody good at what he did that the scientists leading the project decided to try and enhance his already extraordinary ability. They couldn't be satisfied with what they had. They had to try to go one better.'

Joseph understood immediately. 'They used drugs on him, didn't they?'

'Untested psychotropic drugs that affected his thoughts and perception and finished up frying his brain.'

'Without his permission?' asked Joseph. 'Surely that was ridiculously dangerous?'

Corinne answered immediately. 'Anita said that he had given permission for them to administer certain relaxants that would allow him to gain swifter access to a calm, clear mind. But someone had different ideas.'

'So it was hush money?'

'A whole lot of hush money. They had to all intents and purposes killed the goose that laid the golden egg. He was the best they had, and they messed up. Julian came back a totally different man. I do not know how my sister coped, with two young boys as well.' The bitterness in her tone gave way to sadness. 'Well, the truth was, she didn't cope.'

Joseph recalled what Harry had said about their happy childhood, and what Aiden had been told about Julian loving to be with his family. He was puzzled. 'We were given to understand that they were a very happy family, that Julian favoured Lucas and Harry was close to his mother.'

A derisory laugh echoed down the phone. 'Huh. Harry told you that, I suppose. He couldn't tell the truth if he tried. Right from when he was a small boy, he told stories. Now, I'd guess he is a full-blown pathological liar, and a dangerous one at that.'

Joseph felt a stab of concern. 'So what was the real family dynamic, Mrs Blake?'

'On the surface, fine. Behind closed doors, a nightmare. Think about it. The father had lost the plot. Both boys were damaged goods — one had fantasies and the other an anti-social personality disorder, hence the lying. My dear sister Anita never came to terms with the fact that her loving husband had changed beyond all recognition. And she had no time for the children at all.' Corinne swallowed noisily and Joseph guessed that she was on the verge of tears. 'I gave up visiting. I know that sounds harsh, but to see Anita as she had become, knowing that there was nothing I could do to help her, it tore my heart in two. One day, I'll get a call to say she's passed away, *if* anyone bothers to tell me. And it will be a relief, Sergeant.'

Joseph hardly knew what to say. What could you say? The emotion in the woman's voice was almost overpowering. But her words had given rise to a number of questions. If Harry was such a liar, maybe Corinne could give them the truth. 'I hate to do this, Mrs Blake, but I need to know a few very important facts, because from what you've told me, I can no longer rely on the information given to us by Harry. Do you know if Julian killed Bruce, the gardener, because Lucas had lied about being assaulted by the man?'

There was another long silence. Then, 'No, Sergeant Easter, he did not. And I can tell you this first-hand, as that was the last time I visited my sister. I was there when it happened, and I'll never forget it as long as I live. This is the truth. One, it had nothing to do with Lucas, although it was he who made the discovery and called his father. Two, Bruce should never, ever have died. Julian was in a rage because of what he *thought* he saw, but he was wrong. He erroneously believed that Bruce was trying to seduce Harry, but in fact, it was the other way around. Harry had been infatuated with the young gardener from the moment he started working there, and it later transpired that Bruce had done all he could, without hurting the boy's feelings or getting him into trouble, to deter him. Lucas was desperately upset about what happened. He told his mother and me that Harry was

317

always hanging around Bruce, that he said that one day they were going to run away together and invented all sorts of scenarios between the two of them. But when he saw Harry follow Bruce into the tool shed and close the door, he feared the worst and decided it was time their father intervened and stopped Harry before he got into serious trouble. But it all went horribly wrong, Sergeant. It was a fatal mistake on Julian's part.'

'And Harry? What happened to him?' asked Joseph urgently.

'You must understand, Sergeant, that Harry saw the whole thing happen in front of him. The man he adored was murdered right before his eyes, and by his own father, who he also adored. He went into shock, didn't speak for days on end.' Corinne sighed loudly. 'It was a horrific time. I stayed on for maybe a week, and then I went home. By that time, Julian had been taken into custody — he never denied what he had done — and Anita was left with the boys. Again, it sounds heartless, but I knew she didn't want me there and neither did Harry. He was speaking again by that time. I got the feeling he suspected that I might talk about what had happened and he swore to me that Lucas had imagined everything — what he saw and what he believed. He said I couldn't possibly believe anything Lucas said because he lived in a fantasy world.' She paused. 'Harry was very plausible, even as a boy, so even though I knew in my heart that Lucas had told the truth, I couldn't prove it. I decided I was better off a long way away from Arcadia.'

'And you never saw your sister again? You never visited, even after Lucas disappeared?' Joseph asked. 'Because Harry told people you often went to Highgate to help look after his mother.'

'For a while we spoke on the phone, but even that wasn't on a regular basis, Sergeant. There was never any argument, no irreparable split, but for my sanity's sake, I stayed away. I can't cope with lies, Sergeant Easter. If she truly needed me, I'd go to her, but she would have to call and ask.'

Joseph had a feeling that call would never come. He decided not to tell her that Harry had hired someone to impersonate her. It would come out later, but he thought he'd probably put her through enough for now. He had just one more question. 'Mrs Blake, did the boys really get on? Did they care about each other?'

'Yes, they did. When they were very young, they were inseparable.'

'Even with all the fantasies and the lies?'

'I think their differences brought them closer. It was sometimes a little scary. It was as if they shared deep secrets and were laughing at everyone else. Anita told me that when Lucas ran away, Harry was like a lost soul. Then as he grew older, finding his brother again became a crusade.'

Joseph thanked her for both her help and her honesty. He was about to ring off when she said, 'Do you think I should ring my sister, Sergeant? Since she's alone now.'

What to say? 'We understand that when he knew he was coming to the Fens, Harry arranged respite care for her, somewhere she would be properly cared for while he was away.'

'Ah well, maybe that's for the best. And please, Sergeant, will you tell me if you find my nephews? Even if the news isn't good.'

He promised her he would and hung up. What on earth were they dealing with?

CHAPTER TWENTY-NINE

At half past four, when Cat and Ben walked into the CID room, Nikki called everyone together for a meeting. She wanted them all to hear the contents of Eric Dawson's letter and re-evaluate what they knew in light of what it said.

She stood in front of the whiteboards. They were all there — Joseph, Cat, Ben, Aiden, Laura, who had asked if she could listen in, and Yvonne Collins, who was about to go off duty and had volunteered to stay on and help out.

Nikki noticed Hackett standing at the back of the room, which both worried and deeply annoyed her. She wanted her team to know every damned thing, not the diluted version that his presence forced her to deliver. Sick of living in fear of being shut down, her anger at the man and his department — whatever that was — came to a head. Instead of addressing the team, she turned directly to Hackett and spat out, 'You said you wanted Lucas caught. You said you didn't want to hinder our investigation. Well, you are hindering it! I cannot — no, I *will* not continue to keep these officers in the bloody dark because of one name we are forbidden to mention. I don't give a damn about what happened in the past. Your weird scientist doesn't interest me one iota, but catching his murdering son does. If you want that done, I'm your best bet, Hackett. I'm your *only* bet. Plus, if you just take time out from spying on your only allies, you'll realise that in putting an end to this nightmare, we will also ensure that your nasty secret from the past, whatever that is, stays with you.' She drew herself up to her full height. 'If you stay, you will hear the name Julian Hopwood-Byrd mentioned, but only as Lucas and Harry's father, nothing else. If you can't cope with that, then I suggest you leave right now, but don't you dare try to stop me doing my job when innocent people are dying!'

The silence that hung over the room was almost palpable, and it went on for a very long time. Finally, Hackett nodded and walked towards the exit. 'Carry on, Detective Inspector.' He stopped, his hand on the door. 'Just find your killer, and fast.'

As the door closed behind him, there was a collective release of breath.

'Oh my!' breathed Cat. 'Where did that come from, boss?'

'I think we just witnessed a bit of pressure-cooker syndrome,' said Ben almost reverently. 'There really is only so much pressure you can take before something blows.'

Nikki took a deep breath. 'Right, so before he changes his mind, let's not waste a moment.' She looked at Ben. 'Read out the letter that Eric Dawson left us. We need to hear word for word what he says.'

Ben took a copy of the letter from a plastic wallet and read it out.

To whom it may concern.

I suppose this is being written as a kind of confession and as a plea for my beautiful daughter to forgive me, but it is also a true statement of fact that has to be made known, as I fear the future is uncertain for my surrogate son.

I am still not sure if my actions were the wisest, although they were done with the sole intention of saving a boy from danger. They could have been a terrible mistake, but I'm afraid that's something I will never know. I do not regret what I did.

I did abduct Lucas Hopwood-Byrd and he willingly remained with me, as my surrogate son, until he was well into his twenties.

Any teacher will know that some students touch your heartstrings for one reason or another, but although you care deeply about them, there are barriers that you do not cross, because you are their teacher and guide. You are not their parent. Lucas was always special to me, possibly because he was not the same as the other children. His view of the world was so different to theirs that I believed he would struggle to survive in so-called "normal" society. So I watched him closely. I endeavoured to engage the parents, but soon realised that was a pointless task. Inasmuch as Lucas was different to others, so were the parents. So my hands were tied. Lucas moved on to other classes, but I still involved him in projects, as and when I could. He looked to me as his mentor, and I accepted the role gladly. But our relationship changed when my darling son, Josh, was killed.

Lucas had enormous sympathy, something I never expected in such a strange boy. He would sometimes leave little gifts or messages for me, but there was nothing creepy about it. It was not a teacher-crush thing, something a lot of my teaching colleagues had to deal with. It was different with Lucas, a very naïve and simple gesture. Soon after that, he started to talk to me more. Nothing very serious at first, although I soon gathered that his home life was dysfunctional in the extreme. Then his father was arrested for murder and subsequently died, but nothing that I would have expected to happen to support Lucas and his bother Harry was arranged for them. To my knowledge, they had no counselling and no assistance from professionals to see them through the trauma. I found out later that the mother had vetoed it. It was unthinkable, but true.

When he was thirteen years old, he came to my house. There, he gave way to an outpouring such as I have never known to come from a child. He told me everything about his father and what he called his amazing gift. He told me about the murder and how, although he still loved and adored his brother Harry, he was becoming increasingly afraid of his mental state. Coming from a boy who suffered fantasies and delusions, this might have been laughable, but it was far from funny. He said that sometimes Harry would call him Bruce and seemed to see him as the gardener, looking at him in a way that made him feel very uncomfortable indeed.

All this coincided with my moving away from the family home in London. I had procrastinated because it would mean leaving Lucas with no mentor or friend, but the heartache and the pain of losing Josh was too much to bear. I had to go. Then Lucas arrived in a terrible state. He had woken in the night to find Harry standing next to his bed. He was naked and seemed to be in kind of sleepwalking state, and the things he was saying terrified Lucas. Finally he walked away, back to his own room, but Lucas knew that the next night could be very different. At that point, everything became clear to me. I told the boy to pack a bag and slip away when everyone had gone to bed. That day, I instructed the removal company to pack up and clear the house and put everything into temporary storage. Compton Acre was already empty and ready for me to move into, but I took Lucas to the Peaks for a couple of weeks just to get some peace and quiet and to give us time to make some plans.

I didn't realise the extent of his problems, the personality disorder, until a little later and, although life became difficult for us, I never gave up on him. I took him to a private clinic where a drug regime was drawn up for him. He hated the medication, but it saw him through the separation from his family, through college and into full-time employment. When he finally left home, he had rekindled his old love for his brother and put what happened down to some kind of shock reaction to what Harry had witnessed. Once, he even went back to London and followed his brother as he walked his dog, but he soon realised that he daren't risk seeing him again, so he returned to his new life. I prayed that he would continue with the medication so that he could cope with life, live as well as possible. That was all I ever wanted.

Ben looked up. 'The rest is really private stuff for his daughter, boss.'

Nikki exhaled. 'I feel like ripping everything off this whiteboard and starting again. We've been spun so many lies I'm not sure which way is up. The most understandable character in this whole charade is the killer himself. Lucas sees beauty and spirit forms in nature, and if someone destroys them, he exacts retribution, end of story. But right now, we need to make a list of facts, things we know for sure, and ditch all the garbage Harry Byrd has fed us.' She looked at each of them.

'Now, Cat and Ben, you need to fill us in on what Dawson's daughter and brother told you. Laura and Aiden, if you could explain your concerns about Elvinia Torres. I will give you a brief rundown of an Oscar-winning performance that Joseph and I watched on video, starring ageing TV-star Suzie Melrose, who pretended to be Corinne Blake, and Joseph will update you on some good old home truths from the real Corinne Blake, Anita's sister. Ben, you can start. Anyone, feel free to throw in whatever you think relevant as we go. I want a clear overview and remember, our main objective is to find both Lucas and Harry, *before* they find each other.'

It took over twenty minutes to share their combined information and, just as Nikki was preparing to sum it up, Ben's phone rang.

'It's Eric Dawson's brother.' Ben sounded tense. 'Yes, Mr Dawson?'

'I've been thinking of places where Marcus and I went regularly when we were in your area, and I might have a possibility for you.'

Ben grabbed a pen. 'Fire away, sir.'

'My father-in-law used to have a little place on Turner's Drain. It's actually on a tributary that flows around the edge of the golf course and finally meets up with the river. There are only two or three dwellings along that strip, they're all well apart and they all have private moorings, plus you can't see them from the drain. Is that the kind of place you're looking for?'

Was it ever! Ben threw Nikki an excited look. 'Can we have the exact address, sir?'

'The house is called Harriers. I don't know the name of the lane it's in because we always approached by water. It's empty at present. The old man died intestate, silly sod, over six months ago and it went to probate.'

After Ben had ended the call, Joseph said, 'Hold on! That name rings bells from Lucas's old notebook.' He hurried into his office and returned with the tatty old book. 'Yes, he called it Harriers' Haunt and he describes it as a very powerful place surrounded by water.' He frowned. 'And it's one that Harry conveniently left off our famous map of "safe places."'

Nikki turned to Yvonne. 'Go tell Niall! A place called Harriers, on Turner's Drain, along by the golf course. See if we have anyone in the vicinity and if not, get a cartload of officers out there now!'

Yvonne was already out of the office door when Nikki said, 'Grab your stabbies, kids, let's get a fix on this place. We are going to join them!' She turned to Laura. 'Are you okay to hang on here? If we get either or both of these men, we are sure as hell going to need you and the FMO to evaluate them.'

Laura nodded emphatically. 'Of course. I'm not going to pass up a chance to talk to Lucas, now, am I?'

Nikki turned to Aiden. 'And although I hate to exclude you, my friend, will you stay here and field any calls and be our liaison? This could turn out to be a crock of shit and no one's home, and I really don't want to miss anything of urgency coming in here.'

'I will,' said Aiden. 'To be honest, my leg isn't up to rugby tackles just yet. I'll get in contact if anything comes in.'

Nikki gripped his arm. 'Good man. I appreciate it.'

'Got the place, boss!' Cat called out. 'It's on Ferry Lane, approached from the golf-club end of Turner's Drove. I've googled it and it's a small house with a big garden running down to the drain and an L-shaped mooring that not only shields it from the main waterway but has room for maybe three boats.'

Nikki did up her stab-proof vest. Since their last case in which a vest had saved Joseph's life, she insisted they wear them for all shouts that could turn physical. She valued her team and wasn't taking any chances.

As they all hurried out into the corridor, she saw Hackett walking towards them. If he tried to stop her now, she swore she'd run right over him!

Instead, he stood to one side, so she said, 'We have been given a location that our target knew from many years ago, Mr Hackett. There's a good chance he might be there.'

She didn't wait for an answer, but heard him say 'Good luck' as she raced towards the stairs. Slightly mystified at this sudden and unexpected reversal, she heard herself call back, 'Thank you.'

* * *

Lucas heard a noise. Drowsy and a little confused, he climbed up on deck but saw nothing other than some water sprites swimming around the hull. One clung to the mooring rope and laughed at him. He smiled back, envious of the way they lived, spending their days playing in water.

He looked around. He was certain he had heard footsteps — heavy, human ones, not the pitter-patter of faery feet. He stepped from the boat on to the mooring dock and stood on the walkway, staring at the ground.

And then he saw it — a sign. Someone had scratched a symbol on the path that led into the garden. His heart leaped. He knew that cipher well, knew its meaning. He was here!

The triangle with a crude eye drawn in the middle of it had featured often in the games he, Harry and their father had played back in Reston, in the garden or the woods. It had been his favourite, representing their trinity — two sons and their father. It meant, simply, "I am here."

Tears came to his eyes. Now he knew he was forgiven, and forgave in his turn. They would be together, just like before. Only without their father.

He walked up to the point where the mooring met the main waterway, but there was no one there.

He called out, 'Harry! Harry! I am here too!'

Only a water bird responded, with a harsh cry and a splash of wings on water as it took off and flew away.

Only when he got back to the boat did he see the second sign, a single word etched on the jetty, close to his boat: "Oshun." Now he understood where he must go. Oshun's Lagoon.

Harry was there at the lagoon, waiting for Lucas to join him.

CHAPTER THIRTY

There were no search parties in the area close to Turner's Drain, so a group of officers, accompanied by Nikki, Joseph and the team, gathered in the station yard and prepared to search Harriers.

'I've directed two of the inflatable dinghies to move into the area. They're to hang back and observe any movement on the waterway — and, if necessary, block the exit from the mooring,' said Niall, looking at his clipboard. 'We have two cars with six uniformed officers to go in with you. Two are qualified Taser operators. I suggest you and your team approach by the direct route past the entrance to the golf course, while my two vehicles come in the back way to Ferry Lane. Silent approach, of course. It's belt and braces in case he's there and tries to do a runner by road rather than water.' He looked at Nikki. 'I have alerted an armed unit, who'll be on standby, ma'am. I know we don't think he has a gun, but I want to have backup ready just in case.'

Nikki very much doubted Lucas would be armed — it wasn't that kind of case — but it was good to know that Niall had every angle covered if the unthinkable happened.

She nodded. 'We need to move out ASAP. We'll let you know what we find when we get there. If he is at Harriers, you'll know about it.'

During the fifteen minutes or so it took them to reach the place, Nikki's mind was buzzing. Would Harry know about it? Probably not, as Lucas had only discovered it after he'd left home and was learning how to handle a boat. Unless Lucas had found Harry and brought him there for their tearful sibling reunion. She shivered at the thought. She had believed that Lucas had lured Harry to the wetlands in order to kill him, but now, in the light of what his aunt had told them, it was more likely to be the other way around and that Harry was stalking his little brother with the same aim. Or were they wrong on both counts? Was blood thicker than water? Did they truly want to be together again as they had been as children, their terrible past forgotten, and all transgressions forgiven? She just prayed that by the time night fell, she would have her answers.

There was a wide grass verge opposite the entrance to Harriers, and they used it as a rendezvous point. The house itself was unassuming, an old-style three-bed property with very few modern additions. The value lay in the massive garden and its waterway frontage with a private mooring.

'It looks very quiet,' murmured Joseph, 'and unlived-in. I don't think he's been dossing here, do you?'

She agreed. 'He's not an indoor person, is he? He'll stay on his boat, or rough it under the stars.' By now, everyone was assembled. 'Let's check this place out, especially the mooring.'

They had agreed on using a pincer movement, and in no time at all, the two units had checked the exterior of the house and were moving in on the mooring.

'Bingo,' whispered Cat and pointed.

Bobbing on the water behind an ancient rowing boat sat the white cabin cruiser.

'The *Clear Vision*,' said Joseph. 'Must be. It's certainly a Sea Ray 245 Weekender.'

Nikki saw one of the uniformed officers looking at her, waiting for a signal. She nodded. 'Go!'

It was a small craft and took only minutes to search. She soon heard the call, 'All clear, ma'am.'

Nikki grimaced, then looked back at the house.

'Should we check that out?' asked Ben.

'If he's not on his boat, he has to be somewhere close by. But let's do as little damage as possible. I know the owner has died, but even so . . .'

But she knew he wasn't going to be there, and, in ten minutes and with only one forced window catch, she was proved right. A feeling of exasperation rose up inside her. It was the closest they had come to finding Lucas, but as ever, he'd eluded their grasp.

'Boss? It could be nothing, but—' Cat pointed to the garage door — 'it's unlocked and empty. I'm certain that if an estate has gone to probate, you can't touch any of the belongings until the process is complete. I'd say there was a car in here until very recently. I'm sure I could smell fuel when I went inside.'

Nikki looked at Ben. 'Ring Dawson and ask about his father-in-law's vehicle.'

Ben made the call. 'Yes, boss, he had an old-style dark-green Land Rover Defender, and it was here, in the garage. Dawson is spitting tacks to hear that it's gone.'

'Ring that info in to Aiden immediately, Ben, and tell him to check out the reg number, and then to get Niall to issue an Attention Drawn to all units. He can't have got far, and an old Defender is very easy to spot.' Maybe they would see Lucas captured today after all. 'And, Joseph, we need to see inside that cabin cruiser.'

At the mooring, Joseph pulled on a pair of gloves and jumped on board, careful to touch as little as possible. 'Nice,' he murmured, looking at the cockpit and down into the cabin. 'Two berths — there's a sleeping bag on one and it looks like his stuff is still here.' He looked back at Nikki, standing above at the mooring. 'He wasn't going far. He hasn't even locked up. There are clothes, a few toiletries—' he opened the fridge — 'and milk, water, orange juice and some packs of sandwiches.'

Nikki walked along to where the inlet converged into the main waterway and looked around. The empty towpath stretched ahead of her. At her back, the wide drain ran for about a quarter of a mile and then met the tidal river. There was not a single person in sight, apart from the officers cruising slowly around in their two inflatables.

'No movement out here,' one of them called out.

She raised a hand in acknowledgement. So where was Lucas? He hadn't been on the roads coming in, and they had a team at the golf club, checking the perimeters closest to the gardens at Harriers.

Nikki walked back to Joseph. 'He's done another of his famous vanishing acts.'

'Ma'am!' Yvonne Collins beckoned to her from a spot a little further down the path. 'I think this means something.' She indicated a symbol scraped on one of the paving slabs.

Nikki stared at the triangle with the eye in the centre.

'It's the same sign, only more detailed, as the one that Kyle found in that deserted chapel in Fenny Bridge village. The one he saw was constructed out of stones and pebbles, whereas this one is a drawing.'

'The one that surprised Harry?' Nikki asked.

'Yes, he believed it came from Lucas, that it was a message.' Yvonne looked closer. 'Oh, look! There's something else written here, a word . . . er, "*Oshun*"?'

Joseph pulled out his phone and googled it. 'It's the name of a river goddess, boss, a powerful deity associated with water.'

'Oh great! Back to bloody never-never land,' Nikki growled.

'If the triangle had the same effect on Lucas as it did on Harry, ma'am, it's definitely important,' said Yvonne. 'He was pretty emotional about it, even though he covered it up later. And another thing, now I think of it, there could have been something written in the dust close to the symbol, but Harry rubbed it out with his foot. He seemed to be scuffing at something as he spoke to us. I bet it was the same word, could even have been a date or a time.'

Nikki closed her eyes and tried to follow Cam's advice. Ignore the faery stuff and concentrate on the fact that Lucas Hopwood-Byrd was a psychotic killer. She thought hard. 'Okay, let's imagine that Lucas is tucked up in his cosy cabin, deciding what to eat, or maybe planning another murder. And he goes outside to stretch his legs and sees this.' She stared at the symbol. 'Whatever that says, it was enough for him to drop everything and go.'

Yvonne frowned. 'Harry believed that the symbol in the chapel was left by Lucas, so it follows that Lucas must have believed that this one was from Harry.' She turned her gaze to the writing. 'Which would indicate that Oshun is a location.'

'He's gone to meet his brother,' Joseph said.

'You don't think it's a play on the word "ocean," do you?' asked Yvonne.

'The results I found said that she was a goddess of fresh water rather than the ocean,' said Joseph. 'I think it's another "special place" that Harry conveniently left off the map he gave us.'

Nikki frowned. 'If you say Oshun indicates fresh water, then the "special place" won't even be along the river, will it? It's a tidal river, so it must be salt.'

'Not exactly,' replied Joseph. 'The river is fresh water, since it's constantly being replenished from its source. When the tide turns, tongues of salt water flow back into it and the two mingle. The estuary is incredibly productive ecologically. That's why early habitation sprang up around estuaries.'

'Well, thank you, Sergeant Easter, for that informative and educational lecture.' Nikki raised an eyebrow. 'In other words, the river is still a viable option to search.'

'Definitely.' His smile vanished. 'But we need a lot more to go on than that. The waterways here are a massive network. Look, would you mind if I go back to the office? Now we have a name, I need to scour those old notebooks of Lucas's. There might be a mention of Oshun.'

'We might as well all go back,' Nikki said. 'We'll leave a uniformed presence here in case he returns. She looked at Yvonne. 'Well done for spotting that symbol, Vonnie. It's clearly going to be his next port of call, and if we can just discover where it is, we'll be joining him.'

'Hang on.' Joseph ran down the steps to the cabin area. 'Harry said Lucas always kept a diary. I'm just going to check his bags.' He looked in all the bags, under the mattress of his bunk and other less obvious places but found nothing.

'Harry must have been lying about that too,' Nikki said.

Joseph stopped abruptly. 'Hey! He did leave in a hurry, didn't he?' He leaned forward and pointed to an ignition key still dangling from the dashboard. He removed it. 'That could slow up his escape, should he find a way to get back to the boat. Though with our guys surrounding it, I don't think he will.'

* * *

Back in the CID room, Nikki addressed the team. 'It's home time, guys, but if any of you can stay, that'd be great. I don't have to tell you how close we are to catching this guy. We almost had him earlier. So, I can promise that you'll get overtime, and I could even throw in a takeaway if anybody feels hungry?'

'That clinches it for me,' said Cat with a broad grin. 'It was my turn to cook tonight, so hey! Win, win!'

Everyone stayed, as Nikki had guessed they might. She also had a feeling that it had nothing to do with overtime or food. God, she loved this team!

* * *

Joseph dished out Lucas's strange notebooks. 'Some of it is gobbledegook, although some of the sketches are pretty impressive. Skip most of it and try not to get sidetracked. We are looking for the word "Oshun." It's the name of a deity,

332

a water goddess, but we are hunting for her in connection to a location, somewhere Lucas might be.' He looked around. 'Everyone got one?'

There was a murmur of assent.

'Interesting homework, Sarge,' said Ben, staring at a picture of some kind of troll. 'Makes a change from swotting up on *Blackstone's Practical Policing*.'

Joseph glanced across to Nikki's office, where she was speaking on the phone. She had opted to chase up any new intel, and to keep in close contact with Niall, especially regarding that old Defender. So far, there had been no sightings at all.

Joseph returned to his notebook, aware that they only had three or so hours of daylight left to find the meeting place that could turn out to be fatal for one of the brothers. He had hoped that the last notebook, the one with the ramblings and spooky drawings, might deliver up a clue, but it had no mention of the elusive Oshun.

In desperation, he googled the name again and was surprised to find there was so much on her. It made him realise that, while Lucas's nature spirits were a symptom of mental illness in his case, there were still millions of people who believed in gods and goddesses and spirits of all kinds. Some people in hi-tech societies laughed at such beliefs and people like Nikki — practical, down-to-earth beings — found the whole thing beyond comprehension. Yet everyone needs something to believe in, and in the absence of a god, why not turn to nature? It was beautiful, awesome, powerful, all the things a god was supposed to be. Think of thunder and lightning. Who can help but feel they have something supernatural about them?

He blinked a few times. He was tired and his mind was wandering. He needed to concentrate. Strong coffee, that would do it.

As if on cue, Cat knocked on his door. 'I decided that we all needed caffeine, Sarge. It's as strong as I could make it.'

'Thank you, Cat, you're a mind reader.'

She put the beaker on his desk. 'Can you please not mention mind reading? It's much too close to J.H.-B. and his spooky talent.'

Once she had gone, he returned to his water goddess. She was a part of the Yoruba religion. He read on. "*The principal sanctuary of this deity is located in the Osun-Osogbo Sacred Grove.*" Sacred Grove. Now where had he seen that before? He squeezed his eyes shut and tried to remember. Like something forgotten just on the tip of the tongue, he almost heard Lucas's voice. That was it! He had heard it when Karen Cotton recalled her talks with him. He began to rummage through the papers on his desk for those all-important notes. He found them at the bottom of a pile, and began to read:

At times of intense stress, I suppose we all need somewhere to run to, don't we? Some sacred grove where calm and peace can be restored, where things can be made better again. I dream of one day seeing the water goddess herself, the spirit of the river. She's there — I've witnessed the tiniest flashes of her presence on the turning tide in the lagoons. Of all places, that would be my own sacred grove.

Lagoons. He exhaled. He didn't know the marsh areas well, but he knew this was it. Nikki! She knew the marsh. He grabbed the paper and ran to her office. 'Lagoons, Nikki. Where do we find lagoons?'

She looked at him in surprise, then jumped up and went to her large wall map. 'There are several lagoons along the rivers that are designated as wildlife reserves, mainly for waterfowl and other migrant birds.' She looked closer. 'There are two fairly close to where we found Lucas's boat. Here,' she stabbed her finger on the map, 'and here. Not on the drain, but on the river itself.'

He looked over her shoulder to where she was pointing. 'He's gone to one or the other of those, I'm certain of it. I've made a connection between Oshun and lagoons.' He looked at her. 'How would he get to these?'

'By water, definitely. Overland, if he wasn't sure of the lanes, would take for ever. What are you thinking?'

He pulled out his phone. 'I need to check something.' Vinnie answered almost immediately. 'Listen, mate, no time for pleasantries — when you saw the Sea Ray, did it have an inflatable dinghy?'

'Yeah, it did, come to think of it. The last time I saw him he was towing it. It's pretty common, especially if you like fishing or exploring the narrow inlets.'

He thanked his friend and ended the call. 'He didn't use the Defender, Nikki, he went by water, like you said. I saw no inflatable on the Sea Ray.'

Nikki stared at him. 'He's had one hell of a start on us, Joseph, maybe an hour and a half. My initial thought is to saturate both areas with officers, but that could set our batty brothers off into who knows what kinds of madness.' She stood, hesitant, chewing on her bottom lip.

'If you had to decide, which of those two places would most fit the bill as a sacred grove for a river goddess?' Joseph said.

'What? You're asking me?' Then she looked back to the map. 'Okay, my gut feeling says this one, Fishers Mere. It's bigger, has lots of lagoons and marshy pools along the river and a small wood of native trees surrounding the land side of it. There are bird hides, but because of its location, bird-watchers either give it a miss or can't find it.' She frowned. 'Yes, now I come to think about it, the other one is much smaller and is very open and marshy. So in answer to your question, if I was a bloody goddess — which I'm not — I'd pick Fishers Mere.'

Joseph nodded. 'Then let's go without the cavalry. We check the place out covertly, and if they are there, we assess the situation and then alert the troops.'

'Okay, but I suggest we brief Niall and have him move a couple of teams within striking distance. We have no idea what we'll be walking into.'

'And the team?' asked Joseph.

'We'll take Cat and Ben. But they can hang back and observe. We can bring them in if we need assistance.'

'Next question. Can we drive there? Or do we need to go by water too?'

'I know the way by the fen lanes, Joseph. In the time it'd take us to organise a boat, I can get us there.' She grabbed her stab-proof vest from the back of her chair. 'I'll ring Niall en route. You get the others prepped, and then we go.'

CHAPTER THIRTY-ONE

Lucas pulled into a decrepit, rotting landing stage on the riverbank and hauled the small inflatable out of the water. He dragged it out of sight and tied it to some straggly bushes. He had been here several times before and knew that the easiest way to access the lagoons themselves was via the path that ran through the trees and dropped down into the marshy, watery area that nestled between the tidal river and dry land.

As he walked through the trees, he looked out for signs or sounds that would tell him his brother was there.

It was a truly magical place. The longed-for peace flowed around him. Birds sang an evensong and waterfowl cried out to each other. Bright lights reflected on shallow pools, and he saw movement and life everywhere. The laughter of water sprites mingled with the sound of the flowing river, and he felt the touch of gossamer wings on his face.

The shadows were gone. No slimy things slithered between the pools. No contorted bodies or ugly faces smiled evilly at him. Today, all was beauty.

He knew he was alone and, although he was disappointed, he knew that Harry would come when he could. He had left the sign. It was certain.

Lucas made his way to a slightly raised piece of ground with an old, weathered bench on it. With a good view across the lagoons, it had shelter from some stunted and windblown hawthorn trees and elder bushes that grew around it.

He sat, taking deep breaths of the salty air. He felt like an integral part of the place, as if he belonged there with all the other mystical denizens of the lagoons. He sighed with contentment. Here he would stay, waiting until Harry came.

He gazed into the far distance, while a pair of unblinking, glittering eyes watched him, unseen, from the treeline.

* * *

'We'll park here,' said Nikki, pulling into a small expanse of concrete on the far side of a disused barn. 'It means a bit of a hike, but the car won't be seen either from the lane or from the wood that flanks the lagoons. There's a proper little car park at the edge of the trees but it's far too obvious.' She locked the car and headed off across the edge of the field towards the wooded area, the others close behind her.

She was very aware that twilight sometimes crept up on you out here and then the growing shadows made the terrain dangerous underfoot. They had come prepared with powerful torches, but she would have preferred to deal with this in daylight.

With every step that took her closer to the lagoons, more adrenalin pumped through her veins. There were four of them and only two men to bring in. The odds were good, except that neither of the two brothers were what you would call sane. She could plan nothing, as they had no idea what they would find, if anything. She could have got it wrong, and they would encounter nothing but curlews and avocets. But Nikki didn't think so. This place had an air about it. This was where their investigation would end.

They entered the wooded area, treading carefully now, trying to make as little sound as possible and listening out for any sign of the brothers' presence. They stopped speaking, using gestures to communicate, and as the trees thinned out into bushes, crouched down and kept well out of sight of the lagoons.

Joseph suddenly touched her arm and pointed.

It was Lucas, sitting alone on a bench, so still that he might have been asleep. For one awful moment, Nikki wondered if they were too late and Harry had already had his reunion, but then she saw him shift a little, stretch out his legs and cross his ankles. He was perfectly at ease.

'He's waiting,' whispered Joseph in her ear. 'Do we take him?'

She was about to say yes, but before she could answer, another figure broke cover from the far side of the wood. Harry Byrd stood for a while, just staring at his brother. Then he moved slowly forward.

They were too far from either man to catch them unawares. Nikki thought quickly, then turned to Cat and Ben and whispered, 'One of you let Niall know that both brothers are here. Tell them to assemble at the deserted barn on the lane but not to approach unless requested. We'll get as close as we can and try to talk to them. You both stay out of sight and watch for a signal from me.'

They nodded and melted back into the denser part of the wood.

Nikki saw a narrow track that they could follow and hopefully remain unseen until the last moment. There was no knowing what course this meeting would take. It could be heart-rending, or they could be witnesses to some horrendous final act. 'We'll have to make this up as we go along, Joseph,' she whispered.

'Yet again.' He squeezed her arm reassuringly. 'We should be used to that by now. Come on.'

She took a deep breath. They began to edge closer.

* * *

Lucas blinked hard. The setting sun shone directly into his eyes, almost blinding him. Very, very slowly, he rose to his feet. The years fell away. He recognised his brother immediately and was overcome by an emotion so powerful that it rooted him to the spot, unable to move or speak.

Then, as the figure got closer, tears coursed down his face. 'Harry! My Harry.'

'Lucas.'

They ran towards each other and embraced. Harry whispered, 'After all these years, I've finally found you.'

Unable to speak, Lucas could only sob uncontrollably.

After a while, Harry took his hand. 'Walk with me down to the water. I want to show you something special.'

Lucas allowed himself to be led. The tide had turned, the water in the river ran deep and fast, and some of the shallow lagoons were filling up. Harry strode on, while the water rose above his shoes and soaked the legs of his trousers. 'Here! This one. I found it the other day. Lucas! Come and see, it's amazing!'

Lucas felt dizzy. His head spun and lights flashed in front of his eyes, making it difficult to walk. He wondered what his brother had found. They were children again.

'Lucas! It's a portal! Look — in the water. It's beautiful.'

Harry was gripping his arm, so hard it hurt. A portal? But Harry never saw the gateways. He never saw any of his faery kingdoms. So how . . . ? 'Harry?'

'They are calling to you, Lucas. From the portal. You have to go to them. It's your time.'

He stared into the waters but saw nothing but murky weeds and silt. 'Harry, there's no doorway there. Not in this pool. There's nothing.'

The face that looked down at him had changed. The look it now bore was unfathomable.

'You have to pay, Lucas. Killing people is not acceptable, dear brother.'

'But, Harry, they all deserved to die for what they did.' He looked in horror at the sneer on Harry's face.

'I don't care about those fools! I'm talking about the best man that ever lived. It's your fault he died. I've hunted for you ever since you ran away. You knew then and you know now, it's you who must pay for Bruce's death!'

Lucas felt a heavy hand on the back of his head propel him forwards and down. He cried out, 'No, Harry, please, no!' and water gushed into his open mouth.

Harry thrust his head beneath the deepening water a second time, and again he surfaced, coughing and retching, gasping for air.

'Go to your precious spirits!' Harry's face loomed over him. He grabbed his hair viciously. 'Now you'll know what my Bruce felt like when you condemned him to death.'

Beneath the surface, he became aware that they were not alone. Other people were swimming in and out of focus, and he heard Harry's name being shouted over and over again. And Lucas saw the Elf King! He towered over Harry with a terrible look on his bearded face.

Lucas fought to stay conscious. Surely, this couldn't be the Elf King. Because this man had a halo of white light surrounding him, and that face . . . oh, that beautiful face!

Again, Lucas was brutally pushed under the water, and the world slipped away.

* * *

It had happened so fast. One moment the brothers were together on the edge of the water and then Harry was desperately trying to push Lucas's head into the lagoon! Nikki and Joseph leaped into action, but before they were even off the mark, another figure erupted from the opposite side of the woods. He reached the brothers in a matter of seconds.

Nikki was vaguely aware that Cat and Ben and several other people were streaming from the woods and into the marshy inlet. Then Joseph's arm was across her, stopping her headlong flight towards Harry and Lucas.

'Wait!' As his voice carried across the lagoons, flights of birds broke cover and took to the air. He pointed to the big man, who had now reached the brothers.

Nikki stared at him. He was a giant, with long, curling grey hair and a full beard. His clothes were shabby and dirty, but he had a powerful presence.

'Be careful, Nikki,' hissed Joseph. 'He's dangerous.'

As she watched, the man dragged the unconscious Lucas from the pool, while still holding Harry so that both arms were pinned to his sides. Completely ignoring the police, he turned his intense gaze from one brother to the other.

Lucas moved and began to cough. Nikki felt a surge of relief. He was a killer, but it wasn't down to Harry to mete out rough justice. But who the hell was this Hagrid of a man, and where the dickens had he come from?

Joseph started forward, but the man shouted in a deep voice, 'Stay back! All of you.'

The man reached down with his free hand, gently lifted the half-conscious Lucas to his feet and held him tightly. All the time he was gradually edging backwards, away from them and closer to the river.

'We're the police, sir,' Nikki called out. 'Please, let us help Lucas!'

'I said stay back.' The water was over his boots, but still he moved slowly backwards.

Nikki watched, afraid to move, but equally afraid of what the man was about to do.

What he did next would haunt Nikki for a long time to come.

He looked at Harry, smiled sadly, then changed his grip and deftly broke his neck with a strange jerking, twisting motion. In a split second, Harry's lifeless body was hanging over the big man's arm. The man then turned to a shocked and horrified Lucas and said, 'Now we all go together.'

As he backed further into the water, the spell that had held them broke, and Joseph and Nikki rushed forward. Then, to Nikki's surprise, they were once again stopped in their tracks, as another man hurtled past them, heading straight for the water.

'Julian! No!'

Hackett almost screamed the name, and Nikki felt her chest tighten. Julian?

'Get back, Hackett! It's over! It has to be like this! There is no other way for me and my boys!' Julian Hopwood-Byrd was waist-deep in the river now, and already being tugged this way and that by the undertow.

After this, Nikki perceived everything in slow motion. She heard Julian say, 'Lucas! Look! There really is a portal! See! Follow that light! Can you see it, son?' All the time the big man was inching into deeper, darker waters.

Lucas's unfocussed eyes seemed to stare downwards, just as a shaft of fading sunlight cut across the water with a brilliant rainbow glow. 'I see it, Father! I see it!'

'I'll come with you! And I'll bring Harry. We'll go together, my lovely boys! Dive, Lucas, dive down!'

Nikki stood speechless and saw Lucas throw his father a dazzling smile, then dive into the shimmering ray of light.

And then they were gone.

'No!' Hackett ripped off his jacket and launched himself into the river, yelling for Julian.

'Hackett! The current!' screamed Nikki, then turned to Joseph. 'He'll never get out again if he gets caught in that current!'

'Oh shit!' Joseph struggled out of his stab-proof vest and leaped in after Hackett.

Nikki watched, her heart in her mouth, then Hackett surfaced a little further down, and Joseph managed to swim fast enough to catch hold of him. She heard him shout, 'They've gone, man, and you'll be joining them if you don't give up. For God's sake, let them go. You can't help them now.'

To Nikki's relief, she saw Hackett try to turn, and slowly they dragged themselves back to the shallows and out of the water.

Then all hell broke loose. There were police officers everywhere. While an ambulance crew threw foil blankets around Joseph and Hackett, Nikki was left staring into the river, searching for some sign of father and sons and wondering what the hell she had just witnessed.

Then she felt her phone vibrate in her pocket. She answered like an automaton and heard Aiden speaking urgently.

'Something you should know, boss. Elvinia Torres just phoned. She says she should have phoned before, but she didn't know what to do. That's why she was behaving so oddly when we saw her. Bottom line is this. Many years ago she had a letter from Julian Hopwood-Byrd, but it was dated a month *after* he was murdered! She said it was completely kosher. So that means Julian is still alive, Nikki!'

Nikki felt an inappropriate laugh welling up but managed to quash it. She was still in shock after seeing Julian break his son's neck. 'Sorry, Aiden, but she's wrong. Julian is dead.'

'But, Nikki! She swears her information is true. They had been lovers when they were young and still kept in touch. She wasn't lying. He's alive somewhere!'

She sighed. 'No, he isn't.'

'How can you be so sure?' he asked in an injured tone.

'Because I just watched him die.'

She ended the call and stared into the murky depths of the river, as it flowed towards the estuary, the Wash, and the North Sea, carrying with it three damaged souls.

CHAPTER THIRTY-TWO

They were called to an emergency debriefing that same evening, not long after their return to the station. Joseph just managed to grab a hot shower and a change of clothes in the locker room before they were summoned upstairs. They had not expected straight answers and, true to form, the security services gave them almost none. It took the form of a vague statement about the security breach that had occurred when Julian had escaped from a research facility where he worked. It stated that he was involved in top-secret government work, and it was vital that he did not fall into other hands. He was also dangerous and volatile, and it was essential that the public be kept in the dark about him. It had been decided that, in view of his son's activities, the police were to be allowed to track down Lucas, and in doing so, lead them to Julian. They were thanked for a satisfactory conclusion to the affair. Then, as they were leaving, Vernon Hackett took Nikki and Joseph aside. He thanked Joseph for stopping him from pursuing Julian in the river and saving his life. He had come to the conclusion, he said, that they deserved more of an explanation.

'This is off the record, and I want you to forget what I'm going to tell you as soon as I've left, or we'll have to conclude this discussion here and now.'

Nikki and Joseph nodded.

Hackett led the way into a room that was generally used only by the higher echelons for discussing top-security matters.

'We lost an exceptional man to that river, Detectives, one who dedicated his whole life to science, and he was very valuable to us.' He took a deep breath. 'Everything that you heard about the Stargate Project was correct. Julian did indeed have a serious breakdown and was sent home. But the next part of his life differed from the official version. The British government could not afford to let him vegetate at home and spiral even further out of control, so he was approached with an offer that he gladly accepted. Working closely with a team of our top psychiatrists and psychologists, he finally began to recover. Contrary to what the Americans believed, he had not lost his extraordinary abilities, and we came to realise that, despite the fact that it was not accepted as a proper branch of science, Julian had *something* that needed investigation.'

'Out of the frying pan into the fire,' muttered Nikki. 'More experiments. Just a different government pulling the strings.'

Hackett frowned. 'No, Nikki. It wasn't like that at all. In the first instance, he was very disturbed initially. No one knew at the time whether he would ever function properly again after what had happened to him. Second, there was the unfortunate incident that resulted in his gardener's death, and third, he had finally come to accept that both his sons had serious mental health issues. No one was heartless enough to consider any experiments at that point.'

Hackett stared from Nikki to Joseph. 'Because of his fragile state of mind after the outburst of rage that left a young man dead, we decided not to cover it up. Julian had confessed to killing the man and he was in no fit state to stick to an alternative story, so he paid the price with a life sentence.'

'But he was never murdered in the psychiatric unit of the secure hospital, just magicked away. Where to?' asked Joseph.

'Sorry, that one is classified. Just know that it was a different kind of establishment, one of ours. He was still incarcerated, but in quite different conditions. As he recovered, he was given his own department and a certain amount of freedom, enabling him to continue with the work he was so passionate about. Any "experiments," as you call them, were designed by Julian himself, and he worked with a select team, handpicked by him. He was cared for and valued, not used as a lab rat.'

'And his family never knew he was still alive?' asked Nikki incredulously.

'It was best that way,' Hackett replied. 'Actually it was the only way, given their problems. But when young Lucas ran away, we tracked him, and kept Julian in the loop as to his progress. The teacher, Dawson, was actually given a certain amount of anonymous "help" from us in the form of finding a college education, medical assistance and so on, although Dawson was never aware of it. This took the form of exactly the right university course suddenly becoming open to Lucas, and the clinic that Dawson had chosen to help him with his psychological problems was offered the services of a top man in that field, who just happened to be trialling some very expensive and very effective drugs that might benefit Lucas. All gratis in the interests of the trial and the furtherance of medical science, of course.'

'And Harry?' asked Nikki.

'Ah, well. There we messed up. Harry was considered a minimal threat. No one appreciated how damaged he really was and that he would come to hate his brother. His search for Lucas was seen as a mission to reunite with the brother he loved, not a hunt to exact revenge on him.'

'Big mistake,' murmured Joseph.

'It was,' Hackett said dourly. 'Not our finest hour.'

'Then Lucas flipped, and his fantasies took over,' said Nikki. 'Was that when Julian did a runner from your "establishment?"'

He nodded. 'We don't know how he heard about the murders. That kind of news was generally withheld from

347

him. But he did, and I believe that all he wanted to do was to get to Lucas and, well, make sure he was never caught.'

'Kill him himself?' asked Nikki, feeling slightly nauseous at the thought.

'I believe so, but out of love. To save him from further madness.'

'Well, he got his wish.' Joseph puffed out his cheeks and exhaled. 'Neither of them could possibly have survived that river.'

'They didn't,' said Hackett softly. 'Officially, their bodies will never be found. Unofficially, the two brothers were retrieved an hour ago from a sluice close to the Wash. You will hear on the news tomorrow that the bodies of two illegal immigrants were washed up after their boat capsized.'

'And Julian?' asked Joseph.

'The sea usually gives up its dead, in its own time,' Hackett said dispassionately.

'So, two mysteries remain,' said Nikki. 'Where is the massive payout that Julian received from the US, and where is Anita, Julian's wife?'

'You know about the money?' Hackett raised an eyebrow. 'Well done! I must be slipping. I won't ask how you came by that information, as I'm sure you won't tell me in any case. Julian gave most of the funds to his family in the form of irregular sums that trickled into their accounts as if from successful financial investments. The rest was channelled into his project. He provided the funding for years of work.'

Joseph smiled. 'How ironic! The US ostensibly funded your secret project.'

'As you say, ironic,' Hackett said wryly.

'And Anita?' asked Nikki.

'We are going to leave that one to the Met. Harry went right off-piste when he played that little flanker. We have no idea where she is, just that she knows nothing compromising, so she's no threat to security.'

Nikki shook her head. 'And that's all you care about. Poor woman! She could be dead for all we know, a sad, innocent victim of circumstances she did nothing to bring about.'

'Don't be too sure about her innocence, Nikki. Some of Lucas's and Harry's problems could be laid at her door, not through direct abuse but through her failure to recognise their differences and her refusal to get them any kind of help. She seems to have thought only of Julian, about whom she was almost obsessive, and had little time for their offspring.'

Nikki recalled Eric Dawson saying much the same thing when he mentioned that she'd vetoed counselling after their father "died." And Delia Cleghorne had said that she felt sorry for Lucas, whose mother had never appreciated how serious his fantasies were. Goodness, even her own sister had called her hard, following the gardener's tragic death. Then she remembered Harry telling her what a wonderful childhood they'd had, and how close he was to his dear mother. Was that just wishful thinking, or did he really believe it? Poor Harry. Oh, God, what a family!

She studied Hackett. 'So, how are you going to white-wash the murders of Ritchie Naylor, Stuart Baker and Craig Steadman — oh, and let's not forget the damage to that schoolboy?'

'Your superintendent is being briefed on that as we speak. He will update you as soon as I've gone.' Hackett stood up. 'Which will be shortly.' He looked at Joseph. 'Thank you again for what you did. I saw the red mist. I knew his worth and I failed him.' He paused at the door. 'I hope our paths don't cross again, DI Galena.'

Oh, not half as much as I do.

* * *

It was after eleven that night when they were called into the super's office. His face was grey, and he looked exhausted.

To Nikki's surprise, he opened a desk drawer and took out a bottle of Scotch and three glasses.

'It's against regulations, but when you compare this to some of the fabrications and acts of subterfuge that are being set in motion right now, I think we can be forgiven.' He poured them both a drink. 'Medicinal. You've earned it.'

Nikki took a sip and sighed. All she could think of was the fact that it was finally over. Not in the way she would have chosen, but at least it was at an end. 'So, what's the official story, Cam?'

Cam raised his glass to his lips, took a swallow and then began to recite. 'This evening, police were called to an incident at some tidal lagoons outside Greenborough. There they found an unknown male answering to the description of the prime suspect in the case of three local murders and another brutal attack on a youngster. The suspect confessed in full to the officers present but resisted arrest and leaped into the river. Despite heroic attempts to save him, he was dragged down by the undertow and is believed drowned. Case closed.'

'Very tidy,' grunted Joseph.

'And it all fits in beautifully with what really happened,' added Nikki. 'All those blue lights out in the fen lanes neatly explained.'

'Yes, Hackett's people are good at that,' said Cam dryly. 'Tidying up after the shit's hit the fan.' He took another mouthful of whisky. 'Do you know, every single officer and civilian who has had even the slightest sniff at this case will get a personal visit from security? Not long from now, this whole episode will be tied up tighter than a whalebone corset and, after singing from the same hymn sheet for a while, some of those involved will even come to believe it really happened that way.'

'And what do we tell the people who know the truth, Cam? People like Karen Cotton, the Cleghornes and Anita's sister, Corinne?' asked Joseph.

'As little as possible,' Cam said with a sigh. 'I completely trust your judgement regarding these people, and it will be down to the two of you to decide how much to say. And don't forget, Lucas had so many names in his lifetime that he could have died without anyone knowing his real name. Josh, Luke, or Marcus could have ended up as an unknown male.'

'And Julian Hopwood-Byrd is once again classified as murdered while incarcerated,' said Joseph flatly.

'Exactly as history dictates,' replied Cam.

'And Harry?' asked Nikki. 'Let me guess — he's now a missing person.'

'Indeed.' Cam placed his empty glass on the table. 'Now I have some different, but also worrying news for you.'

Nikki's heart sank. What next?

'This isn't something I want to tell you right now, but you're my dear friends as well as valued work colleagues.' He heaved in a breath. 'As you know, I went to the doctor's earlier this afternoon with Kaye. I'm afraid she has some serious heart issues that will probably lead to surgery. We won't know more until further tests are done, but as soon as this investigation is cleared up and the reports done, I will be taking compassionate leave to look after her.'

At once, they said how sorry they were and offered any help they could give, but inside, Nikki was in turmoil. She was desperately sorry for Kaye, and Cam too, but a new superintendent, even on a temporary basis, could be fatal for her and Joseph.

Was this it, the moment they'd been dreading? Was it finally time to make that awful decision? But no matter how many times they had gone over it, she still wasn't ready.

'I'm so sorry,' said Cam softly. 'But I have no choice.'

'We know that, Cam,' said Joseph. 'Of course Kaye must come first.'

'She does,' he said, 'but I also know what this means for the two of you.'

Neither of them answered. What was there to say?

'However, I do have a suggestion — and there's no rush for an immediate answer.' There was a hint of a smile on his lips. 'As this is only likely to go on for around six months, I could speak to my commanding officer about not bringing in a temporary replacement. Instead, I would recommend that you, Nikki, step up to acting superintendent during my absence. What do you think?'

She blinked, as the realisation of what that meant began to sink in.

'It's a lifeline, Nikki, if that's what you want — although you may have other plans, of course. I know it's something that has been hanging over your heads for a long time.' Cam smiled. 'Think about it. Discuss it. I'll do whatever you decide. And now, bugger off, both of you. It's been a bloody long day, and I want to get home to my wife!'

* * *

The night was warm, and Cloud Fen was unusually silent. They never pulled the bedroom curtains and the window was open, but as they lay and looked out into blackness, there was no moon and no stars. The heavy, dark sky suited their mood.

They were both exhausted, but sleep would not come. At two thirty, Nikki got up, made tea and brought it back up to bed.

'Why does the conclusion to this investigation feel like a terrible personal failure?' asked Nikki, partly of Joseph and partly of herself.

Joseph gave a little laugh. 'Because it is less than perfect and you, my darling, like your cases brought to a so-called satisfactory conclusion — all boxes ticked, and a neat line drawn beneath them. Well, not one thing about the Byrd case was straightforward. I mean, even the way we were forced to work was damned near impossible.' He leaned back against the pillows and sipped his tea. 'Right from the start, the one person we believed to be our guiding light was in actual fact a liar and a manipulator. I think you did an amazing job, considering that every way forward was shrouded in a thick web of lies and camouflage. To think, we believed that Harry was the sane one, and a possible victim.'

'How wrong can you be!' Nikki said. 'And where, oh where is the mother? Morgan Flint messaged me earlier that her crack about digging up the garden could soon become a reality.'

They drank their tea, deep in thought. Then Nikki said, 'Well, we may get some answers one day about Julian and where he went when he was supposed to be dead, but they will come from either Elvinia Torres, or Spooky's anonymous source. Spooks said there were some flaws in the timing of the events surrounding his death, but frankly, that's irrelevant now that he's really gone for good. And anyway, I don't care anymore, do you?'

Joseph agreed. 'This is one case I'd be happy to forget about. Not that I think I ever will.'

Nikki saw again the swift movement that brought an end to Harry's tortured life. She shivered, drank more tea and changed the subject. 'Did I tell you that Aiden spoke to me before we left?'

Joseph shook his head. 'I never saw the going of him in all the furore.'

'He's decided that he's not ready to take that post up north. He's going to spend a bit more time in therapy with Laura, allow his leg to get stronger and take some downtime with his wife. He said to say thank you to the team. He knows now that his actions could have been catastrophic for the investigation, but at least he's aware that his head has to be in a much better place before he goes back to work.'

'Well, that's one positive to come out of all this,' said Joseph, placing his empty mug on the bedside cabinet.

Nikki drained her own mug. 'So who do you think was the Elf King?'

'I believe that's the one truth we did get from Harry — that it was different people at different times, and mostly fantasy figures from his faery world. Some of the drawings, especially in the later notebooks, showed a seriously malevolent and dark creature hovering in the background.' Joseph nestled down beneath the duvet. 'But towards the end, I'm pretty sure it became Julian, although I'm sure Lucas had no idea that it was his father. He could have been aware that someone was following him, and decided it was the Elf King.'

'You might be right, Joseph. Julian came here immediately after the first murder, and I'm guessing from his final action that hunting down the boys and killing them was always his intended conclusion.'

'I also believe he tracked his son carefully, probably using his memories of the old maps. Lucas mentioned in his diary that his father was as enthusiastic and encouraging about them as the boys themselves, and even invented places, and joined in games using them. The maps were not all Harry's work. Their dad had significant input too.'

'And if he was following the maps, Julian could then have seen Harry.' Nikki sighed. 'But how did he know they would both be at the lagoons at that particular time?'

'My money is on the fact that it was Julian who left those symbols,' said Joseph. 'And if we look at some of the other "special places," we'll find symbols there too.'

'But we won't be looking for anything, will we? That line you were talking about has already been firmly drawn, by Hackett's people. The case is closed.'

'And we are left with one final decision, aren't we?' said Joseph softly.

'Aren't we just! I would hate the super's job,' she said emphatically. 'Can you honestly see me in some of those meetings? And I've seen some of the key accountabilities of a superintendent, Joseph. "Negotiate and control internal and external budgets within areas of responsibility and partnership arrangements, influencing budget allocation," blah, blah, "making financial savings," blah, blah . . . Oh hell, Joseph, and there are dozens more like that!'

He laughed softly in the darkness and squeezed her hand. 'You'd be simply steering the ship until Cam got back, doing the basics and overseeing good policing practices. There might be some planning of any major events or heading up a major incident, but you could do that with your eyes closed.'

She sighed. 'I suppose. And the alternative is unthinkable, isn't it?'

He raised himself up on one arm and looked down at her. 'Listen, you! Whatever you decide, I'm good with that, okay? All that matters to me is that we're together. If it means different jobs, so be it. It wouldn't be my first choice, you know that, but we've had a damned good run at dodging the bullets with Cam in command, so,' he kissed her lightly on the forehead, 'do what your heart tells you.'

'Pity we can't bend the rules.' She touched his face with her fingertips, 'But we can't.' She smiled up at him. 'As it's just a temporary thing, and because I'm damned if I'll split up a team I'm so proud of, I'll accept the challenge. In fact, Joseph, thinking about it, there are one or two policing issues that have been bothering me, and as acting superintendent, a firm word in the right ear . . .'

Joseph burst into laughter. 'Oh, the powers that be will be *so* pleased you took the post! I can see Cam having to fight to get his old job back! And now, Superintendent Nikki Galena, sleep! We have some tricky days ahead. Just you, me and a bucket of whitewash. I can hardly wait.'

Nikki smiled in the darkness. It might be just another reprieve, but she was happy with her decision. 'And on the bright side, we have a wedding to go to next week.'

'So we have!' said Joseph. 'Which reminds me, I saw this lovely pale pink hat in the window of that store in town. It had little rosebuds and . . . Ouch, Nikki! That hurt!'

THE END

ALSO BY JOY ELLIS

THE BESTSELLING NIKKI GALENA SERIES
Book 1: CRIME ON THE FENS
Book 2: SHADOW OVER THE FENS
Book 3: HUNTED ON THE FENS
Book 4: KILLER ON THE FENS
Book 5: STALKER ON THE FENS
Book 6: CAPTIVE ON THE FENS
Book 7: BURIED ON THE FENS
Book 8: THIEVES ON THE FENS
Book 9: FIRE ON THE FENS
Book 10: DARKNESS ON THE FENS
Book 11: HIDDEN ON THE FENS
Book 12: SECRETS ON THE FENS
Book 13: FEAR ON THE FENS

JACKMAN & EVANS
Book 1: THE MURDERER'S SON
Book 2: THEIR LOST DAUGHTERS
Book 3: THE FOURTH FRIEND
Book 4: THE GUILTY ONES
Book 5: THE STOLEN BOYS
Book 6: THE PATIENT MAN
Book 7: THEY DISAPPEARED
Book 8: THE NIGHT THIEF

DETECTIVE MATT BALLARD
Book 1: BEWARE THE PAST
Book 2: FIVE BLOODY HEARTS
Book 3: THE DYING LIGHT
Book 4: MARSHLIGHT

STANDALONES
GUIDE STAR

Thank you for reading this book.

If you enjoyed it please leave feedback on Amazon or Goodreads, and if there is anything we missed or you have a question about, then please get in touch. We appreciate you choosing our book.

Founded in 2014 in Shoreditch, London, we at Joffe Books pride ourselves on our history of innovative publishing. We were thrilled to be shortlisted for Independent Publisher of the Year at the British Book Awards.

www.joffebooks.com

We're very grateful to eagle-eyed readers who take the time to contact us. Please send any errors you find to corrections@joffebooks.com. We'll get them fixed ASAP.

Lightning Source UK Ltd.
Milton Keynes UK
UKHW012023111221
395493UK00001B/128